THE *Heart* OF THORNEWELL

To Colleen—

God Bless,

[signature]

2018

OTHER BOOKS AND AUDIO BOOKS BY ANITA STANSFIELD

First Love and Forever

First Love, Second Chances

Now and Forever

By Love and Grace

A Promise of Forever

When Forever Comes

For Love Alone

The Three Gifts of Christmas

Towers of Brierley

Where the Heart Leads

When Hearts Meet

Someone to Hold

Reflections: A Collection of Personal Essays

Gables of Legacy, Six Volumes

A Timeless Waltz

A Time to Dance

Dancing in the Light

A Dance to Remember

The Barrington Family Saga, Four Volumes

Emma: Woman of Faith

The Jayson Wolfe Story, Five Volumes

The Dickens Inn Series, Five Volumes

Shadows of Brierley Series, Four Volumes

Passage on the Titanic

The Wishing Garden

The Garden Path

Legally and Lawfully Yours

Now and Always Yours

Heir of Brownlee Manor

The Color of Love

Lily of the Manor

Love and Loss at Whitmore Manor

The Stars above Northumberland

THE *Heart* OF
THORNEWELL

a novel by ANITA
STANSFIELD

Covenant Communications, Inc.

Cover image © Mark Owen / Arcangel

Cover design copyright © 2018 by Covenant Communications, Inc.

Published by Covenant Communications, Inc.
American Fork, Utah

Printed in the United States of America
First Printing: June 2018

22 21 20 19 18   10 9 8 7 6 5 4 3 2 1

ISBN-13: 978-1-52440-571-7

Chapter One

RETURN TO ENGLAND

Africa—1821

ENID HAWTHORNE SAT IN A chair some distance from the bed where her husband lay dying. The moment he'd realized he had contracted the disease that had already taken the lives of many villagers, Alistair had made her promise not to get near him.

"For the sake of the baby if not your own," he'd insisted weakly, barely managing to get to the bed where he'd collapsed, burning with fever and moaning from the pain.

"I want to die with you," Enid had cried. "You can't leave me alone here; you can't."

"Forgive me, my love," he'd finally been able to say a while later, looking at her across the room where she sat. "I never should have brought you here." Enid just listened, not wanting to admit just how fervently she agreed with *that*. "You must leave here . . . now! Don't wait. Get . . . away from here. There's no hope for me now. Don't wait," he repeated. "Take the money we've saved and just . . . go." He forced a wan smile, and even from the distance she saw a tear slide down the bridge of his nose. "I'll be gone soon, Enid. I'll be in paradise. You mustn't concern yourself with me. Save . . . yourself," he said, growing suddenly weaker. "Save the baby." He turned to look at the ceiling and closed his eyes. "You must go."

Those were the last words Alistair had spoken. Enid had remained where she'd been sitting, unable to bring herself to stand up and do as he'd asked. She'd tried to speak to him a few times, but he hadn't responded. She could hear the increasing evidence that he was finding it difficult to breathe. She looked at her hands in her lap and the way they trembled uncontrollably. Every grain of logic told her she needed to heed Alistair's instructions. She'd seen an alarming amount of evidence that this disease—whatever it might be—that was spreading through the village was an inevitable death sentence, and its only mercy was that death came quickly. There were no qualified doctors anywhere near this village, no one who might be able to identify what was taking place or offer advice on how to survive. The people here were isolated from the outside world and living in conditions far worse than Enid had ever imagined possible. They had been warned by the village elders to not even touch the bodies of the dead, or try and give aid to the dying. Given that they would die so quickly, it was not worth the risk of contracting the disease. Enid had miraculously been spared—likely because she'd been remaining at home due to feeling ill and tired because of her pregnancy. But Alistair had been out and about among the people as he always was, day after day. He'd promised her that he would be careful, but clearly, he had not been careful enough.

Enid kept waiting for the evidence that Alistair was dead, while silent tears ran in an endless stream down her cheeks. She couldn't believe this was happening; she felt nothing short of terrified as she wondered what she would do without him. He'd been correct in telling her she needed to leave. There was nothing here for her without him—even if there hadn't been the risk of becoming ill. She needed to return to England, and she believed there was enough money set aside for that to be possible. But how would she possibly manage on her own until she got there? And when she did, what guarantee would there be that anyone might be willing to take her in—widowed, pregnant, and destitute as she was?

Enid began to feel light-headed and realized she'd been holding her breath, waiting to hear evidence of Alistair's breathing. She pushed the air out of her lungs in a loud huff, then listened, only to hear absolute silence beyond the buzzing of flies in the house and the distant sounds of people bewailing the loss of their loved ones. Enid hung her head and wept, realizing her husband was dead and there was nothing she could do to give him an appropriate burial—not without risking her own life, and that of their child. She'd heard stories of such things happening in the past, in other villages. It was likely that the bodies would be gathered up and burned. But she couldn't think of that. Right now, she couldn't think of anything; she just sat there, aware of her sweat-drenched underclothing sticking to her skin, while the trembling in her hands spread up her arms and across her chest.

With no warning, the baby inside of her moved abruptly, as if to remind her of its presence. Startled to the reality of the situation, she spoke some tender words of farewell to Alistair, wanting to believe that his spirit was nearby, and he would hear her. She then hurried to gather her things, glad to know that Alistair had not touched anything in the house before he'd come home ill and crawled onto the bed to die. She packed only the barest essentials and a few sentimental items into a large traveling bag that she would be able to carry without assistance. She found the money they had kept hidden to meet their needs, and she hid it carefully inside one of her nightgowns at the bottom of the bag. She also packed some food wrapped in cloth, and two flasks of water, grateful again that she knew Alistair had not touched anything, and the food had come from her own garden, the water from their own well. After one more tearful farewell to Alistair, Enid left the tiny house where they'd been living for months; she didn't even close the door. She wanted someone to find Alistair's body and care for it properly, but she could only pray that it might happen. She would never know for sure.

Painful memories of watching her husband die and leaving his body behind were overpowered by the horrific images that met Enid as she forged her way down the narrow dirt road through the village. The dead and dying were everywhere, and the mourners were wailing with such wretched sorrow that Enid knew she would never forget the sound they made. She forced herself to only look straight ahead, and to simply put one foot in front of the other. At first, she moved slowly, as if the connection to Alistair might refuse to be broken, but fear finally pushed her along and she walked as quickly as she could manage without running.

When the village was far behind her, Enid found a place to sit in the grass, grateful for the wide straw bonnet that shielded her face and shoulders from the sun. A portion of her grief and fear came tumbling out in heaving sobs she couldn't hold back. After she'd had a good, long cry—and some rest—she forced herself to eat a little bit, even though she felt no appetite. And then she started walking again, knowing that the next village was far away from here. She wondered if that village too might have contracted the disease; then another terrible thought occurred to her. What if she had gotten the illness but hadn't started feeling the symptoms yet? She knew from all she'd witnessed and heard that it was usually less than a day after being exposed to the illness when the symptoms appeared. Not wanting to spread this horrible plague—whatever it was—to anyone else, she made the decision to not go into *any* village until enough time had passed that she knew she was not contagious.

After walking for nearly two hours, Enid spotted a patch of trees—something rare out here on the African prairie. She made her way from the road across a field of dry grass to the blessed shady area. Sticky with sweat from head to toe and with her dark blue dress covered with the dust of the road that was clinging to her, she almost collapsed into the grass that was softer due to growing beneath the canopy of the trees. She ate sparingly again and drank barely enough water to quench her thirst, not wanting to run out before she could find a place to get clean water.

The sun was still above the west horizon when Enid lay down on the grass, using her fabric bag as a pillow. She wept again over the horror of all that had happened this day, then she collapsed into a state of shock as she considered her fears regarding the future. She was completely alone, an unchaperoned white woman in a troubled country. Prayer was all that gave her any hope or comfort at all, even though a part of her was struggling with the way God had allowed this horrible disease to take Alistair from her. They'd had such dreams about doing much good among the native people of Africa. She had followed her husband here somewhat grudgingly, only because she knew that his desire to be a missionary among the African people was a lifelong dream for him. She'd known it when she'd married him, and she'd loved him enough to follow him anywhere. But this was not how either of them had imagined the adventure might end. For now, she just had to concentrate on somehow getting to a port town and procuring passage back to England. But first she needed to make certain she wasn't ill. A part of her wanted to be ill—to die in this very spot and be in paradise with Alistair, free of the long journey and harsh consequences she would face if she lived.

Enid's tears escorted her into a troubled sleep, and when she awoke the sun was peering over the east horizon. She was glad that at least her body had been able to get the rest it would need to get her through another harrowing and unpredictable day. For a long while Enid lay on her back and looked up at the leaves of the trees above her, trying to accept that Alistair was truly dead, and that she had nowhere to go except away from the village where death had come like an evil monster, devouring lives with no respect to age, gender, or skin color. While she pondered all that had happened and what the future might hold, she also carefully assessed how she felt physically. At first, she thought a subtle aching in her muscles might be an indication that she was ill, but then she determined that it was far more likely a result of the tension she'd experienced while sitting and waiting for Alistair to die, and her grief that had followed. She'd also walked a long way and had slept on the ground. Realizing she felt fine, she ate some of the food she'd brought with her, praying that she would be able to get more before the day was out. She knew that by the end of the day she would know whether she was ill, and she would keep moving in the direction of the next village, knowing there were only two options for her. If she was ill, she would find a place to lie down and allow the symptoms to overtake her and pray that death would be swift and merciful. If she was *not* ill, then she would keep going and pray that this village was not also afflicted with the plague that had torn apart the temporary home she'd shared with her husband.

Enid spent the day walking and resting when she needed to, eating and drinking sparingly of what she carried with her. It occurred to her that there were no other travelers on this road, when usually there was a great deal of traffic back and forth—consisting both of people on foot, and with animals and carts. She knew the reason why she saw no one else, but she wondered if the disease had spread to other villages, or if it had been contained. If she could not find a village free of disease before the end of the day, she would have no means of acquiring food and water that might not likely be contaminated. As afternoon slid toward evening, she knew beyond any doubt that she wasn't going to get ill, but she almost felt disappointed to have to accept that she would live and face the many difficulties that lay ahead.

"One problem at a time," she told herself aloud. It was something Alistair had often said, but she'd never felt it was more applicable than now. And the most prominent problem now was determining whether she could find a place to stay where she would be safe and find food to eat.

Enid slowed her steps considerably as a village came into view. She wondered how she might be able to determine if the people here were all right—or if they had been afflicted. She saw an old man sitting in the shade of a lopsided tree by the side of the road, weaving baskets and singing in his native tongue. He saw her approaching and stopped both the weaving and the singing. She wished now as she had many times before that she had put more effort into learning the local language. Alistair had learned more than she had, but they had still relied very much on an interpreter who had become a beloved friend—a man who was now dead.

Enid approached the old man slowly, then stopped and kept her distance, not wanting to alarm him, any more than she wanted to become ill through contact with other people who might be afflicted with this dreadful disease. His black skin looked shriveled by a long life in the sun, but his eyes were kind, and he smiled, revealing that he had very few teeth.

"English?" she asked. "Do you . . . speak English?"

"English?" he said, the word thickly accented. "English!" he added more exuberantly and held up a hand to indicate that she should wait for him. He rose slowly to his feet, as if sitting had stiffened his legs, then he walked at what appeared to be a fast pace for someone his age. Enid became aware of other villagers passing by and looking her way, but no one seemed alarmed. The old man returned with a young lady, perhaps just a little older than Enid. She was exotically beautiful—as most of the women here were; at least that's how Enid saw them. She wore a fabric woven in unique, brightly colored patterns wrapped around her head, as well as her waist. She wore nothing to cover her breasts, but Enid had become used to this being customary among these natives, and she had long ago stopped seeing it as scandalous or improper. This was simply the way of these people, and the women she'd come to know had found it terribly odd that Enid covered so much of her body with clothing, and they were amazed by all the underclothing she wore beneath her dresses. Enid simply found her own manner of dress very hot and uncomfortable for the climate.

The old man motioned toward the woman at his side and said with pride, "English!"

"You speak English?" Enid asked.

"I do," the woman said in an accent that Enid had once had trouble understanding, but now she knew it well.

"Are the people of your village ill?" Enid asked.

"No," the woman said. "When we hear of sickness, we set guards around village to keep sick away."

"How very wise," Enid said, surprised at the tears that stung her eyes. She'd clearly been much more afraid than she'd realized. "I'm so glad to hear that you are all well."

"You are well?" the woman asked, furrowing her brow.

"Many died," Enid said with silent tears streaking her face. "My husband died. I have traveled slowly and completely alone to be certain I was not ill before coming here."

"How . . . very wise," the woman said, trying to imitate the way Enid had said it. "You be very . . . hungry?" the woman asked. "Tired?"

"Yes," Enid said, unable to stop the flow of tears.

"You be . . . sad?" the woman asked.

"Yes," Enid added, fearing she would begin to sob if she weren't careful.

The woman told Enid her name, and that of the old man, but Enid had always struggled to pronounce the local names, so she'd most often allowed Alistair to help her communicate and remember the faces connected with the names. Enid didn't try to say their names; she just pointed to herself and said, "Enid."

They both tried to say her name and struggled with it enough to make her feel less regret over her own embarrassment with speaking names in a different language. Enid regretted more deeply than ever the way she had tried so hard to maintain her distance from the native people and their customs. She'd come to Africa reluctantly, and had relied completely on Alistair to keep track of anything and everything that mattered. She didn't even know the name of the village she'd lived in, or the area in Africa in which it was located. To her it had only been a tiny dot somewhere on a map of a huge, frightening continent. She'd only known where she'd lived as *the village*, and when Alistair had traveled to nearby places, they had only been referred to as *the next village*, or *the village to the east*. He'd come to avoid using names, as if he knew she wasn't interested and wouldn't retain them in her memory. And now she regretted her attitude. Now she was entirely reliant on these people to help her, and Alistair was no longer alive to be a buffer between her and the world in which they lived.

Sensitive to the fact that she didn't want to be perceived as taking advantage of the hospitality of these people, she said to the woman, "I have money." The woman looked confused, and Enid rubbed her fingers together while she repeated, "Money. I have money . . . to pay . . . for food and . . . a place to sleep."

Enid realized then that the woman's expression wasn't due to confusion over her meaning. Sounding mildly insulted, she said, "We serve with glad . . . to those who come to our village with need."

"Thank you," Enid said, feeling the escape of more tears.

"You very sad," the woman stated and stepped forward to wipe Enid's tears with her gentle, dark fingers.

"Yes," Enid said and felt compelled to admit, "and afraid."

The woman nodded to indicate she understood before she took hold of Enid's hand. The old man sat back down to do his weaving, and Enid wondered if he was there to guard the entrance to the village; perhaps the possibility that those who were ill in the next village had either died or didn't have the strength to leave had lessened the need for vigilant guards.

Enid was given a good meal that made her feel more satisfied than she had felt since Alistair had become ill. She was given a safe and comfortable place to sleep, and her rest was long and deep, exhausted as she was in body and spirit. The following day she enjoyed a hearty breakfast while she shared some manner of conversation with this kind woman who spoke enough English to understand most of what Enid said, even though their exchange was slow and challenging. After breakfast, this woman gave Enid food for traveling, fresh water in the flasks she carried, and she arranged for Enid to ride in the cart of a man who was taking his vegetables into a city some distance away in order to sell them. Enid was reassured that from there she could find transportation to the nearest port, where she would then be able to get passage on a ship to England. Once again, Enid offered to pay the woman, but she boldly refused it, telling Enid that it had been an honor to assist her on her journey. She called Enid *the woman alone and full of sorrow*, which once again tempted Enid to cry, but she managed to keep her tears under control.

Enid embraced the woman before climbing into the cart with her bag, amidst a great many vegetables. She waved good-bye and watched until she could no longer see the village where she had found much-needed respite.

Traveling in the vegetable cart was immensely uncomfortable, and the journey seemed to go on forever. Enid just kept reminding herself that it was better than having to walk, and the donkey pulling the cart was moving faster than she could travel on foot—not a great deal faster, but enough to assure her that traveling this way would help her reach her destination more quickly.

When they arrived in the city, the noise and flurry were markedly different than that of the small, quiet villages. Memories of being in such places with Alistair caused a pain in her chest, but she ignored it and remained focused on getting out of this country. Enid offered to pay the cart driver, but he too refused her payment and just smiled as they parted ways. He didn't speak any English, but he did take her to a place where she could purchase a coach ticket, and thankfully the man selling the tickets spoke enough English to be able to help her.

"I need to get on a ship to England," she said, and he nodded to indicate he understood. "I need a coach that will take me to a port . . . where I can get on a ship." He nodded again, then got busy with the papers in front of him before he handed her a ticket. She gave him money, having no idea how much this would cost her, and praying he would be honest with her and not take advantage of her limited funds. She also silently prayed—as she had many times—that the money she had would be enough to get her to her final destination. If not, she had no idea what she would do.

Enid had barely enough time to eat a meal and freshen up in what could barely be called a washroom in a place that could barely be called a café. Her seat inside the coach was far more comfortable than that of the vegetable cart, and she was able to relax somewhat, relieved in realizing how far she had come in a rather short time. Perhaps her prayers were being heard and answered; perhaps God truly was looking out for her and her unborn child. Enid fell asleep, tightly clutching her bag, which she'd chosen to keep on her lap rather than having it strapped to the top of the coach with the luggage belonging to other passengers. She awoke to the realization that the coach was stopping to change horses, and the passengers would have time to eat and freshen up before traveling on. When she boarded the carriage again, she was pleased to find that two of her fellow passengers were English and were also on their way back home. Mr. Winters was mostly quiet, but Mrs. Winters more than made up for his silence with the way she chattered incessantly. Enid was embarrassed to realize she'd fallen asleep amid one of Mrs. Winters' stories, and she came awake, apologizing to this woman who had been very kind despite her continual chatter.

"No need for that," Mrs. Winters said, reaching across the carriage to pat Enid's hand. "You should rest if you're tired."

Now that Enid was awake, Mrs. Winters resumed her talking. Enid retained very little of what the woman said, but she was glad for the way it distracted her from her own eerie thoughts and the shock that kept her from feeling the full reality of all she had lost, and the frighteningly long journey still ahead. And even if and when she got to England, she had no idea what to expect, or what she might do if Alistair's family wasn't willing to take her in. But she couldn't think about that now; right now she just had to get on an England-bound ship. Once she arrived in her homeland, she would deal with whatever came next.

When Enid finally stepped out of the coach to see many beautiful ships docked against the brilliant background of the ocean, she felt some tangible hope of getting nearer to home. She immediately arranged for passage to England, relieved that it didn't cost as much as she'd thought it might. As she counted the money she had left, she could almost believe she had enough to make it back to the enormous family home where she had lived with Alistair prior to his firm decision to leave everything behind and take his wife to Africa so that they could be of service to the people there who were considered savage and inferior by most Englanders. Enid's experiences had changed her views on many facets of life, but it had also made her realize more than ever that her spirit was deeply rooted in England, and she believed that once she set foot on English soil she would feel more like herself than she had since she'd boarded a ship to Africa, with Alistair holding her hand. Alistair had been her rock, her solid connection to the life she loved and understood. He had buffered her from everything that had made her feel afraid or uncomfortable. She had depended on him in every possible way, and now he was gone. But she couldn't think about that now. She was going home.

Enid was both relieved and disappointed when she learned that Mr. and Mrs. Winters would be traveling on a different ship. She had no desire to spend the journey listening to Mrs. Winters' constant chatter, but neither did she want to feel completely alone during the many weeks it would take to sail to England. She recalled all too well the endless sea journey that had taken her and Alistair to Africa. She had hated almost everything about it, and she dreaded having to endure the same again. But there was no other way to get where she needed to go.

Just as on her only other journey at sea, Enid's allotted space on the ship was in the steerage down below, where she had only the barest privacy, and only enough room to sleep. She slept when she could, ate her tiresome three meals a day, tried to help mothers who had more children than they could handle, and walked the decks for fresh air as much as possible. Enid never let her bag out of her sight. It didn't weigh much, but it held what precious few belongings she had. She could have hidden her money beneath her bodice if she'd needed to, and in fact she kept part of it there, and she always slept in her clothes, which was necessary in this situation. But she didn't want to ever lose—or have stolen—the sentimental belongings that were all she had left of her marriage and the life she'd shared with Alistair in a strange, faraway land.

Weeks turned into months as the ship sailed from the southern part of Africa toward the shores of England. They were frequently confronted with multiple terrifying storms that often slowed their progress after having blown the ship off course. They stopped in more than one port for the acquisition of supplies. As much as Enid appreciated having solid ground beneath her feet from time to time, she quickly grew impatient of any such opportunity and only wanted to keep moving toward home—all the while praying that there would be a place where she might be welcomed after all she had endured—a place that would be a home for her and her unborn child.

Enid had begun to feel as if the ship on which she traveled would *never* get to England. The endless expanse of ocean in every direction began to feel like an eternal nightmare that would never cease to torment her. Her only solace came from the increasing movement of the tiny child growing within her—evidence of the love she and Alistair had shared. Then one morning she awoke to realize the ship was stationary. She came up to the deck to see the port of Liverpool before her, blanketed by a light fog that made the city appear far more ethereal than she knew it to be.

Enid couldn't get off the ship fast enough. She found a pub where she could eat some breakfast and use their washroom to clean up as much as possible; however, there was no disguising the fact that she had spent months in the steerage of a ship with very little opportunity to get properly clean or to wash what few clothes she had with her. And there was no ignoring the tightness of her dress over her belly, which had grown significantly since she'd left Africa. After buying some food to take with her, Enid was glad to be able to find an available seat on a coach heading into Manchester, which would travel near to the home where Alistair had grown up. After paying her fare, she was both alarmed and amazed to realize how very little money she had left. It was as if Alistair had left her exactly the amount she would need to get home, and nothing more.

The carriage rolled on throughout the day, stopping only twice briefly. The ride was uncomfortable and tedious, but Enid breathed in the English country air as if it were magical, and its restorative powers gave her strength. She'd finally come home. And she prayed that when she arrived at Thornewell Hall, her husband's brother and his wife would be welcoming. She'd never felt comfortable with Alistair's brother; he had a gruffness to him that had made it difficult to even want to be in his company, even though Alistair had always held to the firm belief that Sebastian was a good man. But Sebastian's wife Marie had always been kind to Enid, as had many of the servants, and Enid longed to feel the embrace of her sister-in-law and the peace she hoped to find there.

The carriage arrived in the village closest to Thornewell Hall as afternoon was slipping into evening. Enid used the very last of her money to get a little something to eat at the nicer of the two pubs available. She used their washroom to try and make herself as presentable as possible, then she headed out on foot toward Thornewell Hall, far more nervous than she had anticipated. A myriad of possible scenarios swirled in her mind, all ending with her being denied a place among the family now that Alistair was dead. She kept telling herself that such thinking was madness, and surely all would be well.

The walk was not terribly long; she'd walked into town and back many times while living at Thornewell Hall—simply for the pleasure of walking—to purchase whatever she might have needed. All of that seemed like another life now, an experience so long ago and distant from the life she'd been living in Africa that it hovered in her mind like a strange dream.

Enid paused and drew in a deep breath when Thornewell Hall came into view in the distance. It was larger than she'd remembered, which seemed odd since it had felt enormous to her when she'd first arrived there as Alistair's bride a few years ago. She wondered how long it had been. She honestly couldn't remember or put the dates together. She had completely lost track of time through the endless months of traveling. Pressing a hand over the baby that grew inside of her, it kicked as if to respond, reminding her that it was real, and alive, and growing. The welfare of this child mattered more than anything, and she took a deep breath and walked on, hoping that if nothing else, Alistair's family would be willing to take her in for the sake of Alistair's child.

It was dark when Enid approached the front door of Thornewell Hall, but there were lights burning in many of the windows. She hoped that supper was over, so she wouldn't interrupt it, and she prayed that she would be received with even a tiny measure of the security and acceptance she so desperately needed.

A minute passed without any response to her knocking. She knocked again and waited. The sound of the door being unlocked quickened the pace of Enid's heart. The door opened just a little, and a familiar face peered out, illuminated by the lantern being held by the housekeeper.

"Mrs. Thorpe?" Enid said. "It's me . . . Enid." The older woman's brow furrowed, and she repeated, "It's Enid."

The housekeeper's eyes widened, and she threw the door wide open as it became evident there was no danger. "Oh, my dear girl!" Mrs. Thorpe cried and hurried to set the lantern down so that she could wrap Enid in her arms. "My dear girl!" she repeated while Enid returned the embrace with fervor. How glorious it felt to be held so tightly by someone who knew her and was so happy to see her. Then she realized that Mrs. Thorpe was crying.

"What is it?" Enid asked, taking hold of the woman's shoulders to look at her more closely. "Why are you so upset?"

"There is much to tell you," Mrs. Thorpe said, "but now is not the time. Come in. Come in. You must be exhausted."

Mrs. Thorpe closed the door and took a moment to assess Enid's appearance as she picked up the lantern again and held it close to Enid. "You *look* exhausted. You've traveled far, I assume."

"I have," Enid admitted, taken aback by the temptation to cry. She hadn't cried since she'd left Africa. There had never been the privacy or safety to do so. But she certainly didn't want to fall apart here, in front of the housekeeper.

"And Master Alistair?" Mrs. Thorpe asked. "Has he stayed behind in Africa to . . ." Her sentence faded as she saw the truth in Enid's expression. "Oh, no!" Mrs. Thorpe said and put a hand over her mouth for a moment. "Oh, no!" she said again, her eyes expressing an expectancy, as if she wanted Enid to tell her she was wrong in her assumption.

"He died," Enid said, "of disease." She cleared her throat unnaturally loudly to force back the emotion behind the voicing of those horrible words. "He went quickly. He told me to leave as soon as I could . . . so I wouldn't become ill." Her voice cracked slightly, and she resisted offering more explanation until she could gain her composure.

"And you've been traveling alone for a very long time," Mrs. Thorpe said with perfect compassion.

"Yes," Enid said, her voice cracking more obviously.

"You need a hot bath and a good meal and a decent night's sleep in a real bed; that's what you need." Mrs. Thorpe took hold of her arm, turning her toward the stairs. As she did, Enid noticed that the once-lovely parlor just off the entry hall now looked like something haunted and eerie. All the furnishings were covered with white fabric.

"What's happened?" Enid demanded, her heart pounding. Something had changed dramatically in her absence, and she wondered what it might have been. Even if someone had written to Alistair to inform him of a tragedy, the letter would have taken many months to get there. Obviously, they had not received word of anything amiss at home.

"The master doesn't receive company anymore," Mrs. Thorpe said as if she were trying not to cry. "He's insisted that we use only the rooms in the house that are absolutely necessary; he's let most of the staff go—sent them off with some generous wages. There's only a few here besides myself and Mr. Thorpe."

Enid wondered over the reasons for such drastic changes. For all of Sebastian's gruffness, this all seemed so completely out of character. All Enid could do was ask once again, "What's happened?"

Mrs. Thorpe looked directly at her, and a tear rolled down each of her cheeks. She sniffled and said, "We lost our sweet Marie." Enid gasped and put a hand over her heart in response to the way it pounded even harder. Before Enid could ask what had caused this tragedy, Mrs. Thorpe went on as if she were glad to have someone to talk to. "She died from childbed fever, my dear, and the baby died not a week later." She shook her head and squeezed her eyes closed. "The master has come close to losing his mind, I think. He's closed himself off, so full of anger and grief. He won't see *anyone*, except those that bring his meals and such. And now . . ." Mrs. Thorpe pulled a handkerchief from her pocket and pressed it over her mouth for a long moment. "Now . . . he must learn of his brother's death. Whatever will we do? His heart is already so very broken."

Enid had no answer to the housekeeper's question. This woman had been so good to Enid in the past, and she was grateful to feel that their mutual trust and acceptance had not waned. But Enid had come home to circumstances she never could have imagined. She didn't want to be an added burden to Sebastian, and her heart ached for his losses. But she had no answers or solutions. She was still tied up in knots over losing Alistair—something she hadn't even begun to come to terms with when she'd been so preoccupied with simply surviving and finding her way home.

"Never mind that," Mrs. Thorpe said, liberating Enid from having to answer the question. "We can take all of that on tomorrow. Right now, you need some tender care, my dear; something I suspect you've not gotten a bit of in a very long time."

Enid couldn't deny the truth of that. She followed Mrs. Thorpe up the stairs and to the room she'd once shared with Alistair. Once inside, Enid forced away the memories that overcame her, and focused instead on helping Mrs. Thorpe remove the fabric coverings that had kept the furniture free of dust. Mrs. Thorpe opened a window, declaring that the room needed some fresh air, then she gathered up the discarded fabric and left, saying over her shoulder that she'd have hot water and some food sent up for Enid right away. Enid thanked her and sat down on the edge of the bed and cried.

Marie, dead? And a baby lost, as well? Enid couldn't believe it. Her grief over losing Alistair—which she'd mostly managed to suppress throughout her journey home—mingled with the shock of these added losses in the family, and her unshed tears rushed up and out of her like lava spewing violently from a volcano. She tossed her bag on the floor and curled up on top of the silky bedspread, crying so hard that she felt as if her chest would burst open. She hugged a pillow tightly and wrapped herself around it, at the same time pressing it to her mouth to muffle her seemingly endless weeping. She couldn't believe it! Marie had been like a sister to her. Given the fact that her own family had completely shunned her upon her marriage to Alistair, Marie had been a tender and caring source of female companionship. Enid had longed to see her again, to share long walks in the garden, to talk about the books they were reading, and to simply talk and talk.

While Enid felt as if her heart would burst from pain, she thought of Sebastian and couldn't imagine the grief he must be enduring. He was so deeply lost in the deaths of his wife and baby that he'd had most of the house shut up; he'd let go of most of the servants. What kind of madness had overtaken him? And now Enid had to tell him that his brother was dead, as well. She'd never even liked the man. How could she face him with such news? And not only was his brother dead, but Enid had come here hoping and praying that Sebastian would take her in—as well as her unborn baby. If Marie were alive, she believed the possibility of that would have been more likely. But in Marie's absence, it wasn't difficult to imagine Sebastian sending her away, and none too kindly. She believed that Alistair was entitled to an allowance, and that in the event of his death, it should by all reasoning fall to her. But Sebastian was the elder brother, and all such things were under his control. She had no idea whether he would deem her worthy of receiving her husband's rightful inheritance. Her future— and that of her baby—was in the hands of Sebastian Hawthorne. And he was so deeply lost in grief that he'd shut himself away from the world. And what did Enid have to bring him but more grief?

Enid was startled by a knock at the door and hurried to wipe her tears in an attempt to appear composed. "Come in," she called, and Mr. Thorpe brought in buckets of steaming water. A young maid that Enid had never seen before followed him into the room, carrying a tray with tea and something to eat that was hidden beneath a cloth of floral fabric.

"Thank you," Enid said.

The maid nodded and scurried out. Thorpe looked at her and sighed. "It's so good to have you back, my dear. Perhaps you can bring some life back to this place."

"It's very good to see you, Thorpe," she said, "although I fear you put too much faith in me."

"Time will tell," he said and left the room, closing the door behind him.

Enid's stomach growled as if it had been brought to life by the smell of food in the room. By the time she had eaten everything on the tray, the same maid came to the room with more water.

"Is there anything else you'll be needing tonight, m'lady?" the maid asked.

"Please . . . just call me Enid," she said, having never been comfortable with such formalities. "And you are?"

"Tilly," the young maid said, looking down in a way that indicated shyness.

"It's a pleasure to meet you, Tilly. Thank you for your help." Enid nodded toward the bell rope. "I promise I'll ring if I need anything, but I'm certain I have everything I could possibly want for tonight. I'll see you in the morning."

Tilly nodded before she picked up the dinner tray and exited the room.

Enid hurried to get cleaned up, dismayed to realize how long she'd been wearing the clothes she'd arrived in, and that everything in her bag was equally dirty. Then she recalled that this had been the room she'd shared with Alistair before they'd left the country. She held her breath as she opened a bureau drawer and sighed with relief to see her own underclothing still there. In another drawer she found nightgowns.

Feeling cleaner and less restricted than she had since long before Alistair's death, Enid crawled between soft sheets into a comfortable bed. It all felt like heaven in contrast to the life she'd lived in Africa. There was so much to face that she didn't even want to think about, and she knew she had a long way to go in coming to terms with her grief over the losses in her life. But she was home. And even if Sebastian was resistant to her staying here, she felt sure that Mr. and Mrs. Thorpe would help her. At least she was among friends in that regard.

Enid silently thanked God for all the obvious blessings and miracles that had brought her safely home. Before she had concluded her prayer, she drifted into an exhausted slumber.

Chapter Two

MASTER OF THE HOUSE

ENID AWOKE TO AN OVERWHELMING wave of relief to realize she was home and safe, but her thoughts went quickly to the reasons she'd come home alone, and the difficulties she'd come home to that she had yet to face. She could hear rain falling outside, which made her grateful that the weather had been more favorable the previous day when she'd been walking from the village. She'd missed the English rain, but today it only enhanced her dark mood. She distracted herself by examining the fine clothes hanging in the wardrobe Alistair had gotten for her when she'd become his wife. She was glad to find a handful of dresses with high waistlines and plenty of gathers that she could wear in her pregnant state and not look ridiculous. She set her eye on a cream-colored piece with a scattered blue floral design.

Even though the sun was barely up, Enid was dressed and had her clean hair pinned up neatly long before she heard any distant evidence of life in the house. She'd become so accustomed to sharing close quarters with children of all ages, and the mothers who were continually trying—usually unsuccessfully—to keep their children from disturbing other passengers. But babies demanded to be fed at all hours, and young children often awoke early and became restless very quickly. Now Enid was greeted only by silence as she walked the halls of this enormous house she had once called home. Alistair had given her his name, and she was pregnant with his child, but she wondered if that was enough for her to be considered a part of the family. If not, she would be without family completely. That thought terrified her far more than any concerns about financial security. She didn't want to be alone in the world, even if her only familial connection was Sebastian Hawthorne, a man who was apparently so lost in his grief that he'd cut himself off from the world as much as it was possible to do so and still survive.

Enid thought about Sebastian as she went up one staircase and down another, through a short hallway, down more stairs, and then through a very long hallway. She wondered as she often had if the luxury of being a gentleman—and having no occupation required—was a stark disadvantage in such situations. If Sebastian had needed to work to provide for his family, would he have been able to lose himself so completely? She thought of his two young sons—Marie's sons—and wondered how they were faring with the loss of their mother and the subsequent disappearance of their father. Of course, she knew they would be well cared for and even loved by the servants responsible for them, but surely that could never compensate for a father's love, when they had to know that their father was in the house. She wondered from what Mrs. Thorpe had said if Sebastian had been interacting with the children at all. She certainly hoped so, for all their sakes. But she recalled Mrs. Thorpe saying that he'd cut himself off from everyone except those who brought his meals and other necessities to him. Enid let out a quivering sigh of concern and tried not to think of how she needed to tell him that Alistair was dead.

Realizing that she felt very hungry, and consequently on the verge of nausea, Enid stopped wandering aimlessly and headed to the kitchen. She wasn't surprised to enter and find Mrs. Miller busy at the stove. The head cook was taller than average and carried around a very full figure—a fact that she jokingly declared was the result of spending every day in a kitchen sampling her own work. Mrs. Miller had been working in this kitchen for many years. But beyond the cook, Enid was surprised to see only Tilly—the maid she'd met the previous day—there helping her. In the past there had been a handful of assistants in the kitchen who helped Mrs. Miller create culinary masterpieces of which both Sebastian and Marie had been very fond. Alistair had told Enid that his parents had been very much the same when they'd been alive, and he believed it was wasteful—both in the extravagance of the food, and the time the servants spent preparing it. But Marie had told Enid it was her belief that enjoying food in such a way was a blessing, and should therefore *be* enjoyed, as long as it was never taken for granted and thanks was always given to God for such abundance. It was also Marie's belief that the ridiculous amount of money that had come through the generations of Hawthornes was best spent on providing a good living for those who worked in the household. As long as they were given fair wages and treated well, it was a blessing for them. Marie had also made certain—as the lady of the house—that the servants all ate the same meal that was prepared for the family, so they could enjoy the fruits of their labors.

Enid stood in the doorway of the kitchen for a long moment, unnoticed, while she took in the dramatic changes. She wondered where those who had once worked here had gone. And she felt certain that Mrs. Miller was surely cooking much simpler menus, given the lack of assistance available to her. Enid didn't mind the idea of less complicated meals, but there were other facets of this situation that left her feeling uneasy.

"Good morning," she finally said, as the smell of sausages frying alerted Enid to the fact that she was becoming more and more hungry.

"Oh, my land!" Mrs. Miller said, turning abruptly to look at Enid as she tossed the spatula she'd been holding onto the top of the stove. "Mrs. Thorpe told me you'd come back," the cook said as she crossed the room and embraced Enid even more tightly than the housekeeper had the previous evening. Enid returned the embrace, grateful for the comfortable relationships she'd developed with many people on the staff prior to her leaving for Africa. She thought of those she'd grown to care for who were no longer here but pushed her sadness away to be confronted at a more convenient time.

"Oh, you look lovely, deary," Mrs. Miller said, "especially considering all you've been through."

"It's very good to see you," Enid said, ignoring the woman's reference to difficulties that Enid was trying not to think about.

"I was going to have Tilly bring some breakfast to your room," Mrs. Miller said. "You met Tilly, already."

"I did, yes," Enid said, exchanging a nod with the shy maid. "But there's no need for anyone to be bringing me my meals when I'm perfectly capable of coming to the kitchen myself."

The cook's expression became cloudy. "Mrs. Thorpe must have told you of our change in circumstances since you were home."

"Yes, she did," Enid said, looking at the floor. "I admit that I'm still rather in shock."

"I believe we all are to some degree," Mrs. Miller said, putting a motherly hand on Enid's arm. "And just this morning I heard you have lost your dear Alistair." She sniffled and dabbed at her eyes with the corner of her apron. "I did not want the two of you to travel to such a place, but I never imagined this to be the outcome." Enid said nothing, and Mrs. Miller sighed. "More to the point, deary, you must know that his lordship takes his meals alone upstairs. There is no family for you to eat with."

"I would be delighted to eat here in the kitchen with the rest of you, whenever that might be. I've been on my own for far too long, and would prefer some company at mealtime."

"Oh, it would be a delight for all of us," Mrs. Miller said, clapping her hands. "I'll have breakfast on in less than half an hour, if that suits you, deary, and—"

"Forgive me," Enid said, pressing a hand over her belly to make it unmistakably clear that she was pregnant. Mrs. Miller's eyes widened, and her smile broadened. Tilly took a quick glance and looked away.

"Oh, deary!" the cook said and guided Enid to a chair. "You must certainly have a bit of something to tide you over," she added as if she'd read Enid's mind. "Would a slice of yesterday's bread and some fresh butter do, or would you prefer a—"

"That would be perfect," Enid said with enthusiasm, recalling how dreadful most of the food had been on the ship. Even Mrs. Miller's most simple menus would far surpass most of what she'd eaten since she'd left here nearly two years ago.

Enid enjoyed her bread and butter and a cup of tea while she listened to Mrs. Miller chatter in a way that didn't slow down her cooking in the slightest. She talked of all the local happenings that had taken place during Enid's absence, filling her in on all the latest gossip, but carefully avoided speaking of the tragic events that had occurred right here under this roof.

When it was time for breakfast, the other servants began to appear, seating themselves at the table and enjoying either tea or coffee while they waited for the others so that the meal could be served. Enid well remembered Beauford the stablemaster, and Lex, one of the stable hands who had always been among the friendliest. They were as pleased to see her as she was to see them, but she was astonished to hear they were the only two men left working in the stables, although they admitted they had little to do beyond keeping the animals cared for and things in order, since the master hadn't left the house—by horse or carriage—since his wife had died.

Mr. and Mrs. Thorpe—the head butler and housekeeper respectively—arrived to take their places. Enid knew the Thorpes had been working in this house since they were very young, and in fact the two had met here, fallen in love, and married, remaining together as they'd worked under the now-deceased Sixth Earl of Thornewell and his wife. Sebastian and Alistair's mother had passed away from an unexpected illness when they had been children—old enough to remember, but too young to know how to contend with the grief of losing their mother. Their father had died from a heart problem not long before Enid had met Alistair; she'd never met the man, but she did know how difficult the loss had been for Alistair and his brother. But Mr. and Mrs. Thorpe had not only cared for the household, they had taken a very personal responsibility for the boys as they'd grown into adults. Enid knew from long-ago conversations with these good people that their inability to have children had been compensated and fulfilled by caring for the Hawthorne household and its residents.

Once Mr. and Mrs. Thorpe were seated, Mrs. Miller and Tilly set the serving dishes on the table and then took their seats. Enid noted how they were all gathered at one end of a very long table that she had once known to be filled—and in fact, the staff had eaten their meals in shifts because there hadn't been enough room. She saw that Thorpe was about to say grace over the food, but before he could, she hurriedly commented, "Is this all? Isn't anyone else coming?"

Everyone looked mildly alarmed. Mrs. Thorpe took it upon herself to explain—as she usually did. "This *is* all . . . except for Gert and Maisy who care for the children, and they always share meals with them. There's Mr. Granger the overseer, but he never takes meals with us, as you'll recall."

"And everyone else is gone?" Enid asked. At the silence she received in response, she clarified, "Did Lord Hawthorne let go of *everyone* else?"

"Everyone except those that went of their own accord," Beauford said, "not wanting to work for him no more."

Enid took note of the awkwardness she had sparked, and she was also aware of the obvious need to get on with breakfast. "Forgive me," she said. "I'm just . . . attempting to catch up with all that's changed in my absence."

"Of course you are, deary," Mrs. Miller said, and Thorpe proceeded with saying grace.

The meal tasted incredibly good to Enid. She'd definitely missed English food, and she might have been embarrassed by how many sausages she ate, and her extra helping of eggs, if not for the way that everyone at the table was pleased to learn she was expecting a baby, and they all seemed to know this was normal for a pregnant woman.

After breakfast everyone except Mrs. Miller and Tilly scattered to see to their work. Enid helped clear the table, but when she tried to help clean the dishes, Mrs. Miller gently scolded her and told her to find something else with which to occupy her time. As Enid left the kitchen, she knew what she was avoiding. The longer she procrastinated telling Sebastian that she was here—and that his brother was dead—the more likely he was to hear it from the servants, if he hadn't already. Mrs. Thorpe had whispered to her after breakfast that he spent his days holed up in his sitting room, as if she'd known—or had expected—that Enid would need to talk to him.

Enid took her time going up the stairs, then she took a minute or two to catch her breath since the baby was becoming bigger and seemed to be pressing on her lungs. When she was finally able to take in a long, deep breath and completely fill her lungs, she drew in every bit of courage she could find and pressed on toward the specified sitting room—a room that had once been a place where she and Alistair had gone to visit with Marie and Sebastian. They'd shared tea there countless times, and together they'd enjoyed much laughter and conversation. Enid hadn't even seen the room since her return, but the descriptions she'd heard of Sebastian's behavior, and the way he'd locked himself away there, made approaching the door feel as if she were about to attend a funeral. It occurred to her that she hadn't been here for Marie's funeral, nor whatever service might have been held for the baby. And then she thought of how there had been no service and no burial for Alistair. She felt a little sick—just as she always did—to think of the condition in which she'd left his body. But she knew the local people well enough to know they would have found a way to gather up the dead and properly dispose of the bodies, and they surely would have had some form of religious service. The people of the village had loved Alistair, as he had them; they would surely care for his body with great respect. In that knowledge alone, she was able to find some measure of peace.

Enid brought her mind back to the present and lifted her hand to knock, but it took her a long moment and another deep breath to force herself to do it. In response to the knock she heard a deep voice bellow, "What?" He clearly believed it was one of the servants; there was no one else in the house except his two sons. Enid wondered again if he'd truly closed himself off from them, as well. The thought tightened her heart.

"May I come in?" she called back.

"You may," he called, "but I might advise against it."

Enid opened the door and was immediately overcome with the stuffiness of the room, as if a window hadn't been opened in many weeks despite the warm temperatures of late summer. The room was also very dim since all the drapes were closed, and only very minimal sunlight was capable of seeping through the heavy fabric.

"You may take the tray," he snarled while Enid's eyes were still attempting to adjust to the darkness of the room. "I'm finished with it."

Once she could see clearly, her eyes focused first on the beautiful chaise, covered with cream-and-rose-colored tapestry; Sebastian had purchased it for Marie during their honeymoon in Paris, and he'd had it shipped home. It had always been Marie's favorite place to sit; she could stretch her legs out in front of her and at the same time remain sitting with her back and head comfortably supported. Enid forced her thoughts away from the fact that Marie was dead, and focused instead on the way Sebastian was lounging on the chaise. He wore dark breeches and black boots, crossed at the ankles. She could make out the stark contrast of the white sleeves of his shirt and the darker color of his waistcoat, but she was unable to discern any further details of his clothing. Still, even in the dimness of the unaired room, Enid had no trouble assessing the depth of his grief; he was practically debilitated by it. He was leaning his head back while he looked toward the window that was covered by draperies.

Knowing she had to get this over with, Enid hurried to say, "I didn't come to take the tray."

Sebastian turned his head abruptly to look at her. Enid found herself remembering an image of Alistair and his brother standing together. Sebastian's hair was much darker than Alistair's, and it had less curl to it. Sebastian was only a little taller, but his shoulders were much broader. Alistair had been thin and almost delicate looking at times. Sebastian was lean and solid and had a commanding air about him. Enid had often wondered if his attitude was a result of being raised to inherit the whole of the estate, or if it was simply his personality. Perhaps both. It took only a second to see that his hair was too long, as was his beard, and he looked generally unkempt. But that wasn't necessarily a surprise. She suspected that the only reason he was adequately dressed had to do with servants coming and going to meet his needs.

"Enid?" he said and put his booted feet on the floor, but he didn't stand. "Is that really you?"

"It is," she said, almost wondering if he might be glad to see her. Then he stood and looked over her shoulder, clearly expecting that she wouldn't be alone. It wasn't *her* that he wanted to see, but his brother. And she had the worst possible news to give him. "He's not here, Sebastian. I've come alone."

"Why?" he demanded, sounding more like the Seventh Earl of Thornewell. "Did you detest Africa so much? Did you leave him? Are you so selfish that you—"

"He's dead," Enid said, and Sebastian sat back down, teetering slightly as he did so. She saw his hands tighten over the edge of the chaise and heard his breathing sharpen. "I'm so very sorry," she said, hearing a quiver in her own voice. She only hoped she could manage to keep from crying until they had completed this conversation.

"What happened?" Sebastian asked without looking up.

"Disease," she said and knew that her hope to do this without tears was pointless. "A terrible disease. It swept through the village like a storm. The contagion was fast. The symptoms took over quickly. There was nothing anyone could do."

Sebastian looked up at her. She couldn't see his eyes, but she sensed his anger. "And yet *you* survived."

Enid told herself not to allow his anger to affect her. He'd just been told of his brother's death, and he'd already been grieving. She just forged ahead with what she knew needed to be said. "I'd hardly been out of the house for weeks. I'd been ill due to . . ." She hesitated and found it difficult to fill her lungs before she finished. "Due to my pregnancy." She couldn't see his eyes, but she could feel the way he looked down at her rounded belly, then back at her face. "When . . . he came home with symptoms . . . he wouldn't let me get anywhere near him." Enid could hear the evidence of her own crying coming through in her words, but she just had to finish. "He . . . went quickly. There was little suffering." She took a ragged breath and sniffled. "Before he died . . . he told me to leave . . . to hurry . . . for the sake of the baby as well as myself." Her breathing became more ragged, her emotion more evident. "I had nowhere else to go, Sebastian." She coughed to avoid sobbing. "I can't even comprehend all that you've lost since we left, and now I've brought more grief to your door, but—"

"Get out!" he said, and Enid feared he was kicking her out of his home without even giving her a chance to defend her position. She was both relieved and deeply concerned when he added, "I don't care if you stay in the house; just stay away from me. I don't want to see you or any evidence of you, *ever*."

"Sebastian, I—"

"Get out!" he shouted, and she did, slamming the door behind her.

Enid leaned against the wall in the hallway, trying to keep her tears silent, trying to catch her breath, trying to comprehend his pain and what it was doing to him. She was relieved that he would let her stay, but she'd come home to a mausoleum. While her feet refused to move, she wept with a hand pressed over her mouth, wondering if it would ever be possible for this house to be filled with light and love again. Her knees gave out and she slithered silently to the floor when she heard Sebastian sobbing like a child, a child who had lost his little brother. It was minutes before she found the strength to get to her feet and creep silently out of his hearing and back to her own room, but it was more than an hour before she could stop crying; and well into the afternoon she was still haunted by the evidence of Sebastian's grief that echoed over and over in her mind. During lunch in the kitchen, Enid was glad for the conversations going on around her, which she barely heard. She was asked more than once if she was all right, but she only smiled and replied that she was simply very tired, that she'd not quite recovered from her journey. The conversations continued, and Enid's mind was compelled back to her dramatic exchange with Sebastian, and the haunting sounds of his grief. She knew he'd be mortified to realize he'd been overheard, but she had no intention of ever letting him know. She wondered what she might be able to do to help ease his pain, but he had made it clear he didn't want to see her *at all*. She concluded that all she could do was pray for him, and she did. Every time the memory of his sorrow crept into her mind, she countered it with a silent prayer on his behalf. But at the moment, it was impossible to see how Sebastian Hawthorne might ever come out of hiding.

Enid wondered throughout the afternoon whether Sebastian's edict included staying away from his sons. Given the fact that he'd not even so much as mentioned them, she decided a visit to the nursery was in order. She wondered if her nephews would even remember her. Matthew might, given that he'd been five at the time she'd departed with Alistair, but Mark had only been three. She knew they would have changed a great deal, and she wondered if she might even recognize them if she'd happened upon them elsewhere. But she had some tender and precious memories of her nephews, of playing games and reading stories together. And she felt eager to renew her relationships with them—especially considering the loss of their mother. And she also wanted to see for herself how they were doing, following the enormous changes in their lives.

Enid found the door to the nursery open—the room where all the toys were kept, and where the boys had spent much of their time, especially when the weather was not suitable for playing outside. Given today's rain, Enid believed there was a good chance she'd find them there. But she only found a young woman with blonde hair on her knees picking up an enormous number of scattered toys.

"Hello," Enid said, and the startled young woman's head snapped up in response. She went to stand up, but Enid stopped her. "It's all right. I don't mean to interrupt. I'm Enid Hawthorne, an aunt to the boys. I was hoping to see them, but . . ."

"They've gone with Gert . . . the governess . . . for their lessons," the young woman said, and Enid heard her sniffle while she continued to vigorously toss wooden blocks into one box, toy soldiers into another, and a great many tiny play horses into yet another. Beyond that, the floor was scattered with toy swords and pistols that had been carved from wood, puzzle pieces that appeared to be from more than one puzzle, and several storybooks. The room was, quite simply, a disaster.

"Here, let me help you," Enid said, going down on her knees to start stacking up the scattered storybooks.

"There is no need, m'lady," the young woman said, seeming embarrassed.

"Please call me Enid," she replied, receiving a surprised glance. "I grew up looking after my younger siblings and often picking up after them. I confess I'm terribly uncomfortable with being placed above the servants in the household simply because I married into the family." The young woman said nothing, and Enid crawled across the floor to where puzzle pieces were scattered, realizing she would have to put them together to figure out which pieces went with which puzzle. "You must be Maisy," Enid said, and again she got a quick glance from the young woman who was still vigorously picking up blocks and toy soldiers; there were so *many* of them.

To explain herself, Enid added, "I was told that Gert was the governess, and you are the nanny. Is that right?"

"Yes, m'lady," Maisy said.

"Enid, please . . . at least when no one else in the family is around. And then . . . Mrs. Hawthorne would be fine."

Maisy nodded slightly and kept working. "What happened here?" Enid asked. "It looks as if the boys purposely dumped out and scattered every toy they own."

Maisy suddenly sat on the floor, hung her head, and began to sob. "Oh, my dear," Enid said, crawling toward her which was easier than trying to stand up. She put an arm around Maisy's shoulders. "What ever is the matter?"

"It was such a pleasure caring for Mattie and Markie when I first came here. They're delightful boys, and they were so well-behaved. But since they've lost their mother . . ." Her words melted into more crying. "It's as if they're . . . lost . . . or angry. Or both."

"Or perhaps they're angry because they feel lost and they don't know how to come to terms with such feelings." Enid tightened her arm around Maisy. "They're children; they cannot possibly understand how to manage such enormous grief."

"I do agree with you . . . Enid," Maisy said. "But they'll not listen to a word I say. They don't respect me as they once did. They throw their toys and fight with each other almost constantly. Lady Hawthorne— may she rest in peace—always made it clear that the boys' parents should handle any significant discipline; that it was my job to watch over them and report bad behavior to their parents. But . . . now . . ."

"Now their mother is gone, and their father has made himself completely inaccessible," Enid said, feeling angry with Sebastian. His grief was certainly understandable. His complete disregard of his children was unconscionable. She took a deep breath and reminded herself not to jump to conclusions. Instead she asked, "And what has their father said about their bad behavior?"

"Oh, m'lady," Maisy said, looking up at Enid, "they've not seen their father once since their mother was put in the ground. Not once. They cry at night for their mother, and ask me why their father doesn't love them anymore, now that their mother has gone to heaven. And what am I to tell them? Because I can't answer their questions, I feel as if they turn their sorrow to anger and they take it out on me. My time with them has come to be nothing but sorrow and strain; sometimes I even feel afraid. Mattie is getting so strong. The boys are tall and strong like their father, and they're growing so fast, and I . . ." Maisy dissolved into tears once again while Enid tried to comfort her and hide the way she was fuming over Sebastian's complete neglect of his sons, and the grief it was causing them and those who had been left to care for them.

While Maisy gained her composure, Enid reminded herself not to act on her anger. It was something Alistair had taught her, and she couldn't deny the value of the lesson. Her own father had been quick to lose his temper, even though he was a good man and he'd never crossed the line of being abusive or cruel. But Enid had unfortunately taken after her father in that regard. She sometimes had a short fuse, and Alistair had been very much the opposite. His patience and kindness had been an inspiring example to her, and she wanted to honor him by practicing all the good he'd taught her.

Enid continued to help Maisy pick up all the toys and put the room in order. She initiated conversation with the young maid that was more personal—avoiding anything to do with the boys and their neglectful father. Enid told Maisy a little about her husband's death and her journey back to England, and she learned that Maisy had run away from home at an early age, wanting to get away from a father who drank too much and behaved very badly when he was drunk. Maisy couldn't remember her mother; she only knew that her mother had been expected to cook and clean and had received no love or appreciation in return. She'd worked in a tavern for a couple of years, which had turned out to be a job where she watched over the owner's children more than she served food and drinks. A friend who was aware of how much Maisy had enjoyed caring for children had heard of an opening at Thornewell Hall and Maisy had applied, not really believing it would come to anything. She'd been interviewed by Marie Hawthorne, who had taken a liking to her, and she'd been here ever since. By comparing dates, Enid realized Maisy had come to work here within weeks of her leaving with Alistair.

Once they'd gotten to know each other a little, Enid glanced around the room and said, "Might I make a suggestion that could possibly lessen the difficulty of this situation?"

"Oh, anything!" Maisy said.

"When my younger siblings left their toys to be picked up by someone else, my mother would lock the toys in a closet and hide the key, and the children were not allowed to play with them until they'd done something to earn back that privilege. And then, it was only one toy at a time." Seeing the intrigue—even delight—in Maisy's expression, Enid went on. "Perhaps not having access to the toys will teach Mattie and Markie to appreciate them, and then if they are only allowed to play with one thing until it's picked up and put away, they will not leave such a ridiculous mess for you to clean up."

"I like that idea very much," Maisy said. "But what if their father—"

"If their father has some objection, then perhaps he will come out of hiding long enough to deal with the problem. And I will gladly take accountability for the decision. If he speaks to you about it when I'm not around, please tell him you were acting on my suggestion. I'd be *more* than happy to speak with him about this situation."

Maisy let out a soft chuckle, as if she would like to see that. Enid only said, "Now, where shall we hide the toys?" A quick look around the room showed many shelves for toys and books, but no closets or cupboards. Enid stood and walked out of the room with Maisy following her across the hall to an unused guest room, where all the furnishings were covered with white fabric. She lifted the covering off a large armoire and laughed. "I think this will do nicely."

Enid and Maisy quickly moved all the toys—except for a few storybooks—to the room across the hall. What they couldn't fit into the armoire, they put beneath the bed. Then they put the fabric that was meant to protect the furniture from dust back in place, and the room looked completely undisturbed. They left and closed the door behind them while Enid said, "Now, I would recommend that you only get toys out while the children are with the governess so that they will never discover your hiding place. Perhaps the two of you can discuss the situation and agree on what constitutes earning rewards."

"Oh, we will!" Maisy said, her countenance entirely different from when Enid had found her lost in a sea of scattered toys. "I do believe Gert will be thrilled with this plan."

"Excellent," Enid said. "And I will do all I can to help. As soon as the boys are finished with their lessons, I would like to see them—even though I'm not certain they'll remember me."

Maisy looked at the watch pinned to her dress and said, "They should be returning to the nursery soon; it's not long until supper now."

Enid and Maisy had barely sat down to wait for the boys when they came bounding into the room, a visibly exhausted Gert following right behind them. Enid exchanged a nod and a smile with Gert; it was evident they both knew each other's identity. Mattie and Markie immediately stopped when they saw someone different sitting there, which distracted them from realizing their toys were gone.

"Hello," Enid said in response to the four little eyes staring at her. "Do you remember me? It's been a very long time."

"Auntie Enid?" Mattie asked with a hint of pleasure in his voice.

"You *do* remember me!" Enid said with a little laugh and opened her arms even though she wasn't certain this seven-year-old boy would be open to a hug from a relative he'd not seen for a very long time. But the child rushed into her arms and held to her much longer and more tightly than she'd expected. She immediately recognized the evidence of a boy who had lost his mother and was receiving no attention from his father. Enid held him close and whispered, "It's so very good to see you, Matthew. I've missed you so!" He looked at her as if to see if she really meant it, and she felt the need to speak her most prominent thought. She didn't believe in pretending that bad things hadn't happened, but chose rather to talk about them in a way that might help a child understand. "I was so sorry to hear about your mother, Matthew. I've felt very sad that she's no longer here. I think you must also feel very sad."

He nodded but seemed to be trying not to cry, and she wondered if there was a reason he felt the need to hold back his tears. "Baby Sister died too," Matthew said.

"I'm so sorry about that, as well," Enid said, taking the boy's hand. "Perhaps we can talk more about that another time." Matthew nodded eagerly, and Enid turned to look at Mark who was staring at her, appearing puzzled. "You probably don't remember me," she said, "but I remember you. I'm Enid, and I'm your aunt. Mattie always called me Auntie Enid. You may call me that too if you like."

Mark only nodded with what appeared to be a cautious acceptance; perhaps he would need some time to adjust to her presence in their lives. Given the lack of any parental presence in their lives, Enid felt compelled to make a conscious effort to spend time with them every day. Perhaps in this way, her being here might serve some useful purpose.

The boys lost their interest in Enid and quickly realized their toys were missing. Enid was astonished at how quickly they both changed from little gentlemen into what could only be described as overgrown toddlers. The absence of their toys provoked fits of yelling and crying, and even throwing themselves prostrate on the floor, kicking with their feet and pounding with their fists.

Enid heard both Maisy and Gert sighing loudly with an air of defeat, and she realized they were flanking her. "Don't worry, m'lady," Maisy said. "This kind of behavior is not uncommon even *if* they had their toys."

"May I?" Enid asked.

"Anything you can do would be appreciated," Gert said. "You're their aunt; we're just here to do what we've been hired to do."

Enid sat on the floor near the location of the tantrum and simply said, "When the two of you are finished acting like babies, I would very much like to talk to you about the privileges of being grown-up boys who know how to behave like gentlemen. From now on, such behavior as this will not get you anything but time alone with *nothing* to play with and *nothing* to eat. And I can assure you that Maisy and Gert will support me in this." She looked over her shoulder to see both women nod firmly in agreement; their relief in having some guidance and assistance with this problem was evident.

Enid wondered if the boys could even hear what she was saying through all of their overly dramatic wailing, but she just sat there for a minute, then asked calmly, "Did you hear what I said? Because we will be eating supper without you if you don't calm down and behave." They did quiet down, but they still looked pouty and retained their prostrate position on the floor. "You will be able to earn the privilege of playing with your toys when you behave properly for both your governess and your nanny. When you behave like babies—which I know you are not—you will not be given privileges. I know this is a change from the way it's been, but we'll talk about it more tomorrow. Right now, I need you to straighten yourselves up before supper arrives, and I need you to eat like the very big boys I know you are. Can you do that?"

Neither of the boys made a sound or gave any response until Tilly brought supper into the nursery and laid it out on the table. When Tilly saw Enid there, she said, "I'll bring more if you'll be dining here."

Enid winked at Tilly and said loudly, "I don't see any need for you to bring more food. I'll just eat the food these young men are apparently not interested in eating." Both boys jumped to their feet and ran to their chairs. "Like gentlemen," Enid said to them and they both sat down with exaggerated proper manners. Enid smiled at Tilly and said, "I do believe I'll have my supper here. I apologize for the extra trouble."

"No trouble at all, Mrs. Hawthorne," Tilly said with a little smile, and Enid wondered if the entire household was aware of the difficult behavior of the boys.

During the meal, Enid asked the boys to tell her about some of their interests and favorite activities, but neither of them had much to say. Now that they were calm, she noticed from their demeanor that they seemed somewhat depressed. Given the situation, she could well understand that, but she wished she knew what to do about it. She believed some daily time with their father could make a world of difference—unless he was so depressed that it would only exacerbate the problem. But she wasn't about to go and talk to Sebastian Hawthorne about this—or any—situation.

After supper Maisy told the boys to get into their pajamas and clean their teeth and then she would read them a bedtime story. "*If* you mind your manners," she added with a firm confidence that seemed to have grown in just the last little while.

With the boys absent, Enid talked for a few minutes with Gert and Maisy about how they might work together to enforce new rules for the boys, and how they could expect a great deal of misbehaving until the children realized that the rules—and the consequences—were going to be firmly in place whether they wanted them to be or not. Enid assured them that the boys would likely catch on quickly—given her own experience of dealing with her younger siblings for many years—and that once their acting out subsided, Gert and Maisy would surely find their jobs much easier.

"And what if their father gets wind of these changes and doesn't like them?" Gert asked as if she were truly afraid of him.

"If that happens, I will deal with their father," Enid said, thinking she might rather die than do so. His shouting at her to get out of his room echoed through her mind, but then she thought of hearing him cry when he'd believed no one was close enough to hear. Her heart ached for him, despite her fear of what he might do if she ignored his edict to never allow him to see her in his house. As long as he kept himself locked away from the world, avoiding him would not be a problem. But no one in the house wanted him to live this way, and Enid wondered how long she could manage to not cross paths with the cantankerous master of the house.

Chapter Three

THE SCOLDING

OVER THE NEXT WEEK, ENID settled into a comfortable routine. She ate breakfast and supper with the servants in the kitchen, and enjoyed becoming reacquainted with those she had known before, and more acquainted with Tilly—who was the only one with whom she shared meals in the kitchen who had not been here before Enid had left. Enid enjoyed helping Mrs. Miller and Tilly with cleaning the dishes, and helping with the laundry. It quickly became evident that they needed and very much appreciated the help, and Enid wondered once again why Sebastian had let so many servants go when the ones he had were— for the most part—overwhelmed by their work. Even though Sebastian never left the house, and therefore didn't use any of the horses or carriages, there were still many animals that needed a great deal of care, and the vehicles in the carriage house needed maintenance in order to remain in good, working condition. Meals still had to be cooked, there was laundry to be done, and a certain amount of cleaning was necessary to keep any household running properly.

Mr. and Mrs. Thorpe were busy practically every minute of the day, and Mrs. Miller and Tilly were working continually. Enid made a point of helping where she could, and she enjoyed the opportunity to feel useful— and earn her keep. She also appreciated the conversation she was able to share with these good people who had once felt like family to her. And they were quickly coming to feel that way again. Still, the amount of work being required of them left her frustrated and confused, and it took great effort to prevent her feelings from turning to anger over Sebastian's obliviousness to all that was happening in his own home.

Enid shared lunch in the nursery with the boys and their nanny and governess. She quickly learned that Maisy and Gert had become very good friends, and even though they each had their different responsibilities with the boys—and they each needed their own time to take care of personal matters—they both shared every meal with the children, and they often worked together to take the boys outside for play or exercise, or to give them their lessons, or oversee their playtime in the nursery.

The first couple of days after the new rules for the boys were in place proved to be hugely vexing for both Gert and Maisy. But on the third day it seemed that both Matthew and Mark had realized their lives would be much more pleasant if they obeyed the women caring for them. The tantrums gradually decreased, their manners became more appropriate, and they spoke to their governess and nanny more respectfully. All this because they didn't want to be left in a playroom devoid of toys, nor did they want to miss the privilege of a good meal. Enid had explained to Gert and Maisy that her mother had often used this threat, but she'd never let a child go hungry—although instead of sharing a hearty supper with the family, the child would be given bread and water in his or her room. Matthew and Mark never tested the threat enough to have *that* experience, but the nanny and governess were pleased with knowing it was an option. Enid was proud of them for the way they calmly and confidently dealt with these new boundaries, and it was quite remarkable how the boys became so much less difficult after knowing that such boundaries were in place. When they were given the privilege of playing with some of their toys— on the condition that they clean them up when they were finished—they behaved as if Christmas had come.

On Sunday, Enid attended church with the rest of household— except for Sebastian who remained home alone. While she sat with Matthew and Mark on either side of her, and Gert and Maisy flanking them on both sides, she was impressed with how well they behaved, and more than once she whispered in their ears how proud she was of them. The boys were given an extra portion of cake after dinner as a reward for their good behavior in church, and Enid spent most of the day playing with them and reading them stories as bedtime approached. It was all going marvelously until Mark looked up at her with sad eyes and asked, "Will you be our mother, Auntie Enid? Our mother went to heaven, and we won't see her again until *we* go to heaven. Will *you* be our mother?"

Enid's heart quickened with compassion while her throat tightened with sorrow. She cleared her throat and fought back her tears, struggling to hurry and come up with an appropriate response. "Markie," she said, touching his face, "I'm so very, very sorry that your mother had to leave while you and your brother are so young." Enid felt Matthew take hold of her arm from where he was sitting on the other side of her. "It's all right for you to miss her, and to be sad. I can't be your mother, but I'm your aunt, and I will do everything I can to be here for you, and perhaps I can do some of the things your mother isn't here to do."

"Like read us stories at bedtime?" Matthew asked, and she turned to look at him. Enid knew that Maisy had been reading them bedtime stories ever since Marie's death, but apparently they didn't feel it was the same.

"Yes, Mattie," Enid said, "if you like, I will read you bedtime stories . . . although Maisy very much likes to do so, and I think we should let her spend that time with you occasionally. What do you think?"

Both boys thought about it, then nodded firmly. Mark said, "Maisy is nice. So is Gert. I like them." He looked up at Enid again. "But you're our aunt."

Enid wasn't certain how their little minds were spinning all of this, especially when there was so much that had happened in their lives that would be confusing and upsetting for any child. She was glad for the distraction when Matthew asked, "How are you our aunt? Your last name is Hawthorne; that's the same as ours. But I thought an aunt would be a sister to one of our parents, and you're not."

"No, I'm not a sister to either your father or your mother," Enid said.

Before she could finish her explanation, Matthew added, his brow furrowed in deep thought, "And you're going to have a baby, so you must be married. You can't have a baby unless you're married."

Enid recognized Marie's teaching in his statement, and she avoided trying to tell her nephews that it *was* possible to have a baby without being married, but it wasn't appropriate. That lesson could wait until they were older. She hurried to explain, "My husband is a brother to your father; that is how I am your aunt." She gave them a moment to take that in, and saw the enlightenment in their eyes. But before they could ask where her husband was, she quickly went on. "My husband—his name is Alistair, and—"

"I remember him!" Matthew declared. "He lived here too, and then you both went away."

"That's right, Mattie," Enid said and forced any measure of grief out of her story. She simply stuck to the facts. "Your Uncle Alistair very much wanted to be a missionary and go to a faraway land to help people who are suffering with great hardships."

"What does that mean?" Mark asked.

"There are many people who don't have enough to eat, and they often don't have clean water to drink. They live in tiny little huts—smaller than the garden shed—with dirt floors and only large, dried leaves as a roof." The boys looked astonished but said nothing, and Enid continued. "I knew when I married Alistair that he wanted to be a missionary, and I agreed to go with him when he decided it was time. But I'm afraid I wasn't nearly as good at helping people as he was. We had a much nicer home than most of the people we were trying to help, but it was very hot there, and I didn't speak the same language as these people, and—"

"Did they speak French?" Mark asked.

"No, darling," Enid chuckled. "They didn't speak French. But there are many, many different languages all over the world." Realizing she had strayed from the point, she forced herself to tell them what really mattered; they could talk more about Africa another time. "While we were living in this village, your Uncle Alistair became very ill. Many of the people were ill. And it was a very serious illness. He died." The boys both gasped softly but said nothing. "Just before he died he made me promise to take the money we had and leave so I wouldn't become ill. And so I came here. When I married Alistair, this became my home, and even though he has gone to heaven, I am still your aunt—which is one of the happiest things I know."

"I'm happy too that you're my aunt," Mark said.

Matthew asked, "Is Alistair in heaven with our mother?"

"I would like to think so," Enid said. "We can't know for certain about things like that, but we can have faith. Faith is believing in something even though you don't have any actual proof that it's real. But we can *feel* faith. And I feel in my heart that those we love are in another place, a better place, and when it's time for us to leave this world, we will see them again."

The boys were completely silent for a few minutes, as if they had a great deal to think about. Mark finally looked up at Enid and said, "Until it's time for us to leave and go to heaven, will you be our mother?"

Enid laughed softly and touched his nose with hers. "I'm your aunt, silly boy. I just explained all that." Sensing the seriousness of the question for little Mark, Enid said more thoughtfully, "I will be here for you as much as I possibly can—just as your mother would be. I think she would want me to do that." As Enid's promise came through her lips, she wondered what their father might think of her making a commitment to be a part of his children's lives when he apparently didn't even want her to ever cross his path *at all*. Deciding that it was the children who mattered most, she just put her arms around them and hugged them tightly.

The chiming of the clock on the mantel alerted Enid to the fact that the boys should have been in bed by now, and she had promised Maisy she would make certain that happened so the nanny could have some time to herself. She urged them along to get ready for bed and they protested only slightly before they left to do so.

"I'll come read you one more story before you go to sleep if you hurry," Enid said, "and then I'll tuck you in."

Enid sat for a few minutes in silence after the boys had run from the room. She considered the impact Alistair's death had had on her, and she couldn't imagine what it had been like for these boys to lose their mother at such a tender age. And the entire situation was so much worse due to the complete absence of their father in their lives. She felt angry with Sebastian in that moment, but reminded herself that she could do nothing about *that* without ignoring his angry edict. And as her father would have said, she had no desire to poke an angry bear. The thought spurred a moment of missing her family, but it was something she felt several times a day—every day—and with practiced efficiency she pushed the feeling away, prompting herself to go and read the promised bedtime story.

After the boys were tucked into their separate beds in the same room, Enid turned down the lantern and moved toward the door, surprised to hear Mark say, "I love you, Auntie Enid."

"I love you too, Auntie Enid," Matthew added.

The ill-tempered, difficult boys she had encountered not so many days ago were nowhere to be found in that moment. She eagerly and sincerely said, "And I love the both of you—very much. I will see you tomorrow at lunchtime—after you've finished your morning lessons."

"We'll be very good for Maisy and Gert," Matthew declared, almost as if he feared not doing so might cause Enid to not keep her promise to see them.

"I'm very glad to hear it," she said. "It's important to be kind to people, especially those who are working with us, and helping take care of us." She added something that she felt needed to be said, "I want you to know that I will love you no matter what. Can you remember that?"

They both said "yes" at the same time.

"Good night, sweet boys," Enid said.

"Good night," they both said, and Enid left the room, but she felt suddenly a little weak and lightheaded and was glad to find a comfortable little settee there in the hallway. As she sat there, she wondered if it had been put here purposely for the sake of being close to the children for any number of reasons.

Enid wondered if her physical symptoms were a result of her pregnancy, or an emotional response to the sensitive nature of the conversation she'd shared with her nephews. She'd spoken so matter-of-factly of Alistair's death, but now that she was no longer in view of the young boys, thoughts of it tightened her chest and pushed a torrent of tears into her eyes that had no choice but to spill down her face. She then thought of Marie's untimely death—and that of the baby she'd recently given birth to—and her tears increased. Enid thought of her own baby growing inside of her, and the deep love she already felt for this tiny new life. She rubbed her belly lovingly, wondering what it might be like after the baby was born, and was momentarily horrified by the very idea that her child might not live. Enid had accepted this baby as a part of her life almost from the moment she'd known she was pregnant. Now, she felt it moving inside of her frequently and she had invested great hope in a bright future for her child. Any other possibility was too awful to even think about. Overwhelmed with a myriad of difficult thoughts and feelings, her tears continued. She managed to remain silent despite this sudden onslaught of grief, not wanting to alarm the boys or to even let them know she was there. The door to their room had been left open—as it always was—since Maisy's room was right across the hall, and she would be able to hear them if there was a problem during the night. But Enid certainly didn't want the boys to know that she was out in the hall crying like a baby.

Enid lost track of the time she sat there overcome with tears, a hand pressed over her mouth while she kept her handkerchief in her other hand which she used to keep mopping her face. A strange sound took her off guard and she held her breath while she listened, wondering what it might have been. Realizing that one of the boys was crying, Enid found it more difficult to stop crying herself. It took a few minutes to compose herself, but the sound of a child crying had not ceased. Enid stood up and crept a little closer to the door without making a sound, and what she heard broke her heart.

"Don't cry, Markie," Matthew said tenderly. "It will be better now that Aunt Enid is here."

"But . . ." Mark whimpered, "she's . . . going to have a baby, and . . . what if she dies . . . like Mama did?"

"I'm going to pray very hard that Auntie Enid will stay with us," Matthew said with a solidity that made it evident he'd taken responsibility for his little brother and was trying very hard to be strong and positive. "Everything will be all right," Matthew added with the same mature tone.

Mark's response was to cry harder and Matthew asked, "What's wrong?"

"Why doesn't Papa come to see us?"

"I don't know," Matthew responded, not sounding mature or confident at all.

"I think he died too," Mark cried, "and they just won't tell us."

"He didn't die!" Matthew almost shouted. "He's just sad!"

"You don't know that!" Mark retorted in a voice tinged with anger. "Or maybe he just left and he's not coming back . . . because he doesn't want us now that Mama's gone."

Enid almost expected some kind of argument to break out, but what happened was worse. Matthew said softly, "I don't think he would leave us, but maybe he *did* die," after which he also began to cry.

Enid stood near the open doorway for a long while, leaning back against the wall, crying silent tears while she listened to her nephews cry their little hearts out. She didn't dare intervene, not wanting them to know that she'd overheard them. They finally became still, and she knew that they'd cried themselves to sleep, and she wondered how often that was the case. Thinking logically, she would guess it was likely a rather common occurrence.

Enid finally went to her own room, where she curled up on the bed and cried. She awoke sometime during the night and changed into a nightgown, and then she cried some more. She cried over the death of her husband, and all the dreams they'd shared that had died with him. And she cried over all the disappointment and disillusionment she'd experienced in her marriage despite how much she'd loved Alistair. She cried over Marie's death, and the baby that Enid knew nothing about—except that it was a little girl. She cried over the broken hearts of two little boys who were trying to be brave and strong, but who were far too young to be expected to do so. At least now that they were no longer being allowed to express their grief through anger or bad behavior, perhaps Enid could help them come to terms with it. But that would take time. Then it occurred to her that their father should have been playing a significant role in helping his sons deal with all they'd lost. He shared their grief more than anyone. But he too was lost in his own form of a childish tantrum, hiding away and expecting to be waited on hand and foot because he didn't want to face the reality of all he'd lost.

Enid wondered what she might have done if Alistair had died when she'd had the privilege of not having to do a thing to take care of herself. But she hadn't had that privilege. She'd been forced to leave her husband's body unattended and walk dirt roads that were littered with people who were dead and dying. She'd had to restrain her grief in order to endure a long and miserable journey. And now she was doing her best to give help where help was needed because Sebastian Hawthorne had apparently made rash decisions in the heat of his grief that were now creating difficulties for everyone in the household—most especially his young sons.

Enid was unable to go back to sleep as her anger toward Sebastian was fueled by a myriad of evidence that he was behaving like a selfish child. She rehearsed the evidence over and over, the worst of it being the heartbreaking conversation she'd overheard between Matthew and Mark, and the very fact that they'd cried themselves to sleep, wondering if their father was even alive.

It was barely dawn when Enid gave up on trying to go back to sleep. She got cleaned up and dressed before she sat in front of the mirror to brush through her hair, roll it up, and pin it into place—all the while fuming inwardly over the deplorable behavior of Sebastian Hawthorne. Did he think he was the only person on earth who had lost loved ones to death? Did he have any idea of the damage his absence was causing? Well, he was about to find out! At the risk of having him banish her from his home completely, she could not let another hour go by without making herself an advocate for her nephews—and she was willing to take on the consequences, whatever they might be. It was time Sebastian took a good, hard look at the truth.

* * * * *

Sebastian stood at one of his bedroom windows and watched the sun as it peeked over the distant horizon. As usual he'd slept in his shirt and breeches; probably the same shirt and breeches he'd been wearing for a few days. Despite finding it impossible to leave his rooms, he'd still managed to clean up and get himself properly dressed every morning. But not so many days ago he'd lost his motivation to do even that. What did it matter? The servants who came and went from his rooms had become accustomed to seeing him completely unkempt, barely dressed in wrinkled clothes, his feet bare and his hair and beard a scraggly mess. A part of him knew that such behavior was ludicrous, and that he was letting a great many people down. He knew that he'd made some rash decisions, but he felt as if he could barely manage to keep breathing, one breath at a time. How could he possibly confront anything that lay beyond the doors of these two rooms—his bedroom and sitting room—where he had imprisoned himself, perhaps with the hope that remaining here might protect him from any further pain, or perhaps believing that he'd done something to deserve this suffering, and condemning himself to such a life was simply a suitable punishment?

Sebastian was startled by a loud knocking, especially considering how early it was. The servants never disturbed him for at least a couple more hours. He wondered who it might be and if there was a problem; surely any problem could be dealt with by someone else. The knocking persisted, and he realized it was coming from the sitting-room door; not the bedroom in which he stood. When the knocking grew louder and more persistent, he took a deep breath and forced himself to face whatever nonsense this might be, hoping to get it over with quickly. He went through the open door between his bedroom and the sitting room and pulled the door open, already angry from having his self-inflicted misery interrupted.

Sebastian didn't know who he had expected to see, but he was completely taken off guard to be facing Enid. He couldn't help noticing that she looked more pregnant even in the short time since he'd seen her; it was impossible *not* to notice. But even *that* brought back memories of Marie. His last good memories of her had been during those final weeks of her pregnancy. Once she'd gone into labor, the minutes of her life had been ticking away. He forced himself to not think about Marie. He wanted to demand a reason for Enid coming here like this when he'd made it perfectly clear he didn't want to see her—at all. But her expression made it clear she was upset, perhaps even angry, and he didn't have a chance to utter a single word before she said, "You and I need to have a conversation, and we're having it now. Lucky for you you're up and dressed, or I would have dragged you out of bed if I'd had to."

"And you think you're strong enough to do that?" he countered in the same snide tone.

"Right now I feel strong enough to slap your face right off," she snarled and stepped into the room, forcing him to take a step back before she closed the door behind her.

Sebastian looked into her eyes and realized that the source of strength to which she referred was anger. She was angry, *very* angry. And he was so taken off guard that he couldn't think of a single retort. He didn't yet know the source of her anger, but he felt certain there were a great many possibilities. And the fact that he felt so angry with himself finally compelled him to admit, "Perhaps you *should* slap me. Perhaps I deserve it."

"Oh, you most certainly do," she said, taking another step toward him. She looked up at him with fire in her eyes. He'd never noticed how short she was; or perhaps the dramatic difference in their height was due to him being taller than average. But with as close as she was standing, she had to tip her head almost all the way back to look directly at him. "I hope you're paying attention, Sebastian," she said, launching into what he knew would be a lengthy tirade; on another day he might have already been yelling back and demanding that she leave. But today he just didn't have the strength. "Listen well, dear brother," she went on, "because there are some things you need to hear, and no one else around here is going to say it because they all work for you, and they will keep silent, either out of respect or fear. Most of them are terrified to even come near these rooms. And who would wonder! Merciful heaven, Sebastian!" She waved her hand in front of her face. "Is the stench in here from you or the room? It would seem a good cleaning in both cases might be in order. Do you let the maids come into the room long enough to clean it? I suspect not. Not that there are enough maids working in this house to have time to clean up after you. What little staff is left are all working to their full capacity just to manage the bare essentials of keeping this house functioning while you hide up here like a pouting child."

Sebastian heard her take a deep breath before she moved her face even closer to his, and he knew she was far from finished. "Do you think you're the only person in the world who has ever lost someone they love?" He heard a quiver in her voice and allowed himself to consider for the first time that she too had lost a spouse. "Your wealth has given you the means to hide here and allow others to wait on you and take care of your affairs, but if you keep hiding it will only become more and more difficult to face the world, and you'll end up dying in this room, alone and unloved."

"Perhaps that's what I prefer," he snapped, knowing even as he said it how childish it sounded. But he wasn't prepared for the way she slapped his face.

"How *dare* you!" she growled. "You, who have been blessed with *so* much that's good have no right to make a martyr of yourself while the people who love you are fraught with worry and overwhelmed with how your ridiculous edicts have changed their lives. You have *no idea* what's going on in this house outside of these walls, or how losing you would affect everyone here. *Everyone!* If you were a butcher or a farmer you would have had no choice but to go back to work the day after the funeral; and with no money to hire help, you would have been forced to do all the work your wife had been doing before she died. There are people like that who live on *your* estate; people who have taken on the role of being *both* parents because there was no choice. And here you sit, wallowing in your own filth, taking sore advantage—in the worst possible way—of the privilege you were blessed with."

As her words began to creep past the crusty exterior he'd placed around himself, Sebastian began to feel mildly nauseous and a little dizzy. The truth of what she was saying stung even more than her slap. He wanted to yell at her and evict her from the room, but he'd become frozen where he stood and found it impossible to move, or to speak.

"Now, I hope you're still paying attention, because what I'm about to tell you is the most important thing of all. You have two sons, Sebastian; living, breathing children who are struggling to understand how their lives have turned upside down. You, of all people, should know how difficult it is for someone so young to lose a parent. And I know very well that *your* father did not leave you alone when you lost *your* mother." Her words pricked him deeply because he knew she was right, but she hurried on. "When I arrived here, your sons were acting out so badly that the nanny and the governess were often in tears. We've been working on those problems and have made marvelous progress, but it *astounds* me that their father was not available to be involved in dealing with such challenges. I've tried to give you the benefit of the doubt, Sebastian; I have great compassion if not empathy for your pain. But your selfishness regarding your children is *disgusting!*" She almost spat the word. "Last night after I'd read them a bedtime story—something *you* should have been doing—and tucked them in for the night, I left the room and overheard them while they didn't know I was listening."

Sebastian felt suddenly terrified of the pain she was about to throw at him, when the growing sunlight in the room revealed the sparkle of moisture in her eyes. Her voice quavered as she barely managed to speak—as if just uttering the words broke her heart. "*Your* sons, Sebastian; *your* sons . . ." She actually pushed at his chest with both hands as if that might dispel some of the anger consuming her. "They were talking," she cried. "They were wondering if you were dead too, but no one would tell them. Or they wondered if you had left because now that their mother was gone you didn't want to be their father."

Sebastian's nausea and dizziness increased, and he took a few steps back, fumbling into a chair, too weak to stand as a reality he'd never considered created a tangible pain in his chest that was not unlike what he'd felt when he'd realized Marie was dead.

"And then," Enid went on, apparently oblivious to his reaction—or perhaps keenly aware of it, "then . . . they cried themselves to sleep. They *cried themselves to sleep*! I happened to overhear it last night, but I wonder how many nights it's happened when *no one* heard them, because they seem determined to keep their true fears and sorrow between themselves. They've exhibited all kinds of anger and cruelty toward the people around them, but underneath it all is just plain grief. Much like their father, I assume. Perhaps you could find some common ground with them in that regard."

Sebastian could only stare blankly at the floor while he heard Enid take another deep breath. She sounded less emotional when she spoke again, but no less determined. "So, this is the way it's going to be, Sebastian. You can throw me out of your house if you wish; you certainly have that right. It's not like this situation is some kind of yibbum or something. But you *will* clean yourself up and show your face to your sons. And if you can't think of anything to say, just tell them you love them. Let them know they are valuable to you . . . valuable enough for you to actually *want* to be a father to them. Stop for a moment and think about the kind of men they might become if you do *not* give them the love they deserve." Sebastian squeezed his eyes closed as the image felt unbearable.

"Marie is gone," Enid said with more compassion than anger. "It's horrible, Sebastian. You have a right to feel your pain. But you have a responsibility to your children that overrides all else. You *must* be both a mother and father to them; you *must*. Because she is gone, and you don't have a choice. She would be *disgusted* by the way you're behaving now. If her ghost came back to you and asked one thing of you—*one thing*—what do you think it would be? Oh, we both know her well enough to *know* what it would be. She would want you to take good care of the children the two of you brought into this world. So, act like a man, Sebastian, and do what any decent man would do, or so help me I will bring Matthew and Mark *here*, and I will show them the evidence of what you have become. You have a right to grieve, but I'm certain you can be the master of the house and a loving father and still find time to wallow in self-pity."

Sebastian didn't even realize she had completed her scolding until he heard the door slam and realized he was alone. He felt as if he'd been snapped out of a dazed fog that had hovered around him ever since he'd lost Marie—and then the baby. In the absence of that fog he was overcome with a whole new brand of pain. Everything she'd said was true, and as much as he wanted to be angry with her, he couldn't come up with a single reason that wouldn't make him look like a fool. He'd already made such a terrible fool of himself; in fact, he felt so completely foolish, so utterly filled with regret, that he couldn't imagine ever coming back to a place where he could be at peace with himself.

Sebastian slid to his knees and pressed his face against the chair where he'd been sitting. He prayed until he began to cry, and he cried until every muscle in his body ached. He was startled by a knock at the door and realized it was time for breakfast. He rose carefully to his feet while he wiped the tears from his face and called, "Come in," keeping his face mostly turned away from Thorpe as he brought in the usual breakfast tray and set it down.

"Will there be anything else, sir?" Thorpe asked, and Sebastian realized that this dear and trusted man had stopped asking Sebastian how he was doing a long time ago, probably after Sebastian had snapped at him one too many times.

"Actually, yes," Sebastian said, and Thorpe became all expectancy. "I would like water for a bath, Thorpe. And . . . thank you."

"A pleasure, sir," Thorpe said, smiling. "The water will be here as soon as you're done with your breakfast."

Sebastian didn't feel much appetite, but eating did help ease his ongoing nausea. And he knew he needed his strength. He had a feeling this might be a very difficult day. Clearly there were some drastic changes he needed to make, but he had no idea how to go about it without making things worse.

While Sebastian soaked in the warm bath water, he prayed silently for forgiveness and guidance. By the time he was dressed and shaved and had his damp hair looking somewhat tidy, Sebastian knew what he needed to do. But he also knew it would be anything but easy and he felt relatively terrified. Just stepping out of his bedroom into the hallway made him a little unsteady and he had to brace himself with a hand on the wall and take some deep breaths before he was able to start walking slowly to where he knew his sons would likely be playing. Or at least he hoped so. He didn't know if he had the strength to go hunting for them. He couldn't believe how terrified he felt to face a couple of children, but Enid's words—the information she'd given him—about all they'd been feeling and experiencing made him sick—literally sick—and he had no hope of feeling better until he spoke to them and told them the truth. He just hoped they would want to see him, and that they would be willing to hear what he had to say. After neglecting them for so long, he couldn't be sure how they might respond. And that's what scared him most of all. If they rejected his efforts, what would he do? Go back to his room and hide? He felt like doing just that, but Enid had been right. He needed to be a man, and his behavior of late had been anything but. His own childishness haunted him now that he could see the truth. And he prayed that he could get beyond what he'd done to his own life—and the lives of everyone who had been affected by his poor choices.

* * * * *

After slamming the door to Sebastian's room, it took Enid a great deal of effort to slow her breathing and calm the pounding of her heart. Given the added strain her pregnancy was putting on her body as the baby grew larger, she didn't want to faint and cause even more of a scene than she already had. The moment she felt capable of remaining steady enough to walk hastily back to the sanctuary of her own rooms, Enid recounted everything she had said to Sebastian, and she couldn't find a single word she regretted. In her heart of hearts, she believed he'd needed to hear the truth. She felt surprised at how little he had said, when she had perhaps expected him to get angry and shout at her as opposed to listening to what she had to say. But perhaps when the shock of her scolding wore off, he would find her and tell her exactly what *he* thought, and give orders to have her expelled from his home. She was willing to take that risk if it helped Matthew and Mark get their father back. And she smiled to herself to think that if he wanted to express his anger toward her, he was going to have to find her first, and to do that he would at least have to leave his rooms.

Enid sat on her bed for several minutes, deeply exhausted and tempted to crawl back beneath the covers and stay there for the remainder of the morning. But she needed to eat, and she didn't want anyone having to wait on her. She also felt an increased need to see the boys and spend some time with them. They needed love and attention from someone who wasn't being paid to take care of them. Even though the boys were very comfortable with Maisy and Gert, and it was fair to say that a genuine mutual caring had developed between the children and their governess and nanny, it simply wasn't the same. Enid had come here willing to do whatever she needed to do to earn her keep so that she would have a home for herself and her baby. She'd devoted time to helping each one of the servants in this house, doing various tasks. But right now, she knew nothing was more important than being with the boys.

With her determination firmly in mind, Enid got ready to face the day and went downstairs to share breakfast with the servants as usual. She left the table before anyone else, saying simply, "I hope you can all manage without me today."

Everyone chuckled softly, and Mrs. Miller said, "We all managed fine before you came back, child. But the work is always more enjoyable with you around."

"Hear hear," a few of the others said.

"Well, you'll have to manage," Enid said lightly in a tone that imitated a mother speaking to her children. More seriously she added, "I'm concerned for the boys, and I feel the need to spend more time with them."

"Amen to that," Mrs. Thorpe said gravely. "Poor little nippers. I'm sure we all agree that no one in the house needs you more than they do. You've already made such a difference in getting them to be more like themselves, but they've got a long way to go." She shook her head and repeated, "Poor little nippers."

Enid heard a few expressions of agreement from the others before she left the kitchen and hurried up to the nursery where she knew the children likely wouldn't have arrived yet. Breakfast was brought here for them after the servants were done eating at an earlier hour. Maisy was likely helping them get dressed for the day, and Enid just made herself comfortable, waiting for them to arrive, glad to let Maisy do her job while she felt the need to once again tally the things she'd said to Sebastian early this morning. She wondered where her courage had come from, and knew it had mostly been rooted in her anger on behalf of the boys. But she feared more than anything that Sebastian would not take her advice to heart; that he would just descend back into his darkness and self-pity. And then what? At the very least, the children deserved to know the truth. It wasn't right for them to wonder if their father was dead, or if he'd left because he didn't care about them. Thinking it through, Enid decided that if their father hadn't shown up before bedtime this evening, she was going to tell them that their father was just very sad about losing their mother, and that he still loved them very much. She was glad that she had all day to think about how to explain Sebastian's extreme grief to children so young, and help them understand it. She had trouble understanding it herself.

Enid straightened her back and put a smile on her face when the door came open. As soon as the boys saw her, they came running with an excitement that warmed her heart. They were happy to see her, as she was to see them, and the hugs they exchanged were long and tight, as if these precious young souls were instinctively trying to soak up any evidence of love they possibly could. Both Matthew and Mark were in much better spirits than they'd been last night before going to sleep—but then, they didn't know she had overheard them. Even at their young age, did they know how to try to put up a good front so that others would not be aware of their difficult feelings?

Breakfast arrived, and Gert came to join Maisy and the children for their meal. Enid sat with them and enjoyed a cup of tea while they ate and visited comfortably. The boys certainly had a good appetite, and they seemed in good spirits albeit somewhat quiet, but Enid was haunted by what she'd overheard last night when they'd believed no one was listening.

After breakfast was cleared away, Gert went to prepare today's lessons for the children, and the boys asked if they could put together one of their favorite puzzles, which Maisy got out for them while she thanked them for being so polite. Enid watched the boys play and visited a little with Maisy, and it occurred to her that with Matthew and Mark having progressed beyond acting out with bad behavior, they had instead become somewhat somber—which was perhaps more honest and appropriate. But Enid had to force herself to keep from once again feeling angry with their father for not being there for them. They were all grieving for the same reasons, and if they could only grieve together it would surely benefit them all.

Enid was glad to hear Maisy distract her with a funny story about an incident she'd had in town the previous week, and how it had ended up putting her on very friendly terms with a woman who worked as a seamstress. Maisy's story was interrupted by a light knock at the door. Both women waited, knowing that the servants generally knocked as a polite warning before they entered without needing any invitation. Enid's heart quickened as she wondered if this could possibly be what she'd been hoping and praying for.

"Come in," Maisy called, tossing Enid a confused glance. As Enid's belief deepened that this could actually be Sebastian, she felt suddenly nervous with the possibility that he might—in his present state of mind—make things worse with the boys rather than better.

Chapter Four

BACK FROM THE DEAD

ENID CAUGHT HER BREATH AS Sebastian stepped tentatively into the room. He looked like a completely different man than the one she'd been reprimanding earlier this morning. His black boots were highly polished. His dark breeches and white shirt were clean and well pressed, and he wore a waistcoat made of an exquisite brocade fabric, woven in different shades of blue, with shiny silver buttons. His beard had been trimmed close to his face, and his hair had been combed back and tied into a ponytail, which Enid assumed was his only option to try and make it look respectable when he was in sore need of a haircut. She saw his eyes dart her way for only a second before he turned his full attention to his sons who were sitting on the carpet, putting together a large puzzle. The boys both looked up at their father with wide, expectant eyes, but neither of them moved or spoke, as if they were in shock. But they'd not seen him at all since their mother's death more than two months ago.

Maisy apparently picked up on the enormity of what was happening and popped to her feet, saying quietly, "I'll be in the next room if I'm needed." She left through a side door and closed it behind her. Enid felt compelled to stay. Unlike Maisy, she was family. And she had initiated this resurrection of Sebastian Hawthorne. She felt some responsibility to make certain this interaction went well—or if it didn't, she would know what had been said so she could help the boys through whatever the results might be.

"Papa?" Matthew said as if he couldn't quite believe it. He came slowly to his feet and Mark followed his brother's example but said nothing.

Sebastian went to his knees and opened his arms. His countenance expressed humility and apology. Enid heard a slight quiver in his voice as he spoke his sons' names and motioned with his hands for them to come closer. The boys' desperation became immediately evident when that was the only invitation they needed to fly into their father's arms, where they both immediately started to cry. Enid watched Sebastian squeeze his eyes closed tightly while he held his sons impossibly close to him and pressed kisses into their hair.

Enid began to feel like she should discreetly leave the room, contrary to her prior belief that she needed to stay. She felt certain now that Sebastian had crossed this difficult boundary, he could handle a simple conversation with Matthew and Mark. He opened his eyes and looked toward her; even though he didn't speak, she could read a silent indication of gratitude in his expression. She nodded very slightly toward him before she stood to leave.

"Please stay," he said, and she sat back down.

His words broke the spell of the lengthy embrace between father and sons, and Matthew looked up at him, asking with a vehemence beyond his years, "Where have you been?" It sounded more like an accusation than a question.

Enid feared for a moment that Sebastian might respond defensively, but he said with kindness, "Let's sit down together and we'll talk about that."

Sebastian stood and took each son by the hand, guiding them to a sofa that was opposite to where Enid sat. She watched him sit down and cross one knee over the other as Matthew and Mark sat on either side of him and he put his arms around them. "First of all," he said, "I owe you both an apology. Do you know what that means?"

"That you're sorry for something," Matthew said.

"That's right," Sebastian said, and both boys looked up at their father as if a miracle might burst forth from him at any moment. As Enid listened to Sebastian explaining the reasons for his absence, and his regret over being so selfish in staying away from them, she believed that a miracle was indeed taking place. She had to inconspicuously retrieve her handkerchief from her pocket to prevent tears from leaking down her face. It became even more difficult to control them as Sebastian himself began to cry as he admitted to his sons how much he missed their mother, and how hard it had been for him to lose her. Then he told them he knew it had been hard for them too, and he should have been there for them. The boys asked him some questions about their mother's death—and that of the baby—which Sebastian answered honestly and with great care. He promised that he would see them every day from now on, and that he would never leave them. The boys cried again in response to his promise and held to him tightly, and again he hugged them and kissed their heads while tears leaked from beneath his closed eyelids.

Enid absorbed the scene before her, and the sharing of grief taking place. They had lost a wife and mother—and a baby as well—and the sorrow had broken them all. But now they were together and talking, and the tears they shared were the beginning of an opportunity to heal. Enid thought of her own loss and felt that she understood them in a way that was deep and profound. A part of her wanted to ignore any decorum and rush across the room to sit on the same sofa and be a part of their healing embrace, as well as the tears they shared in their common grief. But she restrained herself and remained where she was, continuing to wipe away her own tears as discreetly as possible.

It took Enid a long moment to realize that Sebastian seemed to suddenly feel awkward. They'd all apparently said what they needed to say, and they'd all gained their composure, but it had been so long since Sebastian had interacted with his sons at all that he probably had no idea what to do next. Enid cleared her throat quietly and said, "I do believe it's nearly time for their morning lessons." The boys turned to look at her. "You both know where to find Gert. Why don't you hug your father and run along?"

Both boys stood, and they both turned back to look at Sebastian, silently asking for further reassurance, and he was quick to say, "I'll see you later. I promise."

Accepting his promise, they hurried out of the room and Enid was left alone with Sebastian, surrounded by an increasingly awkward silence. She wanted to give him some kind of praise or encouragement, but everything she thought of saying sounded trite or perhaps condescending. He'd done what he should have done a long time ago. She was pleased, but he wasn't a child who needed her approval or appreciation.

Enid was relieved when he stood and said, "I need to speak with Mr. and Mrs. Thorpe; if you will excuse me." He bowed slightly as a gentleman was supposed to do.

"Of course," Enid said, even more relieved with how quickly he exited the room. Only then was she able to take in a breath deep enough to fill her lungs. But she sat there for a few more minutes, taking in the miraculous healing she had just observed between Sebastian and his sons. Her respect for him had just been elevated a great deal. He'd made some mistakes in the way he'd handled his response to Marie's death, but he was humbly willing to rectify them. He'd taken a huge step in doing so with Matthew and Mark, and she hoped that his intention to speak with the couple who ran his household was in the same vein. While Enid considered her growing respect for Sebastian, it occurred to her that the room had a different feeling to it, as if he'd left something of himself behind that left her intrigued. Given the fact that she'd never really liked Sebastian—mostly because he'd never really liked her—she had to admit that what she felt in that moment was entirely unfamiliar and unexpected. She just hoped that he kept his feet firmly on this path of healing and that he wouldn't regress and cause any further heartache for his children. And for the time being, she decided that she was going to do everything she could to make certain he kept his promises to his sons—for their sake.

Enid decided some fresh air would do her good, and walking tended to ease some of the aching in her body that was becoming more prevalent with her progressing pregnancy. She made her way through the huge house and out to the gardens to enjoy what she knew might be some of the final warmth of summer. As she walked, she became aware of a foreign sensation. She'd returned from Africa with the fear of facing Sebastian, but she'd quickly become accustomed to the fact that he never left his rooms, and therefore she'd never had to be concerned about encountering him, no matter where she went in the house or on the grounds. His coming out of hiding was nothing but good; she couldn't dispute *that*. But she didn't necessarily feel comfortable with the idea of coming upon him in any number of places where their paths might cross. He'd been respectful toward her throughout his reunion and conversation with his sons. The very fact that he'd asked her to remain in the room surely showed some measure of trust, especially when he'd exposed his emotions and vulnerability so completely. But all of that was in regard to the children, and Enid had no idea how he felt about her presence in the house otherwise. All in all, she preferred to avoid him.

Enid was dismayed by how quickly she felt worn out. The baby seemed to have grown a great deal just in the last week or so, and her anticipation to meet this child and hold it in her arms was growing stronger day by day. However, she was also finding it increasingly difficult to catch her breath as the life growing inside of her pressed up against her lungs. She sat on a bench in the garden to rest, noting the gray sky above that had quickly grown darker. The air was much cooler than it would have been with the onset of summer rain; she could almost literally feel the coming of autumn in the atmosphere. Not wanting to get caught in the rain, Enid drew as much air into her lungs as she could and headed back toward the house. She assumed lunchtime was approaching and went to the kitchen to see if she could offer some help. The moment Mrs. Miller saw Enid, the cook rushed toward her, full of excitement.

"Oh, deary," she said, "I was hoping to see you. A miracle has happened! The master has come back from the dead, he has. He's asked Thorpe to see that the drawing room and parlors are put back in usable fashion, and for Mrs. Thorpe to hire whatever help is needed in the house."

"That's wonderful news!" Enid said, deeply relieved to know that Sebastian's emergence from hiding was not being limited to his relationship with his children. He was putting right the things that were wrong in his household, and she was genuinely thrilled.

"And he's upstairs now playing with the boys!" Mrs. Miller's eyes filled with tears. "Oh, it's a miracle! He asked to have his lunch sent there so he could eat with them." She hurried back to the stove as if she'd just remembered that food was cooking there. "I assume you'll be eating there also, as you always do."

"Actually," Enid said, "I do believe I'll eat here in the kitchen with you." Mrs. Miller tossed her a confused glance and Enid added, "I'm certain the boys would like their father all to themselves. I think it would be best to allow them some time together alone."

"You could be right, deary," Mrs. Miller said before she went on to repeat her declarations of this being a miracle. Enid kept it to herself that it had not been so many hours since she'd given the master of the house a good scolding. The fact that Sebastian had chosen to respond in a positive way to the things she'd said could very likely be a miracle; he could have chosen to become even more defensive and bitter. Enid was grateful for the miracle, but a little saddened at not being able to share lunch with the children. She wondered if Sebastian would begin sharing *every* meal with the children. And if he didn't eat with them, would he eat all alone as he'd been doing since Marie's death? She couldn't imagine him joining the staff in the kitchen as she had done.

After lunch Enid took a long nap, glad to be able to get some rest after all the turmoil that had kept her awake the previous night, and she was glad to wake up and recall that the boys had their father back, the servants would get the help they needed, and a good portion of the house would be put back to normal. Enid could understand covering furniture in rooms that were rarely used, but she felt sure that Sebastian's edict to do so with the drawing room and parlors had been due to the way they would remind him of Marie. Or perhaps it had been a declaration that he would never again receive company. Perhaps both.

Enid freshened up and went downstairs to see if any of the ordered changes had come about yet. She went first to the parlor situated near the front entrance of the house. She recalled how eerie it had looked when she'd first arrived, which was a stark contrast to the beauty of the room she saw as she stepped into the doorway now. She took in a deep breath while memories of tea times and long conversations and playing cards with family and friends blanketed her. Sebastian had never been fond of Enid, but he and Alistair had always been close, and they had enjoyed sharing the same home as much as they had enjoyed just being in the same room. And Marie had truly treated Enid as a sister. Therefore, the four of them had spent many long hours together in this room, and occasionally they'd entertained company here.

Enid felt a little out of breath again as the effects of her pregnancy were enhanced by memories that took her breath away. She sat down on one of the lovely brocade sofas and just took in the room while Alistair became so alive in her mind that tears slid down her cheeks. More tears came when she thought of Marie, and Enid felt some understanding over Sebastian's reasons for not wanting this room to remain the way it had once been. Although, she knew—and she hoped he was figuring out—that it was impossible to keep life from moving forward after loved ones had passed on. It was mandatory for a person to move forward, as well; whether or not it was easy really didn't matter.

Enid was startled to hear Sebastian say, "So, here you are. I've been looking for you."

She hurried to wipe the tears from her cheeks, hoping he wouldn't notice she'd been crying. Either he hadn't noticed, or he simply didn't comment on it. Perhaps hoping to explain, she said, "I was just remembering all the time we spent here with—"

"I'm trying very hard not to think about it," Sebastian cut her off, sounding mildly angry with her for even bringing it up. He sat down across from her and crossed his legs, looking at her with eyes that held nothing of the humility and softness she'd seen in him earlier when he'd been talking to his sons. She felt decidedly nervous when she realized he had been looking for her, and he was clearly displeased. Now that he'd come back from the dead, would he expel her from the house despite her growing attachment to the boys? Or perhaps that was the reason. Did he not want her involved in his sons' lives?

Instead of trying to speculate, Enid told herself to just give the man time to speak. Sebastian finally cleared his throat and said, "I would be amiss if I did not thank you for bringing my attention to the damage my absence was causing to my sons, and to the other challenges taking place in the house. I honestly didn't believe my absence would make any difference."

"That is surely grief talking," Enid said, hoping to offer some kind reassurance, but apparently that was not the purpose of this conversation.

"However," he said, and Enid's heart began to pound. He *was* going to kick her out! "It's no secret between us that I was never pleased with my brother's choice in a wife." Enid wanted to say that such a decision by his brother or anyone else was none of his business, but she bit her tongue and kept quiet. "But I know he loved you," Sebastian added. "Now that he's gone, however, I am going to spare us both the misery of trying to live up to any kind of pretense. You need to know that I blame you for dragging him off to the other end of the world, and therefore I consider you wholly responsible for his death."

Enid gasped and then held her breath. She couldn't believe what she was hearing! Did Sebastian have no idea of how much she had *not* wanted to go to Africa? His assumptions were astonishing, but before she could even think of an appropriate response, he hurried on.

"I'm not at all interested in your side of the story, so please spare us both the drama of attempting to convince me of your innocence. He's dead. And I am never going to forgive you. I just needed to say that, so you don't have to wonder. Still," he hesitated, and Enid struggled to catch her breath while she tried to comprehend the scorn in his eyes, "you are legally entitled to the annual allowance that would have been his. I will speak with my solicitor tomorrow to make certain you have access to an account at the bank. It will be more than sufficient to meet the needs of you and your child for as long as you both live. The money will go to Alistair's child after your death, so you have no need to be concerned about that. If I had my way, I'd send you off here and now, knowing you are more than sufficiently cared for, because quite frankly I don't want to have you here in my home, and I certainly don't want to see you. But it's quite apparent my sons have taken a liking to you, and they've already lost too much in their lives. For their sake—because you *are* their aunt," he said it as if he wholeheartedly resented the fact, "I'm going to let you stay, and we will do our best to avoid each other. I understand you've been having lunch with the boys, so you may continue to do so, and you may continue to have your other meals in the kitchen with the staff as you've been doing." He said *that* as if he were making it clear he considered her to be in the same class as the servants. Feeling equal to them, she didn't mind *being* in the same class, but she very much minded that Sebastian saw her that way. "I will have supper with the boys," he went on as if this conversation should have no emotion involved in it whatsoever, "and I will be tucking them into bed at night. I've already spoken with Gert and Maisy about the schedule. If you want to spend time with them, please do so before lunch."

Sebastian stood up as if to declare an abrupt ending to his cruel edict. He took a few steps toward the door, then hesitated and asked her a question in a tone that was far more cordial, as if his previous declarations hadn't occurred. "Earlier when you came to my room, you used a word I've never heard before. What does it mean?"

"I'm sorry?" she asked, sincerely having no idea what he was talking about. She was overcome with shock and struggling to hold back any threat of tears that might embarrass her in front of him.

"You said, 'It's not like this situation is some kind of yibbum or something.' I just wanted to know what it meant."

Enid felt herself go warm as the meaning of the word brought on an entirely different reason to feel embarrassed. She had no idea why she'd said it; she'd been angry. But she certainly didn't want to talk to him about its meaning now—or ever. She cleared her throat and forced a steady voice long enough to say, "It's nothing; completely irrelevant."

He hesitated a moment as if he wanted to push her for a more substantial answer, then he left the room and Enid let out a harsh breath of relief to finally be set free from his presence. But only a moment later an unwanted sob burst out of her and she clapped a hand over her mouth in order to remain silent. She couldn't believe it! Her husband's brother actually believed she was responsible for his death! She just couldn't believe it! She squeezed her eyes closed as if that might hold back her tears, but they escaped nevertheless. In her mind she could only hear Sebastian's contempt as he'd said, *I consider you wholly responsible for his death.* And right behind marched the words, *He's dead. And I am never going to forgive you.*

Enid waited only long enough to leave the room to be certain that she wouldn't come upon Sebastian on the stairs. She hurried as quickly as she could manage to the safety of her own bedroom where she locked both doors and curled up on the bed, pressing her face into a pillow that would muffle her heaving sobs. She felt drawn back to the horror of sitting in that chair, sticky with sweat, watching Alistair die but unable to touch him. As Sebastian said over and over in her mind, *'He's dead,'* Enid felt as if she were just coming to fully accept it for the first time. She wondered how she could bear to live under the same roof with Sebastian, but then she wondered how she could possibly leave. She was grateful to know that Alistair's inheritance was available to her, but it wasn't only money she needed; she needed a home and people who cared for her. She needed a family, and the people who worked in this house were very much like that for her. And she could never leave the boys! It would break her heart, but she knew it would hurt them, as well. She was grateful their father at least had *that* correct in his thinking.

Enid didn't realize she'd fallen asleep until she heard a knock at the door and opened her eyes to realize the room was growing dim with evening. "Come in," she called, forgetting she had locked the door. Then, after hearing a key in the lock, she saw Mrs. Thorpe enter.

"Are you all right, my dear? I came to check on you as soon as we'd finished supper. I was worried when you didn't come to join us."

"I'm just very tired," Enid said, glad the room was dim enough that any evidence of her weeping couldn't be seen. "I'm certain it's perfectly normal."

"It is indeed," Mrs. Thorpe said, "but you must eat. I'll have Tilly bring up a tray."

"Thank you," Enid said, sitting up to lean back against the headboard.

"Is there anything else you need, my dear?"

"No, I'm fine. Thank you," Enid said, glad she didn't have to leave the loving care of Mrs. Thorpe.

"Should I call the doctor for you?"

"No, not at all," Enid said. "I'm just tired."

"Very well," Mrs. Thorpe said. "You promise to let me know if you *do* need the doctor."

"I promise," Enid said, and Mrs. Thorpe slipped away.

Enid felt tempted to start crying once more as Sebastian's harsh words assaulted her all over again. But she knew Tilly would be here soon, so she lit a lamp and freshened up before her supper arrived. Surely, with time, the sting of her brother-in-law's disdain would lessen, and with any luck she would never cross his path at all.

Enid felt better physically after eating a good supper, but her heart still felt broken. She wondered why she should care so much about what Sebastian thought, when they had hardly agreed on *anything* for as long as she'd known him. Through prayer and searching her heart, she knew that his accusations had spurred her grief over losing Alistair more prominently to the surface. Still, no matter how much she tried to tell herself that what Sebastian thought of her didn't matter, she couldn't shake the heartache of being deeply hurt by his beliefs about her. But he'd made it clear that he had no interest in hearing her side of the story; therefore, nothing could be done—at least not for now. Perhaps with time his heart would soften; perhaps he was simply so caught up in his grief over his brother's death—which had come on the wake of losing his wife and newborn baby—that he was unable to think clearly, and perhaps with time he would be more rational. In the meantime, Enid was determined to keep her grief to herself and go about business as usual. She was glad to know that she could spend time with the boys in the morning and share lunch with them. And she could spend the rest of the day helping out here and there, which was always satisfying and enjoyable, if only for the company and conversation she was able to share with the servants.

Despite Enid's long nap, she was still able to fall asleep quickly and she slept well—even though she had to get up more than once in the night to relieve herself, a necessity that had become more frequent with the progression of her pregnancy.

The following morning, she was welcomed heartily at breakfast by her friends who had clearly missed her the previous evening. Their kindness helped her feel better. She could avoid Sebastian Hawthorne and still have a good life here in his home.

After breakfast, Enid was surprised when Mrs. Thorpe quietly asked her if they could speak in private. She followed the housekeeper to the little office down the hall from the kitchen where Mr. and Mrs. Thorpe kept all the household records and schedules. She knew they did a great deal of their work right here, since careful planning and organization were at the heart of keeping the household running smoothly. Enid sat down while Mrs. Thorpe closed the door and then sat close beside Enid, rather than sitting across the desk where she might normally sit.

"How are you feeling today, my dear?" Mrs. Thorpe asked in her motherly way, taking hold of Enid's hand.

"Much better, thank you," Enid said. "I simply hadn't slept well the night before and got overly tired. I'm much more rested now."

"I'm very glad to hear it," Mrs. Thorpe said. "However, it got me to thinking that we've not discussed at all the necessary plans for getting this baby here when the time comes. I know you've not seen a doctor since you came back, but did you see one before you—"

"No," Enid said, "I've not seen a doctor at all." She didn't add that the poor quality of medical care in Africa had terrified her about giving birth there. Is spite of her sorrow over Alistair's death, she was relieved beyond words to not have to give birth in a place that was hot and dirty and where their ideas about childbirth were frightening. She felt sure that people were comfortable with whatever they'd grown up with, and she had no disdain or disrespect for the kind and beautiful village women who had assured her they would take very good care of her. For them, it was traditional for women of the village who had given birth to gather around during a woman's labor and to work together to aid her in the process. But the very idea of that had left Enid feeling uneasy. She was glad to be in England where the customs were familiar and comfortable to her—even if giving birth was still a terrifying prospect. She couldn't even bear to think of how Marie had died as a result of having a baby. She just had to go forward with faith, knowing that most babies came into the world without any serious complications for mother or child.

"I think it might be wise to have a doctor see you . . . and make certain all is well," Mrs. Thorpe went on. "But that does present a problem."

"How is that?" Enid asked, confused.

"Mr. Hawthorne will not have the local doctor step foot in this house. He believes the doctor is somehow responsible for the death of Mrs. Hawthorne, although I don't know how that could be possible. He's instructed us to send for a different doctor if the need arises, a man he likes much more—but he lives farther away, and it takes much longer to get a message to him, and for him to come here. Still, Mr. Hawthorne told me to make certain you get the medical care you need—as if I wouldn't do so with or without his approval."

Enid said nothing, but she found it interesting that Sebastian would be concerned for her health—and that of the baby—despite everything he'd said to her. He likely didn't want any more deaths to contend with, and Enid concluded that for all his dislike toward her, she was carrying his brother's baby, and he surely wanted the child to be healthy and strong.

"Well, I have a solution to that problem," Enid said, having already thought this through. She had intended to speak with Mrs. Thorpe about it, but other things had been more pressing. "Before I left for Africa, I became acquainted with a Mrs. Gardener; her husband is the butcher, and they live above the shop."

"Oh, yes, I know the one," Mrs. Thorpe said.

"She's a well-practiced midwife," Enid said.

"Is she, now?" Mrs. Thorpe let out a little laugh. "I had no idea. I suppose we've always just relied on the doctor and I'd never heard."

"I like her very much; I trust her and feel comfortable with her. And she's delivered a great many babies. She's been doing so for years, and I've spoken to women in town who told me their experiences of giving birth with Mrs. Gardener's help were very positive. I suppose such conversations took place back then because I was a new bride and all the women in town couldn't help speculating over my becoming a mother. But now I'm very glad for the information I was given back then. Provided Mrs. Gardener is still there and still engaged in her midwifery, I would like very much for her to oversee my health and the delivery of the baby."

"Well, I'll send Lex with a message for her today," Mrs. Thorpe said. "If she's available, I would like her to come and make certain all is well." She looked more directly at Enid and asked, "Do you know when the baby is due to arrive, my dear?"

"I'm not certain, to be truthful. My cycles were not very regular, and I was never able to calculate what I thought might be an accurate estimate, and then I lost all track of time during my travels home. I can only say that I feel the baby getting very large inside of me, and I'm growing increasingly more awkward and uncomfortable."

"And that is all very normal according to everything I've heard," Mrs. Thorpe said with assurance. "I've been close to a number of women through pregnancy and childbirth over the years." She told Enid a little about those experiences, and she also promised to be with Enid through her labor if that's what she wanted.

"Oh, I would like that very much," Enid said, wanting a woman nearby with whom she felt so comfortable.

Once they had finished their conversation, Enid went upstairs to see the boys. They were as pleased to see her as she was to see them, and they were full of excitement in wanting to tell her about all the fun they'd been having with their father. When they'd run out of things to tell her and returned to their playing, Enid couldn't help noticing how much more relaxed and cheerful they were. For their sake—and for Sebastian's—she felt deeply grateful that he had taken himself out of hiding and come back into his sons' lives.

Enid enjoyed lunch with the boys, as well as Maisy and Gert. The established habit was comfortable, but even better with the boys behaving well *and* clearly feeling happier.

After lunch, Enid hugged the boys and hurried to make her exit, not wanting to cross paths with Sebastian when he came to see his sons in the afternoon. She went to the kitchen with the intention of offering some help, only to be told that word had come from Mrs. Gardener and she would be arriving soon to visit with Enid. She insisted on helping clean the dishes from lunch until the midwife came, but she'd barely put her hands into the soapy dishwater before Mrs. Gardener arrived punctually.

Enid felt a little nervous as she walked toward the front parlor where Tilly had asked the midwife to wait. But the moment she entered the room and Mrs. Gardener stood to face her—offering a genuinely kind smile—Enid's nerves lessened immensely. The midwife's hair was mostly gray, but her face showed very few signs of aging. She was dressed plainly but everything about her looked clean and fresh, including her countenance.

"Mrs. Hawthorne?" the woman said.

"Yes," Enid replied. "But please . . . call me Enid. I don't believe I want such formality during the process of having a baby."

"And you must call me Julia," Mrs. Gardener said. Enid nodded, and Julia added, "I would like to first visit with you and find out as much as I can about your health and what your pregnancy has been like so far. And then I would like to examine you and see if we can determine how far along you are and if everything is as it should be."

"Of course," Enid said and invited Julia to come upstairs with her to Enid's bedroom, where they would have some privacy, and of course where the birth would take place when the time came.

Enid and Julia sat to visit for a long while. Julia took notes as she asked Enid a great many questions, often getting off the topic of her pregnancy as she asked about Enid's experiences in Africa and the death of her husband. She offered genuine compassion, and shared with Enid that her first husband had died of illness before she had married the butcher, who had taken on her two children, and she had taken on three of his, and now they had two more children together. Their youngest children were now nearly adults; some of their children had left the community as they'd embarked on their own lives, but one of their grown sons was working with his father in the butcher shop. Julia was clearly happy with her life, and she enjoyed her work. She declared that little gave her more joy than being able to help bring a baby into the world, and she was glad for the opportunity to assist Enid.

Julia asked Enid to lie on her back so that she could measure Enid's belly, after which she declared, "I believe this baby could come in the next two or three weeks."

"As soon as that?" Enid asked, feeling wholly unprepared.

After completing the remainder of her examination, Julia concluded, "Everything appears to be in order, but babies can come early—or late." Julia went on to give instructions regarding several things that would help Enid feel more prepared, and to know what to expect when labor began. Julia told Enid what a typical childbirth experience might be like, and more than once she said that the pain was normal, and it didn't mean that anything was wrong. She talked about how sometimes babies might be turned the wrong way in the womb, or complications could arise, but she assured Enid that she had experience with being able to handle most of these things, and that Enid should do her best to remain calm and have faith that all would be well.

"By remaining calm and breathing deeply," Julia said, "your pain can be lessened. I will help guide you through that when the time comes. But in the meantime, you mustn't worry."

"You must have heard that my sister-in-law died after giving birth not so many months ago."

"Yes," Julia said sadly, "the entire village was talking about it. Everyone I know feels compassion for the earl. It's truly tragic."

"I can't deny that thinking of what happened to her can sometimes make me feel afraid."

"That is certainly understandable," Julia said, "but . . ."

When she hesitated and seemed mildly nervous, Enid pressed, "But what?"

"If I may speak candidly?"

"Of course," Enid said.

"I have my own theories as to what causes the condition they call childbed fever—which is what took your sister-in-law, and I can tell you that not one of the women whose babies I have delivered ever came down with that ailment."

"What are you saying?" Enid asked, a little breathless. "Are you saying it could have been prevented?"

"I don't wish to speak ill of our local doctor, Enid; his practices are much like every other doctor. But it's my belief that many in the medical profession do not take the simple precautions of basic cleanliness—which is something I am rather fanatic about, I confess. And as I've said, I've never had a patient develop childbed fever. I can't prove that there's a connection, but I believe the theory has merit. That's all I'm going to say, and I only say it to offer you assurance that you mustn't worry about the same thing happening to you. I can't promise there won't be complications, Enid," she said with quiet compassion, "but I can promise that I do have a great deal of experience, and I will do everything in my power to keep you and your baby healthy and safe."

"Thank you," Enid said. "I feel confident we're in very good hands."

Enid asked Julia if she would like to join her for tea before she left. The two women returned to the parlor and shared comfortable conversation over tea and biscuits and one of Mrs. Miller's excellent cakes. Enid was glad to feel so at ease with this woman, and in fact she felt as if they were becoming friends. She certainly felt less anxiety than she would have if she were in the hands of the doctor who had delivered Marie's baby—especially with what Julia had just told her.

After Julia had left, Enid returned to the parlor and poured herself another cup of tea which she sipped while pondering everything the midwife had told her. She felt reassured to know that everything seemed to be fine with her own health and that of her baby, and she felt less nervous about the delivery now that she had found confidence in Julia's abilities and knowledge, as well as the comfortable camaraderie they had quickly established. But Enid also felt troubled as she considered Julia's implications regarding the possible reasons for Marie's death. Of course, she'd said that this doctor's practices were much like every other doctor; therefore, it seemed obvious that any doctor could have made the same mistake. Still, to think that something the doctor did or didn't do might have cost Marie her life felt shocking to Enid. But it was information she would never let pass through her lips. Julia's opinions were her own, and nothing could bring Marie back. Speculating over the reasons for her death would accomplish nothing.

Enid shared supper in the kitchen with the staff, which included two new maids who had been hired that very day. Enid learned they had both worked in the house while Enid had been in Africa, and since Mr. Hawthorne had let them go they had been working in a tavern in the village and they'd very much hated it. Mrs. Thorpe had known where to find them and had sent word, and they'd been eager to come back immediately. They would help lighten the workload a great deal for Mrs. Miller and Tilly.

Enid went to bed early and slept reasonably well, except for having to get up twice in the night to deal with the physical inconveniences of pregnancy. She awoke in the morning to sunlight coming through her windows and the sound of birds chirping in nearby trees. But her serenity was interrupted by a terrible thought and she sat up in bed, overcome with panic. Today was Sunday! Sebastian had carefully arranged their schedules so they could each spend time with the boys and avoid each other. But had he taken Sundays into account? Enid had every intention of going to church, and the boys would be full of questions if she didn't sit with them as she'd been doing since her return. But if their father also intended to go to church, how exactly was that meant to work?

Enid attended to her usual morning prayer, and by the time she'd spoken her amen she had decided that she would go to church as usual, and if Sebastian had a problem with the situation, it would be up to him to do something about it. She could hardly imagine him daring to say something unkind to her in front of the boys—or anyone at church. Or perhaps he would choose not to attend church, since he hadn't done so for months.

Enid tried to stop worrying about it and put on her Sunday best before she went downstairs for breakfast. At the appropriate time, Maisy and Gert brought the boys to the front entry hall of the house, dressed in their finest and ready to go. Just as on previous Sundays since Enid had returned, everyone squeezed into two carriages that were driven by Beauford and Lex—except they now had two more maids, which made the squeeze a little tighter. Enid knew there were more carriages available and concluded that someone else capable of driving one needed to be hired so that everyone in the household could have transportation to church if they desired to attend.

Enid breathed a sigh of relief as they set out and Sebastian hadn't shown up, but as they arrived at the church, she heard his voice outside the carriage and realized he'd been riding on the box seat with Lex who had been driving. It was Sebastian who opened the carriage door, which delighted the boys when they saw him. Sebastian helped his sons to the ground, then he held out a hand to assist Maisy and Gert as they stepped down. Enid swallowed a clump of fear that had gathered in her throat and took a deep breath before she set her hand into his so that he could also help her step down. Before her feet touched the ground, it was clear he'd been expecting another one of the servants, although she wondered why it wouldn't have occurred to him that the boys would ride to church with their aunt. He barely glanced at her as he abruptly let go of her hand and went into the church, holding his sons' hands.

Enid followed and sat on the pew behind Sebastian and the boys, with Maisy sitting next to Matthew, and Gert sitting next to Mark. Sebastian was sitting where Enid had sat previously. She tried not to be bothered by the feeling that she'd been excluded from many aspects of the boys' lives since Sebastian had come out of hiding. If not for his ridiculous edict of banishing her from his presence, it would have been entirely acceptable for the boys' aunt to sit with them and help keep them well-mannered during church. As it was, the governess and nanny were clearly considered of more value to Sebastian than his sister-in-law. She wondered if anyone would notice the change in the seating arrangement and pick up on the implied discord between them; then she focused on the sermon and tried to convince herself that it didn't matter, and she didn't care. But by the time they'd returned home, and she'd gone to her room to be alone, she couldn't deny that she *did* care, and to her it *did* matter. She wiped away a few tears and forced composure upon herself before she went downstairs to eat with the servants, while she knew that Sebastian was sharing Sunday dinner with his sons.

When Enid entered the kitchen, Mrs. Miller looked surprised and said, "I assumed you'd be eating with the family for *this* meal."

"No," Enid said and forced a smile, "I believe it's best to let Mr. Hawthorne have this time with his sons."

"As you wish," Mrs. Miller said, still looking confused. She then said to Tilly, "Remove a place setting from the table in the dining room."

Tilly left to do as she'd been told, and Enid wondered if Sebastian and the boys were already seated, and if Matthew and Mark might question their father over the removal of the dishes, or the absence of Enid, who was their aunt. If so, it would be up to Sebastian to answer any awkward questions, but she wondered what excuse he might come up with to justify this ridiculous separation and have it make sense to a child's mind. Enid reminded herself that the welfare of the children was far more important than her own bruised feelings, but still, it all seemed so ridiculous, and terribly unfair.

Chapter Five

TOUCH OF AN ANGEL

THROUGHOUT THE FOLLOWING WEEK, ENID distracted herself with some interesting books she found in the library, and was glad for the newly hired help when her own ability to offer some assistance in the kitchen or laundry became dramatically impeded by a sudden burst of discomfort associated with her pregnancy. Julia came to check on her and declared that her ankles were swollen and there were veins on her legs that looked terrible by the way they seemed to be trying to escape the skin holding them in place. Julia left orders with Mrs. Thorpe that Enid needed to maintain a careful balance of walking to keep up a healthy circulation, and resting with her feet up to avoid further swelling. But despite all the challenges she faced with this pregnancy, Enid already loved this baby so dearly that she could hardly comprehend a heart capable of holding so much love. Every kick and movement inside of her was a reminder that a new life was about to enter this world; a life born of the love she'd shared with Alistair. Often when Enid was alone, she would rub her belly with her hands and softly sing lullabies, wondering if it was possible for her child to hear the songs it would hear after it was born, when she could hold it in her arms.

As autumn arrived with a burst of cooler rainstorms and a dramatic change of color in the leaves, Enid found herself being waited upon hand and foot as if she were royalty, and she had to keep reminding the maids and Mrs. Thorpe that she wasn't a complete invalid. She continued to spend much of her mornings with the boys, always keeping her feet up while she watched them play. And she always had lunch with them before going back to her own rooms to rest. She was pleased to find that she was thinking less about Sebastian and this strange arrangement. They were doing well at avoiding each other, and she was grateful—as she felt certain he was—for the enormity of the house.

Enid learned from the gossip that came along with her breakfast and supper that yet another maid had been hired, as well as an under-butler who would assist Thorpe with his duties. And two men had been hired to work in the stables and help care for—and drive—the carriages. Enid was glad to hear that the household was getting back to normal. It was a reality that such an enormous house required a great deal of care, and Enid considered the wealth of owning such an estate an opportunity to offer gainful employment to the people who were needed to keep everything running smoothly. She was glad to hear that more such people had joined the Hawthorne household. And apparently the new male employees—all of whom were single and relatively handsome—had caught the attention of the maids, and they enjoyed sitting in Enid's room during their free time, speculating and giggling about any possible romantic implications. Enid enjoyed their company and their conversation, even if she considered some of it a bit silly. But they were young and sweet, and they certainly deserved the opportunity to enjoy such romantic interests.

Julia came again near the end of the week and reported that Enid's veins and ankles were showing some improvement, and she also reported that the baby had moved down—which apparently meant that nature was preparing it to come into the world. Enid's belly had also grown—even over a few days—which meant the baby was growing quickly; another sign that the pregnancy was coming to an end.

Julia helped Enid go slowly down the back stairs and outside for a brief stroll so that Enid could get some fresh air. The sky was overcast and the air was cool, but since they were properly dressed for the weather it was an enjoyable outing. Afterward they went carefully back up the stairs where Julia got Enid settled in bed with her feet up and everything she needed within reach—especially the novel she was currently reading. Julia stayed to visit a few minutes longer, and Enid was grateful for the blossoming of their friendship as well as her growing confidence in Julia's ability to help bring her baby safely into the world.

When Sunday came, Enid was relieved to not be able to attend church—mostly because she didn't want to see Sebastian or feel the exclusion that was implied by the way he kept her away from the boys when he was around. Enid read from the Bible instead of her novel while everyone else was at church, and she found herself recalling the way Alistair had so zealously spoken of certain stories from the scriptures and the guidance they offered for living a good life. For the first time in weeks she allowed herself to miss him, and the tears of mourning came with her memories. But she let them flow, glad to be alone, and then she steeled herself to press forward as a widow, knowing she would soon become a mother to a fatherless child. Her gratitude deepened for being here in this house, surrounded by people who cared for her. She was glad Sebastian had allowed her to stay, and in that moment his cruel assumptions didn't feel quite so hurtful. She knew the truth in her heart, and she knew that God knew. Whatever Sebastian might think was surely irrelevant.

The following day after lunch, Enid stood at one of the windows of her room, noting that the sky was still overcast, and a light wind was beginning to scatter autumn leaves over the ground. She loved such weather and decided that just a few minutes of fresh air would lift her spirits and ease the sometimes-suffocating feeling of being confined to a certain part of the house. She made her trek carefully and slowly, having become accustomed to the aching and discomfort in her body. Stepping outside, she inhaled the breeze and lifted her face toward the sky before she walked slowly just a short distance from the house, then back again. The door wasn't far off when Enid felt a sudden sharp ache across her lower back that reached around her belly, tightening the entire middle portion of her body. She stopped abruptly and wondered if something was wrong, or if this was the beginning of labor that Julia had described to her. After half a minute or so the pain subsided, and Enid continued toward the house, taking slow and careful steps. She reminded herself that Julia had prepared her for this; she'd said that with first babies the pains usually started out with many minutes between them, but she should watch the clock and keep track of the timing. Enid knew at what point she was supposed to send for Julia—if this was indeed labor. Julia had also warned her about the fact that the water that filled the womb around the baby could break at any time. Recalling *that* part of labor, Enid sincerely hoped she would get back to her room before any such thing occurred.

By the time Enid got inside the house and to the back staircase, she was convinced that whatever had happened was nothing, but about half-way up the stairs it happened again. "Oh dear," she muttered quietly and sat down on one of the steps, holding tightly to the banister while she waited for the pain to pass. All her fears regarding the experience of child-birth came rushing into her mind, and she realized she was struggling to fill her lungs with air. The pain passed, and she closed her eyes, focusing on her breathing in a way that Julia had taught her, trying to calm herself with the knowledge that she needed to be strong and steady to get through this, and it had only just begun. She sat there for at least a few minutes, pondering the enormity of what was about to take place in her life, and praying that her labor would proceed quickly, without complications. She wanted to have it over with, and she imagined how it would feel to hold her baby in her arms.

Enid heard a sound and opened her eyes to see Sebastian at the foot of the stairs, frozen and glaring at her, as if this chance encounter were somehow her fault. He'd had his hair cut since she'd last seen him; it hung to the bottom of his neck but was nowhere near long enough to tie into a ponytail.

"Oh, for the love of heaven!" he snarled. "What on earth are you doing?"

"Can I not sit on the stairs to catch my breath?" she asked, unable to avoid mimicking his snide tone. "Should I have sent Thorpe to seek your approval first?"

Sebastian made a huffy noise and started up the stairs, clearly with the intention of going past her with no further exchange—which suited Enid just fine. Another pain assaulted Enid, startling her with an intensity that was far stronger than the last one. A sharp sound came out of her mouth before she had any opportunity to exercise the discipline to hold it back. Her hope that Sebastian wouldn't notice was dashed when he stopped walking and asked—almost as if he really cared, "What's wrong?" Enid couldn't answer until the pain had passed, and he impatiently repeated, "What's wrong?"

"I'm fine," she insisted once she could breathe enough to speak. Knowing she had at least a few minutes between pains, she came to her feet and started up the stairs, hoping to prove to him that she *was* fine. "I just need to lie down," she added, knowing that once she got to her room she could ring for help and one of the maids would be there very quickly.

Enid was nothing but annoyed when she realized that Sebastian was matching her slow pace and remaining at her side as they ascended the stairs. "What *are* you doing?" she asked, pausing to turn and look at him. He appeared baffled and she added, "When you are so fiercely determined to avoid me, why are you not already up the stairs and on your way?"

"Because I don't believe that you're fine," he said with an anger in his voice that contradicted the implication of his concern.

"I just need to lie down," she repeated and headed on up the stairs; never had a staircase felt so long and steep.

Sebastian remained at her side, which made her even more dismayed when another pain clutched her midsection and she had to stop and grip the banister with both hands while she fought back the temptation to groan or scream.

"You see," he declared with a tinge of arrogance, "you are *not* fine. Do you think I don't know labor when I see it?"

Enid couldn't respond, but the very moment the pain let up and she relaxed, Sebastian lifted her into his arms and hurried up the remainder of the stairs.

"What on *earth* are you doing?" she demanded. "I am perfectly capable of walking to my room."

"And it could take you an hour at this rate," he retorted. "Did you think I would just leave you on the stairs in that condition?"

"Please," she insisted, "just . . . put me down and let me walk. I'm fine."

"You're *not* fine!" he countered and turned down the hall toward her rooms.

"I must weigh as much as an elephant in this condition," she said, unable to deny that she felt some embarrassment over the situation. But as she realized how long the walk was from the stairs to her bed, her gratitude for his happening upon her began to replace her dismay.

"I can't tell you," he said, and she almost detected the slightest hint of humor in his voice. "I've never carried an elephant."

He took Enid through the open doorway of her room and carefully laid her on the bed, but she immediately sat up and put her feet on the floor, knowing she needed to ring for the maid before another pain overtook her.

"What are you doing?" he demanded.

"Thank you for your help, Sebastian. I can manage now, and—"

"And what?" he asked and crossed the room to pull the bell rope that would ring for a maid to come. "You have no idea what's about to happen, or how fast or slow the pains are going to be, and I'm not going to have you collapsing on the floor while no one else even knows what's happening. Regardless of what you might think, I *am* a gentleman, and I won't have *your* coming to harm on my conscience."

"I'm not questioning that you're a gentleman," Enid said, coming carefully to her feet, "in spite of certain cruel attitudes and ridiculous assumptions, but you don't have to—" Her desire to just get a drink of water and get her shoes off was foiled by the onset of another pain. Its sharpness made it difficult for her to sit back down, and instead she took hold of the bedpost with both hands and forced herself to breathe deeply in and out, trying to remember what Julia had told her.

"Oh, for the love of heaven!" he said in the same way he'd said it on the stairs—as if she'd done something terribly wrong. "Why on earth are you not on the bed where you're supposed to be?"

Enid waited for the pain to pass while she was brutally aware of Sebastian pacing nearby. When she could speak again she said, "Again, thank you for your help. You've rung for the maid, and I will stay on the bed until she gets here. Now, please . . . leave me in peace."

Enid sat down and was shocked by the way he went down on one knee and began to remove her shoes. "Oh, for heaven's sake, Sebastian!" she growled. "This is not necessary. You are—"

"I'm not leaving you alone," he insisted, keeping his head down. He tossed one of her shoes aside and began unlacing the other one. "Your ankles are swollen!" he declared, looking up at her briefly as if she'd committed a crime.

"Do you think a proper gentleman should be assessing the condition of my ankles?" she snarled, desperately wanting him to leave so she could endure her labor pains away from his scrutiny and his ongoing commentary.

Thankfully Tilly entered the room, although she was quick to take in the picture of Sebastian's presence and the fact that he was removing Enid's shoes. "What's wrong?" Tilly asked.

Before Enid could speak, Sebastian told her, "She's in labor."

"Oh!" Tilly exclaimed. "I'll send for the midwife and—"

"I don't need the midwife yet," Enid insisted as Sebastian tossed the other shoe and stood up straight. "There's no need to—"

"Send for the midwife *now*," Sebastian ordered the maid and Tilly scurried from the room like a mouse running from a hungry cat.

Enid adjusted the pillows on the bed and reclined against them in preparation for the next pain, but she was dismayed by the way Sebastian remained in the room, and even more so with the way he began to pace back and forth on a path not far from the bed.

"I'm laying down now and Tilly is sending for the midwife," Enid said, even though she knew she was stating the obvious. "There's no need for you to stay here and—"

"I'm not leaving you alone," he said again, tossing her a disgruntled scowl.

Enid sighed and closed her eyes, trying to block out his presence, but she could hear his footsteps on the carpet. "Fine. If you're staying, please get me a glass of water. I'm thirsty."

He hurried to pour fresh water from a pitcher into a glass and brought it to her. "Thank you," she said, not liking the way he hovered nearby as if she might not be capable of drinking it on her own. She drank some of it, then said, "I'm fine. Just . . . pace if you must. If you insist on staying, I prefer that over having you stare at me."

Sebastian left her bedside but sat in a chair across the room. Enid drank more water, then set the glass on the bedside table. Another pain came, and she was glad to be lying down, which made it easier to not let on that she *was* having another contraction. As the pain slowly eased, it occurred to Enid that Sebastian's bizarre behavior was likely a result of the fact that Marie had died from complications due to childbirth. Was this harrowing up difficult memories for him? Did he think that helping Enid would somehow ease his sorrow or regret? Did he *have* regrets? Were there things he wished he'd done differently?

Enid turned to look at him, taken aback by the way he was staring at her as if he expected something awful might happen at any moment. At the same moment when Enid felt the urge to cry on his behalf, a horrible memory of her own burst into her mind. She tried to push it away, thinking instead of the perspective she'd just gained regarding Sebastian. His anger toward her didn't seem to matter all that much when she considered the pain he was in. But her own pain rushed into her mind again, as if it refused to remain unacknowledged, given how the present moment seemed to eerily mimic the most horrible experience of her life.

When Enid was unable to get the memories out of her head, she snapped at Sebastian, "Please don't . . . sit there like that!" She knew her sharpness with him was not warranted—despite how he generally spoke to her—but she *didn't* want him here, not while she was in labor, and not when his sitting at the edge of the room with that look on his face was almost literally making her sick.

"Why not?" he asked, but another pain kept her from replying.

While Enid was enduring another contraction, Tilly returned to state that Lex had gone for the midwife. The maid added, "If you'll be all right for a little longer, I'll see to the preparations that Mrs. Gardener requested." Enid nodded toward Tilly, even though she wanted to beg her to stay if only so Sebastian would know that she was no longer alone, and he would leave. "I won't be long," Tilly promised before she left.

As the pain subsided, Enid's glance toward Sebastian assured her that he hadn't moved. She wished she hadn't even looked at him when the memory of Alistair dying became even more prominent. She squeezed her eyes closed and felt tears leak from their corners into her hair. She was hoping Sebastian wouldn't notice, but how could he not when he was staring at her?

"Why not?" he repeated, then asked, "And why are you crying?"

"I'm in labor," she said abruptly.

"Which is painful, of course," he said, "but that's not why you're crying." She refused to comment, and he repeated firmly, "Why don't you want me sitting here like this?" It was clear he'd picked up on how distressed she was over something that seemed so trivial, and he wasn't likely to back down.

Enid took a deep breath and wondered if this might be an opportunity to offer him some important information about his brother's death that might soften his opinion of *her*. Either way, she determined that she just needed to answer the question. "When Alistair was dying," she said and heard, even from a distance, Sebastian draw a sharp breath, "he had come home with symptoms and collapsed on the bed and he insisted that I not come near him . . . because he didn't want me to get ill; he wanted me and the baby to survive. So I . . ." her voice cracked, and more tears trickled into her hair, "I sat across the room . . . and waited . . . for him to die." She cleared her throat and strengthened her composure before she turned to look at Sebastian and said, "Please . . . don't sit there like that. I feel as if you're waiting for me to die . . . or you're thinking about Marie dying . . . and I'm terrified enough as it is. Please . . ."

Sebastian stood up, but his eyes remained riveted to hers. She saw emotion there and for a moment she believed he might say something tender or reassuring, but he only walked toward the door, saying over his shoulder, "The midwife should be here soon."

Left alone with her grief *and* the pain of labor, Enid clutched the bedspread into her fists and groaned, praying this would all be over with quickly.

* * * * *

Once Sebastian was a few steps away from Enid's bedroom door, he practically ran to the other side of the house and into his own room, where he closed the door behind him and leaned against it, as if some kind of monster might have been chasing him and he'd barely escaped with his life. The evidence of Enid's pain haunted him nearly as much as the words she'd just spoken. They pounded through his head with such ferocity that he hurried to the bed before his knees gave out from a sudden weakness. He'd felt nothing but angry with Enid ever since she'd returned. Even his gratitude for her vehement scolding, which had prompted him to get hold of himself and see to his responsibilities was laced with anger. And now he felt freshly angry. Why, of all the people in this house, had he been the one to come across her when she'd needed help? Why, with as little as he'd seen her at all, had he been present to witness the evidence of her labor pains, when it dredged up such horrid and painful memories for him? His concern for her well-being had caught him by surprise, but there was no denying how zealous he had felt about making certain she was all right. And he sincerely hadn't wanted to leave her alone—even for a minute. But he wondered now if that had been more for his benefit than hers. If he could help Enid get through this experience—even in some small way—did he believe it would somehow make up for all his regrets in relation to Marie's death? The very notion seemed ridiculous! And yet, he couldn't keep his mind from darting back and forth to those final days of Marie's life and the fact that Enid was at this very moment descending into a treacherous place from which some women never returned.

Sebastian rolled onto his back and stared at the ceiling, wondering if he would ever stop feeling such pain every time he thought of Marie. Losing the baby had been difficult, as well. But the child had barely entered his life; he'd not spent every day for years dependent upon his relationship with his infant daughter. But every time he managed to push away his painful memories of losing Marie, and the grief that had swallowed him afterward, his mind went to the reality that Alistair was dead. His little brother, his only sibling, his dear friend—dead. He'd felt consumed with anger toward Enid every time he thought of Alistair. She'd taken him away from his home and family to a savage place from which he'd never returned. But now, he felt nothing toward Enid except concern and compassion. He wanted to be in the room with her, as if his very presence might somehow make it possible to give her his strength so that she could bear the pain more easily. He wanted to somehow be able to control the situation so that nothing went wrong, even though he knew there was absolutely nothing he could do that would make a difference.

Sebastian had thought about his brother a great deal since Enid had come back to report Alistair's death. Of course, Sebastian had often thought of his brother long before then, but knowing he was dead had changed the nature of his thinking. Just as with Marie, he believed firmly that they lived on in a better place, and he was glad for that belief—and something powerfully instinctive in him that couldn't deny its truthfulness. But he wondered if his wife and brother were aware of the loved ones they'd left behind, or were they in some faraway realm, oblivious to life on the planet they'd left behind.

Sebastian's thoughts of his brother had never been stronger than they were right now. Alistair's child was being born, and his wife was enduring a great deal of pain and risk to bring their baby into the world. Sebastian's concern for Enid suddenly became so acute that he almost felt as if he'd been shoved off his bed and back to the room he'd fled not so long ago. Of course, he knew he wouldn't be allowed in the room; he'd not been allowed inside even when his own wife was giving birth. And for all that he and Enid were officially related by marriage, and they'd spent considerable time together when their spouses had been present, the two of them were practically strangers. Still, he wanted to be as close as he could, as if he might be able to somehow act as a proxy for his brother in being on hand in case he was needed, and simply being aware of what was taking place—if only because he knew that's what Alistair would have done if he were here.

When Sebastian arrived at the door to Enid's room, he began to pace, just as he'd done when his own children were being born. He tried to force away memories of Marie giving birth to their daughter who had not even lived long enough to be christened. Everything had reportedly gone well with the actual delivery, even though Marie had looked understandably exhausted and mildly traumatized afterward—but that was how she'd looked after giving birth to each of the boys. It was the following day when she began to get ill, and within days after that she was gone. Unable to immerse himself in such sorrowful memories without feeling upset, Sebastian focused on his brother. Whether or not it was true, he tried to imagine Alistair pacing beside him in the form of an angel who had come back to make certain that all was well with his family. He began having an imaginary conversation with his brother in his mind, which made him wonder if he might be going mad; but he couldn't deny that it helped him feel better.

Sebastian was startled to hear the sounds of Enid's ongoing pain. He'd heard nothing at all during the several minutes he'd been there, which left him to assume that her pain was getting worse. He then heard muffled voices—presumably those of the midwife and another woman; one of the maids, perhaps. And he could distinctly hear Enid. He couldn't understand what they were saying, but the calm assurances of the midwife were as evident as Enid's fear and panic; and then there was the occasional sound of a third woman who only seemed to be taking orders. Since he'd not heard their voices before he'd left Enid's door, he wondered if their speaking more loudly was evidence of the situation becoming more intense. His presumptions were aided by conversations he'd shared with Marie following her childbirth experiences, when she'd filled in the details he had missed by being banished from the room.

Sebastian stopped pacing and held his breath when the bedroom door came upon. He wondered who might emerge and suddenly felt as if he was about to be caught doing something wrong. It was Mrs. Thorpe, who stood frozen for a moment before she closed the door and asked in a whisper, "What on earth are you doing here?" Before he could come up with an answer that didn't sound ridiculous, she added, "I was under the impression you wanted nothing to do with Enid, so what is this about?" The housekeeper had been a part of his life for as long as he could remember, and she wasn't known for holding back in her communications with him. The only exception had been when he'd closeted himself away after Marie's death. Mrs. Thorpe had lectured him and pleaded with him, but he'd angrily sent her away one too many times and she began sending his meals and other necessities to his room rather than bringing them herself. She'd cried when he'd come out of hiding, and now she was looking at him as sternly as any mother would, wanting to understand his motives.

Sebastian finally found his voice enough to say, "I was . . . thinking of Alistair, and that . . . perhaps he would want me to make certain all is well." He heard a quiver in his words that betrayed how emotionally distraught he had become. The combination of feelings and memories sparked by the present experience were clearly getting the better of him.

"Oh, my dear boy," Mrs. Thorpe said and put a hand to his face. "What painful memories this must be stirring up for you!"

Sebastian squeezed his eyes closed and tried not to feel embarrassed when tears trickled down his face. Mrs. Thorpe wiped them away with her motherly fingers and said what she'd said many times throughout his life. "I know I'm not your mother, but I've helped care for you since the day you were born, and I'll not let anyone tell me that I don't love you as much as any mother could. We were both with your own mother when she died; we've shared far too much tragedy, my boy."

"Indeed we have," Sebastian said, opening his eyes.

"But we've not talked at all about Alistair since he died," she added. "Perhaps we should."

"Perhaps," he said, "but . . . obviously not now. I just . . . felt as if Alistair would want me to be here. Please don't tell me I have to leave."

"I won't tell you that," she said, "but you must promise me that if the outcome is not favorable, you'll not go back into hiding. We have no control over certain things, my boy; you know that."

"I do know that," he said. "I can't promise I won't be . . . upset." He thought that word sounded mild regarding how he imagined he might feel if Enid or the baby—or both—didn't make it through. But he added firmly, "But I promise you I won't cut myself off; I could never do that to my sons again."

She nodded as if she understood, then said, "I must hurry along and get what Mrs. Gardener needs. Can I get you anything from the kitchen?"

"No, thank you," Sebastian said. "Just . . . do what you need to do to take care of her."

"I will," she said, looking mildly perplexed as if she couldn't understand the depth of his concern when—as she had put it—he'd wanted nothing to do with Enid. He hardly understood it himself; therefore, trying to explain it would be pointless. All he could think now was that his anger toward her seemed petty considering what was taking place.

Sebastian resumed his pacing while he listened to the evidence that Enid's pain was becoming more intense and almost constant. His mind snapped back and forth between memories of Marie going through this, and the present reality of Enid's suffering. He wondered why childbirth had to be so difficult and threatening, but he knew there was no good to be found in questioning the nature of life. He just prayed that Enid and the baby would be all right.

Mrs. Thorpe returned, her arms full of clean linens while she managed to carry a large pitcher of steaming water at the same time. Sebastian hurried to open the door for her since her hands were otherwise occupied. She gave him a quick nod and a brief "thank you" before she hurried into the room and kicked the door closed behind her. Sebastian hated the feeling of being excluded from something so monumental taking place in his home, but given the fact that this was not even his baby, he reprimanded himself for such ridiculous thinking and resumed his pacing while he listened to the evidence of Enid's pain. He hated the way it seemed to go on and on, while he kept thinking that it surely had to be over any minute now.

He was surprised when one of the maids appeared with a tray. He expected her to take it into the room where all the drama was happening, but she set it on a little table in the hall, next to a chair he'd not used, preferring to try and dispel his nervous energy by remaining on his feet.

"Mrs. Thorpe asked me to bring your supper here," the maid said. He wished he could remember her name. "And she told me to tell you . . ." The young woman hesitated and looked down, as if she would rather do *anything* than repeat what Mrs. Thorpe had said.

"Out with it," Sebastian said, wishing it hadn't sounded so sharp.

Apparently now more afraid of him than the housekeeper, the maid said without looking up. "To quote her words exactly, 'Tell him he'd best eat every bite to keep his strength up, or I will see that he's properly flogged.'"

"I see," Sebastian said more kindly. "Well, we certainly don't want to defy the ominous Mrs. Thorpe. Thank you."

The maid curtsied without looking at him and scurried away. Sebastian felt too distracted to eat, but the smell of the food made his stomach growl and he realized it was far past suppertime. He sat to eat and have some tea, although he was unable to finish every bite of the food that had been brought to him. The sounds of Enid's reaction to her labor pains were far too distracting. When he began to feel as if this experience might undo him completely, he hurried back to his own room where he splashed some water on his face and freshened up a bit before he went to check on Matthew and Mark. Maisy had explained to them that their Aunt Enid was in the process of having her baby and they were full of questions for their father—some of them laced with fear, since Matthew especially knew that their mother had died as a result of having a baby. Sebastian did his best to answer every question with honesty but also with a positive out-look—even if he didn't necessarily feel positive about the situation at all.

Sebastian distracted the boys with a bedtime story and tucked them into bed, kissing each of their foreheads while he silently thanked God for such strong, beautiful sons, and that he'd finally come back from the self-imposed foolishness that had kept him away from them. Once he knew they were asleep he left them in Maisy's care—as he always did at night—knowing that her room was near enough to theirs that she would be aware of any problems and would come to get him if he was needed.

With his children cared for, Sebastian returned to his own room and knelt beside his bed, pleading with God to spare Enid *and* the baby. He begged forgiveness regarding the things he'd done that had created challenges for his household, and especially his sons—and for Enid. He couldn't deny that he still felt conflicted over the role she'd played in Alistair's decision to leave here, and his subsequent death. But instead of fanning the flames of his anger toward her, Sebastian prayed that his own grief and confusion would be softened, and that he could let go of whatever Enid had done or not done that had impacted Alistair's life. All of that seemed irrelevant at the moment. For now, they just needed to get through this. Everything else could wait to be dealt with.

Sebastian didn't bother to stop and analyze his own conflicting ideas and attitudes toward Enid. All he could feel was a deep hope that she would survive this—and that her suffering might soon be over. However, his hope kept battling in his mind with a debilitating fear; in his heart he knew his fears were greatly tied into his memories of losing Marie, and again he wondered if something in him had taken hold of the belief that if Enid survived it might somehow make up for what had happened to his wife.

Pushing that and every other thought of Marie away, Sebastian resumed his pacing outside of Enid's room, disappointed that he'd returned only to hear evidence that her labor was still taking place, and the baby hadn't yet arrived. He prayed that it would end soon, unable to imagine how exhausted and overcome Enid must be feeling.

Sebastian froze when Enid cried out with a fierceness that seemed to penetrate the very walls and eaves of the house. He was glad to know that it couldn't be heard where his sons were sleeping, but he held his breath as her cries of pain merged into an unmerciful groan. Sebastian felt a little lightheaded and put both hands to the wall, hanging his head while he forced himself to try and breathe normally. He'd barely taken a deep breath when he heard the wailing of a baby. He laughed with relief, then had to try to catch his breath again. He collapsed into a nearby chair and leaned his head back, silently thanking God that it was over, and praying that all would be well with both mother and child. He knew all too well that as horrible as labor and the actual delivery of the baby could be, the possibility of something going wrong was far from over.

Sebastian was startled from his prayer when the door came open. He looked up to see Mrs. Thorpe stick her head out, as if she knew she'd find him there and he'd be wondering. "It's a girl," the housekeeper said with tired eyes and a bright smile. "She appears to be perfectly healthy."

"That's wonderful," Sebastian said. "And Enid?"

"It's not quite over for her yet, but thus far she seems well—all things considered."

Sebastian nodded to indicate he understood, and Mrs. Thorpe disappeared again, closing the door that separated him from the drama taking place—and the joy of new life. *A girl.* He was an uncle to a little girl. Alistair was a father. Sebastian indulged in fantasies of seeing this child grow up here in his home, of being a part of her life. It occurred to him that he and Enid were not necessarily on good terms, but he hoped that for all their differences she would allow him to be a part of her daughter's life, just as she was involved daily with the lives of Matthew and Mark.

Sebastian's reverie screeched to a thunderous halt when he heard the voices on the other side of the door become frantic—Enid's voice sounding fearful amidst that of the midwife giving imperative orders. He couldn't understand the words, but the tone of urgency was unmistakable. He stood and began to pace again while his imagination ran wild with all the possible, horrible outcomes—the worst being that Enid would join Marie in the annals of women who lost their lives bringing children into the world. And what of the baby? What if she lived and her mother didn't? Sebastian's fantasies of having this little girl grow up in his home didn't seem right without her mother here. Enid had to live. She just had to!

While he was wondering what exactly was happening, a maid ran out of the room and left the door ajar. Sebastian was respectful enough not to go into the room, or even to look, but it was impossible for him to not overhear what was taking place as he pressed his back to the wall next to the door.

"She's going to bleed to death if we can't get this to stop," the midwife said in hushed, frantic tones, followed by imperative and precise instructions to Mrs. Thorpe on what she needed to do to help.

"Should we send for the doctor?" Mrs. Thorpe asked, and while Sebastian wondered the same thing, he was equally reluctant to allow the local doctor anywhere near Enid.

Sebastian was grateful for the midwife's confidence as she said, "No! I know what to do and we're doing it. There is no doctor who would do any differently in the same situation. Besides, there isn't time enough to get anyone else here." She repeated some instructions and added others while Sebastian was overcome with such an overwhelming weakness that his back slid down the wall until he was sitting on the floor, and he pressed his face to the tops of his knees, pleading with God to not let her die, and trying very hard to not allow his terror to come too close to the surface, certain he would either start sobbing or shouting if it did.

Sebastian felt a hand on his shoulder and was grateful he hadn't given in to the temptation to cry when he realized he wasn't alone. He looked up, but no one was there. Certain his distress was causing him to imagine things, he put his face back onto his knees and immediately felt it again. "Alistair!" he whispered with a confidence that surprised even himself, and his heart began to pound. It was almost as if his brother's name had come through his lips even before his mind had had a chance to consider the possibility that what he felt was real, and it was undeniable evidence of the very thing he'd wondered about and wanted to believe. He doubted he could ever explain to *anyone* what had happened without sounding like a fool, but it occurred to him that such an experience was for him and his brother alone. He felt inexplicably grateful for what he'd felt until he began to wonder if Alistair was here to offer comfort, or to take his wife with him to the other side. He again imagined his new little niece being raised here along with his sons—and without a mother. But it felt all wrong. For all that his concern for Enid seemed hypocritical considering his behavior toward her, he never would have wished for this. Was God punishing him somehow for his anger, his lack of forgiveness, his selfishness?

"No," Sebastian murmured and lowered his head again, praying that Enid would survive, and praying for forgiveness of his own shortcomings. He'd already lost too much, too many loved ones, too many lives. And he wasn't ignorant enough to believe that the deaths of his family members affected him alone. Many of the servants had grieved deeply over Marie's death, and that of the baby. And many of them had dearly loved Alistair; news of his death had surely been difficult for them, as well. How could they ever cope with yet another death, another loss? He just couldn't imagine how it would be possible.

Chapter Six

A LOVELY NAME

SEBASTIAN COULD NEITHER WALK NOR sit as he noted an eerie silence on the other side of the door to Enid's room. He was just standing there staring at the door when Mrs. Thorpe emerged, closing the door behind her. He noticed blood on her apron, but it was her expression that tightened every muscle in his body and made him literally nauseous.

"Tell me!" he insisted quietly, but she only hung her head and pressed a hand over her mouth. "Tell me!" he repeated more firmly, taking hold of her shoulders.

Mrs. Thorpe looked up at him and murmured, "Forgive me. I was just so . . . afraid . . . so relieved." Sebastian hung on that last word while he waited for her to continue. "She gave us a fright, my boy," the housekeeper said as her countenance eased into a tearful smile, "but she's going to be all right."

Sebastian let out his breath with a huff of air before he hugged Mrs. Thorpe tightly, as if she were his own mother. He realized she was crying and wondered what kind of trauma she had just witnessed. He let her cry against his shoulder while he looked heavenward and thanked God for what appeared to be a miracle. He didn't know exactly what had happened, but he knew that Enid would be all right. And he didn't allow himself to think about how Marie had appeared to be fine until much later.

"Oh, goodness," Mrs. Thorpe said and eased away, wiping at her tears. "Forgive me. I need to . . . get some things for the midwife and . . ." She didn't finish the sentence as she scurried away.

Sebastian sat down and practically melted into the chair, so relaxed that he was very nearly asleep when Mrs. Thorpe returned with a basket of what appeared to be some clean linens and clothing.

"You're still here?" she asked, and he wondered if that was a hint for him to leave.

"I just . . ." he began but couldn't finish the sentence.

"You're likely anxious to meet your new little niece," she said, even though the thought hadn't occurred to him until that moment. "If you wait just a little longer, we'll have things cleaned up and you can do so."

Sebastian only nodded, grateful for a valid reason to stay. He felt hesitant to leave but couldn't quite define why. Mrs. Thorpe went into the room and closed the door, and Sebastian relaxed again, feeling so sleepy that he couldn't imagine how exhausted these women were who had been helping Enid for so long—not to mention Enid herself who had been enduring unspeakable pain for many hours. But it was over, and mother and baby were fine. He kept his thoughts focused on that fact and refused to indulge in any fears.

Sebastian didn't realize he'd dozed off until Mrs. Thorpe touched his arm and he looked up to see her smiling down at him. "You may go in now, if you like. Mrs. Gardener—the midwife—is going to stay and keep an eye on our dear Enid. She's just folding some clean nappies and blankets for the baby. Everything else is taken care of, and I'm off to get some sleep."

"Sleep well," he said, coming to his feet. "You've earned it. No need to be up early; I'm certain the house will not fall down while you get some rest."

"I'm not so sure," she said with a wink and hurried away.

Sebastian stared at the open door to Enid's room and felt mildly disoriented after all the hours he'd been banished to the hallway with the door closed. He stepped cautiously inside and left the door open. In the glow of a few lanterns scattered about the room, he saw the midwife folding linens on the opposite side of the bed from where Enid was laying. But she blocked his view of Enid's face.

"Hello," she said and smiled at him. "You must be Mr. Hawthorne, the uncle of this beautiful young lady."

"And you must be Mrs. Gardener," he said, nodding at her.

"Please . . . call me Julia. There's nothing like childbirth to remove all formality." Sebastian felt hesitant to move any further into the room until Julia said, "Come in. There's nothing to be afraid of."

Sebastian walked to the other side of the bed and gasped when he saw Enid. He didn't know if she was asleep or unconscious, but even in the dim lamplight her pallor was evident.

"She looks dead," he said and wondered if he should have kept that thought to himself. Or perhaps he was seeking reassurance. He wanted to know what had happened but didn't know how to ask.

As if the midwife had picked up on his concerns, she said gently, "She lost a great deal of blood; it happens sometimes. But we solved the problem and the bleeding is under control. She's naturally exhausted and is sleeping deeply; I gave her something to help with the pain and it will also help her get the rest she needs. It's going to take weeks for her to get her strength back, but there's no reason to believe she won't be just fine."

Sebastian could only stare at Enid while more words came out of his mouth, seemingly beyond his control. He credited the candor and kindness of the midwife for making it easy to say what he was thinking. "But what about . . ." He knew the words in his mind but had trouble getting them to his tongue.

"Childbed fever?" she asked as if she'd read his mind, and he looked over at her, grateful for the genuine compassion in her eyes. "I'll tell you what I told Enid. I have my own theories as to what causes the condition, and I can tell you that not one of the women whose babies I have delivered ever came down with the ailment."

Sebastian had trouble internalizing the implication. Before he could speak, she again answered his unspoken questions. "I would never speak ill of our local doctor, but I do believe that many in the medical profession do not take the simple precautions of basic cleanliness—which is something I am rather fanatic about."

"Are you telling me that—"

"There's no need to get all upset," Julia said, pausing in her work to give him a firm stare. "I'm certain that losing your wife was inexplicably difficult, but placing blame will never bring her back and it will only create more grief for you and those around you. What I just told you is only a theory, and I was simply attempting to offer some reassurance regarding Enid. Our local doctor is a good man, and his methods are no different than most if not all the doctors in this country. He works hard on behalf of the people he serves, and he often does so with little or no payment for his services. He does not deserve disdain from you or anyone else. He's doing the best he can with what he knows."

Sebastian forced away the angry conclusion he had lunged to and said, "But . . . you believe that adding simple measures of cleanliness during childbirth eliminates the risk . . . for infection."

"Or at least greatly reduces that risk," Julia said, continuing to fold the clean linens and lay them in a neat pile. "I have no means to prove my theory, but I will tell you again that I've never lost a mother to childbed fever."

"Then I cannot deny that I wish you had delivered Marie's baby."

Julia stopped again and looked toward him with compassion. "Your daughter," she said.

"Yes," Sebastian said and looked away. "I know that wishing to change something in the past is surely pointless, nevertheless . . ."

"One day the pain will ease," Julia said, making him look at her again. "There will likely always be some sadness with thoughts of those you've loved and lost, but it will get better." Sebastian was wondering how to ask why her words had a tone of expertise when she added, "I lost my first husband . . . and two children."

"I'm so sorry," Sebastian said.

Julia went on with her work. "Yes, so am I. However . . . I'm very happy with the life I have now. I find it ironic that if my husband had lived I never would have married the man I've come to love so dearly. But we needed each other; he's been a father to my children, and I've been a mother to his. And we have two children together. They're all grown up—or getting very close to it. We've shared a good life; he's been very supportive of *my* work. I love bringing babies into the world, but I also love going home to a man who loves me. In some ways my life is better now than it was before; but then it's difficult to compare. Life is simply a journey with many seasons." She looked toward him and smiled. "You will yet find many new seasons of your life, Mr. Hawthorne; I'm certain of it."

Sebastian couldn't think of anything to say; her personal experience and encouragement was appreciated but beyond comprehension regarding himself. He was taken aback when she said, "You look like you should sit down. You must be exhausted."

"No more than you," he said while she pushed a chair near to Enid's bedside and motioned for him to sit down.

"But I'm accustomed to staying awake for a day or more at a time; it comes with the job. I'll catch up on my sleep after I've kept an eye on the new mother for a few more hours, and then I'll stay here in the house for another day or so. My husband is used to it; he keeps everything under control at home."

Once Sebastian was seated, Julia said, "It's time for you to meet the little princess." He watched her pick up a blanketed bundle that looked like a large cocoon. The baby had been lying close to Enid's side, asleep, and he'd not even noticed. "I've looked her over thoroughly," Julia said, smiling at the baby, "and she appears to be as perfect as a baby can be." Julia held the baby toward Sebastian, but he felt hesitant to take it. "Come on," Julia said, nodding emphatically, like she was giving a silent order for him to hold out his hands. "I know you've held babies before. She's not going to break."

Sebastian carefully took the baby from Julia, startled by how tiny she looked in his large hands. He'd forgotten how little these infants could be. For a moment he thought about his baby daughter who had died less than a week after Marie had passed away. But his difficult memories quickly receded as he settled the baby into the crook of his arm and looked at her little chubby face. He caught his breath as one fact stood out clearly: she looked very much like her father. He didn't know how it was possible to recognize the features of a grown man in the face of a newborn girl, but it was impossible to deny. This child was a precious gift that Alistair had left behind, and Sebastian was overcome with awe and gratitude.

"Hello there," he said to the baby, then he asked Julia without looking up, "Does she have a name?"

"Not yet." Julia laughed softly. "Her mother was somewhat distracted, but I'm sure she has something in mind. Until a little one is named, I just call them Baby."

"Hello, Baby," Sebastian said, and the tiny little girl squirmed slightly in her sleep, grunting like a baby piglet and scrunching up her tiny face, making her uncle chuckle. "You look like your father, little one," he added, as if she could really understand him.

"Your brother," Julia said.

"Yes," Sebastian replied. "I fear you know far too much about me."

"I don't know anything that isn't common knowledge around here," Julia said, putting the folded nappies and blankets into a bureau drawer. "But I'm very happy your brother left something wonderful of himself behind."

"As am I," Sebastian said.

"I'm going to rest on the sofa in the sitting room," Julia said, making Sebastian look up at her, feeling a twinge of panic. "I'll leave the door open so I can hear if I'm needed. Any time you're ready to leave, just lay the baby next to her mother. I'm used to this and I know how to keep myself from sleeping too deeply. I'll check on them both every little while."

Sebastian just nodded and watched her leave the room. Alone with Enid and the baby, he pondered his gratitude that all was well. He became utterly mesmerized by Baby—as Julia had temporarily named her—and her uncanny resemblance to Alistair. Sebastian knew that many people considered *all* babies to be beautiful, but even with setting his own bias aside, he believed this little girl to be especially so. Her features were fine and balanced—like a porcelain doll. And her thick, gold-colored hair added to her cherubic appearance. Sebastian touched her hair, and her face and her little hands; the rest of her was wrapped up tightly.

Sebastian turned his attention to Enid, and despite what Julia had told him, he concluded once again that she looked dead. If he hadn't been able to see her blanket moving up and down gently with her breathing, he might not have been convinced that she was indeed living. In addition, Enid looked as white as porcelain, and appeared equally fragile. Despite the baby being so tiny, she looked strong and healthy; Enid looked the opposite, and Sebastian felt deeply concerned. While he watched Enid sleeping, he didn't think at all about their troubled past; he thought only of the future, while he prayed that Enid would be in it, alive and well to be a mother to her daughter, and a mother figure to his sons. They'd all become utterly reliant upon her—even if he'd not wanted to admit it—and everyone in this house needed her to live, but especially the children.

Julia came in more than once to check on both baby and mother—just as she'd promised. She didn't speak; she just glanced at both Enid and the baby to be assured that nothing had changed, then she returned to the sitting room through the open door.

The baby squirmed in Sebastian's arms. He watched her while she stretched her arms, and her face contorted comically in time with the same little grunting sounds she'd made before. For a minute or two he feared she would wake up and he had no idea what to do. He knew Julia was in the next room, but she surely needed her rest. But Baby resituated herself in her little cocoon and slept on. Sebastian began to feel sleepy as he watched her perfect example of slumber, and he fell asleep with her cradled in his arm, leaning his head into the corner of the large, comfortable chair in which he sat.

Sebastian came awake to growing daylight in the room and the sound of a gentle moan. At first, he thought it was the baby, but a quick glance told him she was still sleeping. When he realized Enid was coming awake—and feeling pain—he wondered for a long moment what to do. He doubted that she would appreciate seeing *him* here, and he couldn't begin to figure out how he would explain his reasons for remaining nearby all these hours. He was relieved when Julia came into the room, looking as if she'd just awakened, proving what she'd said earlier about being able to sleep lightly enough to hear if she was needed.

The midwife whispered to him as she passed by, "We will need a few minutes of privacy. Why don't you take Baby into the sitting room?"

Sebastian nodded and stood carefully, keeping the baby secure in his arms. He went into the sitting room and sat down across from a sofa where there was a pillow and blanket, which had obviously been Julia's makeshift bed. He wondered if it would be better for him to return the baby to Julia's care and leave now that the drama was over and he'd had the opportunity to become acquainted with his niece. But he didn't want to go. He couldn't explain his instinctive need to remain nearby; he wanted to be needed, and perhaps he feared that if he let either Enid or the baby out of his sight, something terrible might happen to one or both of them. Of course, he knew that such things were entirely out of his control, but he could find very little logic in his own thinking right now. He rather felt caught up in a whirlwind of emotions and memories, where the past swirled around with the present and he had moments where it was difficult to discern the difference—which made him wonder if the losses he'd experienced had somehow caused him to lose his mind to some degree. All he knew for certain was that he wanted to stay nearby, and he hoped that Julia—who was obviously in charge of this situation for the time being—would not tell him he needed to leave.

* * * * *

Enid was finally able to push past the heaviness of her eyelids and looked up to see Julia's friendly face, wearing a warm smile.

"My baby," Enid muttered, her throat dry.

"She's absolutely perfect, and she's been sleeping like a little angel."

Enid took that information in with deep relief as Julia lifted her head and helped her drink some water. Julia carefully put Enid's head back onto the pillow and asked, "Do you remember what happened, sweetheart?"

"I was . . . bleeding too much," Enid said. "And then . . . I don't remember. I think that . . . I thought I was going to die."

"You're going to be just fine," Julia said, "but you *did* lose a great deal of blood, and that's going to make you very weak for quite some time. You'll need to be patient with yourself as you heal. There are many people here to help take care of you and your little girl. You've both come through just fine, and that's what matters."

Enid nodded and said, "I want . . . to hold my baby."

"Let me help you with some personal matters first, and then we'll get her straightaway."

Enid was especially grateful for Julia's help as it became evident just how weak and sore she was. The soreness was apparently the result of any childbirth experience, but the excessive weakness was due to what Julia called hemorrhaging—the loss of too much blood following the delivery. Once Enid was settled back into bed, leaning against the headboard with a stack of pillows behind her, she only wanted to hold her baby. She heard Julia say loudly, "You can bring her in now," and a moment later Enid looked up to see Sebastian—of all people—holding her baby.

Julia was quick to answer the question she had accurately guessed Enid would ask. "Mr. Hawthorne has been getting acquainted with his new little niece, and watching over her very well."

"She's done nothing but sleep," Sebastian said, "so I hardly did anything of value."

With a smile on his face, Sebastian carefully eased the baby into Enid's arms while he said, "She looks so much like her father; it's uncanny."

"Oh, she does," Enid said after only a glance at her daughter's face. Unable to look at anything except the baby she became oblivious to everything else around her—even Sebastian.

"What will you call her?" Julia asked.

"Sarah Marie," Enid said without hesitation; she'd already given the matter a great deal of thought.

Enid recalled Sebastian's presence when she heard him say, "After my mother and my wife?" She couldn't tell if he was pleased or upset.

Enid looked up at him, her firm gaze indicating that it was up to her to choose her child's name, and she would not be swayed by any opinion of his. She looked back at her beautiful, perfect child and heard Sebastian say, "It's a lovely name."

Enid was relieved that he wouldn't protest, but even more relieved when he said, "I should be going. I'm glad that all is well." She sensed that he was hesitant to leave, that he wanted to say more, but he paused for only a moment before he hurried out of the room, making it much easier for Enid to just focus on the miracle she was holding in her arms. During her labor she had wondered many times how enduring such horrible pain could ever be worth it, but now she understood what she'd heard so many women say about the incomparable rewards of childbirth. She'd gladly do it all again just to have this beautiful little girl. The fact that little Sarah *did* look so much like her father only added to the miracle. This baby was living, breathing proof of Alistair's existence, and of the love that Enid had shared with him.

He would live on through this child, and right at this moment, nothing could make Enid happier. She was relieved beyond words to have the worst behind her, and to know that her baby was healthy and strong. Her own healing seemed irrelevant by comparison.

* * * * *

Sebastian felt exhausted but also disoriented after spending so many hours close to Enid and the baby. He focused on practicality, knowing that Julia would take very good care of mother and child. After getting cleaned up and putting on fresh clothes, Sebastian knew it was near the time the boys would be awakened to begin their day. He got to their room just a moment before Maisy did and told her that he would wake them and see that they made it to breakfast on time. He was pleased with how delighted Matthew and Mark were to see him when they woke up, and he sat with his arms around them while he gave them the good news that their Aunt Enid had given birth to a little girl, and therefore they had a new cousin. They asked many questions, some of which he answered directly, and others which he skirted around, not certain how to tell boys so young about some of the more delicate matters of childbirth. The boys were thrilled with knowing about the baby and anxious to see her, but Sebastian told them, "I will talk to Enid about when *she* feels it would be a proper time for you to meet the baby. She needs a great deal of rest, and it will be up to her."

Sebastian explained very briefly that the childbirth had been difficult for Enid and she would not be feeling normal for quite some time, and therefore they wouldn't be seeing her every day as they usually did. It was clear that they understood, but Sebastian was not prepared to hear Matthew ask, "Is Aunt Enid going to die like Mother did?"

Sebastian found it difficult to breathe, let alone speak, but he forced himself to do both in order to remain calm and offer an appropriate response, so as not to upset the boys. He knew he couldn't promise them that nothing more would go wrong; if it did they might never trust him again. But at the same time, he didn't want them being afraid—even though he understood their fear completely. He finally cleared his throat and said, "Right now everything is fine, and there is no reason to believe that anything will go wrong. We will pray that Aunt Enid and the baby will both be all right."

The boys both nodded but he sensed their concern. How could he forget that they'd not only lost their mother, but their baby sister as well?

It had been so traumatic for him that he'd not been there for his sons as he should have been, and he wondered if they were still holding onto grief as he was. He made a mental note to talk to them about it at some future time, but first he needed to heal a little more from his own grief.

Sebastian distracted the boys from their concerns by helping them get dressed for the day. They shared breakfast together before Sebastian admitted to his sons that he'd gotten very little sleep and he was going to take a nap. He promised to see them later and left them happily playing in Maisy's care.

Sebastian returned to his own room and removed his boots and waistcoat before he crawled into bed and sighed gratefully for the comfort that greeted him. In his mind he reviewed all that had happened since he'd come upon Enid on the stairs, pretending that she was fine and didn't need any help. She was as proud and stubborn as . . . well, he concluded, as himself. His thoughts brought him to the point where he'd been sitting with the baby in his arms, and with that pleasant memory he drifted into a deep sleep.

* * * * *

Enid found it impossible to embrace the complete measure of joy she felt in now being a mother. This beautiful little girl had changed Enid in ways she could neither quantify nor explain, but the changes were deep and life altering. She could have just stared at tiny, little Sarah every waking moment, but it quickly became evident that what she'd gone through to bring this baby into the world had taken a severe physical toll, and the luxury of just enjoying time with her little princess came in increments far too small. It took a great deal of time, effort, and help from others for Enid to perform the simple human tasks necessary for living and getting through the day. She was grateful beyond words for all that Julia had done for her, and that this midwife who had become her friend was willing to remain in the house for a couple of days, just to make certain that all was well with Enid and the baby. Mrs. Thorpe was also extremely helpful and regularly on hand, as was Tilly, who had apparently been reassigned to wait on Enid hand and foot through her recovery, while the newly hired maids would assist elsewhere.

Enid was glad for the level of comfort she had come to feel with these women, given the personal nature of childbirth and all that was required to assist her in recovering. All three of them had been with Enid during her labor and delivery, and now they were kind and respectful in helping her with every little thing. She couldn't take even a few steps without someone helping her remain upright—even though Julia had insisted that she get on her feet every few hours to help prevent other problems that could arise from staying down too long. Enid was so weak that she needed help eating; she found it difficult to believe that she wasn't capable of even lifting a spoon to her mouth without her arm aching.

Little Sarah was kept close by, usually right on the bed near Enid. Julia helped Enid learn how to feed the baby, even though her milk hadn't yet come in. Enid marveled at Julia's knowledge of how mother nature had given a woman all she needed to bring a child into the world and care for it, but she was also open to the reality that such things were often challenging and might not go according to plan, and that God always provided options. In Enid's case, Julia explained that with her excessive loss of blood, it might take time for her to produce enough milk to keep the baby satisfied; therefore, she'd given instructions to Mrs. Thorpe on how to properly prepare goat's milk for the baby if it was needed. Everything had been taken care of, and every need of both Enid and the baby was being met. Enid hardly went a moment without wondering how it might have been if she'd been expelled from this house with nothing but her dead husband's money. Even if she'd been able to afford having her basic needs met—and even hiring proper medical care and someone to assist her—it wouldn't have been the same. Here, she felt at home; she felt like she was among family—at least as close as she would ever be since her own family had cut her off completely. *That* was something she chose to *never* think about; the loss was simply too unbearable. She indulged herself for a few moments, simply wondering how it might be if her parents actually wanted to see her and meet their beautiful new granddaughter; but doing so only made her cry, and she was already excessively weepy—which Julia said was a normal reaction following childbirth.

In addition to being weak, Enid was experiencing a great deal of pain and soreness. Julia had medicine Enid could take to ease the pain and help her sleep, but the midwife recommended only small doses that would allow her to be awake and alert for her meals—which she very much needed in order to get her strength back—and to be involved with Sarah's care as much as possible.

After eating a good supper, Enid gladly took one of those small doses, very much feeling the need to rest, but too aware of her pain to be able to relax. She came awake to a room filled with the dim light of dusk and concluded that the baby either hadn't fussed while she'd slept, or someone else had taken care of her. She thought of how just twenty-four hours earlier she'd been in severe pain with hours of labor yet to go. She heaved a sigh of deep relief, knowing all of that was now over.

Enid rolled very carefully to her other side, unable to keep from groaning when it hurt so much to move even a little. She was astonished to see Sebastian sitting in a chair near her bedside, the baby in his arms.

"Are you all right?" he asked, apparently in response to the indication he'd heard that she was in pain. If she'd known he was here she would have put more effort into remaining silent.

"According to Julia all is well and perfectly normal in light of having given birth." She heard a terseness in her voice that she regretted, but his attention was as confusing now as it had been when he'd insisted on staying with her while she'd been in labor. Then she recalled that he'd been here early this morning when she'd awakened, and he'd likely been at her bedside for hours while she'd slept.

He nodded and said, "Forgive me if I startled you. I confess that I rather enjoy spending time with my niece." He looked down at the sleeping baby. "She has a . . . comforting effect."

Enid felt a softening toward him—or at least toward his desire to be here with the baby. She knew Alistair's death had been very hard on him, and it was natural for him to be drawn to his brother's daughter. Just as she very much loved her nephews, she couldn't begrudge Sebastian wanting and needing a relationship with his niece.

When she said nothing, he asked, "Is my chair at an acceptable distance from the bed?" She couldn't tell if his tone was tinted with humor or sarcasm regarding the comments she'd made during her labor when his sitting in a chair across the room had reminded her all too much of Alistair's death.

"It's fine," she muttered, wishing he would ask her to tell him more about what had happened with Alistair. Perhaps if he would be willing to listen to her side of the story—as opposed to the distorted version he'd come up with in his own mind—he might come to see that she'd done nothing to warrant his disdain. Enid forced aside thoughts of the discord between them, and instead took in how content he looked, holding the baby in his arms. He'd just admitted that she had a comforting effect. In that moment it was easy for Enid to imagine Sebastian being significantly involved in Sarah's life—just as she was with Matthew and Mark. For the sake of the children, it didn't seem so difficult to set their differences aside.

"I need to thank you," Enid said, and he looked surprised.

"For what?"

"For your help . . . when I was in labor, for staying with me. I know I was being stubborn and . . ."

"Cranky?" he offered when she hesitated. He then showed an unexpected smile and added, "You had every right to be cranky, and I wish I could have done *more* to help."

Silence merged into a mildly awkward tension, which was eased only by his attention being fully focused on the baby.

"How are the boys?" Enid asked, glad to have thought of something to say.

"Very well," he said, still looking at Sarah, which Enid preferred. "Of course, I explained that you'd had the baby and you wouldn't be able to come and see them until you got feeling better. They are, however, anxious to meet their cousin—and to see you, of course. When you're feeling up to it, I'll bring them for a brief visit." He looked up. "If that's all right."

"Of course," she said. "I miss them; I'd love to see them."

"They miss you too," he said, looking at her with anything *but* disdain showing in his eyes. Confused by the contradictions in him, she looked away.

Enid listened as Sebastian commented again on how much little Sarah looked like her father, and he made a point of saying that he was grateful Alistair had left this beautiful child behind. Enid gave single-word responses to indicate she agreed, but she wished they could talk about Alistair's death and clear the air of the smoggy implications hanging around them whenever they were in the same room. Trying to ignore them often felt suffocating to Enid. All her efforts to simply focus on the present and his affection for the baby were continually interrupted by memories bursting into her mind—memories of him telling her that he blamed her for Alistair's death and that he would never forgive her. And perhaps even worse was his declaration that he would not even allow her to tell him what had really happened and why.

Realizing her thoughts were going in the same circles over and over, she made a more assertive effort at initiating conversation. "So, any gossip in the household?"

"Not that I know of," he said, looking a little surprised.

"Come now," Enid said, "surely there's something going on that you could tell me about to ease my boredom, since I won't be able to make it down to the kitchen to hear such things for myself."

"I'm certain Mrs. Thorpe can bring you whatever gossip you might want to hear," he said.

"She's very busy, and you're just sitting there," Enid said. Still he offered nothing, and she asked more specifically, "How are the new servants working out?"

"Very well from what I'm told," he said. "Thorpe has told me they're all fitting in nicely, and they're reliable and hard-working."

"That's good, then," Enid said. "And what of the tenants on the estate? No drama among them?"

"Not that I know of," he said, sounding mildly irritated.

"And no scandal with the vicar or—"

"You should know I'm not one to indulge in idle gossip and—"

"And you should know that neither am I," Enid declared. "You should also know me well enough to know when I'm teasing you. I know very well that you try to remain abreast of what's going on in the lives of the people you are responsible for. I don't consider any news of events in their lives to be idle gossip. And I would never expect there to be any scandal with the vicar; if there were, I don't think I would want to know. I was hoping to provoke a smile into that sour expression of yours. But it seems the only thing that can make you smile is my daughter."

Sebastian's response was only another long stretch of silence. But he surprised her when he admitted, "I confess it's difficult to find anything worth smiling over, and the children seem to be the exception. I'm trying very hard to remember all that we have to be grateful for, and the list is very long. But the things that bring me sorrow often overshadow any gratitude I can muster, and the weight feels too hard to bear."

Enid was glad Sebastian was focused on the baby and not her when she felt certain her astonishment over such a confession could not be disguised. Had his involvement in Sarah's birth—and the presence of Sarah herself affected him so deeply as to provoke him into speaking of his grief openly and with humility? While she was trying to come up with a suitable response, he looked up at her with a vulnerability in his eyes that sharply contrasted with something in his expression that silently challenged her to counter his confession with words that might give him an excuse to never be so open with her again. Did he really believe she was the kind of person to be so unkind, so lacking in compassion?

"I understand, Sebastian; I really do."

"Yes, I suppose you do," he said as if *her* grief had never occurred to him before. He turned his attention toward the baby again, touching her chubby little face while she slept. He actually smiled, albeit faintly, and said, "Perhaps Sarah will bring some much-needed joy to our home."

"I'm certain she will," Enid said, liking the way he'd referred to *our home*. Considering his mention of all they had to be grateful for, she felt compelled to add, "Thank you, Sebastian, for letting us stay."

His eyes darted toward her and one eyebrow went up; she could almost imagine he'd forgotten how he'd once told her that he would personally prefer that she left. "Of course," he said, and to her surprise he added, "This is where you and Sarah belong."

Enid was glad to hear him say it, and grateful that Sarah's birth had apparently escorted them beyond any outward disgruntlement toward each other. She knew—just as she felt certain he did—that nothing had changed regarding their deep disagreement, but perhaps it was best to simply leave all of that unspoken and simply strive to live together in peace as a family— even considering the odd nature of their family unit.

The baby began to stretch and groan in a way that Enid had come to recognize as the signs that she was coming awake. Sebastian watched her and kept smiling, but as soon as she was fully awake and began to fuss, he was quick to hand her over to Enid. He thanked her for allowing him to visit and hurried away, pausing only long enough to hear her say, "Perhaps you could bring the boys to meet Sarah right after lunch."

"I will," he said. "We won't stay long. I know you need your rest."

Enid nodded, and he left the room, leaving her appreciative of the softening between them, but at the same time confused over the nature of Sebastian Hawthorne in general. She pondered the strange situation between her and her brother-in-law for just a moment before she turned her focus to her precious new daughter. Enid loved touching the wisps of blonde hair on Sarah's head, and she loved the hint of a dimple that showed in her right cheek at times. Yes, she certainly looked like her father, and Enid felt a deep peace to think that all the difficulties she'd endured because of her marriage to Alistair had at least given her this precious daughter. It had all been worth it and more.

Chapter Seven

CONTRADICTION

SEBASTIAN CAME BACK AFTER LUNCH as promised, bringing Matthew and Mark with him. Enid watched from her currently permanent position in her bed as Sebastian sat on a sofa, with his sons on either side of him. He held the baby while the boys examined her with awe, asking questions that made both Enid and Sebastian smile. He looked toward her once to *share* a smile, and she wished she didn't have to wonder if his heart had softened toward her. She hated the way his angry words still haunted her. Sebastian carefully unwrapped Sarah while she slept to show the boys her tiny feet and allow them to count her toes. He helped them each hold Sarah for a few minutes before he took her back, almost as if he selfishly wanted to hold her as much as he possibly could. The experience was sweet and tender until Mark looked up at his father and asked, "Is she going to die like our baby did?"

Tears rushed painfully and without warning to Enid's eyes and she had to fight hard to keep them from falling. She felt an overwhelming onslaught of compassion for what Sebastian and his sons had been through, and an undeniable spark of fear in wondering if something horrible could happen to her daughter. After losing Alistair she couldn't imagine being able to cope with losing her baby as well. But Sebastian had lost both his wife and baby. She was grateful the question had been directed at Sebastian, because Enid knew she couldn't speak without her tears breaking loose.

Sebastian cleared his throat tensely and spoke in an even tone. "We don't know exactly what was wrong with our baby," he said, looking at Mark, then Matthew, then Mark again. "We have no reason to believe that little Sarah Marie here won't be just fine. If something goes wrong, I promise I will tell you."

"No secrets?" Matthew asked.

"No secrets," Sebastian said. "I promise."

"I like her very much," Matthew said, gently touching the baby's golden hair.

"I like her too," Mark said. "When will she be able to play with us?"

Sebastian chuckled, the tension of a moment ago completely absent. "Not for a while yet, but she'll change very quickly, and I'm certain she will love to have the both of you play with her; you'll see."

"She has the same name as our baby," Matthew said.

Enid gasped, and Sebastian looked up at her almost guiltily, as if he knew he should have told her. He quickly looked down at the baby again and simply said, "Yes, she does. It's a lovely name."

A few minutes later Sebastian stood and returned the baby to Enid, telling the boys, "Your aunt needs to rest. We'll come back another time."

"Can we come back later?" Mark asked him in a whiny tone.

"Perhaps tomorrow if Auntie Enid is feeling up to it," Sebastian said, herding the boys out of the room while he waved toward Enid and said, "Thank you. Take good care of yourself."

"Of course," Enid said and waved at them all as they left the room. Once they were gone, Enid had no reason to hold back her tears. Now that she'd become a mother, she'd gained a great deal more empathy for Sebastian's grief, and she could only pray that her little Sarah Marie would remain healthy and strong. She couldn't even imagine losing her! But what was this about her little niece who had died having the same name as her daughter? What kind of coincidence was this? Alistair had loved the name Sarah, which had been his mother's name. And it had been Enid's idea to use Marie as a middle name—both in honor of her sister-in-law whom she loved deeply, and because she very much liked the sound of it. How could two brothers—who had been living on opposite ends of the world—have chosen the exact same name for their daughters, who would have been only months apart in age if the elder of the two had survived?

Enid willed herself to regain her composure when Julia came into the room in response to the baby's fussing. She was grateful beyond words for Julia's knowledgeable and kind assistance, but she could already tell that the weeks it would take to get her strength back were doomed to be slow and frustrating.

Later in the afternoon, following a long nap, Enid had just finished feeding the baby when she heard a soft knocking on her door, as if the visitor hadn't wanted to wake her if she'd been sleeping.

"Come in," Enid called, surprised to see Sebastian enter the room.

"Did you get some rest?" he asked, leaving the door open.

"I did, yes."

"May I?" he asked, motioning toward the chair that had remained near the bed for those who had come to visit with Enid.

"Of course," she said, wondering what he might say.

She didn't have to wonder long when he immediately said, "I'm sorry about earlier. It's not the first time one of them has asked me if the same thing might happen to your baby that happened to . . . their sister. I didn't think it would come up again in front of you."

"You have nothing to apologize for," Enid said, *in that regard*, she added silently, trying to think only of the present topic of conversation. "They're naturally curious, and losing their sister was most certainly difficult for them."

"Yes, I'm certain it was," Sebastian said, leaning his forearms on his thighs, gazing at the floor in front of him. "I'm ashamed to say that I was not there for them when it happened. They are likely more traumatized by it because of that."

"But you're helping them adjust now," Enid said, attempting to reassure him. "We can't change the past; it's how we move forward that matters."

"I want to believe that," he said, and Enid was touched by his humility. She was also somewhat taken aback by the very fact that they were sharing such tender conversation.

After long moments of silence, Enid decided to express her most prominent thought. "Now that I'm a mother . . . I want to say that . . . I can't comprehend how it must feel for you to have lost a child. I'm so very sorry."

"Thank you," he said without looking up.

More silence pressed Enid to ask, "Forgive me if this sounds insensitive, but . . . do you know *why* she died?"

He looked up at her for only a moment, but it was long enough for her to see that he understood her reasons for asking. "She developed a fever, but the doctor said he couldn't say for certain whether it had anything to do with what had taken Marie. He had no answers regarding either of their deaths. He just kept saying, 'Sometimes these things just happen.' Apparently, that was meant to simply explain away the deaths of my wife and baby. *Sometimes these things just happen.*" Sebastian sighed and leaned back in his chair, looking firmly at Enid. "There's no reason to believe that Sarah won't remain healthy and strong. We're just not going to consider any other possibility."

"I pray you're right," Enid said with a shaky voice, surprised by the way Sebastian leaned forward again and took hold of her hand. He squeezed her fingers in a silent gesture of comfort and she squeezed back, wishing they could talk about Alistair and clear the air. Not wanting to bring the subject up at all for fear of destroying such a tender moment, she took advantage of more silence to say something else that needed to be said. "Why didn't you tell me . . . about the name?"

"Our little Sarah Marie was never christened; the name was never made official. I was a little . . . surprised when you told me your daughter's name, but it only took me a moment to feel that it's right, rather appropriate, truthfully."

"Are you sure?" Enid asked. Even though she believed it was her right to name her own child whatever she chose, given how kind he was being, she wanted to be respectful. "If there is any reason you're not comfortable with it, or—"

"I can't imagine her having any other name," Sebastian said. He let go of Enid's hand and leaned back again, chuckling softly. "She's not been here two days and I've already become completely attached to her."

"So have I," Enid said, glancing at the baby where she slept beside her mother.

Enid watched Sebastian closely, trying to understand the different sides of him, wondering if she could trust that his present kindness would last. She only realized she was staring at him when she became aware of him staring at her. She resisted the urge to look away and ignored the way her heart quickened. Feeling compelled to clarify the situation, she simply asked, "Sebastian, what is going on with you? What's happening? Please talk to me."

She saw by the way his eyes moved that he was thinking, likely pondering whether he could trust her. She wanted to tell him he could, but she feared it would only sound patronizing. He cleared his throat and looked away, giving her the sense that he was going to admit to something he didn't necessarily want to say. "Truthfully," he cleared his throat again, "I keep wondering why you remind me of Marie." With that much out in the open, he looked at her again. "The two of you had *nothing* in common; why would you keep reminding me of her now?"

Enid wanted to feel defensive over his declaration that she'd had nothing in common with his wife; they'd been very close, and he knew it. Although, it was as if he *didn't* know it. Given his distorted accusations regarding Alistair, she wondered if there were some things he simply chose to ignore or refused to see. But she reminded herself to focus on the present conversation, hoping perhaps they could work in tiny steps toward sharing a mutual trust, given that it seemed they would be helping to raise each other's children.

"Perhaps it's more to do with the experience . . . of my just having had a baby, rather than anything in particular. Although," she couldn't resist adding, "Marie and I were very good friends, Sebastian. I would think that means we had much in common."

He looked up at her abruptly with something in his eyes that made her wonder if he would argue that last point. She held his gaze firmly, wishing to silently convey that she was more than willing to defend the truth of her relationship with Marie—and anything else he might have assumed about her that wasn't true. The gaze they shared became intense, as if some invisible force kept them staring at each other. At first it felt to Enid like a battle of wills, to see who might look away first. But she saw his countenance soften, and something in his eyes completely contradicted everything unkind he'd ever said to her. While she was attempting to figure out what he might be thinking, she recalled him saying only a couple of minutes earlier, *I keep wondering why you remind me of Marie.* And then she saw it. Without a doubt she saw in his gaze clear evidence that what he was feeling had nothing to do with their familial connection or being attached to each other's children. Enid's heart quickened, and she *did* look away, wondering what on earth she was supposed to make of his silent implications.

"Are you all right?" he asked.

"I'm fine," she said and closed her eyes, relaxing more into the pillow behind her head, if only to be more convincing when she added, "I'm just very tired."

"I'll let you rest," he said, coming to his feet as if he felt relieved to be set free from the tension that had descended over the room, but then he hesitated to leave, as if he didn't actually want to go. She finally heard his footsteps on the carpet, along with him saying, "I'll check back later, if that's all right."

"Of course," she said, at the same time wondering how she was supposed to contend with what she'd just realized about Sebastian's feelings for her—which were in such direct contradiction to so many things he'd said to her in the past, and the way he'd always made it clear that he didn't approve of his brother's choice of a wife, and that he would only tolerate her because she *was* his brother's wife. Now Alistair and Marie were both gone; Sebastian and Enid were left behind. But it was ridiculous to think that just because they were drawn together due to the love they had for each other's children, it could possibly mean anything more than simple companionship—like unto a brother and sister at best. Enid couldn't imagine ever being able to share anything more with him, especially given his opinions of her.

Enid tried to rest. She *did* feel tired, just as she usually did. But her mind was thoroughly preoccupied with attempting to understand what she had just seen in Sebastian's eyes, and the way it had made her feel. She gasped aloud when the memory of him looking at her that way provoked a fluttering in her stomach and a quickening of her heart. What did *that* mean? Was she as attracted to him as he was to her? But if she considered his attraction to be rooted more in their circumstances as opposed to anything real in and of itself, then it was surely best ignored until it passed as something superficial and entirely without substance.

By suppertime, Enid felt downright agitated by her inability to get Sebastian out of her head. Knowing that her meal would soon arrive, she reprimanded herself for getting caught up in such feelings and speculations and decided again that the only reasonable option was to simply ignore anything she might have seen or sensed. If a day came when Sebastian actually *spoke* of his feelings, she would address the matter appropriately. Until—or if—that day came, she would simply treat him as the uncle to her daughter and enjoy his company while she was stuck here in bed and he wanted to spend time with the baby.

After Enid had finished her meal and fed the baby, Sebastian came and asked if he could hold the baby for just a little while, declaring that he wouldn't bother her for long. Enid watched him with Sarah and felt warmed by the depth of attachment he'd formed with his niece so quickly, but she also noticed that he kept his focus so completely on the baby that he didn't look at Enid at all. It was as if he was fully aware that he'd betrayed feelings toward Enid—feelings he preferred to keep to himself, and the only way to do that was to not so much as glance at her. He returned Sarah to Enid's arms without looking at her, thanked her for being patient with his visits, and hurried from the room.

The following day, Julia declared that Enid had passed the point where Julia felt any concern for her health—or that of the baby. The midwife returned to her family, promising to continue to come every couple of days to check on them both, and making it clear that they could send for her any time of the day or night if needed. Enid quickly missed Julia, not only for her pleasant company, but for the security she'd offered in her perception and skills, which had kept Enid feeling safe regarding her baby as well as her own health. But in Julia's absence, Tilly became more actively involved in helping Enid with everything she needed. They'd become completely comfortable with each other, and Enid had overcome any embarrassment she might have felt prior to giving birth in having Tilly assist her in personal matters she could not always manage on her own, given how weak she was from her severe loss of blood. Tilly was also very good with the baby, encouraging Enid to do all she could to care for and feed little Sarah, but readily on hand to fetch whatever was needed or to help hold and care for Sarah in ways that Enid simply couldn't manage at present. Observing Tilly with the baby, Enid felt inexplicably grateful that she had not been banished from this house, left alone to deal with learning to be a mother while her own health was so fragile. She'd grown to love Tilly dearly, and she felt decidedly comfortable with the prospect of Tilly becoming an official nanny to Sarah. Enid wanted to maintain a continual influence in her daughter's life; she wanted Sarah to see her mother's face more than any other. Enid also knew that—practically speaking—it was impossible to live in such an enormous house, where the kitchens and the laundry were so far away from the bedrooms, and not have assistance in caring for children. Tilly and Enid were comfortable enough with each other that Enid could ask for help when she needed it, and know that she could always leave Sarah in Tilly's care even if it was simply to allow her to spend time in another part of the house or go for a walk in the gardens—none of which she could do in such a huge home without knowing that someone was listening for her baby while she slept, or able to help with the simple but necessary tasks that were a continual part of caring for a baby.

Enid knew she had many weeks of healing left before she could even consider leaving this room, but when she did, she wanted to know that Tilly would be available to watch over Sarah. And in the meantime, Tilly had become invaluable in being on hand for every little thing. She'd been sleeping in a room across the hall so that she could hear if she was needed, and Enid asked Tilly how she would feel about making this a permanent situation—if it met with Mrs. Thorpe's approval. Tilly was thrilled, and so was Mrs. Thorpe when Enid spoke to her about it. The housekeeper visited Enid at least once a day personally, and it was evident that she'd assigned Tilly to assist with the baby because she'd believed it would be a good fit, and that the young woman was more than up to the task.

As Enid became accustomed to what she was capable of doing in her current condition—and what she simply could *not* do—she became more adjusted to caring for her daughter with Tilly's assistance, and they established a comfortable routine. Sebastian worked his way into that routine by communicating with Enid over what would work out best without upsetting the baby's naps and feeding schedule, and Enid's need to rest. Once a day he brought the boys to spend some time with her and the baby, and Enid had taken to reading them a story when they came, while Sebastian held Sarah. She liked it when Matthew and Mark cuddled up close to her on the bed and she could read from whatever storybook they had brought with them. She had grown to love these boys, and she was glad to be a part of their lives.

Sebastian occasionally stopped by just to check on her, staying only a minute or less, but he always came alone later in the day, wanting to just hold the baby, and he even enjoyed helping feed her warm goat's milk from a bottle when Enid's milk supply wasn't enough to satisfy the baby. While Sebastian was in the room, they sometimes shared conversation that was trivial for the most part—as if they both mostly wanted to avoid anything that wasn't—or sometimes they both remained silent, although it had become a comfortable silence, and Enid enjoyed just watching Sebastian's love for Sarah with each passing day. Occasionally they would talk about more significant things—even if it was in a very nonpersonal way—and she sometimes felt surprised at how similar they were in their thinking. At times he was open and honest, and at others he could quickly become defensive or grow suddenly silent. Still, Enid loved their conversations. She tried not to think about how attached she was becoming to her husband's brother. Most of the time she did well at convincing herself it was merely her need for company and conversation, or it was the fact that they'd both loved Marie and Alistair, and they'd both suffered losses. All of that was true, but something deep inside herself kept forcing its way to the forefront of her mind, whispering to her that what she was growing to feel for Sebastian was far more than all of that combined. He'd come to avoid looking directly at her at all, but she suspected the reasons, and she had to wonder if he was thinking about her as much as she thought about him. In all practicality, the very idea of such an attraction was ludicrous. It had not been so many months since he'd lost Marie, and even less time since she had lost Alistair. The fact that they were both lonely and sharing time with each other's children had nothing to do with the feelings Enid was trying so hard to suppress. The fact that Sebastian had never recanted or apologized for his cruel declaration of blame and anger toward her made the possibility of their ever sharing anything more than what they already shared inconceivable.

Weeks passed while Sarah changed every day, and Enid loved every precious moment she spent with her daughter. She contemplated a great deal the decisions and events in her life that had brought her to this place at this time, and to be the mother of this beautiful child. The pain and soreness of giving birth had continually improved, but the weakness from losing so much blood seemed no better. Julia assured her this was normal, and Enid just needed to be patient, that in some cases there was a sudden burst of healing once enough weeks had passed for the body to create new blood to make up for the loss—at least that was her theory. Enid tried to be patient with herself in the need to heal, and she was grateful to be so well cared for. But the walls of her room were beginning to feel prisonlike at times, and she longed to roam the house, and even more so to go outside. She often managed to carefully make her way to one of the windows in her room where she could enjoy the view of the lovely grounds below, and the wooded hills in the distance. The leaves were becoming more colorful every day, and more of them were being blown to the ground by frequent breezes. Some days were warm and sunny, as if summer were determined to hold on for as long as possible, and other days were cold and stormy as if winter were declaring its imminent invasion. But Enid had always enjoyed going outdoors in any weather; only a dreadful storm could keep her from venturing out. She looked forward to the day when she would once again feel strong enough to walk and explore, rather than just looking out her window.

As Enid and Sarah both remained healthy long past the point when Marie and her baby had become ill and died, a sigh of relief seemed to fall over the entire household. But Enid felt it most with Sebastian. She hadn't realized the tension that had been present in his countenance during their daily visits until it went away. He became more prone to laughing over the funny noises and expressions that were becoming a part of Sarah's personality, and he was more playful, even silly sometimes, with his sons. Her conversations with Sebastian became more relaxed and comfortable, and she'd come to feel very dependent upon his daily visits, even if that meant pushing certain feelings aside, and completely ignoring the discord that had seemed to just magically go away. Enid was not naive enough to believe that it *had* gone away; she believed there were a great many difficulties they were both merely avoiding, but perhaps neither of them were strong enough, considering the losses in their lives, to do anything *but* avoid certain matters. And perhaps that was all right for now.

Given the general benign nature of their conversations, Enid was surprised one evening to hear Sebastian ask, "Do you think you will ever marry again, Enid?"

"Why are you asking me *that*?" she countered, listening to rain run down the windows.

He seemed mildly uncomfortable, and he typically kept his focus on the baby in his arms, as if it kept him from having to look at Enid at all. "You're young; you must surely consider it a possibility. If I were to marry again, I would remain here. But if you marry again, you would leave, and of course Sarah would go with you. I confess that I'm not fond of the idea."

Enid knew it was his attachment to Sarah that concerned him most, but before she answered his question, she couldn't resist asking, "Would *you* marry again?"

He looked directly at her for the first time in weeks, but he turned his attention back to Sarah before he said, "I don't know. It's difficult to even imagine such a possibility."

Enid didn't know how to respond to that, and finally decided that she didn't have to. Instead she focused on his original question. "Well, I believe you can put your mind at ease over my taking Sarah away from here. I have no intention of marrying again or ever leaving this place. I can't imagine being able to leave the boys. I doubt you'll ever get rid of me. I'm content to be the widowed aunt."

"Why?" he asked, astonished—and looked at her again. She found it ironic to consider how many weeks they had been sharing conversation every day without him ever meeting her eyes. And now that he was, the feelings she'd been trying to suppress came uncomfortably close to the surface.

Enid looked toward the window to avoid his gaze, but she was determined to be honest. "I don't know that I found marriage necessarily enjoyable," she admitted, hoping it didn't sound like an affront toward Alistair. She kept to herself the truth that she'd been slowly coming to terms with: she had loved Alistair very much, and she missed him, but she'd had many reasons to feel unhappy in their marriage; reasons she was still trying to understand. Sticking to the present conversation, she added, "I think I far prefer being able to make my own decisions, and not have my life controlled by a man just because his ring is on my finger. My mother was little more than some kind of extension of my father, as if she'd lost herself somehow through their years of marriage."

"And that's how you felt about *your* marriage?" he asked, and again she feared how he might respond if she spoke ill of Alistair.

"Given the personal nature of this conversation, should I assume by your question that you want me to answer it honestly?" She looked at him, wanting to see how he would respond to her boldness. "Since we're talking about your brother, I don't want you to consider anything I say to be an affront to your relationship with him. But you've been married; you should know that there is no relationship like unto marriage. Being married to someone forces us to face ourselves in a way no other relationship can— but only if we choose to see ourselves honestly."

Enid saw his brow furrow before he said, "That statement sounds as if it has a great deal of thought behind it . . . as if you're speaking from experience."

Enid looked down and wrung her hands. "May I speak candidly without having you get upset? I know how much you loved your brother, but he was less than perfect." She looked up at him and attempted a gaze that would let him know how serious she was when she asked, "Can I trust you with such personal matters when you may very well not agree?"

He thought about that for a long moment and said, "I can't possibly know or understand *your* experiences, just as you could never know or understand mine. I'll respect whatever you have to say, but you don't have to talk about it at all if you don't want to."

Enid considered how *desperately* she wanted to talk about it. She wanted to be free of Sebastian's cruel edict against her concerning Alistair. His words still haunted her, and she wanted to be able to let them go. She wanted him to know the truth, and for his heart to be softened against believing that she'd somehow wronged his brother. He'd told her he'd never forgive her, but many weeks of introspection had not given her any reason to believe that she'd done anything that required forgiveness.

Following a quick, silent prayer that this would go well, she took a deep breath and said, "I suppose I followed my mother's example without even realizing it. I believed that it was a woman's place to make herself an extension of the man she married; to be completely supportive of his endeavors and beliefs. And that's what I did. But I look back now and realize that I had begun to lose myself." She felt mildly embarrassed by her explanation and wondered if *any* man could understand what she was talking about. "I simply prefer to never have to contend with that again," she concluded, hoping it would end the conversation.

Sebastian asked tonelessly, "Are you saying that you regret marrying Alistair?"

Enid shot him an astonished glare. "Not at all! I loved him, Sebastian; and he loved me. We had our challenges, as every marriage does, and I was not keen on life in Africa, whereas he took to it like a fish to water, but . . . no, I don't regret it, and I wish he were still alive—as I'm certain you wish that Marie was still here."

"If he were alive," Sebastian said, still toneless and stone-faced, which made it impossible to discern even a tiny clue as to how he was feeling about this conversation, "you would have had this baby in Africa. Do you think that whatever medical care you might have received there would have prevented you from dying? Do you think the baby would have survived there without you in such living conditions?"

Enid realized from the way he said it that it was something to which he'd given a great deal of thought. But she didn't draw attention to that; she simply answered, "I don't know. For all that I wish Alistair was alive, I can't deny that I was terrified to give birth there." Sebastian remained silent to the point where it became awkward, and Enid said, "Coming back around to your original question, I don't intend to ever marry again. I believe that eventually I would have learned to find myself again as Alistair's wife, and I believe he would have been supportive in that, but perhaps there's still just too much pain associated with losing him. I'm not entirely certain of the reasons, Sebastian, but I have no particular desire to marry again, so you needn't worry about me leaving and taking Sarah with me, and I will always be here for your sons. That's what matters most, isn't it? The children?"

"Yes, of course," he said, but she wasn't certain he agreed entirely, and it made her wonder what *else* he believed might be important about her staying. Or perhaps he would prefer her leaving, and it was more his attachment to Sarah that provoked his kindness toward her. She didn't want to think about any other possibility, even though her own thoughts of him completely contradicted her attempt to convince him that this was only about the children.

Enid was relieved when the conversation was put to rest. Sebastian returned Sarah to her arms as he always did; he thanked her for allowing him to come and visit—as he always did—and he left the room, saying he'd see her tomorrow. Enid was left with a strange sensation hovering around her while she held her sleeping daughter and listened to the rain. She wanted her life to be simple and free of complications. But having Sebastian in the center of it felt to her as if the opposite was taking place, as if some kind of whirlwind was gaining momentum and it was beyond her control to stop it or escape it. All she could do was take life one day at a time, and right now every day was one step closer to getting her health back and being able to resume the normalcy of her life.

When Sarah was a month old, Enid still felt excessively weak, but she was slowly becoming able to do more to care for herself and her baby, and she could move around the room more—and sometimes even make it to the sitting room—even though it meant having Tilly or Mrs. Thorpe remain close at her side to help keep her steady. Her limbs quickly ached from weakness if she tried to do too much or walk more than a dozen steps at a time, and if she stood up too quickly, she would inevitably become dizzy or lightheaded, and she certainly didn't want to faint or collapse and cause any kind of trouble for those who helped take care of her.

After lunch on a sunny day, Sarah was well-fed and napping, and Enid wanted to get out of this room—even if that simply meant going to the sitting room where the windows were larger and let in more sunlight. Enid got out of bed carefully and put on her dressing gown, then she had to sit on the edge of the bed for a minute to catch her breath. She reached over to the bedside table and picked up the book she was currently reading, then stood and began a slow and steady trek toward the sitting room, desperately needing a change of scenery, and not willing to wait for anyone to show up and help her.

She was almost to the door of the sitting room when someone knocked at the bedroom door. Given how weak she felt, she considered it perhaps a miracle that one of the servants might have shown up at such an opportune moment.

"Come in," she called, taking hold of the back of the chair with her free hand while she mentally calculated the number of steps to the sitting room door, wondering if she'd been foolish to think she could do this on her own.

"What are you doing?" Sebastian asked, and she turned toward him, surprised that it was him while at the same time wondering why she should be. It wasn't so unusual for him to check in on her, even if she still found it difficult to understand his motives. He'd continued to be so open and honest about some things, and yet so closed and mildly defensive about others. But despite her confusion, she couldn't deny being glad to see him.

"I was just trying to get to the sitting room," she admitted. "I really need a change of scenery, but it's a longer walk than I anticipated."

Sebastian crossed the room, and she expected him to allow her to hold to his arm for support as she walked, but without warning he scooped her into his arms and carried her into the sitting room, where he set her on the chaise where she was able to sit upright but keep her feet elevated. She knew there was a similar piece of furniture in nearly every sitting room in the house, but she'd never appreciated its comfort and purpose more than she did in that moment.

"Thank you," she said to Sebastian.

"Are you comfortable?" he asked. "Do you need any pillows or—"

"I'm fine." She chuckled and looked toward the windows. "I do believe these windows allow more sunlight into the room. It feels lovely to just be in a different room."

"We should have gotten you out of there days ago," he said, as if he felt personally responsible.

"I've come in here a few times," she explained, "but not without help, and never for long. I suppose I'm growing weary of having to be so dependent upon Tilly and Mrs. Thorpe, but perhaps I was a little too zealous about thinking I was capable of such an adventure on my own."

Enid was surprised when Sebastian sat on the edge of the chaise, next to where her legs were stretched out. There were more than a dozen other places to sit, and she wondered why he would choose to sit so close. He then looked into her eyes, making no effort to hide what he was feeling. Enid was taken off guard and was perhaps even shocked to see so clearly what he'd been trying to hide for weeks. Her heart quickened, and her stomach fluttered, but her mind went to Alistair and she wondered if such feelings were some kind of betrayal. He'd only been dead a matter of months, even if it felt like much longer, given all that had happened since then.

"There's something I need to say," Sebastian muttered with a huskiness in his voice she'd never heard before.

Enid felt relieved over the possibility of him saying something that might break this terrible tension between them, but at the same time she feared how whatever he might utter could change everything, and she didn't feel at all prepared for such change.

"I feel guilty," he began, almost as if his own feelings were in perfect synchronization with her own. "When I consider how much I think of you . . . and the way I think of you . . . and the way I feel toward you . . . I feel guilty, wondering what Marie would think if she knew; or perhaps she *does* know . . . and I wonder if she would approve, or if she would feel betrayed."

Enid could hardly breathe as her mind struggled to accept that he had just admitted to everything she had been wondering for weeks. She saw the raw vulnerability in his eyes and could only say, "I feel the same . . . when I think of Alistair."

He squeezed his eyes closed and let out a shaky breath, as if hearing her admit to her own feelings had come as a deep relief, and she wondered how much courage it had taken for him to say what he'd just said. He opened his eyes again to look at her, and the silence between them seemed endless but necessary, as if they both needed to catch up to all they had just finally been able to say aloud. She saw him smile and his eyes softened, as if he'd been searching for something in her gaze and he'd found it.

"Stay . . . right where you are," Sebastian said, tightening his gaze on Enid in a way that made her want to look away, but she couldn't find the will to do so.

"As if I could go *anywhere*," she countered lightly with the hope of easing this tension between them that was becoming palpable. She was surprised by the way he lifted a hand to push a stray wisp of hair back from her face, but she was entirely unprepared for the way he pressed his lips to hers.

"What are you doing?" she demanded, pushing him away.

He didn't answer the question, but neither did he look away. Disappointment and confusion were equally evident in his eyes. It only took Enid a long moment to assess that his reasons for kissing her were deeply tied into his confession—and she could not deny the fact that she had wanted him to kiss her. She would be a fool to think that he hadn't perceived her desire for his affection, which made it wholly unfair for her to reject him the way she just had. It took her only another moment to decide that she needed to rectify the problem—and she needed to do it now.

Enid took hold of his face with both of her hands and lifted her lips to his. She felt as well as heard him take in a sharp breath as their kiss became fully mutual, excitingly sweet, and passionately tender. It lasted only a long moment, but Enid opened her eyes to see him looking at her while she found herself considering in a way she never had before how very different he was from his brother. She wondered if he would kiss her again; she wanted him to. But he eased her into his arms and her head found a comfortable place against his chest. She could hear his heart beating and relished the simple solace of just being held this way. She felt him kiss the top of her head as she pressed her hands against the silky fabric of his waistcoat.

"Sebastian," she murmured, knowing it had to be said, "is this real . . . or simply a matter of convenience?"

"Perhaps it's both," he said and again pressed a kiss into her hair.

Enid liked that answer and felt comforted by it, but she wanted to ask him if he still blamed her for Alistair's death, and if he still held to his determination to never forgive her. The very contradiction of this moment in contrast to the memory of his cruel declarations was difficult for her to comprehend. She needed to know how he really felt, given all that had changed between them—but not now. For now, she just wanted to bask in the serenity of this moment. They had both loved and lost and grieved; they were both lonely and dependent upon each other in many ways. And they had both crossed a bridge into admitting how much they'd grown to care for each other. Now that she was in his arms and had accepted his kiss, they could never go back to the way things had been before. The future was impossible to predict; the past could never be changed. Right now, Enid only wanted to be with Sebastian in this moment and absorb into herself the comfort of his closeness and the hope that perhaps, after all, she wouldn't end up spending the rest of her life alone.

"Talk to me," she whispered and looked up at him without relinquishing her embrace. "Tell me what you're thinking."

"I don't know what to think, Enid," he said with a humility she had never thought possible, given all that she had previously believed about him. "Since I lost Marie . . . and the baby . . . everything in my life has felt chaotic and wrong. I reacted badly, and I know that. I'm trying to do right by my sons . . . and the household . . . and you. But I still feel . . . lost. Except that . . ."

He hesitated, and she gently encouraged him. "Except that what?"

Sebastian tightened his arms around her and moved his face a little closer. "Except that right now . . . I don't feel lost at all. Right now . . . everything feels exactly as it should be, but even that confuses me, because . . . it's complicated; you know more than anyone that feeling this way about each other . . . under the circumstances . . . is complicated."

Enid wanted him to be more specific about what exactly he considered these complications to be. There were questions she wanted answered, things she needed to understand. But now was not the time; she was content to once again rest her head against his chest and bask in the warmth of not feeling alone. She had no idea what, if anything, might come of this. But for now, it didn't matter. She felt him press another kiss into her hair, and she tightened her arms around him, choosing not to think at all about Alistair or Marie.

Chapter Eight

HAUNTED

Sebastian felt completely out of his mind as he kissed Enid again and pressed a hand to the side of her face, simply because he'd wanted to do so more times than he could count. When his thoughts began to swirl with all the possibilities of what this could mean for their future, he was overcome with a sudden need to be alone; otherwise, he feared that he would start babbling promises he didn't feel at all prepared to keep. He hadn't come here intending for this to happen, but given how many times he'd imagined what it might be like to just kiss her and hold her in his arms, he shouldn't have been surprised by the way it just happened with hardly any thought at all.

"I should go," he said, forcing himself to let go of her. The disappointment in her eyes was soothing, somehow. Still, he needed to leave even if he could never explain his reasons to Enid. He stood reluctantly, taking hold of her hand as he did. He pressed a lingering kiss there before he let go. "I'll be back later . . . as usual."

Enid nodded, and he wondered if she shared his thoughts, that after what had just happened between them, nothing would ever be *as usual* again. Only time would tell if that was a good thing, or otherwise. Would they end up loving each other? Or was it possible that some form of hate would evolve between them due to all the complications he had no desire to talk about? How could he talk openly with Enid about things he couldn't even think about? And how could he expect her to understand the contradictions in his own mind, when he could hardly make sense of them himself? He only knew he wanted to be with her every possible moment, and when he wasn't with her he found it difficult to think of anything except her.

Knowing that Tilly would help Enid back to her room, Sebastian closed the door of Enid's sitting room behind him and walked slowly down the hall, as if fighting some magnetic force that was trying to pull him back and not put too much distance between them. At the top of the stairs he felt a little unsteady and sat down, putting his head into his hands. "What am I doing?" he murmured and tugged at his hair. Had he been a fool to express his feelings so openly when he hardly knew where they stood with each other? He was acting impulsively on this bizarre attraction he felt for her, and nowhere inside himself could he find any gentlemanly logic to explain the way he'd just spoken to her, and kissed her, and held her in his arms. There were things about her that he sorely disliked; things that made him angry. So, what kind of madness was this?

Sebastian forced himself to some level of normality—at least enough to be able to continue normally with the remainder of his day. He saw Enid again briefly, and was glad for the maid in the room helping with the baby, which prevented him from giving in to his desire to kiss her again and gush forth every detail of his thoughts and feelings regarding her. He wanted to never leave her room, but at the same time he felt as if he could breathe more deeply once he was out of her presence.

When nighttime came, thoughts of Enid made it impossible for Sebastian to sleep. There were so many things he wanted to say to her, but the words just swirled around in his mind until he felt as if he would *lose* his mind. He finally got up and lit a lamp so that he could see clearly enough to attempt writing her a letter. He crumpled and tossed one attempt after another into the fire and finally gave up when his head grew heavy and his eyes ached. He managed to sleep but woke up to daylight with unbridled words swarming in his brain. He forced himself to forge ahead with his normal routine, feeling almost giddy to recall that his routine involved seeing Enid. As much as he adored Sarah and loved holding her, it was Enid who had won him over—heart, mind, and soul but he had no idea what to do about it.

Sebastian arrived at Enid's room and found the door had been left open. He entered with some trepidation, not certain what to expect from her. He saw her sitting up in bed as usual, reading a book. The moment she heard the floor creak from his footsteps, she looked up at him, and there was no mistaking how glad she was to see him—and was perhaps equally as glad as he was that they were alone.

"Good morning," he said and stopped where he stood, just wanting to look at her.

"Good morning," she replied and smiled while she held his gaze.

"What are you reading?" he asked.

She glanced down at the book as she set it aside. "I'm afraid I could hardly tell you," she said. "I've not been able to concentrate."

"Why not?" he asked, hoping she might be sharing his present ailment.

Looking up at him again, she said with no hesitation or embarrassment, "I keep thinking of you; wondering what you're doing, what you're thinking, when I might see you again. And I keep wondering if . . ."

"If what?" he asked when she hesitated.

"If . . . what I think might be happening between us is only my imagination run wild; or maybe it was a dream."

"If it was a dream" he said, stepping closer, "we've been having the *same* dream." He knew he should maintain a gentlemanly distance—especially given that she was sitting in bed. And he certainly didn't want one of the servants to come in through the open door and catch any hint of the changes taking place between himself and Enid. But before he sat down, he put one hand on the wall above the headboard of the bed and leaned over to kiss her. While his eyes were closed and his lips were touching hers, he felt her hand on his face, and he absorbed her meek response. His heart quickened from the way she eagerly accepted his affection. If she rejected him, he wondered how he might cope. He drew back and noted the dreamy look in her eyes as they came open. He smiled at her and forced himself to sit in a chair that would keep him at a safe distance.

Sebastian was wondering what he could possibly say when his thoughts were still muddled and chaotic. Tilly came into the room to help with the baby, and Enid initiated conversation with him that was more typical of things they'd talked about before they'd crossed this boundary into a new and unexplored territory, where it seemed they both felt somewhat lost but unable to go back.

Days merged into weeks while Enid slowly regained her strength and more color in her cheeks. Each day Sebastian seemed to need at least a minimum amount of time holding Sarah or he couldn't seem to function, and each day he brought the boys to spend time with Enid. They all seemed dependent upon each other to feel that a day was complete—a matter that made perfect sense regarding the children, and perhaps no sense at all regarding how he felt about Enid and his need to just be in the same room with her.

At least once a day he took the opportunity to kiss her, and always relished the way she seemed as sustained as he by their shared affection.

They were rarely alone long enough to discuss in any depth the changes taking place between them, but their time together strengthened Sebastian's hope that perhaps she could fill the void in him that Marie had left behind. He knew he would never cease to love Marie, and no one could replace her. But Enid filled the emptiness in him, and he longed to have it last forever. When he and Enid *did* have time alone to talk, their conversations often reverted to their feelings for their deceased spouses, as if it needed to be thoroughly discussed so that they could move beyond their losses, and it was certainly something they had in common, something that helped them understand each other.

Each night Sebastian attempted to put his feelings on paper by writing a letter to Enid, but every effort met with the same fate of being crumpled up and thrown into the fire. Following every failed attempt, he always crawled into bed once again with his deepest sentiments still unexpressed.

While Sebastian felt himself slowly coming to terms with the grief that had undone him completely following the deaths of his wife and daughter, he was finally able to gather the courage to share a conversation with his sons that he knew was long overdue. Instead of reading the usual bedtime story, he told them he wanted to talk to them about something very important. He humbly and sincerely admitted to how difficult their mother's death had been on him, and that losing the baby soon afterward had only made it worse. He apologized for getting so caught up in his own pain that he hadn't been there for them. He was amazed at how clearly they understood what he was trying to tell them, and how easily they forgave him for his neglect when he should have been the father they had needed. He then asked them to tell him about their own feelings over losing their mother and baby sister. They had much more to say than he might have expected, and he marveled at how much they understood about loss and grief; he suspected Enid might very well have had something to do with that. When he asked how they knew so much about such things, they both admitted that Auntie Enid had talked to them many times about their feelings. Why should he be surprised to realize that she had been helping them deal with their grief while he had been oblivious? Together Sebastian and his sons wept over the losses they had shared, and when he finally tucked them into bed, he felt as if they had just climbed a mountain that had brought them miles closer to being able to move forward with their lives—together.

* * * * *

Sebastian was thrilled—along with everyone else in the house—when Enid reached a sudden burst of healing. Almost overnight she had more strength and energy, which Julia said could sometimes be the case when the body had been given time to rebuild the blood that had been lost.

Sebastian came to her room as usual in the morning, only to hear her announce, "I am getting out of this house if it kills me! I can't bear this confinement any longer without going mad." Tilly was getting clothes for Enid out of her wardrobe, and Enid was sitting in front of her mirror, brushing out her hair.

"And what exactly do you have in mind?" Sebastian asked.

"It's a beautiful day," Enid replied. "I suspect we might not have many more such days before winter completely takes over. If you'll come back in about half an hour I will be ready to leave this room, and if you're any kind of gentleman you will escort me on a walk in the gardens and make certain I don't fall over."

"Well, I wouldn't want to be anything less than a gentleman," he declared with a chuckle. "I'll come back."

"You must make certain she doesn't overdo," Tilly said to him. "I fear that her desire to get out might be making her unrealistically ambitious."

"How well you know her," Sebastian said to Tilly with a wink that made her smile.

Enid tossed a comical glare toward both of them and continued brushing her hair. Sebastian left the room, feeling almost giddy at the possibility of being able to take Enid out of the house. Perhaps it was ridiculous to think that their relationship might look different to both of them when viewed outside of the rooms in which she been confined for several weeks. He only hoped that when she saw him in some other environment she might still be able to see him as a man deserving of her company and affection. He paced nervously in his own sitting room, waiting for a half hour to pass, watching the clock far too closely. After thirty-five minutes he forced himself to walk slowly back to her room, where he quietly entered the open door to find Enid sitting in the chair near the window, her silky brown hair wound up and pinned to the back of her head, and wearing a yellow dress that made her look like sunshine personified. He'd grown accustomed to seeing her mostly in bed, always wearing ridiculously modest nightgowns that were buttoned to her throat, with her hair down around her shoulders or in a long braid. This was the Enid he knew and remembered from before the day when childbirth had almost taken her life. Except that everything had changed between them, and his heart quickened at the thought of just being with her.

"You look beautiful," he said, and she turned toward him. Her smile and the sparkle in her eyes made her even *more* beautiful.

"Hello," she said. "Are you certain you're up to this?"

"I should be asking *you* that," he said, walking toward her.

"I don't think I can go far," she admitted, "but I feel as if I will suffocate if I don't get out of this house."

"Let's go, then," he said, picking up the heavy shawl next to her, which he wrapped around her shoulders before he held out his hand to help her to her feet.

Sebastian could feel more strength in her even as they walked out of the room and down the hall. She took hold of his arm, but he didn't feel her leaning against him for support as she had for weeks now when he'd helped her move around her rooms. At the top of the stairs she hesitated and took a deep breath, as if they were daunting. Sebastian just scooped her into his arms and carried her down.

"What are you doing?" she demanded, at the same time wrapping her arms around his neck.

"No point having you waste your strength on the stairs; you should save it for enjoying the fresh air." She didn't protest, and he set her down near the door that exited onto the patio that merged into the loveliest part of the gardens. "Perhaps I should have carried you outside a long time ago."

"Perhaps you should have," she said, mimicking the way a parent would speak to a child guilty of bad behavior.

Sebastian chuckled and opened the door for her. He loved watching the way she stepped outside and closed her eyes, lifting her face toward the sun and breathing in the late autumn air.

"Let's walk," she said after he'd closed the door. Once again, she took hold of his arm and they ambled slowly between rows of bushes where only a few dwindling roses remained, and down passageways of neatly trimmed shrubberies. She said nothing, and Sebastian didn't interrupt her apparent desire for silence. He simply enjoyed being by her side while he imagined how this might feel for her. He'd never been forced to remain indoors for as long as she had been, so he honestly couldn't comprehend the experience, but the serenity in her countenance spoke volumes.

"I need to sit down, I think," she said at a moment when there was no bench in sight. He was about to pick her up and carry her to one when she sat down on the grass and motioned for him to sit beside her. He sat where he could be at the best advantage to just look at her, while he contemplated how thoroughly she had filled the void in his life that had been left by Marie's death. He'd grieved so deeply that he'd often believed there was no life at all for him without her. He hadn't thought it possible that he would *ever* come to love another woman again. And even if he'd indulged in such thoughts, he never would have imagined feeling this way about Enid.

"Are you all right?" he asked.

"Yes, I'm fine," she said. "Julia has drilled into me the need to take things slowly. I'm a little weak and tired, but much better than I have been."

"I'm very glad to hear it," he said and took her hand to kiss it. He watched her eyes as he did so and found her watching *him* with fascination, as if she were trying to discern his motives.

To break the spell of a deepening tension, he began to talk about the children and their recent antics. He told her a particularly funny story of how Mark had just yesterday mixed up the words butter and brother, and he'd asked for more brother on his scone. Enid laughed as if doing so was releasing all her pent-up frustration over the weeks it had taken her to heal. He loved the sound of her laughter, and the way that once she'd started laughing, everything he said seemed to be funny—whether it actually was or not. When he couldn't think of anything else to say, he impulsively leaned over to kiss her. He allowed his lips to linger tenderly near hers while he whispered, "I love you, Enid." He kissed her again before she could respond, and his heart began to pound as he realized he'd just admitted it aloud, and he had no idea how she would respond. He wondered if he'd ever felt so vulnerable in his life. When he'd been courting Marie, he'd not felt afraid to admit to his feelings, but he felt afraid now, and he wondered why.

Sebastian drew back from his kiss and watched her eyes come slowly open. She looked at him as if she were searching deeply for something, and he returned her gaze firmly, wanting her to see the evidence of his sincerity.

"I love you too, Sebastian," she said, pressing a hand to his face, but he caught a glimmer of something troubled in her eyes. He chose to ignore anything but the joy and pleasure of this moment as he closed his eyes and turned his face to kiss the palm of her hand.

While he was trying to absorb the possibility of sharing a future with Enid, the rumble of distant thunder surprised him. He looked skyward the same moment Enid did, and she said, "Those clouds rolled in very quickly. I didn't even notice."

"Nor did I," he said, and they shared a smile before he came to his feet and held out a hand to help her up. "We should get inside before it starts to rain. Julia would scold me if I let you get wet on your first outing—especially with such a chill in the air."

"I dare say she would," Enid said, and they walked together at a slow pace back toward the house. It began to sprinkle just before they got to the door, and they were splashed with a few heavy drops that made it evident their timing was good; another minute or two and they would have been soaked. They stood just inside the open doorway, watching the downpour in silence for a couple of minutes before Sebastian suggested they go to the library where they could be comfortable until it was time for lunch.

"And if you're up to it," he said, loving the way she once again took hold of his arm as they walked, "you can join me and the boys for lunch."

"That sounds lovely," she said as he closed the door before they sat close together on one of the sofas. "I should probably go and feed the baby first, but I'm certain Tilly has everything under control."

Enid was glad when Sebastian kissed her again. She'd become strangely accustomed to his kiss, and his company. She wanted to spend every waking minute with him. She loved to touch his face and his hair, and she loved being in his arms—a place where she'd come to feel safe and secure. But throughout the course of all these weeks as their relationship had merged from being barely tolerant of each other, to a friendship that was something akin to brother and sister, and then unexpectedly into this mutual attraction, Enid had tried in vain to bury her memories of the cruel things he'd said to her after he'd come out of hiding. She was haunted by the other side of Sebastian, the man who had politely tolerated her prior to her departure to Africa with Alistair. He had not minced his words when he'd told her he believed Alistair's death was her fault, and that he would never forgive her. And now he had told her he loved her. He had been kind and tender and sensitive—in many ways even more so than Alistair had ever been. But Enid could never go forward without knowing for certain that his beliefs about her had changed. Dozens of times she had been determined to ask him about it, to know where he stood on the matter. And each time she'd been deterred by how rarely they were alone together, given the time they spent with the boys, and the way the servants were often coming and going. When they *were* alone the doors were always open and Enid had not wanted Tilly or anyone else to overhear them talking about something so sensitive, nor did she want to mar the mood between her and Sebastian during moments when his adoration was growing more evident, and she couldn't deny the thrill she felt at the possibility of what it might mean for her future—and his.

Now, however, he had declared his love for her—and she had felt no reason to keep from admitting that she loved him too. But was love enough? Given the experience she'd gained in her marriage to Alistair, she knew it wasn't. They'd loved each other deeply, and she had literally gone to the other end of the world for him—even though she'd not wanted to and had mostly hated the experience. Alistair had been a kind and gentle man; he'd never treated her badly, had never raised his voice to her. But she had quickly realized that his passion for the work he was doing among the African natives was far stronger than his passion for her. In fact, she could look back now and see that he'd never really been passionate toward her in any respect. Enid hadn't fully realized this until she began to see in Sebastian's eyes something that she'd never seen in those of her husband. Even Sebastian's kisses—as appropriate and gentlemanly as they'd been—had stirred something in her that she'd never experienced in her marriage. Until Sebastian Hawthorne had fallen in love with her, she'd never fully realized just how much had been missing in the life she'd shared with Alistair—but she'd been young and naive when she'd met him. She'd never known or felt anything else; therefore, she'd had no means for comparison. She wondered now what might have happened if Alistair had lived. Would she have eventually been able to fully admit that there was something crucial missing in their marriage? Would she have grown increasingly discontent? But given the fact that her convictions would never have allowed her to betray her husband or treat her marriage vows as anything less than sacred, what might she have done? Enid had no idea, but wondering had haunted her almost as much as she was haunted by wondering if Sebastian still held some deep contempt toward her, which he was merely keeping carefully hidden. She didn't question the sincerity of his love for her, but that didn't necessarily mean it had vanquished things that still troubled him, but which he chose not to address. Well, it *had* to be addressed. Enid could not go any further with this relationship, not knowing how he really felt about her relationship with his brother.

Unable to bear Sebastian's fervid gaze, nor the way he tenderly explored her fingers with his own, Enid stood and walked to the window to watch the rain fall. She marveled that not so long ago the skies had been clear and sunny. She hoped that wasn't somehow symbolic regarding the joy she'd felt over their declarations of love in the garden, and the conversation she was about to embark upon. She felt terrified to bring it up, but knew that she had to. He would either tell her that he'd realized he was wrong and they needed to talk about Alistair and clear up any misunderstandings they might have had in the past, or he would tell her that nothing had changed in that regard, and all the feelings they had shared would come to a blinding and painful halt. The pounding of her heart led her to believe it would be the latter, but she couldn't put this off any longer.

"Is something troubling you?" he asked from where he remained sitting on the sofa. She was glad for the way his perception would force her to answer his question—and she needed to answer it honestly. But at the same time, she wanted to avoid it forever; to simply remain in this eye of the storm with him where all was calm and everything between them seemed perfect, but her deepest instincts told her that what they shared wasn't entirely sound. On the surface, everything seemed right and good, and the possibility of sharing a future together seemed natural, and almost perfectly destined. But Enid knew their foundation was shaky and unsteady. If he was holding onto even a degree of his negative beliefs toward her, it could not be ignored, or it would surely come up at some future time—perhaps at a point where it would cause further damage for them and those they loved. At all costs, she had to consider the children, and it was thinking of them that motivated her to just gather her courage and answer the question.

Keeping her eyes focused out the window on the continuing downpour, she began by simply answering his question. "Yes," she said, hearing a shakiness in her voice that she hoped he didn't notice. "Something *is* troubling me."

"What is it?" he asked, coming to her side as if he would gladly alleviate anything that distressed her if it were in his power. She knew that it *was* in his power to solve this problem, but she wasn't so sure he'd see it that way.

Choosing to avoid his gaze, which she hoped would make this easier, she just hurried to say what needed to be given a voice. "I never expected this to happen between us, Sebastian."

"Nor did I," he said, but she ignored him and forged ahead.

"In fact, given the nature of our relationship in the past, coming to feel this way for you—and you for me—was the *last* thing I ever would have predicted."

"What are you trying to say?" he asked, sounding concerned. She still resisted the urge to look at him, fearing she would be deterred by the love she knew she would see in his expression.

Enid took a deep breath and leaned a hand against the window for support. "When I came to tell you what I thought about the way your hiding away was impacting the boys—and the household—it took a great deal of courage. Such behavior is not common for me."

"And I can never express my gratitude for your courage," he said. "I needed to hear what you had to say. I was so lost, and I would have continued to spiral downward if you hadn't snapped me out of it."

"I'm finding the need to gather all my courage now," she admitted.

"Why?" he demanded, a fearful edge to his voice. Still, she couldn't look at him or she knew she wouldn't be able to finish.

"The night that Sarah was born," she went on, "your kindness and concern took me by surprise. Your attachment to Sarah also took me by surprise. I know she helps you feel close to Alistair, just as she does for me. But your attention to *me*, and the feelings that have developed—as wonderful as they have been—have left me confused, and . . . haunted."

"Haunted?" he echoed, as if he had no idea why she could ever feel such a thing. Had he truly forgotten the horrible things he'd said to her? Had he buried them so deeply that they simply didn't exist in the conscious part of his mind? Or had he come to terms with his negative feelings without bothering to clarify his change of heart with her? She desperately prayed it would be the latter, but her instincts told her it was the former.

"Yes, haunted," she said, feeling some anger—or at least a stark frustration that was taking her to the verge of anger. "As hard as I've tried, I can't get out of my mind the conversation we shared after you'd brought yourself out of hiding. Although, I don't know if I said hardly a word. It was more a lecture than a conversation."

Enid heard him draw a sharp breath and she suddenly found it easy—or at least necessary—to turn and look at him. "Every day I wonder if your feelings on the matter of Alistair's death—particularly your feelings toward me—have softened as we've grown to love each other, or if you still feel the same way about it now as you did then. And I must know. I have to know the truth."

"I would never tell you anything but the truth," he said, but she saw a hardness in his eyes that made her heart pound. She had tapped into that place deep inside of him that was full of grief, and anger, and blame—and she was terrified.

"So, what is the truth, Sebastian? Have you simply buried how you really feel about the matter, or have you been coming to terms with it? You can't be honest with me if you can't be honest with yourself. I need to know the truth." She took a deep breath and acknowledged the core of the problem. "You told me that you considered me wholly responsible for his death, and that you would never forgive me." She allowed a moment for that to sink in while she watched his countenance change. She could almost literally feel her heart breaking into little pieces, creating a physical pain in her chest as the truth became evident. Everything they had shared—and the possibility of sharing it for a lifetime—came crashing down around her as the foundation cracked and crumbled and disintegrated right before her eyes. Still, she managed to keep her gaze firmly upon him, making it evident by her silence that she expected him to speak.

Sebastian finally cleared his throat a little too loudly and said, "What does it matter how I feel about Alistair's death? It doesn't change what we've come to feel for each other."

"What does it matter?" she echoed, unable to believe what she was hearing. "Do you think that such feelings left unresolved wouldn't eventually come between us in one way or another? Your ignoring the truth does not make it go away. Your blame and lack of forgiveness will eat away at our relationship, Sebastian, like a cancer that grows and grows until it devours everything good. I don't understand—when you are such a good man—why you feel this way toward me . . . why you've never even given me a chance to tell you what *really* happened."

Sebastian took an abrupt step backward, almost as if she'd slapped him and he feared she would do it again. Enid's heart crumbled a little more when the old Sebastian came forward, and the love he'd declared for her was nowhere to be seen. "I don't want to hear your version of what you think happened, Enid. I don't think about it, because thinking about it makes me angry and I don't want to feel that way."

"So you *haven't* forgiven me?" she said and allowed him a long moment to respond. His silence implied that he hadn't. Enid again looked out the window at the pouring rain, unable to bear the disdain in his expression. She had needed to know where she stood, and now she did, and the pain was nigh to unbearable. She felt herself trembling and wanted to hurry to her room where she could be alone. But she had to hold herself together until this conversation was complete. She certainly wasn't finished yet. "I see," she said. "I have to say how astonished I am at the very idea that you believe I'm in need of some grand gesture of forgiveness—which you are not willing to offer. I have prayed and pondered endless hours to try and understand what I might have done wrong, and I cannot find one tiny iota of any action on my part that warrants the need for forgiveness from you—or even from Alistair."

"Then perhaps I'm not the only one ignoring the truth," he said with a bitterness that made her wonder where the Sebastian she'd come to love had gone.

With her anger now closer to the surface, Enid countered, "And what makes a generally wise and insightful man such as yourself believe you can feel such contempt toward me, and at the same time just try to pretend such feelings don't exist—so that we can share some kind of fantasy romance that will inevitably crumble when it's all twisted up with blame and anger?"

Enid drew as much air into her lungs as she could manage and blew it out slowly before she added, "Well, I won't have it; I can't live with it. I won't pretend that you love me as much as you claim while you hold such contempt for me." She drew the courage to look at him, if only to drive home her point. "Your feelings are yours, Sebastian, and you have to decide what to do with them, but I cannot live with such harsh contradictions in our relationship. I've wondered ever since you first kissed me if that meant your anger toward me had been resolved. Now I know. Clearly it has not."

Enid took a long glance at Sebastian and saw nothing but the arrogance and self-righteousness that had once been his most common demeanor. She felt herself begin to tremble, and knew there was nothing else she could say, and nothing more she needed to know. The truth was evident—horribly and devastatingly evident. She hurried toward the door, saying over her shoulder, "I will speak with Mrs. Thorpe about arranging a schedule where we can spend time with each other's children and not cross paths any more than is absolutely required."

As her hand took hold of the doorknob, he said, "Do you really think such harsh measures are necessary?"

Enid looked at him and declared, "I think that I cannot bear to even see your face—at least not until I can find a way to forgive you."

"And what, pray tell, might you need to forgive me for?" he asked with an arrogance that made her want to walk back across the room and slap him.

Enid lifted her chin and just said it, wishing her voice wasn't so shaky. "You made me fall in love with you, all the while holding onto ugly and hateful feelings toward me. You broke my heart, Sebastian Hawthorne. And when you're lonely and miserable, don't think for one moment there is anyone to blame but yourself. This matter is between you and God. I want nothing to do with it." She opened the door and started away, wanting to run to the safety of her own room, and deeply frustrated by how slowly she had to go, due to her physical weakness. Praying that Sebastian wouldn't come after her, she just kept moving, even though she had to stop more than once to catch her breath and try to get control of the trembling that was overtaking her entire body.

Once in her room, Enid locked the doors, kicked off her shoes, and crawled into bed, where she cried into her pillow to muffle the sound. Her tears quickly dissipated into a silent shock. A part of her wished she hadn't said anything, that she'd been able to pretend as he'd been doing that everything between them was as it should be. But she knew she never could have lived with it. And she knew that eventually it would have come between them. Better that it was acknowledged now before anyone else had more than a suspicion that a romance had been blossoming between them. Considering all that had happened and the way she felt now, Enid wondered how her life had come to this. She could do nothing now except move forward one day at a time and strive to be a good mother, a good aunt, and to make a positive contribution to the household—all the while doing her best to completely avoid Sebastian. She'd grown accustomed to his company, his tender words and sweet kisses, and she missed him already. But that was irrelevant. She would not degrade herself by living with such a lie.

Enid got up to open the door when Tilly brought Sarah to her to be fed. After the baby had gone back to sleep, Enid felt tempted to hide in her room, but she knew that she had to face life eventually, and the sooner she gathered her courage and faced reality, the better. Knowing it was lunchtime, she didn't want one of the servants coming to look for her. And she was sick to death of being in this room, even if getting anywhere else in the house would take a great deal of effort. Since she and Sebastian had both been eating lunch with the boys, they might be expecting her there, but she just couldn't—not even for the sake of the boys. A schedule needed to be established for her and Sebastian to have their separate time with the children. For the moment, she went slowly and carefully to the kitchen, sitting down on the stairs more than once to catch her breath. Once there, everyone declared how good it was to see her up and about. She declared with a convincing smile that she wanted to give Mr. Hawthorne some time with his boys, and enjoyed sharing her meal with the staff. As soon as the meal was over, Enid said quietly to Mrs. Thorpe, "May I speak with you alone?"

"Of course, my dear," the older woman said and led the way to her little office near the kitchen from where she managed the household in partnership with her husband. Mrs. Thorpe motioned Enid toward a chair and closed the door before she sat down herself. "Now, what can I do for you?"

Enid drew air into her lungs and searched for the right words. She didn't want to speak ill of Sebastian, but she also needed to be honest—and she knew she could confide in Mrs. Thorpe. She also knew that very little went on in this house of which this woman and her husband were not aware. Enid just hurried to say, "I fear that we must once again arrange a schedule in which I will be able to spend time with the boys—and Mr. Hawthorne will be able to spend time with Sarah—but we would prefer to avoid each other."

"Oh, my," Mrs. Thorpe muttered on the wave of a long sigh. "I had so hoped he'd gotten past all of that. I won't be nosy enough to inquire over the problem, but I think I could guess."

"You likely *could* guess," Enid said. "And it's surely better if you can remain neutral and be able to say in all honesty that I didn't tell you any specific details of the reasons for my request. Although, I treasure your confidence, as you well know, and I am well aware that of all the women who work in this house, you are the one who does *not* spread gossip."

"No, I never would," Mrs. Thorpe declared, as if the very idea of repeating anything private or personal might be a criminal act.

"Confidentially speaking," Enid went on, finding some relief in being able to at least say this much to *someone*, "he has a cruel opinion of me over certain matters that can never be outweighed by any measure of kindness. For me to pretend otherwise is to compromise my integrity and my self-respect. I know there are certain facets of living under the same roof in which we cannot avoid each other, but as much as possible, it's mandatory that we do so. We were able to manage previously according to *his* wishes. It seems we will need to manage to do so again. I would be very grateful if you would speak with the maids and Mr. Hawthorne and work out a schedule that's acceptable. I fear that if I try to do so myself, I may not handle it very well."

"I'll take care of it," Mrs. Thorpe reassured her with confidence. "And we will hope and pray that our dear Sebastian might overcome his anger and prejudices; I fear if he does not, he will only grow more miserable and difficult over time."

"I fear the same," Enid said, "but I cannot change his mind, and I certainly cannot change *him*, and it would be a fool's errand for me to even try. This is the best option." Enid stood up, wanting to end this conversation before she began rambling about the present turmoil of her opinions on the matter, until she ended up spilling *everything*, and that simply wouldn't be appropriate. "Thank you for understanding," Enid said, "and for your trustworthiness in keeping my confidence. I know you will handle the situation in the best possible way."

"Is there anything I can get for you, my dear?" Mrs. Thorpe asked.

"No, but thank you," Enid said. "I do believe I've worn myself out. I'm going to just spend the rest of the day with my Sarah; perhaps you could have supper sent to my room."

"Of course," Mrs. Thorpe said, and Enid made her way slowly and carefully back up the stairs to the safety of her own rooms where she didn't have to interact with anyone but Tilly while she rested and enjoyed the company of her daughter, forcing herself not to think of how Sebastian Hawthorne had broken her heart.

* * * * *

Enid spent a restless night while she vacillated between anger toward Sebastian and sorrow over the way he'd hurt her. With the beginning of the day, she felt exhausted and knew she had overdone it the previous day and she would do well to take it easy and try to recover. As always, Tilly was on hand to help with the baby, and Mrs. Thorpe herself brought Enid's breakfast to her room so that she could tell her she'd spoken to Mr. Hawthorne, who had been agreeable about her proposed schedule. Enid would spend some time with the boys during the latter part of the morning after they'd finished their lessons. She would take the baby with her so that they would be able to see their new cousin and hold her, and they would share lunch. Tilly would take Sarah to see her uncle each afternoon following her usual nap, and the nanny would remain nearby to make certain the baby's needs were met. Enid was glad for the established schedule, even though she hated it. She missed Sebastian and she wanted to see him, talk to him, share conversation and company with him. This was all so ridiculous! But her only other option was to spend time with a man who was selectively arrogant and presumptuous. And she just couldn't do it. His hypocrisy and contradictory nature could make her go mad if she allowed it.

Chapter Nine

THE WIDOWED
MRS. HAWTHORNE

THROUGH THE FOLLOWING WEEKS, ENID was glad to feel her body gradually returning to normal. She'd never faced any serious illness before, and recovering from childbirth had given her an entirely new appreciation of the gift of good health. With her renewed strength, she did not take for granted the ability to go for long walks through the gardens or around the house. Just being able to get up and down the stairs to share meals or simple conversations with others in the household seemed an enormous blessing.

Autumn was swallowed abruptly by winter with one brutal storm where harsh gusts of wind blew the remaining dead leaves from the trees, and snow settled over Thornewell Hall and its surrounding land. Enid commended herself for managing her conflicted feelings toward Sebastian as well as anyone could. During the days, she was glad to be able to never see him, even though she knew he was spending an hour or two each afternoon with Sarah, and Enid always had her time with the boys. The only time she'd seen Sebastian in more than a month was when they both attended church, but they kept their distance from each other without exchanging so much as a word or even a glance. And Enid did well at pretending that this distance between them wasn't breaking her heart. Sometimes at night she would allow herself to think of him, and the love she'd come to feel for this enigma of a man, and she couldn't help contemplating how things might be if he weren't so angry and stubborn. But wishing for another person to be any different than they were certainly accomplished nothing. She knew that well enough. Still, sometimes she just missed him so much that it felt as if her chest would burst open from the swelling pain in her heart—a pain worsened by memories of Alistair's death and all the uneasiness she still felt over how it had happened. She wished she could talk to Sebastian about it;

no one else loved Alistair as much as his brother did. But he'd made it clear he would not talk about it, and so she kept her difficult memories to herself, allowing herself to cry for her deceased husband only when she was all alone at night.

On rare occasions—when Enid was feeling especially sorry for herself—she indulged in missing her family and wondering what her parents and siblings were doing. Were they well? What changes had taken place in their lives? Inevitably such thoughts brought on an anguish that she had become well practiced at avoiding. If she thought about her family and the reasons why they had banished her, the pain was just too much to endure. So she thought of them rarely, and when she did, it was only possible to think of them briefly or she would become consumed with grief over all she had given up to marry Alistair—a man now dead. At times the loneliness weighing down upon her felt nigh to unbearable. She'd grown to love many people in this household; she enjoyed their company, and she liked to be able to work with many of them whenever possible. But it wasn't the same. She had no confidant with whom she felt there was sufficient trust to unburden herself of such personal matters. Sebastian had eased her loneliness a great deal as they'd spent time together with the children and sometimes alone, just talking and laughing together. She missed him dreadfully—even after all these weeks. But even with him, she'd never been able to talk about the subjects that weighed heaviest on her heart—Alistair's death, and the loss of her family. Years earlier—when she had come to live in this house as a new bride—word had come to her through the servants that Sebastian had been astonished and disgusted to know that Enid had been disowned by her family, and that he felt certain there had to be terrible scandal behind such a thing happening. He'd been reported as saying, *"What kind of people would be anything but thrilled to have their daughter marry into such wealth and privilege? I can't even begin to understand the possible reasons, and I'm not certain I want to know."* Even though his words had been repeated to Enid and she'd not heard them firsthand, they had been told to her by more than one person in the household, and she knew from little snippy comments he'd made several times in her presence that it surely had to be true. But just as with the circumstances surrounding Alistair's death, he'd never bothered to talk to *her* about the situation. He had just assumed the worst and made her out to be some kind of villainess. She marveled even now that he had believed his attraction to her, and his need for company, had made him believe that such things didn't matter. She scolded herself every day for getting caught up in her own romantic notions without assessing his true feelings toward her. If she'd confronted him the first time he'd gazed at her with that dreaminess in his eyes, she could have halted the evolution of these feelings that she now had to contend with every day. One of her biggest challenges was striving to not be angry with Sebastian for the way he invaded her thoughts every hour. Thankfully she felt well enough to keep very busy.

It was easiest to push away any difficult thoughts when Sarah was awake and needing attention. She was changing every day, and loved to look directly at Enid, responding with smiles and sweet cooing sounds when Enid spoke to her. It was as if Sarah had so much she wanted to talk about, but she hadn't yet acquired the ability to do so. The baby was doing better at sleeping during the night, waking up only once to be changed and fed, but quickly going back to sleep. During the days she was on a predictable schedule of two naps—one of them being late morning and usually through lunchtime, which made it convenient for Enid to spend time with the boys and not have the baby fussing. She always took Sarah to the playroom where Matthew and Mark gave the baby a great deal of attention, and they both had a way of making Sarah smile and try to speak to them with her indiscernible noises. As soon as the baby got fussy, Enid would leave long enough to go feed Sarah and put her down, leaving Tilly to listen for her, then she would return to play with the boys and have lunch with them. Usually during the middle of the afternoon, Tilly would take Sarah back to the playroom to spend time with her uncle. Tilly almost always remained in the room, since Sebastian had no idea what to do if the baby got fussy, and he certainly had never changed a nappy. But Tilly reported to Enid that Sarah's uncle clearly enjoyed his time with the baby, and he was very sweet and tender with her. Enid would have preferred to witness that for herself, but under the circumstances it just wasn't possible.

Sarah always took another nap late in the afternoon, although they never let her sleep too long because it interfered with her being tired enough to be put down for the night at a reasonable time. All in all, Enid was finding peace and contentment with her new way of life—at least as far as it was possible, given the limitations that were not in her control. She thanked God every day that she and Sarah had a home and people around them who loved and cared for them. Many women in her position—widowed with a child to care for—were not nearly so blessed; she knew that to be true. Therefore, she didn't let a day go by without taking notice of how very blessed she was and offering her gratitude to God for all He'd given her despite all she'd lost.

One morning after breakfast, Mrs. Thorpe took Enid aside and showed her an invitation that had come from a baronet and his wife who lived on a neighboring estate. "Their winter ball is a long-standing tradition," Mrs. Thorpe said, "and the invitation is specifically addressed to Mr. Hawthorne and yourself. I'm certain that people in the area are aware of your situation, and I think it's marvelous that they've invited you."

"But . . . if Mr. Hawthorne is going," Enid said, "it would surely create nothing but an awkward situation, which I sorely wish to avoid."

"I very much doubt that he will go," Mrs. Thorpe said. "He's never been fond of such social gatherings. Marie had to beg and plead to get him to go; she did enjoy such things. But without her I can't imagine he'd even consider it." Mrs. Thorpe's smile widened, and her voice became more animated. "But *you* should go, my dear. It would do you so much good to dress up and get out and socialize with people beyond your own household."

"I don't know," Enid said, looking at the invitation more closely. "I've only attended two—maybe three—such events in my entire life. I didn't grow up in this world, you know. But I felt secure with Alistair at my side; how can I go without him and—"

"You just *go*," Mrs. Thorpe said with such enthusiasm that Enid wondered if being involved in such an endeavor brought her joy, or perhaps she was concerned with Enid's reclusiveness. Perhaps both.

"I'll think about it," Enid said.

"And in the meantime, you should go into town and order a gown and everything else you'll need to go with it—just in case you decide to attend. If you wait, there won't be time to have something made. Just getting beyond the house and gardens would do you some good. I believe a shopping trip is in order. If you get the gown and don't use it, you'll have it on hand should the need arise in the future."

"I'll think about it," Enid said again, handing the invitation back to Mrs. Thorpe. "Thank you for letting me know."

Enid walked away, certain that such an undertaking along with all the preparations that went into making herself appropriately adorned for such an event would be exhausting. She imagined herself arriving at such a grand social gathering—on her own—and felt decidedly nervous over the prospect. But she also felt the inkling of a desire to go. Perhaps it was her perpetual feelings of loneliness; perhaps she was bored with the daily tedium of her life. Whatever the case, by the following day she had talked herself into it. She informed Mrs. Thorpe before breakfast that she was going into town;

Gert would accompany her, and Beauford would be driving the carriage and watch out for them. Enid had already arranged with Tilly to care for Sarah while she went out. Given Enid's difficult recovery from childbirth, she'd never had enough milk to satisfy Sarah. Gradually the baby had shown a preference for the bottle; and Enid's own milk had all but disappeared. She felt a little sadness over the fact, but she could still hold her baby close and feed her with a bottle, and it certainly made matters less complicated when Enid needed or wanted to leave the baby with the nanny. Tilly and Maisy would make certain the boys were cared for during the time when Gert normally taught them their lessons. The governess had left a couple of assignments for them to complete and felt confident that Maisy would do well in overseeing the work.

Mrs. Thorpe was clearly thrilled, and Enid felt grateful for the way this dear woman looked out for her in so many ways. As the carriage rolled away from the house, gaining speed, Enid commented to Gert, "I don't believe I've left the house at all since I've returned—except to go to church."

Enid knew the servants went back and forth to town regularly and if there was anything she needed they could acquire it for her. Given her pregnancy and subsequent difficult childbirth, Enid had chosen to stay at home. She'd never even considered that a simple excursion to town to do a little shopping could be so exhilarating. Gert was clearly excited and thanked Enid for asking her to come along.

They went first to the dress shop, where Enid was glad to find only one other customer. She was prepared to wait until the shopkeeper was free, but another woman who worked in the shop came out from behind a curtain at the back of the shop and approached Enid with a smile.

"I need to have a ball gown made," Enid said, "and I need everything to go with it, I suppose."

"I'm certain we can help you with all of that," the woman said with a polite nod. "I'm Mrs. Morse, the head seamstress here. I can help you choose the fabric and style you like, and I will personally see to making the gown to meet with your approval." She nodded again, and Enid realized she needed to introduce herself.

"I'm Enid Hawthorne, and this is Gert," Enid said, motioning toward the young woman who was already intrigued with examining a display of fabrics.

"Oh," Mrs. Morse said, "you are the widow of the younger Mr. Hawthorne."

"That's right," Enid said, wondering why hearing herself referred to as a widow by a stranger felt disconcerting.

"Then you've recently returned from Africa," Mrs. Morse added.

"Not *too* recently," Enid said. "It's been many months. I had a baby—a daughter—and I confess that my confinement following her birth has felt eternal."

Enid hoped she wasn't saying too much. She knew that some people were put off when the established boundaries between social classes were crossed, but Enid had grown up in the same class as Mrs. Morse and had married into the Hawthorne family, and initiating conversation seemed the right thing to do.

"Congratulations on your new arrival," Mrs. Morse said with a smile, putting Enid at ease. "It must feel good to get out."

"It does, thank you. And I confess that I'm not certain that attending a grand social is the best of ideas, but I'm following the advice of our trusted housekeeper who believes that I *should* go, and that having everything I need is a good idea in case I decide to do so."

"Excellent advice," Mrs. Morse said before she guided Enid to look at a variety of fabrics. She positioned Enid in front of a long mirror while she draped lengths of fabric across Enid's chest to see what might appeal to her. The seamstress explained that in her experience she'd learned that the right color was always the best place to start; she had a theory about how the wrong color could make a woman look drab or even ill, while the right color could make her look vibrant—and it was different for every woman. Gert enjoyed helping Mrs. Morse keep the varieties of fabric organized, neatly folding the ones that were obviously not a good match for Enid's coloring. The three women finally agreed wholeheartedly on a fabric that was the color of red wine. The satiny surface had a subtle uniqueness to its texture that made it shimmer slightly as it moved in the light, and Mrs. Morse enjoyed showing Enid and Gert how easily it draped over her arm, which would make it the right choice for a gown that would flow with Enid's movements as she walked and danced, as opposed to certain linens or taffeta that would be less fluid. Enid found her mind riveted on the reference to dancing. She hadn't danced in years and wasn't certain she could even remember how. It was only Mrs. Morse's enthusiasm over the gown—an enthusiasm mirrored excitedly by Gert—that kept Enid focused on seeing this through. She could decide later if she actually wanted to attend the ball.

With the fabric selected, Mrs. Morse showed Enid drawings of different styles of gowns, telling her that she could choose sleeves from one drawing, a bodice from another, and a skirt from still another. Or if one particular dress appealed to her, then that would be fine as well. Mrs. Morse set aside certain drawings, declaring they wouldn't work well with the type of fabric being used. This woman obviously knew what she was doing, and Enid felt certain she was in good hands—although choosing the perfect gown didn't feel like an important priority to her. For that reason, she was grateful for Gert's enthusiasm and input. The young woman had apparently noticed the everyday dresses that Enid wore, and commented on how a certain waistline suited Enid's figure well, as did a gathered skirt—but not too heavily gathered.

After Enid had made all her decisions regarding the work of art that Mrs. Morse would create on her behalf, the seamstress showed Enid a variety of slippers, gloves, and handbags that were for sale; or custom orders could be accommodated, since they worked directly with a cobbler in town. "In fact," Mrs. Morse said, "if you like, we can have slippers made from the very same fabric as the gown."

"Oh, my," Enid said, "that seems so extravagant." She sighed loudly. "In fact, all of this seems so extravagant." She knew the money that had been going into her bank account every month was more than ample to purchase a dozen such gowns and anything else she might desire, but her humble upbringing, combined with her time living among the impoverished African natives, made such luxury seem utterly self-indulgent.

Gert surprised Enid when she spoke up in a very forthright manner. "Forgive me if I'm being too bold, m'lady, but you are far too demeaning of yourself. It gives all of us who know you and work with you great pleasure to see you doing something for yourself. You're the kindest and most gracious woman any of us has had the privilege of working for, and I think the entire household would be saddened if you did not dress yourself up like a princess and go to the ball."

Enid was taken aback but countered, "You make it sound as if *my* indulgence actually brings pleasure to the servants. Do you not think that—"

"It does give us pleasure, m'lady," Gert said. "We have our own brand of entertainment, and enjoy our social gatherings. You have been through many difficulties, and you deserve this. It's my opinion that you should make the most of this, and perhaps something good will come of it. We all want you to do this and have a glorious time."

"I couldn't agree more," Mrs. Morse said, alerting Enid to the fact that the seamstress was still standing there and had heard the entire conversation.

Enid sighed again before she said, "Very well, I shall order slippers to match the gown."

Both Gert and Mrs. Morse seemed immensely pleased, and Enid didn't feel at all like Mrs. Morse's pleasure had anything to do with simply wanting to sell her products.

After leaving the dress shop, Gert suggested they take some time and walk the high street since they were already there, and just enjoy their outing. Enid appreciated Gert's suggestion when she began to feel more relaxed than she had in a long time. She knew Sarah was being well cared for, and the day was sunny and pleasant despite the winter chill. But they were bundled up sufficiently and she was enjoying Gert's company. They went into a shop that had a variety of items crafted from pewter, and Enid had the sudden idea to purchase fine pewter tankards for each of the men who served in the Hawthorne household. She asked Gert if she thought it might be strange or inappropriate.

Gert responded by saying, "I think that you don't have to compare what you do to anyone else's standard, but personally I think it's a lovely idea. Whether they actually drink out of them or just set them on a shelf, it's a token of your appreciation that I think will be meaningful."

Enid appreciated Gert's insights and her encouragement, and she also recognized how comfortable she'd come to feel with the governess. Perhaps without her even realizing it, she'd become better friends with Gert than she'd taken time to notice or acknowledge. And the same was true with Tilly. She didn't feel quite as close to Maisy, but she was certainly comfortable with her.

With her purchases wrapped and put into a bag that made them easy to carry, Enid and Gert continued ambling through the village and stopped at a reputable pub to get some lunch. Enid noticed that Beauford was usually nearby no matter where they went, watching out for them from a distance, and he was within her sight in the pub, eating his own lunch. After they'd eaten, Enid felt drawn to a shop that sold perfumes and fine bath products for ladies. She looked around and said to Gert, "What do you think would be most appreciated by the women we work with? Be honest with me, and yes, I'm including you in this so don't even think of protesting, or . . . how did you put it to me? Demeaning yourself?"

"Very well," Gert said and sighed while she looked around the shop. "Such a thing as scented bath salts or soap is very nice, but it's rare that any of us would bother to heat and carry enough water to truly enjoy them. Truthfully, perfume is something I would consider a true luxury. It can be applied quickly no matter how busy a woman might be, and it feels very . . . indulgent . . . and feminine."

"Perfume it is," Enid declared. "Smell them and tell me which one you like best and it's yours. And I think we should get different fragrances for each of the women."

Gert smiled and set about closing her eyes while she inhaled the different perfumes with the kind assistance of an elderly woman who ran the shop. Enid and Gert spent nearly an hour choosing the right fragrances, all of which were in different glass bottles, all unique and beautiful. As they were each wrapped, Enid wrote the names of the women they were for on each package, because she would never remember once they got home.

Leaving the shop, Gert said, "You are very generous."

"I am very grateful for all that each one of you do to make my life easier," Enid said. "I'm blessed with the money left to me by my husband. It feels good to use it to brighten—if only in some small way—the lives of those I care for."

"Well, it has certainly brightened mine," Gert smiled. "So, thank you."

"A pleasure," Enid said before they went into a toy shop and Enid chose some new storybooks and toy animals for the boys. After that, they purchased some new clothes for the baby, and by then they were both worn out and glad to find refuge in the carriage as it took them home.

Enid went first to check on Sarah and found her sleeping, with Tilly nearby, who reported that all was well. She wished she could go to the playroom and give the boys the gifts she'd purchased for them, but it was a standing rule that she was not to go there in the afternoons if she wished to avoid Sebastian—and she certainly did. Therefore, she antici-pated giving the boys their gifts in the morning and decided to rest while Sarah completed her afternoon nap.

That evening after supper, Enid brought out her gifts for the servants. Their surprise and pleasure warmed Enid deeply, and she exchanged more than one discreet smile with Gert as they observed the men admiring the fineness of their tankards, each one crafted with a different design. And the women raved about the luxury of having perfume while they compared scents and declared that they each liked their own the best, although they thought that sharing occasionally might be fun. They all thanked Enid profusely, but each time she simply expressed how grateful she was to each of them for all they did for her and her daughter.

Enid was surprised when Gert whispered to her, "A little token of appreciation can go a long way. I worked in a household before where it was quite the opposite. I must say that as long as you're here, I would never hope to work anywhere else."

"You're very kind," Enid said and impulsively squeezed Gert's hand.

"You make it very easy to be kind," Gert replied, and they turned their attention back to the women who were practically giggling while they now compared the unique beauty of each little perfume bottle. Enid felt gratified by the day but couldn't deny that she'd gotten a great deal more pleasure out of buying gifts for the people she cared about than she had out of choosing a ball gown for herself. It occurred to her then that Sebastian was the only person for whom she'd not purchased a gift. But there was surely nothing he needed, and she suspected that any gift from her would only be somehow misconstrued. The thought saddened her, so she pushed it away and went upstairs to spend some time with her daughter before they settled in for the night.

* * * * *

Throughout the next few weeks, Enid began to feel like her normal self again. Any sign of weakness was completely gone. The winter weather offered some unexpectedly pleasant days that were perfect for going outdoors to soak up the warmth of the sun that eased the chill in the air. Enid loved to bundle Sarah up in a matching crocheted hat and jacket that protected her from the cold. The baby clearly loved being outdoors and lay contentedly in her pram, tucked beneath a thick baby quilt, while Enid pushed her along garden paths and sometimes sang to her.

Enid didn't see Sebastian at all, even though she saw the boys every day and she knew that he spent time with Sarah each afternoon. Beyond that first Sunday, he hadn't attended church since their falling out, and she felt concerned for him in that regard. She didn't want her being there to keep him away, but neither was she willing to deprive herself of something that was deeply important to her. She often caught herself missing Sebastian— or worrying about him—but she'd developed the habit of uttering a silent prayer on his behalf before she forced her thoughts elsewhere and focused on all that was good in her life.

As this grand social event approached, the servants all seemed to take for granted that Enid would attend, and for some reason many of them had taken a personal interest in the matter; the thought of her going apparently provided some source of excitement for them. Enid vacillated about whether she wanted to go, but she *did* determine that she wanted to arrange a party for the household staff—and perhaps include the families who lived in houses on the Hawthorne estate, many of whom worked the farms that belonged to the Earl of Thornewell. She spoke to Mr. and Mrs. Thorpe about her plan and they were immediately excited. Thorpe agreed to get permission from the master of the house, and then they would proceed with plans. Enid wondered whether Sebastian might not be in favor of the idea and therefore might *not* give his consent. Considering his enormous financial resources, she determined that if he stood in the way of such an event, she might have to break her own rules of separation and give him another of her scoldings. And besides, she planned to use the money from her own allowance to fund the event.

In the meantime, Enid realized that if she *didn't* attend the upcoming ball, the women she worked with would be very disappointed. On the same day when she finally committed to going, her gown and slippers were delivered. She'd gone into town for a fitting when the gown had been nearing completion, but as she tried it on now in the privacy of her own room— with some help from Gert—she felt as if some other woman was looking back at her from the reflection in the mirror. When she'd married into this world, she'd never put any stock in the social aspects of being a part of the Hawthorne family. Alistair had not been fond of such things, so they'd rarely attended. Given all she'd been through since that time, she'd never imagined an indulgence such as this. But now, as she looked at herself adorned in this magnificent wine-colored gown, something warm and healing took place inside of her.

When the day of the winter ball arrived, Enid was dismayed to be told by Mrs. Thorpe that Sebastian had informed her he would be attending the event. Before Enid could speak, Mrs. Thorpe added, "Don't worry, my dear. I'm well aware that both of you are determined not to even *see* each other at all. Separate carriages have been arranged—although I must offer my opinion that this ongoing feud between the two of you is a bushel full of silliness."

"I couldn't agree more," Enid said, "but his attitude toward me is so clearly prideful and judgmental. Would you expect me to subject myself to such behavior when he will not even allow me to tell him my side of the story?"

"No, of course not," Mrs. Thorpe said, more kindly. "It's not you I'm frustrated with, my dear, but rather the situation. And yes, I understand that his stubbornness and pride are at the root of the problem. However, we both know there is a great deal of grief in him beneath his anger. I pray every day that he will be able to come to terms with these things and move beyond them."

"My prayers are the same," Enid said, allowing herself to think of how much she missed Sebastian—but only for a moment; any longer than that would have her fighting back tears. She took a deep breath. "But nothing can be done about it today. I am going to this ball with no thought of anything but enjoying myself."

"As you should," Mrs. Thorpe said, her mood brightening.

During the hours preceding the ball, Enid felt like a queen with the way she was fussed over and assisted in getting ready and looking her absolute best. The women who had become more friends than servants to her were all genuinely delighted on her behalf, but for Enid it didn't feel right that they weren't on equal social standing; she felt as if they should *all* be able to attend this event. They all seemed a little stunned by her declaration, and a subtle awkwardness descended that made Enid realize they were all comfortable with their station and wouldn't expect the situation to be any different. Enid changed the subject and relieved the tension, reminding herself that she was going to make it up to them with her plans for a party devoted especially to the servants. For tonight she was just going to do as she'd told Mrs. Thorpe, and think only of enjoying herself.

When the women declared that Enid was *finished*, she looked at herself in the long mirror and felt as she had when she'd initially tried on the gown—only more so. For a tiny moment she felt like a child playing dress-up by putting on her mother's best dress and jewelry to pretend that she was all grown up. But that moment passed quickly as she studied her own reflection and felt almost like royalty. Though a bit nervous, she felt prepared to interact with the high society who would be in attendance, and she wanted to just enjoy cordial conversation with new people, and perhaps she might even dance if she were asked. She had no expectations; she just felt eager to get out of the house and enjoy an activity that was entirely different from her normal routine. Perhaps all those endless weeks of being confined to bed had increased her enthusiasm over such a prospect.

During the carriage ride, Enid enjoyed the view of the scenery out the window as the sun was descending toward the west horizon. Being all alone, she thought of the absurdity of Sebastian riding in a different carriage to the same event. In retrospect, she wondered if she should have told Mrs. Thorpe that surely she and the esteemed Mr. Hawthorne could behave like adults long enough to endure riding in the same carriage. She wondered what the staff might be thinking of this ludicrous feud between them—so ludicrous that it necessitated the use of separate carriages to attend the same event. Enid felt like a fool for engaging in such foolish behavior until she considered the source of this issue between her and Sebastian. If she allowed herself to recall the initial conversation that had started all of this—wherein he had blamed her for Alistair's death and had declared that he would never forgive her—she was tempted to cry; therefore, she did her best to *never* think of it. The fact that she had allowed herself to become romantically involved with him without addressing the issue was the greatest source of her chagrin; she was angry with Sebastian, but perhaps even more so with herself for getting caught up in her attraction to him without acknowledging their irreconcilable disagreement over a matter that was no small thing by any means.

When the carriage arrived, Lex opened the door for her and offered his hand to help her step down. He'd told her with a smile how lovely she looked before they'd departed, and he offered the same smile now as he said, "You enjoy yourself now."

"Thank you, Lex," she said, knowing from experience that he'd brought along a book to read, and a lantern to light the carriage interior so that he could wait there and not be bored. She also knew it was customary for the carriage drivers at such events to often meet in the stables or carriage house to enjoy games of cards or dice until their employers were ready to leave. "You do the same," she said before looking up at the magnificent mansion before her. The home she lived in was enormous and grand, but this looked like a palace in comparison, and it was all lit up with a seemingly infinite number of lanterns burning in every window and at every outcropping of the intricately designed roof.

Enid focused on the path from the carriage to the elegant marble steps that went up to an enormous portico where the huge doors of a large entrance had been left open for guests to enter. While climbing the steps, Enid could hear the music of many stringed instruments. The beauty of the music alone already made her efforts feel worthwhile. She loved such music and had rarely been exposed to it. She thought of the very few socials she had attended with Alistair prior to their departure for Africa, and felt a little sadness in recalling his distaste for gatherings of so many people, and how he hadn't liked dancing, and how he'd always wanted to leave as soon as they could do so without creating a scene. Enid had never been one to protest or create contention—especially over such silly things; and she'd always wanted to please her husband. But right now, she found it strange to look back and be able to acknowledge her disappointment over their different views on such things. As she stepped into the splendid ballroom, the magnificence took her breath away, and she was strangely relieved to not have to contend with her husband's lack of enthusiasm. Tonight she could stay as long as she wanted, and do whatever she pleased. She was a respectable widow who had passed the appropriate season of mourning that would make it socially inappropriate to wear anything but black or to dance or interact with anyone of the opposite sex. Taking in the magnificence of the artistic decor of the beautifully lit room, Enid felt absolutely no guilt in being grateful to not be subject to Alistair's whims, which he had exerted with no consideration of her own. She knew she was partly to blame; she had allowed herself to remain quiet over many things that had been disagreeable to her. But she had learned from her experiences. She doubted she would ever marry again, but if she did, she would not be repeating her mistakes.

Enid felt a little breathless as she took everything in, and she was glad to spot an empty chair nearby where she sat to just absorb the view and listen to the ongoing music. She was mesmerized by the exquisite clothing worn by men and women alike; the variety of styles and fabrics made the room look like a sea of wildflowers in motion as the ladies' skirts twirled around them while they danced, guided by the hands of gentlemen who had been well schooled in dance as a necessary art that was an essential among this social class. Enid had been able to dance only a little when she'd met Alistair, but he'd arranged for her to have lessons when they'd been courting. She'd always found it ironic that he'd wanted her to be able to dance appropriately so that she could fit in with his class, and yet he'd had very little interest in dancing with her.

Enid sat and watched as that dance ended, and another began, then another, while in her mind she settled several difficult and confusing memories, replacing them with the determination to move forward from this point in her life as the woman she knew she truly was. She committed to herself to always live in truth and to not be afraid to express that truth appropriately. Considering her recent mishaps in her relationship with Sebastian, she added that as one more experience that had taught her the folly of not speaking up when her instincts were telling her to do so. She would never be that woman again.

Enid was startled out of her deep thoughts when she saw a man's hand appear in front of her at the same moment she heard a deep voice say, "May I have this dance?"

Enid looked up to see a man with a very handsome face, dark hair, and vivid green eyes. He added with a little smile, "I know we've not been officially introduced, but I hope you won't think me vulgar to overleap that step. I've been watching you and I just cannot resist the possibility of sharing a dance." Enid couldn't help smiling while she was trying to think of the best thing to say to accept his offer. His smile grew, and he added a wink, "Since no one here seems inclined to introduce us, I will tell you that I am Colonel George Whitaker. And you are?"

"Enid Hawthorne," she said, putting her hand into his—which was still outstretched in front of her. "And I would love to dance." She stood up and saw his smile grow wider still. "If I waited for someone to make introductions on my behalf," she said, "I would be sitting here all night."

He seemed to appreciate her validation of his overlooking what was considered a social requirement. As they walked slowly toward the dance floor where people were gathering while the orchestra waited, he said to her, "I'm guessing that you are the widow of Mr. Alistair Hawthorne."

"That's correct," she said, looking ahead instead of at his face.

"Dreadful thing," he said with compassion. "Of course, everyone around here has heard of what happened. I've wondered how you ever managed to get back to England on your own."

"And what conclusion did you come to?" she asked, now looking up at him as they took their places facing each other in long lines of men and women doing the same.

"You don't look any worse for wear," he said, again winking, and she realized he was paying her a compliment. More seriously he added, "And from the first moment I heard your tale repeated, I decided that this Mrs. Hawthorne was surely an incredibly brave woman."

"You know nothing about me," she said, humbled at the praise.

"I know that you followed your husband to Africa and then came back entirely on your own following his death." He said it as if that somehow exalted her to the status of a goddess. Not knowing how to respond, Enid was glad when the music began. She was also glad that it was a lively number, and one she knew well. She couldn't help laughing as the men and women turned in circles around each other while doing spirited steps, then they took hands and glided together across the floor before repeating the sequence again and again. By the time the music ended, Enid was out of breath but still finding it difficult to keep from laughing.

The colonel smiled at her and said, "Am I to assume that you find something humorous, Mrs. Hawthorne, or—"

"More like delightful," she explained. "I can't remember the last time I danced."

"Then we must do it again so that you can keep laughing," he said as if just hearing her do so would be nothing but a pleasure for him.

Chapter Ten

THE SUITOR

ENID INSISTED THAT SHE NEEDED to sit down and catch her breath, and she wasn't disappointed when the colonel sat next to her. Such attentiveness might have been annoying if he were disagreeable company, but he was kind without being overbearing, and there was a sparkle in his eyes that she couldn't help but enjoy. He looked at her as if she were a rare piece of art in a museum, and his gaze made her feel beautiful. And right now, making the most of such an experience was all that mattered. She'd been through a great deal of sorrow and difficulty—some of which had been so kindly acknowledged by the colonel—and this moment in time felt healing to her. She just wanted soak in every facet of the event and not worry about anything beyond this night. A memory burst into her mind of Sebastian looking at her the same way the colonel had, but his harsh attitudes toward her made it all irrelevant. She forced all thoughts of Sebastian away and focused on the kind gentleman sitting beside her.

Feeling the need for conversation so as to avoid any awkward silence, Enid said, "May I ask how you became a colonel?"

The music began again, and he had to speak somewhat loudly to be heard above it. "You may ask me anything you like. My older brother inherited our father's estate—as is the case in such matters—but I felt the need to make something useful of my life, so I put my interests into the military. I've served for many years and traveled to many places," he added, and Enid didn't think he looked old enough to have done so for *too* many years; by her calculations he was in his late twenties, perhaps early thirties at most. But then, if he'd joined on the brink of adulthood, that would certainly amount to *many years*.

"I can't say that my military career was necessarily a pleasant experience, but it was certainly humbling."

"I can only imagine how difficult it must have been," she said.

He looked mildly surprised by her comment, and she was surprised when he countered, "You may likely be the only woman here who could say that and mean it. You, who have actually experienced what the world can be like beyond the sheltered drawing rooms of our beloved England."

Enid looked down for a long moment, allowing her memories to pass quickly through her mind before looking up at him again. "Yes, the world beyond England is impossible to imagine without seeing it firsthand; I cannot deny that."

"So," he said in a lighter tone as if to purposely brighten the mood, "my brother inherited a title, and I earned one. Nothing wrong with that, I believe."

"Nothing at all," she agreed. "May I ask if you and your brother are close?"

The colonel smiled. "I told you that you could ask anything you like. And I'm glad to say that we are. Now that I've retired from my military service, I've taken up residence in one wing of the house, and he lives in another with his family. We get along well and I'm even learning how to assist him in running the estate."

"That's wonderful, then," she said, glad to hear that he'd retired. For some reason, she hesitated in wanting to admit that she didn't like the idea of him leaving. She'd only known the man for a matter of minutes, she reminded herself. Still, she liked knowing that he'd returned to England for good and was settling down.

Enid danced with the colonel again, this time at a slower pace, which she found gave him more opportunity to look directly at her as they moved around each other and between other dancers. He occasionally took her hand to guide her through the turns and steps, but whenever they were facing each other, her quick and discreet glances toward him always revealed an unyielding gaze and a growing sparkle in his eyes. Following the conclusion of the dance, the colonel guided Enid to a chair and declared that he would return momentarily with some refreshment for her. A couple of minutes later he appeared with a glass of punch for her and one for himself.

"Oh, thank you," she said, taking the delicate glass filled with pink liquid. "I confess I am quite thirsty."

"I knew you must be," he said, sitting beside her, "given that I was, as well."

Even though they had to speak a bit loudly to hear each other over the music, they talked long after they'd finished drinking their punch and a young under-butler had come by to take their empty glasses. Enid learned that Colonel Whitaker had grown up—and now lived—on an estate that was several miles in the opposite direction from Thornewell Hall. His elder brother of whom he'd spoken earlier was married to a woman he respected, even though he confided that she was a bit dull and not a good conversationalist, and he very much enjoyed stimulating conversation. The colonel's brother and his dull but respectable wife had three children, all of whom were a treasure to the colonel. He loved playing with them and spoiling them. He also had two sisters, one of which had married years earlier and lived three counties away, which meant that the rest of the family saw her very rarely. His other sister had never married and described herself as the spinster aunt who would end up living under her brother's roof for the remainder of her life. However, the colonel spoke fondly of her and declared with admiration that she was not unhappy with the way her life had turned out, and she was always genuinely cheerful and a delight to be around. Everyone in the family loved having her there, and she helped a great deal in caring for the children—so much so that they rarely had need of the nanny. When Enid asked about his parents, he told her that his mother had died when he was very young, and he barely remembered her, but his father had always been kind and attentive to his children and had done everything he could to make up for the absence of a mother in their lives. His father had passed at about the same time the colonel had reached maturity, and his death had spurred the colonel's decision to pursue a career in the military.

"And now you know everything about me," Colonel Whitaker said. "You have a clever way of steering the conversation away from yourself, Mrs. Hawthorne. Tell me of *your* family."

Enid didn't want to talk about the family that no longer wanted anything to do with her. She missed them so much sometimes that she simply couldn't bear to think how they were, what they were doing, and if they missed her. She chose instead to *not* think about them, and she certainly didn't want to talk about them. Instead she said, "You already know that my husband died in Africa." Sensing that he was curious over details that local gossip would have never produced, she added, "It was a dreadful illness that swept very quickly through the village. People were getting sick, then dying a day or two after exposure to the disease. I believe I was spared because I had been staying inside, due to illness from my pregnancy. Alistair had promised me that he would be very careful as he went out to assist the people in need." She tossed him a wan smile, then stared at her hands that were clasped in her lap. "That's the way he was; always putting the needs of the people he served above his own." She sighed and added silently, *And above those of his wife.* "But he came home with the symptoms already making him very ill. He got himself to the bed and collapsed, insisting I not come anywhere near him, and that I pack my belongings, take the money we'd saved, and just leave." She sighed more deeply, not wanting to get into any more detail than that. She was still haunted with thoughts of leaving Alistair's body there on the bed, and she couldn't think about the journey home without recalling how miserable it had been, and how terrified she'd felt nearly every waking minute. "So, that's what I did," she concluded.

"As I said," he declared, "you are a very brave woman."

Enid chuckled uncomfortably. "I just did what I had to do."

"Which surely must have taken a great deal of courage," he added. Given that she didn't know how to respond, she was glad when he continued. "And you came home to discover that your sister-in-law and her baby had died during your absence."

"Yes," Enid said, again looking at her clasped hands.

"I cannot imagine the losses you've suffered, Mrs. Hawthorne. Allow me to offer my condolences."

"Thank you," she said. Then hoping to lighten the mood, she added, "We are all doing reasonably well, I believe. My nephews have shown evidence of much healing in the months since I've returned. They are delightful boys."

"And you had a child?" he asked; it was evident that gossip hadn't reached his ears as to whether her baby had survived, or whether it was male or female.

"Yes," she said brightly, "her name is Sarah. I'm happy to say she's in very good health and an absolute delight to everyone in the household."

"That's *very* good!" he said as if it was the best news he'd heard in years. He then surprised her by saying, "I should very much like to meet the young Miss Hawthorne at some time in the future . . . if that would be agreeable to you."

Enid looked at him, realizing he was asking permission to call on her—officially and respectfully. His request to meet her daughter made the petition more personal. But he clearly knew that; something in his eyes led her to believe that he wanted to make it *very* clear that his interest in her was indeed personal. Enid didn't know whether to feel thrilled or terrified. She enjoyed his company very much, but she sincerely felt no interest in marrying again, and she didn't want to lead him to believe that a visit might lead to courting. Of course, such a declaration surely wasn't necessary when they'd only just met, and she concluded that one visit couldn't hurt. Enid smiled at the colonel and said, "I'm certain that could be arranged."

His countenance revealed great pleasure just as the orchestra struck up a lively tune. The colonel offered his hand to Enid, which she gladly took, and they were soon dancing again, and again. Enid was so wrapped up in thoroughly enjoying herself that she almost tripped when she caught a glimpse of Sebastian through the mass of swirling dancers. Of course, she had known he'd be there; it was the fact that he was staring at *her* that interrupted her enjoyment as abruptly as if cold water had been thrown on her face to awaken her from a dream. She didn't want to see Sebastian; she didn't want to think about him at all. Most of all, she didn't want to feel the way she felt. In that moment she was nothing but angry with Sebastian Hawthorne for luring her into a romantic bliss that had eased her loneliness as surely as it had filled her with hope for a rich and bright future with him. She was perhaps equally angry with herself for believing that the feelings they'd come to share had magically erased his contempt. She didn't want to see him here tonight; she wanted to enjoy herself—and she had been doing just that until she saw him. It was bad enough to encounter him at all when there were so many people here that it surely could have been avoided. But why was he staring at her like that, as if she had somehow betrayed him by enjoying the company of another man?

"Are you all right?" the colonel asked when she missed more than one step and then couldn't get herself back into the rhythm of the dance.

"Just . . . a bit lightheaded, I confess."

"Perhaps some fresh air would help," he said, holding firmly to her arm as if to support her without crossing any inappropriate boundaries.

"That would be lovely, thank you," she said, grateful for the ease with which she was able to exit the ballroom and get away from Sebastian's searing gaze.

Once outside, Enid felt immediately better. She took in a deep breath of fresh air and didn't realize how hot the crowded ballroom had become until she was encompassed by the cool evening. The cold air of winter was a relief in contrast to the heat indoors. "Oh, that's much better," she declared. "I must confess that this gown doesn't necessarily make it easy to breathe." What she really meant was that the corset beneath it was just a little too tight to be able to take a deep breath, and the other layers of underclothing were just plain hot. But she wondered if her implication had been too suggestive and hurried to add, "Forgive me if that sounded too personal."

"Not at all," he chuckled. "The decorum that requires a gentleman to wear a proper coat and waistcoat for such events is certainly not compatible with crowded rooms and vigorous dancing. Therefore, it would seem we suffer from the same ailment, even with differing requirements for our genders."

"Sometimes the decorum is rather silly, isn't it," she stated, and he chuckled again.

"Shall we take a brief stroll until the cold air gets to us?" Colonel Whitaker asked, offering his arm.

"That would be lovely," she said as she took it. They walked slowly around a large fountain where the sound of water was soothing to Enid as it spewed out of the mouths of marble cherubs. An area of the garden was well lit with lanterns and they walked a little farther until they *did* start to feel cold and returned to the house. But instead of going to the ballroom, the colonel led her to one of many parlors that had been prepared for this evening's guests. It was well lit with a fire crackling in the fireplace, and only a few people talking quietly at one end of the room. Colonel Whitaker guided Enid to a sofa at the opposite end of the room where they sat together and resumed their conversation. Enid loved the way he spoke hypothetically about many topics that were fascinating as well as stimulating, and he was eager to hear her opinion, showing respect toward her even when they disagreed over certain matters of science, political happenings, and even religion.

They went back to the ballroom, where Enid was glad to see no sign of Sebastian when she scanned the room. The colonel got her another glass of punch and they shared another dance before it became evident the party was winding down and many of the guests were leaving. The colonel stayed with her until her carriage was brought around in one of three lines of wheeled vehicles waiting for their passengers to emerge from the castle-like structure to begin their trek home. Enid spotted Lex on the box seat of the carriage she'd come in. She was surprised when the colonel insisted on walking her to her carriage, and even more so when he asked, "May I call tomorrow? I don't want to make a nuisance of myself, and you must be honest about whether or not you want me to, but—"

"That would be lovely," she said and meant it. She had enjoyed his company, and she would welcome a break in her mundane routine, as well as a distraction from her often troubled thoughts. "Come for tea, and you can meet Sarah."

"How splendid!" he said as if he'd been invited to meet royalty.

Colonel Whitaker thanked her for a delightful evening and took her hand to help her step into the carriage. As she did so, Enid detected from the corner of her eye that the carriage directly in front of this one also belonged to the Hawthornes. And Beauford was on the box seat, which meant that Sebastian was either in that carriage or would be coming this way soon. She hoped to get inside her carriage quickly and avoid him.

"Thank you for a lovely evening, Colonel," she said. "I'll look forward to seeing you tomorrow."

"It is I who have been blessed by your company," he replied with a cordial smile that lit up his eyes. "I am greatly anticipating the opportunity to continue our visit tomorrow."

Enid smiled back at him before she stepped into the carriage. She decided that she liked the way he could be so proper without being stuffy or pretentious. As far as she could tell, he was kind and respectful and a man of integrity. She had no intention of encouraging him toward any romantic involvement, but she couldn't deny that he'd contributed to her having a glorious evening, and she was genuinely pleased over the prospect of seeing him again tomorrow.

The carriage door closed behind Enid and she sat down, only to gasp when she realized that Sebastian was sitting across from her. "You scared me!" she scolded.

"Did I?" he asked as if he were pleased with himself.

"What on earth are you doing here? If you were not opposed to sharing a carriage, we wouldn't have needed to make such a fuss over bringing *two*."

"I told Beauford to go on without me," Sebastian said. "I thought perhaps we should talk."

"About what?" she asked, not caring that she sounded so snappish. His own attitude betrayed no humility—quite the opposite, in fact.

"I see you had an enjoyable time with the colonel," he said, and she realized that the two men knew each other. But of course, they would. If Colonel Whitaker had known details of Alistair's death and other circumstances, he would know of Sebastian too—and the other way around.

"I did, thank you," Enid said. "Not that it's any business of yours."

"Enid." He drew out the two syllables of her name ridiculously long. "Why are we behaving this way? This is utterly ridiculous!"

Enid shot him a sharp glare, at the same time assessing that the carriage hadn't yet started moving. They were waiting in a long line of vehicles and couldn't move until those in front of them did so. While planning her possible escape, Enid said to him, "Why? If you're trying to tell me that your feelings have changed about how I supposedly destroyed your brother's life, then I would be glad to hear it."

He said nothing and looked down, letting her know beyond any doubt that his feelings had *not* changed, which made her utterly furious. He was behaving badly regarding the attentions of another man toward her, and questioning the reasons for the rift between them, while at the same time being completely unwilling to acknowledge his own ludicrous and unyielding attitude.

Enid didn't bother saying another word before she opened the door and practically jumped out of the carriage without any assistance. She lifted her skirts and nearly ran toward the carriage that Beauford would be driving, calling his name to alert him to her presence.

"I'll be riding home with you," she said when she got to the side of the carriage.

His brow furrowed into something of a scowl while his lips almost smirked, as if he found this ongoing feud between her and Sebastian confusing but also amusing. She didn't care if the servants found entertainment in her argument with Sebastian; she just didn't want to be anywhere near him.

"As you wish," he said and began to get down to help her until she stopped him.

"Stay where you are," she said and opened the carriage door, climbing in with little trouble since she felt no concern whatsoever over whether anyone considered her present behavior to be ladylike. She closed the carriage door and barely let out a long sigh before the carriage began to move, which meant that Sebastian couldn't follow her and impose his company upon her throughout the ride home.

Enid forced away thoughts of Sebastian and instead relived in her mind how enjoyable the evening had been. She looked forward to the colonel's visit, and she also looked forward to the party she would be overseeing for the servants. They'd all been so thoroughly kind to her, and they all worked so hard; they certainly deserved some fun and celebration, and Enid smiled to think of the opportunity to make it happen. She had a ridiculous amount of money in the bank, which kept increasing every month with the ongoing accrual of Alistair's monthly allowance. She couldn't think of any better way to spend it.

Enid didn't realize she'd drifted off to sleep until she felt the carriage come to a halt, and she found herself curled up on the seat. She hurried to sit up and try to get her bearings before Beauford opened the door, and she barely managed to do so before he held out his hand to help her step down.

"Thank you so very much," she said to him. "Get some good rest now."

"And you," he said. "'Tis a pleasure, as always."

They shared a smile and Enid went into the house and up to her room where she found Tilly dozing on the little sofa there, waiting to help her get out of the elaborate gown and the corset beneath it. While Tilly helped Enid, the maid was thrilled to hear that the outing had been a success and Enid had had a wonderful time. Enid avoided any mention of Sebastian's intrusion; focusing instead on telling Tilly that Colonel Whitaker was coming for tea. Tilly was genuinely excited over the very fact that Enid would receive a gentleman caller, and that he wanted to meet the baby. Given that babies were most often kept hidden away in polite society, Tilly considered this a kind gesture from the colonel, and Enid had to agree with her.

When Enid needed no more help in getting ready for bed, Tilly left the room, saying over her shoulder that she would inform Mrs. Thorpe about the colonel's intended visit, and that Enid should sleep as long as she liked in the morning, so that she could be well rested in order to receive company in the afternoon.

Before Enid went to bed, she stood over the crib where Sarah was sleeping and just watched her precious little daughter for many long minutes. It had been lovely to go out, but even lovelier to come home and know that she shared her life with this beautiful, perfect child. She finally went to bed, knowing it was about two in the morning. While attempting to fall asleep, Enid once again recounted the magical evening she'd enjoyed: the music, the lights, the beautiful colors of ladies and gentlemen dressed so finely and dancing with well-practiced steps and elegant twirls. Enid loved the memories and held the details close, and she hated it when Sebastian forced his way into them, making her thoughts trip and stumble, much as she'd done when she'd seen him staring at her while she'd been dancing. She forced her thoughts back to the colonel and his pleasant company, but again Sebastian intruded. And again, she put her mind firmly upon the colonel, looking forward to his visit tomorrow. Then with pleasant anticipation she fell asleep.

* * * * *

Enid slept through breakfast, knowing that Tilly had taken care of feeding Sarah when she'd awakened in the night. Feeling rested enough to face the day, she found that a tray had been left in her room with some scones and butter and jam, and tea that was still hot, which meant Tilly had likely brought the tray only minutes before Enid had awakened to find it. Tilly had a special sense about such things.

Enid ate only enough to tide her over until lunch before she freshened up and got dressed. She fed Sarah and took the baby along as usual to spend some time with the boys and share lunch with them. She feared that Sebastian might cross their established boundaries and intrude upon her time with his sons, just as he'd shown up in her carriage last night. But he didn't, and she was relieved.

Enid left the boys at the usual time, not wanting to risk seeing Sebastian at all. She took Sarah with her down to the kitchen where the women who worked in the house—at least those with whom Enid shared a personal relationship—gathered around the table to take a break from their work to hear a report of Enid's evening out. Their genuine enthusiasm touched Enid, and she wished they all could have gone to the ball. They were all so delighted over the prospect of her having a gentleman caller, but when they began to speculate over the possibility of the colonel becoming a potential suitor—and perhaps even officially courting her—Enid halted the conversation by firmly declaring, "I doubt that I will ever marry again, so let me assure you that I have no romantic intentions regarding the colonel, and I will make that clear to *him* if I even sense that his view differs from mine. I enjoy his company, and that is all."

"But surely," Mrs. Thorpe said, "if he's asked to meet your daughter, he might already be thinking of you in that light."

The idea struck Enid with a bit of a shock. They had gotten along very well, but she'd not said anything to encourage him to believe she might have a romantic interest in him. Not wanting to be unfair to him in any way, she stated once again, "I will make it clear to him where I stand." When the faces looking back at her all appeared disappointed if not distraught, Enid added in a tone that she hoped would lighten the mood, "Now, why would any of you be wanting me to seek out a husband? If I were to marry, I would have to leave here, and I don't know that I would *ever* want to leave here. How could I possibly manage without any of you?"

These women who had become friends to her—and some of them much like family—expressed agreement with that theory, but they still seemed disappointed that Enid had no romantic interest in the gentleman who would be coming to see her that afternoon.

* * * * *

Enid felt decidedly nervous as she waited for the colonel to arrive. She paced the drawing room, wishing they had agreed upon a more specific time. He'd said he would come for tea, but that didn't mean he might not arrive earlier than the generally accepted time when tea would be served in any household. She knew she could have waited upstairs and one of the maids would have come for her when he arrived. But she'd decided that she preferred to be here, where she could hear—if only barely—when a visitor came to the door. She wondered *why* she was so nervous, and didn't necessarily like any of the conclusions she arrived at. Was she attracted to the colonel in a romantic way as the servants had implied? If so, was she simply not acknowledging her own feelings? If she was truly determined to never marry again, and she'd given the colonel the wrong impression, then it certainly made her nervous to think of having to let him know that pursuing her was in vain. However, she realized she didn't necessarily *want* to discourage his attention when she'd found it so pleasant. Did that mean she *was* attracted to him romantically? Or did it simply mean that she'd thoroughly enjoyed his company and considered him nothing more than a potentially good friend? And through all her stewing over the matter— while wearing a path in the carpet as she paced back and forth—thoughts of Sebastian continued bursting into her mind, to be immediately banished by her determination to not think of him at all. But inevitably he appeared in her thoughts over and over, and it only made her angrier with him. She knew how she felt about him, and she wouldn't try to deny it. But she also knew that her love for Sebastian could never survive what stood between them, and she wouldn't delude herself into trying to hope that it would. If Sebastian had the decency to just deal with the matter appropriately, their relationship could have been entirely different, and she would have spent the previous evening dancing with *him* instead of the colonel; and she certainly wouldn't have invited the colonel to tea.

When such thoughts only created more confusion over how she felt about the colonel and his interest in her, Enid forced herself to sit down, where she closed her eyes and breathed in and out deeply, trying to completely clear her mind. She thought about Sarah and smiled to think of the perfect joy she found in her love for her daughter. Sarah had the power to force every problem or difficulty out of her mind and place them in their proper perspective. Enid was truly beginning to feel relaxed when she heard the distant sound of the heavy knocker at the front door, and the evidence that a maid had answered. A slight whoosh of air went through the room as the door was opened, then a deep thud echoed through the nearby hall as the door was closed. A moment later a maid entered the drawing room to announce that Colonel Whitaker had arrived.

"Thank you," Enid said, still sitting and glad to note that she felt relatively calm. "Bring him in here and tell Mrs. Thorpe that we will take tea whenever it is ready."

"Very good, m'lady," the maid said as she curtsied and left the room, only to return a moment later with the colonel.

Enid rose to greet him as the maid left and closed the door. "My dear Mrs. Hawthorne," he said, taking her hand to kiss it as he bowed. Enid was genuinely glad to see him and couldn't deny her pleasure over his enthusiastic greeting. He stood up straight after bowing and looked at her with that sparkle in his eyes that she'd been keenly aware of the previous evening. "How lovely you look!" he added, and Enid couldn't help but smile.

"How very kind of you to visit," she said, noting that he seemed reluctant to let go of her hand. As she sat back down on the sofa, she motioned for him to be seated in a chair where they could face each other to visit comfortably.

They chatted about the ball and both agreed it had been very good fortune that they'd encountered each other there. Then they chatted about the weather and some local news. An elderly man who lived in the village had died; he'd been a tailor all his life, and both his son and his daughter had taken on his trade and were well equipped to continue running the shop. The colonel also mentioned that the cobbler's wife had given birth to a healthy baby boy the previous week. And a kind young man who worked at one of the local pubs had just become engaged to be married. Enid was pleasantly surprised by how much the colonel knew about the happenings of ordinary people. He obviously wasn't held back by social position when it came to interacting with other people.

While enjoying their visit, Enid began to feel mildly uneasy. The colonel's behavior was completely appropriate; he was a perfect gentleman, and very respectful toward her. Conversation between them flowed effortlessly. They agreed on many matters, and it seemed they might never run out of things to talk about. Still, Enid felt uncomfortable, and while she listened to the colonel tell her an amusing story about his brother's children, she half listened while she tried to ascertain the reason for her discomfort. It only took her a minute to assess all the information she had—from the servants' comments as well as the colonel's behavior—that there was a distinct belief that this relationship was headed toward something romantic. And while she had strong personal feelings otherwise, she had not said or done anything to discourage the notion. Now what was she supposed to do? She didn't want to send the colonel away; she enjoyed his company. But he was a kind and good man and she didn't want to have to say something to him that would leave him disappointed, or perhaps even upset.

Enid was rescued from her inner turmoil when a maid brought tea into the room, and she and the colonel became pleasantly occupied with the comforting aroma of hot tea and the lovely variety of little cakes, biscuits, and delicate sandwiches. They talked about their personal preferences regarding the delicious repast they were enjoying, and the colonel was highly complimentary of the cook's abilities. Enid promised to pass along his compliment; but thinking of how she might feel after he left, her thoughts went again to her dilemma. She reminded herself that this was only tea, and it was the first time he'd come to her home. It wasn't as if she'd led him on through the course of many visits over weeks or months. She didn't have to decide how to handle the situation right now, or even today. With that thought, she relaxed more fully and just enjoyed the colonel's company.

Only minutes after they'd both had their fill of tea and the accompanying food, Tilly brought Sarah into the room. The baby had awakened from her nap and had been changed and fed. Tilly smiled as she declared, "Here's the little princess." She turned her over to Enid and added, "I'll just be in the next room if she fusses and you need me to take her."

"Thank you, Tilly," Enid said. "I'm certain we'll be fine."

Tilly nodded and stole a glance at the colonel before she left the room. Colonel Whitaker immediately left his chair and sat down on the sofa next to Enid so that he could have a perfect view of the baby in her arms.

"Oh, she is beautiful," the colonel declared. "Much like her mother," he added with a wink. Enid found it odd to consider that if she were truly attracted to the colonel, such a comment combined with his winking at her would have likely prompted a quickened heartbeat or a fluttering in her stomach. She'd felt such things when she'd been getting to know Alistair Hawthorne, and she'd felt them in response to Sebastian's attention—even if she didn't want to admit it. As much as she had quickly grown fond of the colonel, she knew that even if she was interested in marrying again—which at this point in her life she certainly was not—it would be wrong to allow this man to believe that pursuing her was worthy of his time and attention.

The colonel fussed over Sarah and made her smile, while Enid considered ways to let him know that she had no interest in anything beyond friendship. She again reminded herself that such a conversation didn't need to take place today. She needed time to be able to think clearly without the distraction of his company.

"You know," the colonel said while his interest remained mostly on the baby, "I've told you practically everything about my family, and I realized last night after the ball that I know absolutely nothing about *your* family."

Enid bristled but did well at not allowing him to see how the topic ruffled her. He'd mentioned the same thing the previous evening and she had managed to keep the topic contained to facets of her life that she was willing to talk about. But he was asking again, and she sought for a way to skirt around what she knew he was wanting to know. "You likely know more about the Hawthorne family than I do," she said, "given that you've lived in the same area your entire life."

"I doubt that I know *more* than you do," he said, "but I believe you know very well that's not what I mean. I know nothing about where you came from, Mrs. Hawthorne. What kind of family did you grow up in? Where are they now?"

Enid cleared her throat if only to give her a few more seconds to think of how to answer his questions. She decided on firm honesty, and hoped it would quickly put the matter to rest. After taking a deep breath, she gave him the simplest answer. "My parents were not pleased with my choice of a husband. They cut me off completely. Given the fact that I have no contact with my parents or siblings, it's easier for me to not talk about them. Forgive me if that sounds harsh, but it's been difficult and I'd simply . . . rather not speak of it."

"Very well," he said, looking confused. "But . . . may I ask . . . why?"

"Why what, exactly?" she had to ask, not wanting to give up any more information than necessary.

"Why would they disown you for marrying into a fine family with wealth and security?"

Enid looked away, marveling at how everyone she'd ever spoken to about the matter always immediately assumed that when a marriage guaranteed her social and financial security—and marrying into a family as fine as the

Hawthornes would—nothing else could possibly make sense. But no one knew the whole truth. Even as much as she'd confided in Marie at one time, she'd never told her the real reasons for her family's behavior. And she certainly wasn't going to tell this man whom she barely knew. She simply said, "Forgive me, Colonel. But I really prefer not to talk about it."

"Very well," he said. "I apologize if I've put my nose in where it doesn't belong. I certainly respect your desire to—"

The colonel was interrupted when the door came open. And while Enid had expected to see a maid coming to get the tea tray, or Tilly coming to check on the baby, she was anything but pleased to see Sebastian entering the room. He wore a big smile, as if nothing in the world was amiss.

"I heard that we have company," he said brightly, and the colonel came to his feet, showing an equivalent smile.

The two men shook hands as the colonel said, "How very good to see you, Sebastian. It's been far too long."

"Indeed it has, George," Sebastian said, and Enid realized she'd completely forgotten this man's given name. But her mind was more focused on Sebastian's ridiculous intrusion. She knew very well that he was not keen on receiving visitors, and he had no prior connection to the colonel beyond a mere acquaintanceship. She was certain Sebastian's intrusion was spurred by ulterior motives, and it made her angry.

Following the handshake, the colonel sat back down, while Sebastian took Sarah from Enid without asking permission. Not wanting to draw any attention to the discord between herself and Sebastian, she had no choice but to allow him to take Sarah.

"There's our little queen," Sebastian said with a chuckle as he sat down, his attention completely focused on the baby. He talked to her in a silly voice that made her respond with a happy cooing sound that was almost a laugh, which in turn made both men chuckle. Enid smiled, hoping the men were focused enough on the baby to not notice how forced her smile was. She wondered if she'd ever felt so uncomfortable as Sebastian and the colonel began exchanging pleasantries about trivial things. And all the while, Sebastian held Sarah and kept her calm and entertained as if to declare that he was an important part of the baby's life, and he spent enough time with her to know how to care for her. While that was certainly true, Sebastian's flaunting that fact at this particular moment further incited Enid's anger. What if she *did* have an interest in pursuing a romantic relationship with the colonel? How would Sebastian's place in her life—and that of her daughter—impact such a possibility? But surely Sebastian knew his presence was likely to make her uncomfortable, and it certainly created an undeniable awkwardness in the room. For all that the colonel appeared to be enjoying his interaction with Sebastian, he was not as relaxed as he'd been prior to Sebastian's arrival. Enid wanted to scream at Sebastian and tell him to leave, but she didn't want to utter even a word, fearing she might betray how furious she felt.

When the colonel politely tried to include her in the conversation, she had to swallow hard and force a steady voice to respond as if nothing at all was amiss. She noticed Sebastian smirking subtly at her and abruptly looked away, not wanting him to have the satisfaction of seeing how frazzled she was by his presence in the room.

During a lull in the conversation, the colonel declared, "I think I must be going." He came to his feet and both Enid and Sebastian did the same. "I'm certain I've overstayed my welcome."

"Not at all," Enid said in an especially kind voice that she hoped would irk Sebastian.

"It has been a distinct pleasure," the colonel said, once again kissing her hand and bowing.

"The pleasure has been all mine," she said.

The colonel and Sebastian exchanged appropriate farewells before the colonel made his exit. The moment the door was closed, Enid whispered so as not to be overheard, "What on *earth* are you doing here?"

"Simply enjoying the company," he said, again smirking slightly.

"I know for a fact you detest such formal visits," she snapped, still whispering, not certain if there was a maid outside the door. "And he was *my* guest, not yours."

"And why is that?" he asked, his pleasant demeanor fading. "Is this the blossoming of some romantic tryst?"

"That is *none* of your business," she snarled quietly and took the baby from him. "You are more than welcome to live your life any way you please, and I would ask that you extend me the same courtesy."

"And do you really consider it appropriate to be entertaining a suitor not so many months after the death of your husband?" he asked.

Enid stopped on her way toward the door, frozen instantly by her own astonishment over such a statement. The only response she could think of was, "Your hypocrisy is appalling!"

Enid hurried out of the room before he could say anything more, and before her own anger made her say something she might regret. Holding Sarah tightly in her arms, she attempted to soak in the comfort she always drew from her daughter, praying that it might dispel the absolute fury burning inside her.

Chapter Eleven

DIGGING FOR ROOTS

BY THE TIME ENID GOT to the top of the stairs, Sarah was crying—no doubt due to the baby's ability to sense her mother's mood. It was far from the first time the baby had become fussy when Enid was tired or upset or anxious. Once within the safety of her own rooms, Enid willed herself to calm down as she paced slowly with the baby and patted her softly, cooing gentle sounds that completely belied her inner rage. She was still thoroughly overcome by the audacity and arrogance of Sebastian Hawthorne.

Enid was startled from her fuming when she heard Tilly ask, "Is everything all right, m'lady?" The maid had obviously come in through the open door between the bedroom and sitting room, where she had likely been reading while she waited until she was needed.

"Yes, of course," Enid lied and let out a stilted chuckle, attempting to sound more convincing. "Perhaps she's hungry; I've likely lost track of the time."

"I believe she might be," Tilly said. "I've just had some milk brought up for her a few minutes ago so that you can—"

"Of course," Enid said and hurried into the sitting room, which had become somewhat of a nursery. Even though Sarah didn't sleep in this room, during the days she was often changed and fed here, and so the necessary amenities were discreetly kept in a cupboard. Enid laid the baby on a little blanket that was often left on one of the sofas where the baby could be changed. Tilly provided Enid with what she needed, but the nanny knew that Enid preferred to do even the little tasks during the time she was with Sarah. After the nappy-changing ritual was complete, Enid held Sarah close and began to feed the baby her bottle.

Once Sarah was contentedly eating, Tilly asked, "Would you prefer that I leave, m'lady?"

Enid felt a little disoriented by the question. Sometimes Tilly sat in the same room and read quietly, and sometimes they would chat and enjoy each other's company. At other times Tilly would go and take care of something personal or help elsewhere in the house when she was not needed here. But she'd never had any problem either declaring that she had other things to do, or simply taking a seat, because Enid had made it clear she was always welcome to do so. They'd become completely comfortable with each other, and even very friendly.

"You are welcome to stay, of course," Enid said as she clarified what she believed was a well-established routine between them. "Or if you have somewhere else you need to be, then . . ."

"I don't need to be anywhere else," Tilly said, taking a seat but not appearing to be very relaxed. "I simply wondered if you prefer to be alone."

"Why would you wonder that?" Enid asked in a mildly sharp tone that she immediately realized made her sound like a hypocrite.

"If I may speak candidly?" Tilly asked, easing back into her chair a little further as if to make herself more comfortable—or to imply that she did not intend to leave.

"Of course," Enid said, even though she wondered if she really wanted to hear Tilly's opinion of the reasons that Enid was clearly upset, even though she'd claimed not to be.

Enid felt decidedly nervous when Tilly seemed to be gathering courage, although she sounded completely confident when she said, "You can't be surprised to know that the entire household is aware of this . . . discord . . . going on between you and the earl. It would not be possible to be certain that the two of you were never in the same room together, without the servants knowing who is eating which meal in which room and when—among other things."

"No," Enid admitted, "I shouldn't be surprised, but perhaps I simply . . . didn't want to think about it. Ignoring the fact that he's actually living under the same roof has perhaps been the only way to make the situation tolerable."

"And yet it's not working," Tilly stated as if it were a firm conclusion resulting from much consideration. Enid made no effort to disguise her curiosity over what might have brought Tilly to this belief; or perhaps showing curiosity was an attempt to disguise her embarrassment. Tilly added firmly but with perfect respect, "The two of you are often in foul moods; the only time that either of you are pleasant and cheerful is when you are in the presence of the children. Yet, in all truthfulness, m'lady, if the children are *not* present, there isn't a single person working here who wants to encounter the master of the house, and gradually it's becoming the same with you." Enid felt her own eyes widen in astonishment as the nanny went on. "I've grown to enjoy your company, as you well know, and I've never enjoyed any work I've done in my life as much as I've enjoyed caring for little Sarah. However, being in your company has not been so pleasant of late. That's the truth of it. I do not say so in a spirit of criticism, m'lady, but rather concern. I wonder if you have *anyone* with whom you would speak your thoughts and feelings honestly. If not, then—as my mother always told me—when chaos is trapped in our heads, and turmoil is trapped in our hearts, it will only smolder and become venomous until we can let it out and find a way to make sense of it."

Enid sighed and took in what she was hearing, feeling humbler now as the truth of Tilly's concern began to sink in. "Your mother sounds like a very wise woman."

"She was, yes; may she rest in peace," Tilly said. "You know that I have no family left to speak of, but I have found friendship here in this household. There is more than one person I trust completely with whom I can unburden myself. And I know that you have no contact with your family. Is there anyone that *you* can unburden yourself upon? I'm not saying that it has to be me; for all that we have grown comfortable with one another, I would not assume to have such a place in your life. But I do believe you have enough respect for me to accept my opinion that you need to talk to *someone*; otherwise your thoughts and feelings of confusion and frustration will only—"

"Become venomous," Enid said, quoting Tilly's mother.

"Yes," Tilly said on a lengthy sigh.

During a few minutes of taut silence, Enid considered everything Tilly had said. Sarah made it clear that she was finished eating, and Enid stood and carried her to the opposite sofa, handing her to Tilly. "Would you try and get a burp out of her?" Enid asked. "I'm certain she can sense that I'm upset; she's more likely to relax if you do it."

Tilly said nothing as she held the baby against her shoulder and patted her little back. Enid began to pace the room slowly in an effort to release her nervous energy while she considered how she might go about being free of the *chaos trapped in her head and the turmoil trapped in her heart*. Realizing she couldn't find that answer on her own, she finally admitted, "I *do* trust you, Tilly. You've proven yourself to not only be the very best of nannies, but you *have* become a friend. You must know that it's no small thing for me to leave my baby in your care, when Sarah is the most important person in my life. And we have shared many conversations of a personal nature; you know things that no one else in this house knows, and I've never questioned that you would keep such things in confidence."

"If you wish to talk, m'lady, I am here for you. I am glad to help in any way I can."

"Thank you," Enid said. "We can start by having you call me Enid when we are alone together. I consider you a friend, and therefore I must feel that we are equals. I know it's important for social status to be maintained—for reasons that are complicated; we've talked about that. But when we are alone together—as we often are—I need to feel that there are no barriers between us. You've seemed uncomfortable with calling me by my given name despite my having requested it before, and I suppose I can understand why, but you know that I came into this family with nothing that made me deserving of being elevated above anyone else. It's only through my marriage that I have any status in this house . . . and this community." Enid finally sat down and looked directly at Tilly. "If we are to declare our friendship in this way and cross certain boundaries of confidentiality that we have not crossed before, we must see each other as equals in every respect."

"Very well, Enid," Tilly said. "Allow me to assure you that nothing you ever tell me will pass through my lips except when we are sharing private conversations. Your every thought and feeling is safe with me."

Enid drew in her promise with a deep breath, and instinctively knew she was telling the truth. She quickly said to Tilly, "And I promise the same."

"Now that we have *that* clarified," Tilly said, "may I ask why you are *especially* upset this afternoon? Did your visit with the colonel not go well?"

"Oh, it went extremely well," Enid said, "until Sebastian strolled into the room, behaving as if he and I commonly made ourselves present at each other's social engagements."

Tilly spoke with an air of truly being Enid's friend and equal. "Neither of you have had a single social engagement since he lost his wife and you returned a widow."

"Precisely," Enid said, hearing anger rise in her own voice, "but given the well-established ways that we avoid each other in this house, I cannot imagine what made him think that it was all right to intrude upon my visit with the colonel. He actually took the baby from me as if he were trying to declare to the colonel that his role in Sarah's life is of great significance."

"And is it not?" Tilly asked. "He is Sarah's uncle, and has been close to her from the beginning."

"Yes," Enid drawled, "but that has nothing to do with the colonel, and Sebastian's behavior was completely inappropriate given the status of our relationship."

"I agree that the earl intruding upon your visit with the colonel was certainly uncalled for," Tilly said, "and I can certainly understand why it upset you. But I can also understand why he did it."

"Why?" Enid asked. His reasons had not even occurred to her. She simply believed that his intrusion had crossed inappropriate boundaries, which gave her every right to be angry with him.

"He's jealous," Tilly stated as if it were simple and obvious and the only plausible explanation of the problem.

"Jealous?" Enid echoed in a tone that made it sound as if she'd never heard the word before in her life.

"Of course," Tilly said. "Everyone here knows that he's in love with you—and we've all had good cause to believe that you loved him, as well. If I speak truthfully on behalf of the staff, I have to say that we are all confused over what changed. The two of you were certainly discreet, but it was evident that you enjoyed each other's company and you were spending a great deal of time together. Then suddenly it ended; you asked for a schedule to be worked out so that the two of you would never see each other, and you've both been in a foul mood ever since. Even though you do well to remain cheerful and positive, and you've never been unkind to me or anyone else, I've come to know you well enough to tell that you're . . . well . . . unhappy."

Enid stood up and began to pace again. "Unhappy?" she countered. "Angry, more like," she added, angered all over again over the reasons that Sebastian had broken her heart. His attitudes toward her had left her feeling betrayed and deeply hurt.

"If I might impart another of my mother's wise adages, it was her firm belief that anger is an emotion rooted in another emotion. As she put it, anger is like a weed that will just keep growing if left unchecked, until it overtakes any beautiful or productive plant within its reach. But the roots beneath the weed are something else entirely: fear, pain, betrayal, sorrow, frustration. You get the idea. So . . . it's evident you're angry; *quite* angry, if I may say so."

"Yes, I cannot deny that I am certainly angry," Enid said while she continued to pace.

Tilly was still patting the baby's back. "Perhaps it would be beneficial to ask yourself *why*. If you can push aside the anger, what emotions lie beneath it?"

Enid stopped pacing and silently asked herself these very questions, as if one part of her mind could interrogate another part of it and come up with the answers. She became suddenly out of breath as the answers rushed into her mind like some kind of mental explosion, which then rushed forcefully through her entire body, making her suddenly weak. She hurried to sit down, holding tightly to the sofa cushion on which she sat. Tilly said nothing, as if she wanted to allow Enid the necessary silence to assess what she was coming to realize. Enid finally looked at her friend and said in a quivering voice, "It's everything; all of them. Each emotion you mentioned, and perhaps more." She hiccupped a quiet sob and admitted, "He broke my heart, Tilly."

"Oh, dearest," Tilly said and moved with Sarah in her arms to sit right next to Enid, taking hold of her hand as soon as she had the baby settled. "It's not necessary for you to tell me the details, but I do think it's important for you to acknowledge the truth of what you're feeling."

Enid nodded, fully agreeing but unable to speak.

Following minutes of silence while Tilly just sat beside her like a sentinel who might protect her and help keep her strong, Tilly said, "Given what happened today, may I ask if you have feelings for the colonel? Do you believe that he could heal your broken heart?"

Enid looked up at Tilly, as if doing so might help her better understand the question. After letting it sink in, she said on a shaky breath, "No. The colonel is a kind man . . . and a good one from everything I know thus far, but . . ." her voice broke with emotion, "I suspect he could never be anything more than a friend to me; I doubt I could ever feel for him the way I do for . . ." Enid couldn't finish the sentence; she couldn't say his name aloud in that context without breaking down into unbridled sobbing.

"So . . ." Tilly drawled, "are you angry with the earl for intruding upon your visit, or . . ." She paused in a deliberate way, as if to allow her question to be taken very seriously.

"Or what?" Enid demanded, not certain if she was wary of the question, or if she wanted Tilly to put a voice to what Enid didn't want to say.

"Or is it possible that you are angry with yourself for loving him, which makes it impossible for you to even consider the possibility of finding that kind of love with anyone else?"

A river of silent tears finally overtook Enid as the truth came into the open. Tilly let go of Enid's hand to pull a clean handkerchief from her pocket, which Enid took gratefully, pressing it over her eyes. She admitted on the wave of a sob, "How can I love a man so much when I'm so *angry* with him?"

"By angry, you mean . . ." Tilly obviously expected Enid to finish the sentence, but she didn't want to say it again. She was relieved when Tilly guessed accurately. "You're angry because he broke your heart; you admitted that much. I don't understand the reasons, Enid, but I do know that we human beings are complicated creatures. I wonder what might be the roots of *his* anger, and why it is that anger seems to be drowning out anything and everything else between the two of you."

Enid wiped her face again with the handkerchief and looked up at Tilly. "Where did you learn to be so wise, my friend?"

Tilly smiled. "Not once has anyone ever told me I was wise. I suppose if I have any wisdom, I learned it from my mother. She was very sensitive to people's feelings . . . and the reasons they might behave in certain ways. She had a way of helping guide people through their challenges without hardly realizing she was doing it."

"I dare say you are very much like your mother," Enid said.

Tilly seemed pleased but perhaps mildly embarrassed. Enid could only feel grateful for the wisdom she'd been offered, but it had given her a great deal to think about, and she suddenly felt exhausted.

As if Tilly had read her mind, she said, "Why don't you lie down for a while before supper. You must be tired. Consider what we've discussed, and we can talk more anytime you might feel up to it."

"Thank you, my friend," Enid said and hugged Tilly awkwardly with the baby between them.

"Thank *you*," Tilly said, "for trusting me. I pray that you can find your way through this and be happy; you deserve to be happy."

Enid nodded, feeling another rush of tears threatening to burst forth. She touched the baby's face as she stood, then hurried into the bedroom and closed the door behind her, needing to be alone. As much as she felt exhausted and wanted to take Tilly's advice to lie down, she went to her knees next to the bed instead and pressed her face into the soft bedding while she pleaded with God to show her how to come to terms with all that she was feeling, and how to handle the seemingly impossible situation with Sebastian. And she also needed help in being able to communicate appropriately with the colonel so as not to give him any false impressions. She wished now that she'd never attended that social. Then she never would have met the colonel, and she wouldn't have yet another complication in her life to contend with. But it occurred to her that perhaps the colonel coming into her life might have been the determining factor that had forced her to look at all of this from a different perspective. She couldn't change Sebastian's attitudes or opinions, but she could come to terms with her own—which she could see now she had *not* been handling well. With any luck and with God's help, perhaps she had taken the first difficult steps to being able to learn how to move forward in her life—with or without Sebastian.

* * * * *

Enid awoke when Tilly gently nudged her, saying softly, "It's almost time for supper. And Sarah needs to be fed. I know you prefer to do it yourself."

"Thank you," Enid said and sat up in bed to lean back against the headboard as Tilly efficiently shifted Sarah into her mother's arms and handed Enid the bottle of warm milk. "I slept much longer than I thought I would," she said to Tilly, who had sat down nearby as she usually did to be on hand if she was needed. As Enid remembered losing herself in prayer, she honestly couldn't remember crawling into bed. Recalling her reasons for praying so fervently, she was ambushed once again with the confusion and turmoil she felt regarding Sebastian. But at least she didn't feel angry anymore. Tilly's explanation of learning to discern the root of her emotions had helped her immensely. Now that she understood more clearly *how* she felt; she just had to find a way to make peace with her feelings.

"Are you all right?" Tilly asked.

"I'm better, I think," Enid said. "You've given me much to think about, and I thank you for that." She went on to explain the path of her thoughts, and her earnest desire to be able to get beyond all that currently weighed her down. Enid was glad to be able to talk openly with Tilly; that in itself had helped her feel calmer.

When Sarah was full, Tilly took her from Enid, insisting that she should freshen up and eat some supper. "Would you like to go down to the kitchen," Tilly asked, "or should I ring to have a tray brought up for you?"

"I believe I'll go downstairs," Enid said, feeling a little disoriented after her long nap. Perhaps eating with the servants as was her routine would help set her mind straight. She thanked Tilly for her help and arrived in the kitchen only a few minutes after the meal had begun. While she ate, Enid enjoyed listening to the friendly chatter among those at the table, but she didn't want to answer questions about the ball she'd attended, or the colonel's social call. She reported that both experiences had been enjoyable and steered the conversation elsewhere, hating the way she could think of little else except Sebastian's intrusions—the way he'd been staring at her while she'd been at the ball; the way he'd been waiting for her in the carriage; the way he'd invited himself to join her and the colonel during their visit. She had to keep reminding herself of Tilly's advice to look beneath the anger—but she was finding it difficult to do so when most often she still just felt angry. Even now, when she could have been enjoying a relaxing meal with people she cared for, her mind was distracted with thoughts of Sebastian. And it made her angry.

After helping clear the table and clean the dishes, Enid went back upstairs to play with Sarah and get her ready for bed. After she'd been fed again and put down for the night, Tilly settled into her favorite spot in the sitting room to read and listen for the baby while Enid decided a brisk walk might help ease her restlessness. The combination of a late nap and her plethora of difficult thoughts made her certain she wouldn't be able to sleep for a long while yet.

Enid was disappointed to step out onto the patio and realize how terribly stormy the weather had become. Even as bundled up as she was, the wind was throwing around a combination of rain and snow that was far too brutal. She closed the door and removed her outdoor clothing, settling for a brisk walk through the long hallways of Thornewell Hall while she mentally dug for the roots beneath her weeds of anger. She lost track of the time she'd spent walking, but felt suddenly tired despite her nap. It was as if all that was going on in her mind was as exhausting as scrubbing floors and washing linens all day. She headed toward the library, just wanting a place to sit comfortably and relax until she felt ready to go to bed.

Still holding the lamp that she'd been carrying throughout her walk, Enid opened the door to the library, surprised to find the room lit by a blazing fire. She closed the door and set down the lamp, instinctively moving toward the fire to ward off the subtle chill of winter that was almost continually present in the house. It wasn't until she was enjoying the fire's warmth that it occurred to her a fire wouldn't have been lit in the room unless someone had been here. And the only other person in the house who would be allowed to take such liberties in the library was . . .

"You're welcome," Sebastian said from behind Enid and she turned, more startled than she should have been, given that she'd just figured out he was likely in the room.

"For what?" she asked, wondering if she should hurry and leave in order to continue avoiding him in every possible way, or if she should take advantage of the opportunity to say some things that had been swimming in her head for weeks. She knew she could never make peace with the situation until she said the words to him that needed to be voiced. But she wasn't sure she wanted to do that *now*.

Enid heard him sigh loudly, but she could barely make out his form sitting across the room, leaning back in an overstuffed chair, his booted ankles stacked on the low table in front of him. "For lighting the fire," he said. "I hadn't predicted you would come here in need of warmth, but since you have . . . I'm glad the fire has benefitted us both."

"Indeed," she said and felt her anger toward him rising despite all her efforts to keep it in check. *What are the roots?* she asked herself over and over, but considering the emotions beneath the anger only made her angrier. Deciding now was *not* a good time to try and express her feelings, Enid hurried toward the door, setting her eyes on the direct path there, and planning to pick up the lamp she'd brought with her. She could be out of the room in seconds.

"Now that I'm warmed up," she said, beginning her planned trek to safety, "I'll leave you in peace."

"No need for you to go," he said and shot to his feet almost as fast as he stepped in front of her to prevent her from leaving.

Enid looked up at him, now able to see his face clearly in the firelight. The desire and adoration in his eyes made her stomach flutter and her heart quicken—but it all combined to fuel her anger. She looked down and said firmly, "If I had known you were here I would not have bothered you." She stepped aside to try and go around him, but he moved and blocked her way again.

"Sebastian," she said, sounding far less impatient than she felt, "this is ridiculous. We both know that—"

"You're right," he said, "this *is* ridiculous." Enid felt certain that their individual interpretations regarding the absurdity of the situation likely bore no similarities. "Do you have any idea how it makes me feel to see you . . . *flaunting* yourself about with other men?"

"Flaunting?" she echoed, glaring at him, her tone incredulous. "I have never *flaunted* myself in any way around *anyone*. My desire to engage myself socially is absolutely none of your business."

"I don't know how you can look me in the eye and even say that your becoming involved with another man is none of my business."

"I am not *involved* with anyone," she said. "If you would bother to ask me about my feelings regarding the situation, as opposed to simply making assumptions which you then construe to be fact, you wouldn't be making such a fool of yourself."

Enid inhaled sharply when he took hold of her chin and kissed her before she had a chance to realize he'd intended to. "You make a fool of me, Enid," he whispered.

Enid turned her face away, hating the way his kiss affected her when she felt so angry with him. "Don't try to blame me for your foolishness, Sebastian. You've done that all on your own." She took a deep breath before she added, "And *don't* kiss me when you—"

Sebastian took hold of her chin again, forcing her to face him, completely ignoring what she'd just said by kissing her again, more passionately this time.

"No!" Enid managed to say and attempted again to move around him, but he blocked her way and kissed her yet again. She recalled vividly one of her mother's most important teachings; she'd often told her daughters that a woman should *never* allow a man to have power over her, physically or otherwise. Enid had struggled over that principle in her marriage when it came to lines that were often blurry and subtle. But there was nothing subtle about Sebastian's current behavior, and Enid wouldn't stand for it. She'd given him fair warning, which he had ignored. Amid his attempt to kiss her again, Enid slapped him hard across the face. He took a teetering step backward and pressed his hand over his face where she felt certain she'd inflicted a sharp sting.

Enid's anger bubbled up and grew more difficult to control, fueled as it was by the astonishment on Sebastian's face, as if he had no idea why she would have needed to take such drastic measures to snap him out of his atrocious behavior.

"Your arrogance is appalling!" she said, pushing against his chest with both hands, which forced him to take a few more steps backward, putting more distance between them. "Kissing a woman—or demonstrating any other form of affection—without her permission is completely inappropriate and unacceptable—and you should know that."

"But you *wanted* me to kiss you," he said as if it were a fact.

"So, you can read my mind?" she countered hotly. "Is that what you interpreted from my clearly using the word *no*? No means no, Sebastian. I will not be subjected to your confusion and contradictions. I'm not some toy for you to play with when you feel lonely or unhappy."

"And I never thought that you were," he said, sounding defensive. "I know how you feel about me, Enid. I know you love me and I love you."

Enid hated this conversation, but she was determined to be honest and say what needed to be said—and to get through it as quickly as possible. She took a deep breath and said, "I cannot deny my feelings for you, Sebastian, nor my attraction." She hated hearing the quaver in her own voice, but perhaps he needed to see the evidence of how difficult this was for her. She drew courage enough to look him directly in the eye. He needed to know she was serious. "However, neither of us are naive enough to think that love or attraction is ever enough to sustain the kind of relationship that you keep implying you want to share with me. No gentleman would share such affection with a lady and assume it was given without implications of courting and marriage. If your affection has been given to me without such expectations, then you are even less of a gentleman than I've assumed you to be. But don't think for one moment, Sebastian, that I can live with the underlying hatred you feel toward me, and—"

"Hatred?" he echoed, aghast. "Enid, I do not hate you or—"

"You blame me for Alistair's death!" Enid countered, surprised at the anger in her own voice. She'd been aware of the anger she'd felt, but it wasn't like her to express it so vehemently. But perhaps that was the only way to say what she needed to say. "You've made it repeatedly clear you will *never* forgive me, when I cannot come up with a single reason why I need forgiveness from you or anyone else. If you were even slightly interested in hearing about *my* life beyond my time living *here*, you might realize just how judgmental and brutally arrogant your attitudes toward me are. But you have also made it clear that you have no interest in hearing my side of the story." Enid took a step toward him and he stepped back, as if he might be afraid she would slap him again. "You tell me you love me, but you know *nothing* about me. *Nothing!* Love is not just a feeling, Sebastian. Love is comprised of trust and respect and commitment. You were raised with Christian beliefs, and yet I wonder if you have any idea how your prejudicial behavior so harshly contradicts them." She heard him gasp and realized that he felt truly insulted to be told he was not behaving like a Christian. She hoped that meant she sincerely had his attention, because she wasn't finished yet. She'd wanted to say these things to him for months now, and she wasn't going to leave this room until she'd said it all. "Perhaps," she went on, "it would serve you well to study the teachings of Jesus—if indeed you claim to be someone who follows His example in the way you live." She moved her face closer to his and the words that had been circling in her head since the day he'd broken her heart came tumbling out of her mouth. "'Oh, thou hypocrite! Judge not and ye shall not be judged! Charity rejoiceth not in iniquity, but rejoiceth in the truth!'"

Enid took a deep breath, noting that Sebastian looked stunned and overcome. But that's exactly how she wanted him to feel. She hoped that what she was saying might penetrate the walls of pride and arrogance with which he'd surrounded himself. In conclusion, she declared firmly, "You know nothing about me, Sebastian. How can you claim to love a woman when you don't even know where or how she grew up? Or anything about her family? You know nothing of what I experienced in Africa, or through my journey home. And you don't know your brother nearly as well as you'd like to think you do." Her voice became heated and tears stung her eyes as that quaver in her voice deepened. "I watched him die, Sebastian, and you have *never* asked me *anything* about the reasons. Do you have any idea of why he went to Africa? And why his own choices resulted in his death? No!" she answered for him. "You do not! If you want to keep him on some kind of pedestal of perfection in your memory, you need to make everything you didn't like about him and his choices *my* fault, and you don't even care to know the truth."

Enid inhaled a calming breath and exhaled slowly, feeling more at peace for having at long last let go of things she'd known he needed to be told. It was up to him what he did with the information; she had done all she could do, and she had a clear conscience.

"You can hate me if you must, Sebastian; if it helps you to feel better, then hate me. So be it. But don't be thinking that you can love me and at the same time hold such contempt for me in your heart—a contempt that would eventually destroy any feelings of love. And don't be thinking that I will ever again be foolish enough to give you or any man so much as a kiss without knowing beyond any doubt that any demonstration of affection or any declaration of love comes with absolute trust and respect."

Enid couldn't think of anything else to say, and Sebastian looked as if she had slapped him multiple times. She felt relief in being free of the thoughts and feelings that had haunted her for so long, but she also felt sorry for this man she had grown to love. If he had actually heard what she'd just said, if he took it to heart, perhaps there was some hope of them sharing a future. But she couldn't wait for that or expect it. The matter was out of her hands. After giving him a good, long stare that she hoped would give the message an added emphasis, Enid picked up the lamp and left the room. By the time she got to the stairs she was feeling sorry for *herself*. She loved him, and he'd broken her heart. He'd made it impossible for her to love anyone else, and at this moment, she hated him for it. She reminded herself that feeling hateful would only hurt herself, and she needed to work on coming to terms with that; she needed to forgive him and not judge his actions, lest she become a hypocrite as well. If nothing else, she didn't want any form of her behavior—or even her thoughts and feelings—to have any similarity to those that Sebastian had exhibited, and which had caused her so much grief. Now, more than ever before in her life, she knew she needed to not just act like, but to truly *be* a Christian woman.

* * * * *

Enid slept little that night. It was as if the memories of her tumultuous relationship with Sebastian kept invading her dreams, startling her awake. Tempted toward anger, she had to keep reminding herself that she'd come to recognize the roots beneath that nasty, angry weed inside herself. She'd sorted through the complex emotions at the heart of all she felt, and had concluded that she could now sum everything up into one sad but simple root: sorrow. Identifying just how deep the root of sadness went, and how it had wound its way around and around within the soil of her thoughts and feelings, Enid could only resign herself to a need to grieve. She had loved Sebastian, and she had lost him. In many ways, Alistair's death felt easier to cope with. As difficult and horrible as it had been, death had taken him irrevocably away from her, and it was a facet of life that the brain was able to comprehend. But Sebastian lived under the same roof, and yet he was as unreachable as his deceased brother.

Enid prayed and cried herself to sleep numerous times, only to be awakened again and again because of strange dreams. When the light of dawn began to fill the room, she accepted that it wasn't likely she would be able to go back to sleep. She'd fed Sarah once in the night, and she knew that the baby was likely to wake up again soon according to her usual pattern. While Enid looked toward the window where the sunlight was slowly becoming brighter, she felt a distinct impression that if she truly had compassion for Sebastian, she needed to help him find his way past whatever might be at the root of *his* anger. Now that she'd thoroughly examined her own roots, she found herself somewhat amazed at how she was able to turn the situation around and consider that there surely had to be painful roots inside of

Sebastian, things she simply didn't know about or understand. Suddenly she could see that his confusing behavior clearly had to be the result of his own confusion. Considering how much effort it had taken her to get to the roots of her own anger, she could understand how Sebastian might simply feel trapped in confusion and not know how to find his way out. Looking at it that way made it easier for her to feel forgiveness for his bad behavior, to feel more concerned about him than upset with him. She didn't know if it might ever be possible for them to be together the way she would prefer, but she did know that she wished him no ill will and she wanted him to be happy.

Sarah woke up and Enid changed her nappy before she leaned against the headboard to feed her. Tilly arrived right on schedule with a bottle of warm milk from the kitchen. From her own room, Tilly was keenly tuned to hearing Sarah cry and knowing when she was needed.

"Good morning," Enid said.

"Good morning," Tilly replied.

"Please sit down and be my friend," Enid implored. "I need your insight very much, I think."

"Talk to me, Enid," Tilly said, sitting close by.

Enid gave Tilly a summary of all that had happened since they'd last talked, and all that Enid had been thinking and feeling. They fed and burped Sarah while they talked, then laid her on the bed where she made happy noises as the conversation continued. When Enid had said all there was to say, Tilly smiled at her and took her hand. "You are far wiser than you think you are, my friend. If you're feeling that there is something you need to do to help him, then you must figure out what that might be and do it."

"But I have no idea," Enid said, somehow hoping that Tilly would simply spew forth an answer to her dilemma.

"If you know that you need to do something," Tilly said, "then I'm certain that more prayer and thought on the matter will illuminate in your mind exactly what you need to do. Just give it some time. You've made good progress already, and dare I say . . . you're feeling much better?"

"I am, yes," Enid said, hearing the sadness in her own voice. "Or at least . . . I don't feel angry anymore."

"And the rest of what you're feeling will be healed with time," Tilly said.

Enid nodded toward her friend, certain that was true. But she didn't want to heal from a broken heart; she wanted Sebastian to be able to acknowledge the true source of the estrangement between them so they could be together.

But perhaps that was just too much to hope for, and it was certainly beyond her control.

Chapter Twelve

TURMOIL

"MAY I SAY SOMETHING THAT'S been on my mind regarding all of this?" Tilly asked.

"Of course," Enid said. "You don't need my permission to say whatever you like when it's just you and me."

Tilly smiled, and her eyes took on a faraway look that Enid had learned often came with thoughts of Tilly's mother, and she wasn't surprised when Tilly said, "It's one of my mother's pieces of wisdom that I recalled after we talked last." She focused more on Enid and said, "She used to say that it would be a crime for a person to be unhappy or unfulfilled simply because of poor communication." Tilly tipped her head to the side. "She stressed very strongly in our home that most problems in the world could be solved by simply speaking the truth and knowing that what you speak will be heard and respected."

Enid thought about that for a long moment. "Do you really believe that? It sounds far too simple a principle to actually be able to solve *most* problems in the world."

"Simple perhaps, but not easy," Tilly said, and Enid felt sure that too was another of her mother's adages. "Obviously we only have control over our own ability to communicate our thoughts and feelings appropriately, and it's something we have to learn. It also most often means overcoming a great deal of fear to be able to speak the deepest feelings of our hearts—especially when we don't know how they will be received." Tilly leaned forward just slightly, as if to imply that what she was about to say had great importance; Enid prepared herself to hear the point that Tilly had been working toward expressing. "Perhaps you should consider the possibility that Sebastian's anger and arrogance are rooted in his own broken heart. You have said he knows nothing of your relationship with his brother, and nothing of you or your upbringing. But is the same not true the other way around? Perhaps if you can help him come to see the truth from your perspective, he might be more willing to open up and show you the truth from *his* perspective."

Enid replied too quickly and perhaps defensively. "He's made it clear he doesn't *want* to hear my side of the story. That is the very thing that makes it impossible to get past this barrier. He would only have to give me some indication that he was willing to hear what I have to say, and I would gladly tell him everything."

"If getting to the truth through conversation isn't working, then you must figure out another way to help him see and understand your perspective."

"Like what?" Enid asked, sounding even more defensive. She softened her voice and added, "I'm sorry. My frustration is not toward you. I truly appreciate your insights, Tilly, and your wisdom continues to amaze me. I suppose I am afraid to tell him certain things when he's been so . . . difficult," she said in lieu of other more derogatory words that came to mind; she was trying to think and speak of him more kindly.

"And how do you think he would respond if you respectfully asked him to simply listen to what you had to say; if you ignored his edict instead of being angry over it."

Enid took that in with a long, deep breath that filled her lungs completely before she blew the air out slowly through her mouth, closing her eyes as if that might help her more fully absorb the possibility that she'd been so focused on how badly Sebastian had handled his feelings toward her regarding Alistair's death, that she'd not stopped to rethink how she had responded to his attitude, which had perhaps only added fuel to the fire rather than extinguishing it.

Sarah became fussy with a restlessness that had become more prominent of late. She was becoming more aware of the world around her and she wanted to be entertained. She wanted something new to look at or to have people talk to her and make funny noises—something that her cousins were very good at. Tilly stood and picked up the baby, saying, "I'll take her to play with the boys and look after her. I'm certain you'll figure out what you need to do. As long as you know you've done everything you can, then you can put the matter to rest no matter how he responds."

"I appreciate your confidence in me," Enid said with light sarcasm. The two women exchanged a wan smile, and Tilly left the room with Sarah.

Enid slithered back beneath the covers and even pulled them over her head, wishing it could be possible to just slink away and hide from this conundrum that in some ways seemed so simple to solve, but in reality, felt tantamount to moving a mountain. The thought popped into her mind that with faith, mountains could be moved, and she threw the covers off her face to look up at the ceiling, silently asking God to help her know what she could do to solve this problem. After several minutes of vacillating between prayer and deep thought, it occurred to Enid that big problems didn't necessarily get solved all at once; there likely wasn't one grand gesture she could make that might create an irreparable shift in the chasm between her and Sebastian. So she altered her prayer to ask for just one thing she could do, one step she could take, that might help solve this problem—even if it could only be solved in tiny increments.

Still feeling confused about what she might be able to do, Enid got out of bed and prepared herself for the day. Her time with the children completely distracted her from her dilemma, then after lunch she returned to her room to feed the baby and put her down for a nap, hoping for a nap herself, given her recent lack of sleep. But she had barely gotten Sarah to sleep when a maid came to inform her that the colonel had come to visit and had been left to wait in the drawing room. Enid felt completely taken off guard. She knew it would have been all right if she sent word back with the maid that she was unable to receive his visit at this time—especially given that he'd come without sending word ahead. But she also knew that she needed to speak with him and clarify her view of their relationship, and if she let this opportunity slip by she would only continue to dread the prospect of the conversation. Given how caught up she'd been with thoughts of trying to solve the problems with Sebastian, she'd overlooked trying to mentally prepare herself on how to go about appropriately speaking her mind to the colonel.

Having told the maid that she would be down to see the colonel shortly, Enid freshened up and checked her appearance in the mirror while she silently prayed for the right words and the proper frame of mind. She sat down on the edge of her bed to review her prior conversations with the colonel, and her assessment of his fine qualities. She wondered for a moment if she was seeing the situation backwards. Perhaps she would be far better off to encourage the colonel's interest in her with the probability that she could marry a fine man, move away from here, and never have to deal with Sebastian again. The possibility seemed practical in that moment, and it offered the solution to some problems she didn't want to face. But she immediately thought of how leaving this house meant leaving the boys, and the idea of not seeing them every day felt impossible. Then her mind went—almost against her will—to Sebastian, most specifically their interaction in the library the previous evening. Now that she'd gotten past the anger he'd incited in her with his appalling behavior, she was suddenly overtaken with a vivid memory of how it felt to be in his arms and have him kiss her. A quiver of excitement and joy went from the top of her head all the way to her toes and back again. How could she possibly ignore such feelings and believe that she could forget him and be truly happy?

Reminding herself that the colonel was waiting, Enid pushed away every thought except the need to have a straightforward conversation with this kind man. As she hurried down the stairs, she uttered another prayer for assistance and attempted to gather all her dignity and decorum, determined to be kind and appropriate, and secretly hoping they could remain as friends, for he truly was enjoyable company.

"Colonel Whitaker," she said as she stepped into the room. "What a lovely surprise!"

He rose from where he'd been sitting and kissed her outstretched hand while he bowed slightly as he'd done on their previous meetings. "I hope I didn't call at an inconvenient time," he said, reluctantly letting go of her hand. "I did very much want to see you . . . especially after I made such a hasty exit yesterday. I didn't want you to misread my intentions, and I thought it prudent that we have a frank conversation. I hope I'm not being too presumptuous to make such a request."

Enid felt evidence of her prayers being answered when it almost seemed as if the colonel's thoughts had been in the same vein as hers—although she doubted that clarifying their intentions would turn out the way he might hope. Still, this was a good start, and it was easy for her to be seated and say, "I agree that we should talk." She motioned for him to sit back down while she glanced at the doors of the room to be certain all of them were closed so their conversation wouldn't be overheard. She wasn't entirely surprised that the colonel chose to sit right next to her, but the gesture put her more on edge.

Through a long moment of strained silence, Enid began to feel mildly nervous. The colonel had been the one to declare the need for a conversation; therefore, she expected him to initiate it now that they were together and alone. She tried to avoid looking directly at him while she waited to hear what he might say, and she tried to figure how she would be able to make her own desires clear and not hurt him, given his obvious personal interest in her.

"May I speak candidly?" he asked, surprising her by the way he took her hand into his. He turned slightly on the sofa to look at her more directly, and she felt compelled to offer him the respect of returning his gaze. It was evident that what he intended to say was important to him, and she owed him the respect that she hoped to receive in return, given what could prove to be a very difficult conversation.

"Of course," she said and meant it. "I believe we should both be completely truthful with each other. Anything less could surely become the source of unnecessary difficulty."

"My thoughts exactly," he said and smiled, but it was a sad smile.

"I've enjoyed every moment I've spent with you, Mrs. Hawthorne," he said, and her heart quickened as she anticipated a declaration of his desire to officially court her, or for their relationship to hold some hope or expectation for a future together. And she would have to decline and tell him the truth of her feelings.

"And I with you," she said, knowing it was the truth, but hoping that her saying so wouldn't make this more difficult.

"However," he said and looked down. With that one word, Enid was surprised, realizing that what she'd imagined he might say would not have begun with *however*. She waited impatiently for him to continue, sincerely wanting to have this over with. But until she heard what he had to say, she couldn't speak her own thoughts. "However," he repeated and cleared his throat, "it's become readily evident to me that your heart lies elsewhere." While Enid was trying to absorb exactly what he meant, he looked up at her with undeniable sadness in his eyes and added, "Given how short a time we've known each other, I keep telling myself that I shouldn't feel any sorrow to accept that pursuing any notions of a future with you would be futile, but I confess that I do feel regret. Yet, it is not in me, my dear Mrs. Hawthorne, to try and convince you that I am a more appropriate suitor of your heart. You must follow *your* heart, and I must do as any gentleman would do and graciously bow out and not create any further complications in your life."

Enid felt immensely disoriented as her mind swirled with confusion. She looked at the floor while she attempted to sort out everything he'd just said and try to understand what exactly would have brought him to such conclusions. Her relief at not having to find a way to halt this relationship was overshadowed by her confusion over his declaration. Realizing she would never understand without further clarification, she looked back up at him and simply said, "I don't understand, Colonel. I must confess I was prepared to tell you that while I very much enjoy your company and you've been so very kind to me, I don't have feelings for you that would justify pursuing anything between us beyond friendship. I've been concerned about not wanting to disappoint you, but I certainly did not want to lead you on in any way; that would be terribly unkind. Still, perhaps I am being presumptuous in thinking that you had any feelings for me that would—"

"You are not presumptuous in that," he interjected, and Enid caught a glimpse of something in his eyes that made her look away. He was in love with her, and yet before she had even been able to express her feelings on the matter, he had declared that any notions of their sharing a future would be futile, and he intended to graciously bow out of her life to avoid causing any complications.

"Then I must ask your forgiveness," she said, even though she still felt confused over his motivations.

"There is nothing to forgive," he insisted. "You've been nothing but kind and honest with me. And perhaps you do not fully realize what might be obvious to others. I've come to learn that such can often be the case."

"I still don't understand, Colonel," Enid said. "What is it that is so obvious to you that I might not realize?" As soon as she asked the question, Enid's stomach tightened; she knew now to what he was referring, and her first impulse was to feel angry. But Tilly's wisdom quickly reminded her that anger had other roots, and even if she didn't have time right now to analyze exactly what those might be, she had willpower to suppress her anger and appropriately finish this conversation.

"It is quite clear to me, Mrs. Hawthorne, that you are very much in love with the earl—and he with you."

Enid looked away abruptly, feeling as if the air in her lungs had suddenly become trapped, and she could neither breathe in nor out. Hearing it voiced that way by someone who had only observed her interaction with Sebastian for a very short while left her stunned. She finally found the ability to take a breath and she hurried to say, "The earl does little but infuriate me, Colonel." She heard him chuckle softly, but she didn't feel like he was laughing at her in any way; perhaps more accurately he was mildly amused by her own obliviousness to her feelings for Sebastian that ran much deeper than her fury. The truth was, she knew exactly how she felt about him, and their relationship was complicated at the very least. Given the fact that she knew the truth—and the colonel had clearly seen it—she knew it would only be right for her to admit that his observations had merit. "However," she added, "I cannot deny that whatever you might have picked up on yesterday between myself and the earl is certainly . . . complex. Truthfully, I was angry over his intrusion upon our time together."

"Yes, that was evident," the colonel said, avoiding her gaze. "However, the reasons underlying your apparent frustrations with each other seemed readily evident."

"I confess that I underestimated your perception, Colonel; I'm not certain that most people would have been so discerning."

He chuckled again without any sign of humor. "I've been told as much many times; I'm not certain if it's a gift or a curse." He took a deep breath and turned to look at her, at the same time drawing his shoulders back as if he were gathering courage. "However, the only thing that matters right now, Mrs. Hawthorne, is that I must—in good conscience—gracefully distance myself from your life. I cannot deny that I feel disappointed, but dragging this out would very likely only make the situation more difficult for both of us. I want you to know that I wish you every happiness. Perhaps . . . with the passing of time . . . if we find ourselves still unattached . . . and our paths cross . . . something good might evolve. But for now, I believe it's best to accept this as the best course."

Enid took a long moment to absorb how easy he had made it for her to be able to unburden herself of all she'd needed to communicate to him. She finally sighed and said, "Your kindness and insights are appreciated more than I can say, Colonel. More than anything, I admit that at this point in my life I am mostly confused, and I suppose . . . I'm trying to find my bearings given all that has brought me to this time . . . and these circumstances." She tightened her hand in his and stated with all the firm resolve that she felt, "You are such a good man, Colonel. Even with our brief acquaintance you have refreshed something in me that had become parched. I thank you for your kindness and your company, and I too wish you every possible happiness."

He smiled in a way that was more genuine; his relief in having had this conversation was evident, but no more so than the hint of sadness in his eyes. "You are truly precious, Mrs. Hawthorne," he said and lifted her hand to his lips to kiss it, rising to his feet the moment his lips parted from her fingers. "I hope we might one day again encounter one another. As for now, I bid you good day."

"Thank you," Enid said, remaining seated, overcome with a strange weakness. "And the same to you." She watched him leave the room and sat there for a long while reviewing their conversation with all its implications. She felt sadness at the realization she would likely never see the colonel again, or if she did cross his path in the future, she knew she could never love him the way he deserved to be loved. She'd enjoyed his company, and now he was gone from her life as quickly as he'd entered it.

Enid's thoughts turned to Sebastian and her ongoing desire to figure out how she could help smooth over the situation between them—or at the very least help Sebastian come to terms with whatever might be the source of his often-unreasonable behavior. While she was beginning to think that she might never get any insight into what she might do, an idea appeared in her mind seemingly out of nowhere. The thought of it made her uneasy for several reasons and she stood up to pace the room to release some of her sudden nervousness. While she walked, she prayed and thought through all the possible positive or negative results of her taking such a step. She'd considered this idea months ago when Sebastian had first declared his belief that it had been her influence in Alistair's life that had led him to make decisions he'd disagreed with. And at the time she had immediately believed it would do more harm than good; but perhaps the timing had just been wrong. Perhaps now it was the right answer.

She finally concluded that she could not possibly predict the outcome, but she felt instinctively confident about taking this step. Enid hurried upstairs where she first checked on Sarah to find her still sleeping, with Tilly nearby. Enid told Tilly there was something she needed to take care of, then she went to her room where she got down on her knees at the side of the bed where Alistair had once slept. She reached beneath it and pulled out a small chest, which had been crafted to look like a very small version of a trunk used for traveling. She blew the dust off the top and opened it, taking a deep breath as Alistair's life and the tragedy of his death seemed to pass through her mind all at once. With fresh determination she closed the chest and went in search of Sebastian.

* * * * *

Sebastian left his sons in Gert's capable hands for their afternoon lessons and went to his sitting room where he made himself comfortable with the intention of reading from a novel he'd been trying for days to become engaged with. But he just couldn't get past the first chapter, and he found himself reading the same paragraphs repeatedly without retaining their meaning. Most often he ended up with the book open on his lap while he just looked out the window or gazed at the wall, as if doing so might help him find some obscure, unexpected answer to the dilemmas in his life. He was startled by a knock at the door; assuming it was one of the servants, he absently called, "Come in."

He heard the door open—and then nothing. He turned to see Enid standing in the doorway, holding a box of some sort. "What are you doing here?" he asked, wishing immediately that he hadn't sounded so snippy, especially when he was truly happy to see her. He desperately wanted her to let go of the circumstances of the past over which they didn't agree so they could move forward together in their lives. But her ongoing stubbornness over the matter had left him nothing but frustrated and confused.

"There's something I believe you need to see," she said, stepping farther into the room. "May I sit down?"

"Of course," he said, motioning with his hand toward the other end of the sofa on which he sat.

"I must confess that I considered showing these to you soon after I'd returned from Africa, but my concern was that it might be difficult for you, and so I didn't."

"What on earth are you talking about, Enid?" he said, noting the small chest that she set on the sofa between them. She opened it and he could see that it contained a row of leather-bound books with nothing imprinted on the spines, which were all facing upward. The set of books almost filled the box; there was likely room for only a couple more. But he felt confused.

"These are Alistair's journals," she said, and he suddenly felt very afraid of what he was looking at and the potential of what might be written there. "Did you know that he kept a journal?"

"I did not," he admitted.

"He began the habit soon after his eighteenth birthday when a friend gave him a journal as a gift. He found it satisfying and felt that it was important for him to record the significant events of his life for his own benefit, and to leave something of himself behind for his posterity. His writings are not lengthy or necessarily consistent. Sometimes he'd go days or even weeks without writing a word, and then he'd fill many pages. This box was left here when we went to Africa, so all these, except the last one, were written prior to that time. He didn't write much while we were there; he was far too busy with other things. I brought his one final journal home with me and added it to the box."

Sebastian glanced at Enid, then back at the row of books. He had to ask, "And you've read them all?"

Enid felt like the question sounded accusatory, as if her doing so might have been an invasion of privacy toward his brother. Realizing she needed to take his words at their value and not read something into them that might or might not be there, she simply said, "I have. He shared passages from them with me occasionally, and never gave me any indication that they held anything he didn't want me to read. More than once he told me that after his death they would perhaps help his children understand him in ways he might have found difficult to explain to them. Of course, when he said such things, I'm certain he believed he'd live a long life and there would be many more volumes." Sebastian heard her take in a ragged breath and he realized this was difficult for her. "After I returned here following his death, I read them all in order. I found nothing in them that I didn't already know. I believe they helped me come to terms with his death, and I'm glad that Sarah will one day be able to have these as a record of her father." She took another lengthy, strained breath. "You are his brother, his nearest blood relative besides my daughter. You should read what he felt about his own life, the things that he considered important enough to write down. Forgive me for being so slow to put them into your hands." She rose abruptly to her feet. "Take all the time you need, and just . . . get them back to me when you're done. I'll give them to Sarah when she's old enough."

Enid headed quickly toward the door, as if she couldn't get away fast enough. Sebastian felt rather disarmed by her unexpected visit—and the record of his brother's life that she'd brought with her. Despite a certain trepidation over reading what his brother had written, he still felt the need to say, "Thank you, Enid."

She paused only long enough to say, "Of course," before she left him alone with what felt like his brother's ghost.

Sebastian stared at the row of books for many minutes, asking himself why he felt so afraid to read what his brother had written about his life. Arguments between them from many years ago crept from the hidden places in his mind to the forefront where he could not even force himself to ignore them. He and Alistair had always been dramatically different in their personalities, their goals, their perspectives. They had gone through a phase of stark disagreement that had put an immense strain on their relationship, but then they had settled the differences between them, and they'd become very close. Sebastian had fond memories of the years they'd spent living under the same roof while Sebastian had mostly run the estate that had been left to him by their father, and Alistair had been helpful and supportive. Even after Sebastian had married and Marie had become a part of the family, he had remained close to Alistair and they had continued to work together. And then Alistair had met Enid, and everything had changed. Observing the changes in Alistair, Sebastian had been opposed to his brother's plans to marry her after having known her a rather short time. While he'd tried to remain supportive of his brother's decisions, Sebastian had always felt that Enid had changed his brother, and therefore she had come between them. Sebastian had just begun to feel comfortable around his brother's wife, and accepting of the situation, when Alistair announced that they would be going to Africa as missionaries. Alistair had mentioned this idea only once years earlier, and he and Sebastian had argued over it. Sebastian believed it was a fool's errand and destined for disaster; he believed there were plenty of struggling people right here in England who could benefit from his brother's desire to devote his life to doing good and serving those in need. And Alistair had never brought it up again—until a few months after he'd married Enid, a woman who had been suspiciously secretive about her upbringing or family. Sebastian had felt leery and uncomfortable over that fact. It had never made sense to him why her family would have cut her off completely when she had married Alistair. He was a good man with the ability to provide well for a wife and children and give them a good life. What kind of people would snub their noses so boldly over such a match?

All these things combined had left Sebastian with a general dislike for Enid, and he was never comfortable with her influence on his brother. And then he and Enid had ended up here together, both alone and grieving over the loss of their spouses. He'd never expected to fall in love with her, but he had. And he loved her so much that this chasm between them created an almost tangible pain in the center of his chest that had become nearly constant. She had told him he knew nothing about her and he'd never bothered to ask. He couldn't deny that was true. She had told him he didn't know his brother as well as he thought he did. The idea left him unsettled, but instinctively he believed she was probably right. He didn't know what he was going to read in his brother's journals, but he felt wary—even frightened—to find out.

As Sebastian finally gathered the courage to reach for the first book, he recalled vividly how he'd told Enid soon after her return here that he blamed her for Alistair's death, he would never forgive her, and that he had no interest in hearing her try to defend herself. He knew that was the greatest source of her anger toward him, and the reason she'd put distance between them and a firm halt to their romantic relationship. He'd convinced himself that he had been completely justified in his opinions, and she had just needed to accept them and not be so upset about it. He'd chosen to ignore every inkling of the possibility that he might be wrong. And now he had a feeling that he might have been *terribly* wrong, and before him was the proof. He would never know until he actually read what his brother had written.

Sebastian took a deep breath and opened the first volume. He immediately recognized his brother's handwriting and once again had the sensation that he was facing Alistair's ghost. It was as if they were about to have a conversation; Alistair was about to tell Sebastian the deepest feelings of his heart, and Sebastian could imagine him saying, *Just open your heart and hear what I have to say before you pass any judgment.* Is that what Sebastian had done? Passed judgment again his brother? Against his brother's wife? The very idea left him a little queasy—mostly because he realized it was likely true.

Sebastian noted the date and mentally counted the years in his mind; just as Enid had said, this would have been soon after Alistair's eighteenth birthday. Alistair began by simply declaring his desire to keep a journal, since a good friend of his had always done so and had found it a positive practice for many reasons. He wrote that he liked the idea of having a place to record his thoughts and feelings where he could be completely honest and not upset anyone else by having his beliefs conflict with those of the people he loved. Sebastian felt mildly uneasy over that statement and had to read it over a few times while memories of some of his arguments with Alistair—preceding the date when he'd written this—came back to haunt him. Pushing that thought away for now, Sebastian just kept reading.

Not even halfway through the first journal, Sebastian was finding it difficult to even breathe normally, while Enid's voice pounded through his head. *You don't know your brother nearly as well as you think you do.* From Alistair's own words, speaking to him from beyond the grave, Enid had already proven that statement to be absolutely true.

At one point, Sebastian slammed the book closed before he threw it at the wall. When that didn't begin to release his growing turmoil of emotions, he erupted to his feet and began pacing frantically as everything he'd believed for years collided with the reality that he had been horribly wrong in so many ways.

Sebastian was startled from his silent tirade by a knock at the door. He glanced at the clock while he gathered his composure, realizing he'd lost track of the time.

"Come in," he called, sitting down first.

Maisy entered, and he wasn't surprised to hear her say, "Forgive me, m'lord, but you missed supper and the boys asked me to make certain you're all right."

Sebastian knew he was in no condition to spend time with his sons and be able to pretend that everything was fine. Grateful to have someone who could make certain they were cared for, he said, "Truthfully, I'm not feeling very well. Could you give them my apologies and tell them I'll spend some time with them as soon as I'm feeling better?"

"Of course," she said, her expression showing concern. "Should I send for a doctor, sir?"

"No need for that," he said. "I'm certain it's a just a little cold or something," he lied, "but I don't want to give it to the children."

"Of course," she said again. "I'll alert Mrs. Thorpe and have some supper sent up for you."

"Thank you," Sebastian said.

"Is there anything else you need?" she asked.

"No, thank you, Maisy," he said. "Tell the boys I love them. Give them a kiss for me."

"Of course," she said yet again, but this time with a smile.

After she left the room, Sebastian realized that he actually *did* feel ill. He knew it wasn't a cold, and it wasn't contagious, but he didn't want *anyone* around while he attempted to come to terms with what he was just beginning to learn about his brother. Considering his ruse of being ill, Sebastian picked up the book he'd thrown—along with the box containing the other journals—and took them to his bedroom. He slid the box beneath his bed and removed his boots and waistcoat before he slid beneath the covers and made himself comfortable, leaning his back on some pillows stacked against the headboard.

Mrs. Thorpe herself brought his supper, and repeated all the questions Maisy had asked him. He had to be especially insistent with this woman who had always felt responsible for him in a maternal way. She finally left him alone to eat his supper after he promised to ring if he needed anything at all. Sebastian felt hungry and the food smelled good, but he was only able to eat about half of his meal due to a growing smoldering in his stomach. Knowing he could eat nothing more, and knowing he needed to keep reading even if he didn't necessarily want to, Sebastian picked up the journal again and continued turning pages, taken back in time with the way that Alistair wrote of incidents of the past that he'd been involved in or affected by. Some of what his brother had written evoked pleasant memories of good times they'd shared, and some of his words lured Sebastian more and more toward a place that felt distinctly uncomfortable and disorienting. He turned up the wick on the lamp so that it would give him more light as his eyes became tired. He finished the first journal and pulled out the box to retrieve the second. He read that one and got more than halfway through the third before he finally couldn't keep his eyes open any longer. After extinguishing the lamp, he lay in the darkness for a long while before he was able to relax, wondering why his brother had kept so much of himself hidden. Sebastian asked himself if he might have inadvertently done or said something to incite his brother to be so private about his most personal feelings. As soon as he had gathered the courage to ask himself such a question, from somewhere deep inside himself he knew the answer. But he had no idea how he would ever come to terms with it. Preoccupied by the possibility of where this journey with his brother's writing might take him, Sebastian finally slept, haunted by strange dreams and a deep ache over a new level of grieving for his brother's death and the reality that they would never be able to bridge the gaps that had existed between them—far more often than Sebastian had ever imagined.

* * * * *

Enid felt concerned when word came to her that Sebastian was ill and keeping to his room. She suspected that he was feigning illness because he wanted to be left alone, and that was most likely due to her putting Alistair's journals into his hands. She hoped his seclusion was an indication that he was actually reading them. And even though she had no doubt that his doing so would be difficult for him, she still hoped that it would not be *too* difficult. What she wanted most was for him to simply read them so that he could know things she didn't want to have to tell him—as if he would believe her if she did. And then she hoped that they could talk about it; talk about Alistair; talk like mature adults about this man they had both loved and lost.

Enid kept a prayer in her heart for Sebastian and took Sarah with her to play with the boys during the time their father was usually there. She hoped to distract them from his absence, and if he showed up, she would make a gracious exit. But he didn't show up. Throughout the remainder of that day and into the next, Enid kept telling herself that it would take a certain amount of time for him to read through all of Alistair's journals. She knew because she'd read them herself, but she'd done so a little at a time; not from beginning to end in complete seclusion. She also felt certain that Sebastian could very well be upset by some of what he read; he might even feel angry. And he likely didn't want anyone to see any evidence of such emotions. But when two full days had gone by and he hadn't come out of his rooms, Enid began to feel concerned. After a third day had passed, and then a fourth, Enid's concern had grown to a mild panic, which she kept to herself except in private conversation with Tilly, who kept telling her that the earl surely needed time to come to terms with discovering things he'd never known about his brother. Enid couldn't argue with that, but her real fear was based in the memory of her returning here from Africa to discover that he'd been holed up for months, neglecting his sons and leaving his household barely functional. If what he read in Alistair's journals sent him into a similar type of grief, Enid wondered if there was anything she could say or do to bring him out of it. She considered it likely that he might misdirect his anger toward her; that he might still find a way to blame her for all the ways that Alistair had withheld much of himself from his family—specifically his brother when it had just been the two of them for many years.

After five days of Sebastian's absence, the boys' questions about their father's supposed illness became more worrisome. Enid suspected they too might fear his disappearance from their lives, considering that it had happened before. She did her best to reassure them, and to spend as much time with them as she could. When Mrs. Thorpe came to Enid, expressing her own concerns that were very much in line with Enid's thoughts, Enid wondered if she needed to go to Sebastian's room and confront him—or at least remind him that his children needed him, as did the rest of the people who cared about him. She quickly searched her feelings and said to Mrs. Thorpe, "Let's give him another day or two, and if he hasn't come out of hiding, I will try my best to talk with him."

"Very good," Mrs. Thorpe said, seeming relieved to have someone else make a decision that might put an end to this situation.

Chapter Thirteen

THE RECKONING

ANOTHER DAY PASSED AND STILL Sebastian was taking his meals in his room, and he was refusing to see anyone but Mrs. Thorpe or the maids who came and went briefly to see that his needs were met. But they had nothing to report because he'd said nothing beyond thank-you and simple requests, which amounted only to his wanting fresh water for bathing about every other day. Mrs. Thorpe reported that from what was left on the trays that came out of his room he likely didn't have much appetite. Enid could only think that she was at least glad to know he was eating *something*, and he was attending to his personal hygiene.

More than anything, Enid just wanted to go to him and tell him how much she loved him. She wanted to hold him in her arms while he struggled to come to terms with the difficulties of his life, and the losses he'd experienced. But she couldn't cross a boundary Sebastian had put so firmly in place. Could she? Was it possible that he needed her, that perhaps he *wanted* to talk to her, but he was too proud—or just too caught up in his grieving—to know how to cross his own boundaries?

When still another day had passed with no evidence of change, Enid knew she had to keep her promise to Mrs. Thorpe and do her best to try to talk to Sebastian. While Sarah was taking her afternoon nap, Enid went to the library to find some solitude so that she could consider the best possible way to approach him, while she silently prayed for guidance. Her intention had been to go for a walk outside, but it was snowing. She loved the relaxing ambience of the library, and the view from the windows that was so different than the view from her own rooms on the other side of the house. Deeply invested in her thoughts and concerns, she stayed near the fireplace while she looked out a nearby window. The snow had a mesmerizing effect that soothed her nerves, but not necessarily her concerns. The very thought of knocking on Sebastian's door and confronting him made her stomach churn with dread. But if he wasn't going to come out, someone besides the servants had to go in—and she was the only adult in the house who was *not* a servant.

Enid thought about the last time she'd forced herself into his room and confronted him. She'd done it on behalf of the children and the household—and she had the same valid reasons now. But now everything was so much more complicated, given the personal relationship they'd come to share, and the anger they'd felt toward each other. She loved him, and she believed he loved her. But she didn't know how to mend all the troubling issues that stood between them. She needed a miracle, and until she could get past the inner turmoil that kept her from marching up the stairs to face him, all she could do was keep praying for just that—a miracle.

Enid closed her eyes and focused on the noise of the crackling fire. She felt a strange but distinct peace wash over her, as if she were being reassured that all would be well. Completely immersed in her silent respite, she let out a gaspy scream when she heard Sebastian say, "So, *there* you are."

She turned to see him standing there, and she resisted the urge to look heavenward as a gesture of astonishment in response to her prayers for a miracle. Because she'd left the door open, she hadn't heard him come in. It took only a moment to see that he actually *looked* ill. He was pale and perhaps a bit thinner. His eyes looked tired, and his countenance seemed strained. His hair was clean and damp, but he looked somewhat disheveled, as if he'd bathed and put on clean clothes, but hadn't put any effort into finessing his appearance. And he clearly hadn't trimmed his beard during the week while he'd been hiding.

Enid's heart quickened as if to remind her how much she loved him, and how just seeing him made her long to be free of all that stood between them. When the silence between them became taut, Enid said, "Yes, here I am. You were looking for me?"

"Yes, I was," he said and closed the door, implying that he wanted to speak with her and not be overheard.

Enid resisted the urge to hold her breath as he walked across the room to face her. His eyes showed a humility that helped her believe he wasn't angry, and that this wouldn't turn into another tense confrontation. Still, she felt nervous, waiting for him to speak.

"Enid," he finally murmured and took her hand, glancing down at it as he did. He looked directly into her eyes again, and Enid's quickened heartbeat became even faster. She was managing to keep breathing evenly until she saw the sparkle of moisture gather in his eyes at the same moment his bottom lip quivered slightly. "Enid," he repeated, a slight tremor in his voice, "the depth of apology I owe you is beyond my ability to express. I . . . cannot even find the words to begin."

Enid couldn't keep her own voice from trembling as she muttered, "I think what you just said is sufficient."

"No," he insisted, "it's not even *close* to sufficient." He cleared his throat and gathered his composure. "We need to talk about this, Enid; we need to talk about *all* of it. I can see now that I was using anger to keep myself from having to think about—or face up to—my suspicions that my brother had difficult feelings toward me; and perhaps with good reason. Either way, none of that is your fault, and I was wrong—so wrong—to be angry with you, and to blame you for whatever might have been wrong between me and Alistair." He took a deep breath and she realized he was speaking more quickly than usual, as if he'd memorized what he needed to say, and he had to keep going. Enid was so caught up in the evidence of her prayers being answered that she had no trouble remaining silent.

"Come, sit with me," he said, walking backward while he kept hold of her hand. He guided her to one of the sofas and sat down beside her, keeping her hand in his. "It's obviously not necessary for me to repeat anything from Alistair's journals, since you've also read them. We both know how *he* felt, and why he did what he did. I don't need to tell you that reading them—and trying to accept the truth of his feelings and opinions—has been very hard on me. Initially I felt so angry . . . but it didn't take long to realize I could only be angry with myself. I know he's gone . . . and I can't change the past . . . and I know that I need to forgive myself for not being the kind of brother he deserved, but . . ." That tremor returned to his voice, but he took in a deep breath and steadied it. "But I don't think I can forgive myself until I ask for . . . your forgiveness. And then . . . I just have to believe that Alistair will somehow know—wherever he is—how grateful I am that he wrote down so much of himself, which has allowed me to see and understand the truth."

Sebastian let go of her hand and leaned his forearms against his thighs, looking at the floor as he went on. "I remember very clearly the argument I had with Alistair after he'd told me he wanted to go to some faraway land and be a missionary. I told him it was a ludicrous notion, that it was dangerous, and that I needed him here with me to help me manage the estate. I think it was the worst argument we'd ever had; truthfully, we'd never argued that much—which I suppose just makes *this* argument stand out all the more. He kept telling me that he'd wanted to do this for a very long time, but he'd been afraid to tell me, fearing I would react exactly as I did—with anger. The truth that I should have been able to see . . . that I should have told him . . . was simply my fear that something would happen to him; and that I would miss him. I didn't want him to leave. We'd always been close; I didn't want that to change. The deaths of our parents were difficult for both of us, and thankfully we were blessed to have Mr. and Mrs. Thorpe to help care for us. But Alistair and I were the only family we each shared. Perhaps something inside of me just needed to believe he and I were more alike than we really were, that we wanted the same things, thought the same way. I can see now that it was my own fears regarding such false notions that came between us. I should have honored the differences in us, not resorted to anger over them."

Sebastian slipped into silence except for a few sniffles that indicated he was crying, but Enid wondered if he had ever truly grieved over his brother's death, or if he'd just eclipsed the pain with his anger. She saw him discreetly wipe a hand over his face, and she resisted the urge to say anything at all, sensing that he just needed to unburden himself, and she needed to know exactly what he was thinking and how he felt before she said anything that might veer the conversation in the wrong direction.

"He changed when he met you, Enid," Sebastian said in a voice that made it clear how difficult it was for him to say what he was saying. "After reading his journals, I can look back now and see that he was happier, but at the time . . . I think all I could see was his becoming more distant from me. I see now that he could be himself with you . . . and because I had so selfishly dismissed—and even demeaned—his dreams and desires, he had simply stopped talking to me about them. I had believed he'd given up the notion of becoming a missionary; in truth, he'd just kept it to himself to avoid any contention between us."

Sebastian took a deep breath and leaned back on the sofa, looking at Enid firmly as he said, "I blamed you for coming between me and my brother, but the truth is that a wall existed between us—a wall *I* had put there—long before you came into his life. Now, I can only feel grateful that he found someone who accepted him just as he was; someone who supported him in fulfilling his life's passion. I've been so angry about his death, thinking only that his foolishness brought him to such a horrible end. Now I understand that he died doing what he loved most, and I believe with that understanding I might be able to finally find some peace over his death."

Enid felt in awe of all he was saying, and the absolute sincerity with which he spoke. It was the miracle she'd been praying for, and he'd finally been able to see and understand the truth concerning what had stood between them ever since she'd come back. But there was something in those last couple of sentences that pricked a sensitive and painful place inside herself, and she felt a tightening in her chest. She bolted to her feet and moved back to her spot at the window where she could gaze out at the snow and try to calm her breathing before Sebastian noticed.

"What's wrong?" he asked, coming to stand beside her, which made it impossible to hide how affected she was by their conversation. "Did I say something to upset you? If I've misunderstood anything—anything at all— please help me understand."

To hear him genuinely say *that* to her became a warm distraction from her own internal battle. "You've come far, m'lord," she said, "from declaring that you had no interest in . . . How did you put it? That you were not at all interested in my side of the story?"

Sebastian looked down, embarrassed. "A part of me knew I was behaving deplorably, but . . . I just couldn't get past my own confusion and . . . anger—and guilt. I don't expect you to forgive me, Enid, but I hope that you can—"

"Sebastian," she said, tentatively reaching out to touch his face. Her touch startled him, and he looked up. "I forgave you a long time ago," she added and heard him take a sharp breath while his eyes mirrored his disbelief. "My anger has not been based in a lack of forgiveness, Sebastian, but rather in my frustration and confusion over having all of this stand between us when it was all just a gross lack of communication. I have felt like the proverbial scapegoat in the Old Testament, where all the sins were laid on my head, and I was banished from your presence into an emotional wilderness."

"Why did you not give the journals to me sooner?" he asked. "If Alistair's own words could clear up the problem, why did you wait so long?"

Enid looked down and watched her hands twisting the handkerchief she'd unconsciously pulled out of her pocket, probably fearing that her strained emotions could result in tears. "Perhaps my thinking was not clear in that regard; I can only say that I didn't want to mar your memories of the relationship you shared with Alistair."

"So, you chose to have me remain angry with *you*, as opposed to allowing me to see the truth?"

Those predicted tears pressed into her eyes and she looked away. "He's your brother," she said with a quiver in her voice.

"And you are the woman I love," Sebastian said, his voice quivering as well, which made Enid look at him, surprised by his emotion as much as the words he'd just said. "After Marie died, I didn't think it would ever be possible to feel that kind of love again, but . . . for all of my trying to wish these feelings away when I was blinded by my own selfish anger, I could never deny how much I've grown to love you . . . how much I need you in my life . . . how desperately I hope that we will be able to repair the damage I've caused, and that we never allow Alistair to come between us. We both loved him; he should be a common bond, not a source of dispute."

Enid heard herself laugh softly, which provoked Sebastian's brow to furrow in question. "Forgive me," she said and dabbed at her eyes with her handkerchief, "but that is exactly what I've been wanting to say to you for weeks."

He smiled, his eyes reflecting his relief. "Does that mean we've found a common stepping stone from which we might move forward . . . together?"

Enid took his hand. "Yes, I believe it does," she said.

Sebastian kissed her hand, keeping his lips against her fingers a ridiculously long time before he tightened his hold on her hand as if he were trying to prevent her from escaping. He met her eyes with a penetrating gaze and asked, "Then why are you upset?" The question jolted Enid back to the realization that she had indeed been upset, and the reasons came rushing back, tightening her chest and making her stomach smolder.

Enid pondered what—or how much—she should tell him, and concluded that she honestly didn't know. She kept a tight hold on his hand, as if she didn't want him to escape while she turned again to look at the snow falling silently outside. "I don't know if I want to talk about it," she admitted, which gave her more time to consider how much would be appropriate to share.

"Talk about *what*?" he asked.

Enid sighed loudly. "You must realize this is an awkward position for me to be in. I don't believe that secrets should be kept in a marriage; a good marriage requires complete trust and complete confidence." She sighed again. "If you love me as much as you claim—and given that I cannot deny how very much I love you—I have to assume that—"

"Yes," he interjected.

"Yes, what?" she asked, looking at him abruptly.

"Yes, my intention is to marry you . . . if you'll have me."

Enid assessed his sincerity and looked back to the view out the window. "Well, then . . . if my deceased husband was a man you didn't know, then it would be only right for me to share with you my experiences from my previous marriage; the good, the not so good, what I learned about myself, about life, about marriage. But he's your brother, and just as I hesitated to give you his journals for fear that I might harm your memories of him, your perception of him—I hesitate to tell you certain things about what it was like to be married to him. The more time that passes, the more I'm finding it easier to remember the good and let go of the bad." She laughed softly, not because anything was funny, but because she was overcome with the irony of all that had brought her to this moment. "Initially following his death, I missed him so much that all I could recall about our relationship was the good, but as time went on, my memories became clearer and more accurate; I came to see the truth, but I think I'm still trying to accept it." She drew a deep breath of courage and again looked at her deceased husband's brother, trying to comprehend the depth and breadth of what they shared, and how much healing had taken place just since he'd entered the room a short while ago. She gathered her courage and asked, "How honest should I be with you about my previous marriage? I think that I would like you to be able to tell me anything good or bad about your relationship with Marie. I loved her dearly, but I can accept that she was surely human and less than perfect—as we all are. But this situation is different. I *only* knew Marie as your wife. Alistair is your brother. So, please . . . tell me, Sebastian . . . are there things that I should simply put into the category of being better for me to not share with you for that reason?"

His silence implied that he didn't have an easy answer. After a long moment he said, "I never considered such a dilemma, Enid; but you certainly make a fair point. Right now, I . . . I feel so overwhelmed with everything I've been learning about him that was so different than what I'd believed. Is it all right for me to just admit that . . . I need some time?"

"Of course it's all right," Enid said firmly and let go of his hand to touch his face again. Oh, how she loved being able to do so! "As long as you don't lock yourself away and hide from me, we can take all the time we need to figure all of this out."

He nodded and seemed relieved. "Might we talk some more . . . perhaps after the children have gone to bed . . . here in the library?"

"I would like that," she said, overcome with how grand it felt just to think of spending time with him instead of being alone, apart from chatting with Tilly or the other servants. As if a maternal clock chimed in her head to make her aware of the passing of time, she declared, "I need to feed the baby."

He nodded his understanding and she took a step back. "I'll see you later, then," she said, but he pushed his arm around her waist which made her take two steps toward him.

"Wait," he murmured and gave her little warning before he kissed her. Enid was quick to lift her arms around his neck and engage herself completely in his tender expression of affection. "I love you dearly, Enid," he said, and she had to try to convince herself that she wasn't dreaming; this really was the same man who had created so much turmoil in her life.

"I love you too," she whispered and eased her lips to his again, grateful beyond comprehension for the miracle that was finally bridging the estrangement between them. They had a long way to go—probably much longer than he realized—but they'd made remarkable progress.

"Please forgive me," he said softly, moisture brimming in his eyes.

"I already told you that I have," she replied.

"I suppose it's just difficult for me to believe; I've been so unkind—even cruel."

"I won't argue with that," she said, but she said it with a smile that seemed to put him at ease. More seriously she added, "But I can't say that I've handled the situation perfectly. You are surely not the only one in need of forgiveness."

"There is nothing you've done that would require—" Enid stopped him with another kiss.

"We're starting over right now," she said, her face still close to his. "Whatever we need to work out, we'll do it together."

He nodded and smiled and kissed her again before Enid insisted that she had to go and feed the baby. She knew Tilly could handle caring for Sarah, but Enid treasured her time with her daughter, and she couldn't deny the need to distance herself from Sebastian right now to let her mind catch up to all that had just happened. Before she left the room, she looked once more into his eyes, holding onto the distinct evidence she'd seen there that his anger toward her was indeed completely gone, and the love and adoration she'd once seen in his eyes had returned—except that it was somehow more vivid, more real, less guarded. She hurried up the stairs, overcome with joy as long as she didn't think about the conversations they still needed to share. Beyond the dilemma they'd overcome regarding her marriage to Alistair, and his subsequent untimely death, there was still so much about her that he didn't know. And despite knowing that his love was sincere, a part of her wondered if Sebastian could overlook certain facts about her upbringing that Alistair had been able to accept. Oh, how she prayed they could get beyond all this careful navigating through the past to move together into the future, with no secrets between them, and nothing to hold them back from being perfectly happy together.

* * * * *

Sebastian watched Enid leave the room before he turned to look out the window at the falling snow. After days of feeling incapable of doing anything but trying to come to terms with adjusting his entire perspective about his brother—and Enid's place in all of this—he was deeply relieved to be out of the confines of his own rooms, and even more so to have been able to speak with Enid and say things he should have said a long time ago. Her genuine and generous forgiveness warmed his heart and tempted tears that he fought to blink back.

Soothed by the relief of having that hurdle behind him, his thoughts turned to the dilemma Enid had put before him. Something he'd said about Alistair had upset her, and from what she'd said, he had to believe it was based in the likelihood that his brother had been a less-than-ideal husband. But what man wasn't? Now that he'd had even a few minutes to consider her question, the answer was very clear. She'd been right when she said that marriage should be based on complete trust and confidence. If his intention was to share his life with Enid—and it was—then it surely had to be far more important that she feel comfortable in telling him whatever she had a need to share, than any concern over how it might affect his opinion of his deceased brother. He needed to let Enid know that she was more important to him than any possibility of his own feelings being hurt over misconceptions or assumptions on his part. He'd already contended with coming to understand that Alistair had passionately wanted to serve as a missionary in a faraway land where he could make a positive impact on the lives of people who were impoverished and whose lives were difficult in ways that no man with his upbringing could ever comprehend. It had been Sebastian's chastening attitude that had made Alistair decide to keep his dreams and goals to himself. Sebastian had drawn from his own logic to try to convince Alistair that his desires to travel and live among the poor and serve them in this way were utterly absurd. And he'd been so vehement about it that Alistair had vowed to never again speak to Sebastian concerning the matter. Sebastian now knew that to be absolutely true; he'd read it written in Alistair's hand in one of his journals. And somehow Sebastian had assumed that Alistair's silence meant he had given up on the idea, and when Alistair had announced that he and his new wife were making plans to travel to Africa, Sebastian had placed all the blame on Enid, unable to even acknowledge the possibility that he and his brother could be so divided and out of touch with each other. They *had* been divided and out of touch, but only because Sebastian had silenced Alistair from being able to speak openly about his hopes and dreams without being criticized.

Alistair was gone now; there was no way to apologize or ask his forgiveness. He hoped that in the place beyond this life where he believed the spirits of the dead lived on, his brother had some awareness of the softening that had taken place in Sebastian's heart, and all that he had learned about himself during these past days when he had locked himself away with the words his brother had written. He felt completely changed, and he believed he had his brother to thank for that. And Enid. Her willingness to forgive him so quickly warmed his heart once again, and the love he felt for her—and that he knew she felt for him—gave him the hope of being able to create a bright future with her at his side. Still, he knew there were facets to this situation they had yet to confront; there were many things they had to talk about and sort out. He felt some nervousness and even trepidation over what might yet surface, but he also felt a growing confidence that together they could get through anything. The conversation they'd just shared strengthened his belief in that, and he smiled with the anticipation of being able to spend some time with her later this evening.

* * * * *

While Enid fed Sarah and then held her close, patting her little back, she reviewed the conversation she'd just had with Sebastian, and how everything had changed over the course of an hour. It was a miracle! She felt elated and lifted by hope—until she considered all that he didn't know about her. She'd opened the door to be able to talk to him about the challenges she'd faced in her marriage, and it was up to him to decide whether he was comfortable with that. She believed that he would be, given the remarkable changes she'd seen in him thus far. But he still knew nothing about her life before she'd married Alistair, and the truth about *that* was something she dreaded telling him. She honestly had no idea how he would respond. He might feel an aversion that would outweigh everything else and he would decide that despite how much they loved each other, and how far they'd come, he didn't believe marriage to her was a good idea. There was a reason she and Alistair had chosen to keep her past a secret from his family, and since she knew that the family she'd grown up in would never be around to interact with her new family, the secrecy had never been difficult. But she could not marry a man without him knowing the whole truth. She just prayed that she would know how to tell him—and when—and that he would receive the truth with an open mind and a softened heart.

Despite knowing they needed to have some difficult conversations, Enid looked at the clock and counted the hours until she could see Sebastian after the children were down for the night. With the possibility that they might be able to fully open their hearts to each other and share a future, she wondered if she'd ever been happier. She could only hope and pray that her happiness would not be dashed once she laid out the full truth for him to see.

* * * * *

Enid placed a sleeping Sarah in her crib and took a long moment to just touch her wispy hair and gaze upon her peaceful, beautiful countenance. She then glanced at the clock, and her heart quickened to realize that the boys would have been put to bed by now, and Sebastian was likely waiting in the library. With Tilly nearby to listen for the baby, Enid quickly checked her reflection in the mirror and resisted the urge to walk quickly. She was delightfully anxious to see Sebastian, but at the same time dreading their potential conversation. Moving slowly down the stairs, she rehearsed how she might tell him things that any woman should tell her potential husband. Recalling how sincere he'd been about declaring his desire to marry her, Enid contended with a sweet fluttering in her stomach that made her smile. But they had some important steps to take before she could ever—in good conscience—officially agree to be his wife. And practically speaking, it still had not been such a long time since they'd both lost their spouses, and perhaps they simply needed more time to be certain they were ready to move forward together.

Enid stepped through the open library door to see Sebastian sitting on one of the sofas, his booted feet stacked on the table in front of him, his head leaning back comfortably, and his eyes closed. A fire sparked and crackled in the fireplace, casting strange shadows over the room, which was only otherwise lit by a couple of lamps that were incapable of shedding enough light to compete with the fire's blaze. It was still snowing outside, although more lightly now, which added to the cozy effect of the room as Enid closed the door behind her, alerting Sebastian to her presence, and he lifted his head to look at her, immediately smiling. He'd trimmed his beard since she'd seen him earlier, and she was freshly taken aback by how handsome he was.

"Hello," he said, coming to his feet.

"Hello," she replied, and he stepped toward her, taking both her hands into his, and kissing her cheek in a slow and lingering way that implied he wanted to be close to her. She looked into his eyes when his kiss was finally complete, deeply assuaged to see undeniable evidence not only of his adoration but his humility; she had no doubt that the changes in him were genuine, which increased her hope that they could get beyond the issues causing her anxiety, even if she instinctively believed that doing so could take time.

They sat close together, and he took hold of her hand. Much to her relief he spoke immediately, opening the door for her to be able to pick up this delicate conversation where it had left off. "You asked me a question earlier, and I told you that I needed time to think about it. Well, I've thought about it, and I believe that if we are considering the possibility of spending the rest of our lives together, there is nothing that takes priority over our being able to share anything and everything that will strengthen the bond between us. Yes, Alistair is my brother, but he's gone now. I've had a hard, fast lesson in coming to accept that he was not the man I had led myself to believe he was; in many ways he was a far better man than I gave him credit for. But I know that reading his journals gave me only his perspective. You were married to him, and marriage is surely the best and perhaps only relationship that exposes our truest selves. I want you to know that I'm not going to keep my brother on some kind of pedestal of greatness just because he's my brother and he's dead. I want to remember him realistically—both his strengths and his weaknesses. I've learned about his life from his perspective, and now I want to hear about him from his wife—the person who knew him best. I'm willing to see him as your deceased husband and not my brother at times when you need to share those things with me, because I don't want any secrets between us, and I don't think Alistair would want that either."

Enid heard what he was saying and was once again struck by the miracles unfolding. With all the anger she'd felt toward him, she never could have imagined him saying such things to her—and meaning what he said. She'd longed to be able to tell him the truth, but now that the opportunity was before her, she had trouble knowing where to begin. As if Sebastian sensed this, he squeezed her hand and said, "Just . . . start at the beginning. Tell me how the two of you met, and . . . how your relationship evolved."

Enid thought about that for a moment and realized the story of Alistair's and her courtship involved other complications from her past that she felt more hesitant to tell him than anything else. Hoping those details could be postponed until another conversation, she said, "I think I would prefer to talk first about the issue that came between you and me. Now that you're willing to hear what I have to say, I need you to know that Alistair was obsessed with his desire to do missionary work. He had talked about it here and there when we'd been courting, and I told him he was surely more adventurous than I and I wasn't certain I would be up to such an endeavor. Looking back, I realize that his steering away from talking about it was not for the reasons I had allowed myself to believe. I think I wanted so much to believe that for me he would let go of such notions and that we could simply settle down here in England and have a family and live a good life. After we were married, I quickly came to realize he had simply chosen not to talk about his true passion in order to circumvent any discord between us—which I suppose means that you and I have something in common in that regard; to keep the peace, he left us both in the dark over his true intentions, all the while making plans for when we would leave and how we would go about following his dreams—as husband and wife, side by side. Quite frankly, I was terrified, but I believed it was a woman's duty to accommodate herself to her husband's life; so that's what I did. I buried my fears, I prayed hourly for courage, and I did my best to focus on how much I loved him. I'd given up everything for him, and I couldn't turn back; he was all I had."

"And why is that?" Sebastian asked with an intensity that reminded her she was also guilty of withholding a great deal of information.

Enid knew he needed to know everything, but she meant it when she said, "The answer to that question is very complicated, Sebastian. Let's get through one conversation at a time. I promise that I will answer your every question in time, but . . . I do need time."

"That's only fair," he said, which helped soothe her concerns. "You've given me far more time than I deserve. I just want you to know you can trust me."

"I do know that," Enid said, even while something inside her felt afraid. And she couldn't deny that it had only been a matter of hours since she'd seen this miraculous change in him. If she was going to share her most difficult secrets, perhaps time was the only thing that could truly convince her he'd changed enough to be privy to the truth about her past.

Sebastian nodded to indicate he understood, and he accepted her promise to tell him everything when the time was right. "Go on," he said.

"I didn't want to leave here," she said, hearing the sadness in her own voice as she recalled how difficult it had been. "I felt so safe and comfortable here. Everyone who worked here was so kind to me. And I'd found a true friend and sister in Marie. Saying good-bye to her was like . . ." Enid paused to compose herself and force back a sudden threat of tears, not only in recalling her sorrow in having to leave behind her friendship with Marie, but how she'd returned to learn that her sister-in-law had died tragically.

Enid cleared her throat and jumped past that point, which she considered obvious enough. "The journey to Africa was long and miserable, and our arrival there was terrifying. There's no way to even describe what it's like there to someone who has never seen it. I didn't speak the language; the clothes I wore were so out of place, and certainly not made for the climate. But I persisted and did everything I knew I needed to do. I confess I had some very fulfilling experiences. I grew to love the people there, especially the women. There was often someone around with a minimal knowledge of English who could interpret for me, but I never fully understood the conversations going on around me. I felt like the women cared about me and accepted me, but I was always on the outside, always so different from them in every way except for the fact that we were all women."

Enid flexed her neck and sighed, determined to get to the most important point. "I did my best to accompany my husband as he helped the people in ways that I could only admire. But I couldn't keep up with him. He was so driven by his desire to serve the people there that I quickly became invisible." Enid gathered courage and looked at her husband's brother, a man she'd grown to love, the only man with whom she wanted to share her life. "It was as if he saw the work he was doing as the sole purpose of his life, the only thing that gave him any real happiness. I gradually came to accept that his main reason for marrying me was mostly because it was more appropriate for a missionary to be accompanied by a wife. I'm not saying he didn't love me; I know that he did. But it was more like an intellectual kind of knowledge; I *knew* it far more than I ever *felt* it. He was so deeply and thoroughly passionate about the work he was doing that there was no passion left over for me. I began to feel like the cook and the housekeeper and the silent companion required to stand at his side for certain events and occasions. He could have lived to be an old man there and would have been completely content. I only wanted to come back to England. But I was his wife, and I had made sacred vows. I felt trapped there."

Enid became distracted by the sincere compassion showing in Sebastian's eyes. She looked down, fearing that if she lost herself in his sympathy she would not be able to hold back the hovering threat of tears. Knowing she couldn't lose her momentum now, she forced herself to go on.

"One of the manifestations of my invisibility was his general disregard for anything I had to say. For a long time, I tried very hard to be involved; I often offered suggestions based on my observations among the women and children, but he had his own way of wanting things done and it felt to me as if he barely listened to anything I had to say, and then only to be polite. I felt as if he had an unlimited supply of kindness and love to offer the people there, but he had none to give me. The fears I'd experienced before we'd left here began to overtake me again. It became more and more difficult for me to go out of the house, and when I tried to talk to him about my feelings, he was clearly frustrated with me, which added to my feelings of inadequacy as a wife, and of being a source of disappointment to him. This only seemed to make him feel even more justified in remaining mostly aloof from me. I became so . . . lonely and . . ."

"What?" Sebastian asked when she hesitated, startling her slightly as she came to the realization that her mind had been wandering.

"I just remembered something I'd forgotten," Enid said. "There was a very wise old woman in the village. She came to visit me occasionally, although we couldn't communicate at all without someone to help interpret. Sometimes we would just sit together and share tea, and nothing at all needed to be said for me to just feel like she cared." Enid felt herself smile. "Occasionally we would be able to actually visit with the help of someone who spoke some English. I'll never forget the way she told me that . . . being lonely is not about being alone, it's about not feeling loved." Enid sighed. "I remember crying that day after she left. It was as if she'd observed and sensed the truth, and she had stated it very clearly."

"Oh, Enid, I'm so sorry," Sebastian said. "I never could have imagined that it was so difficult for you. I—"

Enid stopped him by bolting to her feet as if doing so might give her some distance from the sorrow and grief being unearthed by her delving into such unpleasant memories. She moved to window even though it was impossible to see anything through the darkness. But with her back to Sebastian it was easier to say, "I was so happy to find out I was pregnant. I'd always wanted to be a mother, and I believed that having a child would give *me* a greater purpose—even though I was terrified of giving birth and raising a child in a village that barely had the means for survival. And I considered the simple fact that I was pregnant a miracle."

"Why?" Sebastian asked, and Enid wished she could take back those last words. His question was legitimate, but she didn't want to answer it. She reminded herself that they were both mature adults, they'd both been married, and they were working toward sharing marriage themselves. She could surely find a way to appropriately tell him the truth.

After searching for the right words, Enid finally said, "Because in order to become pregnant a certain amount of intimacy must take place, and it rarely did." There. She'd said it. And even from across the room she heard him gasp as her meaning sank in. "He as much as admitted that he believed such happenings between a man and a woman were solely meant for the creation of life; he seemed more relieved than happy when I got pregnant— almost as if he could check that off his list and focus more fully on his work."

Enid was glad to have that out in the open, so it could stop circling in her head, but she hurried on, not wanting to focus on the most sensitive aspect of her relationship with Alistair. She hurried to say, "Given that he was so in the habit of disregarding my observations or advice, when a terrible illness began sweeping through the village, killing people quickly and brutally, I begged him to stay in, to keep his distance, until it passed. But he insisted that he needed to assist the people, and that he would be careful. I didn't see him for two days, and I began to fear he had fallen ill somewhere and was already dead or dying. Then he came through the door, visibly ill, barely able to walk. He told me to stay away, not to touch him at all. He dropped onto the bed and I sat in a chair across the room. Before he lost consciousness, he told me that I needed to leave, that if I stayed even long enough to see his body cared for, the baby and I would inevitably die as well. We had money hidden, and enough supplies in the house for me to be able to travel on foot for some distance, with the hope that I could get to a ship and sail to England."

Enid's tears finally began to flow, and she allowed them to come. She was talking about the most difficult experience of her life; she felt entitled to cry about it. "He told me he loved me—for the first time in many months. He told me that once I made it home he knew that you would make certain we were cared for. And then I watched him die. He told me not to wait, but I couldn't move. I just sat there until I knew he was gone. And then I couldn't leave fast enough. With every step I took I felt as if the disease that had killed him was stalking me like some kind of monster. I remained completely alone and waited to go into the next village until enough time had passed that I knew I wasn't ill; I didn't want to make anyone else ill. Miraculously, the village I went to had not been infected by illness, and I was able to get what I needed to begin my journey home—which felt longer and more miserable than the previous journey. Perhaps it was the illness of my pregnancy that made it worse; perhaps it was the very fact that I was completely on my own. Arriving here at last was the greatest relief I'd ever experienced. I knew I would be safe here; there were people here I knew and loved, and I knew they would help care for me and the baby. But I was met with the news that Marie had died, that you had locked yourself away, and that the house had become like a mausoleum."

Enid felt suddenly at a loss for words. Sebastian knew the story from there. She'd said what she needed to say, and he'd listened with kindness. While she was waiting to hear what he might say, she heard him sniffle, and then she heard him again, and she knew he was crying. Preferring to hide her own tears that were sliding steadily down her face, Enid remained where she was, certain they likely each needed a few minutes to shed their tears privately.

"And then," Sebastian said, his voice quivering, "you had the courage to put me in my place and bring me out of hiding. But after you saved me from myself, I turned around and heaped more pain upon everything you were already carrying."

Enid couldn't respond. What he'd just said was true, but she'd already told him she'd forgiven him, and she'd meant it. Still, hearing him voice it that way prompted a sudden rush of tears that she preferred to keep to herself. If she spoke, her efforts to keep her emotion silent would be foiled. With her eyes squeezed shut she didn't even realize Sebastian was standing beside her until he spoke and startled her. "I'm so very sorry, Enid."

Now that he could clearly see the evidence of her tears, along with the way she could feel her chin quivering, she abandoned her efforts to keep her emotions under control. Tearfully she reminded him, "And all is forgiven, Sebastian. My purpose in telling you all of that was not to revisit our past disagreements. I needed you to know the truth of my relationship with your brother, and I've feared what your reaction might be to hear me speak of him with such an emphasis on his weaknesses. I tried so hard to focus on his strengths, Sebastian, but adding up everything over and over, I cannot deny how lonely and unhappy I was in my marriage—even before we went to Africa."

Enid felt some relief to see a slight smile appear on Sebastian's face as he wiped her tears with his handkerchief. He took hold of her chin and kissed her quivering lips before he said softly, "It would seem we both came to learn the hard way that Alistair tended to keep his true nature hidden from those he loved, until it was causing damage that could not be undone. I love my brother no less to know the truth, Enid, but in putting all the pieces together, I have no trouble admitting that despite all the good he did for a great many people, he was selfish and perhaps even deceptive with his family—and I believe no one should be more important than family when it comes to our commitment and loyalty. No one suffered more than you from his weaknesses, Enid. The thing is, I can see now that selfishness is something I had in common with him; and I too have kept parts of myself hidden away—sometimes literally. Thanks to you, I'm learning to be a better man, and perhaps if Alistair had lived a longer life, he would have had the chance to do the same."

"I'd like to believe he's in a better place . . . and still learning."

"I'd like to believe that too," Sebastian said and kissed her again before he used his handkerchief once more to dry her face. "I love you, Enid. I don't want the ghost of my brother to ever come between us."

"I love you too, Sebastian," she said, "and as long as we are committed to communicate any feelings that arise regarding him—or anything else for that matter—we'll be all right."

"I agree," he said, and then he just gazed at her, his eyes full of love and adoration—so much so that it felt as if his heart was completely exposed to her; even in his silence, his humble vulnerability was readily evident.

As Enid took in what she found so easy to see, something remarkable occurred to her, and she was quick to share her thoughts. "He never looked at me that way."

"What?" he asked, sounding confused even while the meaning in his gaze became more intense.

"I believe he loved me, Sebastian, but . . . he never looked at me the way you're looking at me now. He always seemed to look . . . through me . . . or past me . . . but you *see* me." She placed her hand against the side of his face and he briefly closed his eyes as if to savor her touch, at the same time placing his hand over hers as if he wanted to savor it forever. "May I say," she added, and he opened his eyes again, "how lovely it is to not feel invisible?"

"You may certainly say that," he said. "And may I say that I can't even imagine how that's possible. Ever since you came home and put me in my place, all I could see is you. Everything has centered around you. Even in all my ridiculous anger toward you, my mind was continually preoccupied with you. Every time you walked into a room, the atmosphere brightened, and it was difficult to not just stare at you. You've become the center of my life, Enid—you and the children. Nothing matters more to me now than devoting my life to your happiness—and theirs."

"Well, that all goes together, doesn't it?" Enid asked, unable to keep from smiling in a way that completely dispelled any sorrow as she leaned closer to him and wrapped her arms around his neck.

"Yes, I believe it does," he said and kissed her.

Chapter Fourteen

DISCLOSURE

"Will you marry me?" Sebastian asked with no warning, still holding Enid in his arms.

Enid knew her answer to the question. The only remaining problem was that she knew he was asking it without knowing everything a man should know when committing himself fully to a woman. She stepped back to put distance between them, and his concern was immediately evident. Before he could ask what the problem might be, she quickly explained, "There are still unresolved issues between us, Sebastian. I want to say yes; I want it more than anything. But we can't get caught up in this moment and forget that there are still things you don't know about me."

"I can't imagine that there would be anything you could tell me that would change my mind."

"And perhaps there is something about my past that you simply can't imagine," she said, hating the way her mouth went dry and her palms became sweaty. She'd dreaded this conversation ever since she'd had the first inkling of attraction for this man. As she'd grown to love him, she'd known they could never share a future if he didn't know everything about who she was and the life she'd lived before she'd married Alistair.

"Whatever it is, Enid," he said, "it doesn't matter."

Enid was glad to hear him say so, but she also knew that what she'd said was true: he could never imagine the full truth about her past. She also knew that she wasn't ready to tell him. They'd come a long way very quickly—perhaps *too* quickly. Reaching deep inside for her practicality and reason—without allowing herself to let go of the happiness she felt over the love they shared and her hope for a bright future with him—she looked up at him and said, "I want nothing more than to be your wife, Sebastian, however . . ."

"However?" he echoed, sounding panicked.

"I'm not telling you no," she hurried to assure him. "I just need time. We've both experienced some enormous changes in our lives, and it would be foolish to think that the love we feel for each other has erased all the grief we've had to endure. For myself, sometimes I feel like I've healed from all the drama of losing Alistair—and everything else I endured regarding going to Africa and then finding my way home. But at other times the grief overtakes me, and I feel like I've lost myself somewhere along the way." She put both her hands on the sides of his face. "I love you, Sebastian; I want to be with you forever. I just . . . need time. And I think you do, as well."

He swallowed hard and cleared his throat without letting go of her gaze. "I can't deny that you're probably right. Neither can I deny some disappointment. I want nothing more than to marry you as soon as possible, but perhaps that's an impulsive and selfish idea. Or maybe I'm afraid if I don't make you mine I will lose you."

"I'm not going anywhere, Sebastian," she said and kissed him before she smiled and suggested, "Can we not simply share an official courtship? There's no reason to hide our relationship from anyone in the house or even the community. We can spend time *together* with the children, instead of apart. And we can talk as much as we like and get to know each other better while we each come to terms with all that's changed in our lives." Enid sighed and attempted to ignore the blatant disappointment in his eyes—even though she knew it mirrored her own. She readily admitted, "In all honesty, Sebastian, I too would like to be married as quickly as possible, but . . . in my heart I truly believe we will have a better marriage if we wait. Please tell me you understand."

"I *do* understand," he said, "and I can't deny that you're probably right; I've already accepted that you are far wiser than I could ever be."

"Oh, I don't think that—"

"Of course I'll wait," he said, "but I would feel better if we had some approximate end in mind; a time when we could plan on becoming officially engaged. Give me some hope, Enid. I sense there are things you are hesitant to tell me, but you can't avoid such things indefinitely."

Enid knew he was right on all counts, and she was easily able to say, "When winter is ending . . . when spring is beginning to show . . . ask me again." His smile gave her relief, and she was glad to impulsively add,

"And tomorrow evening you can officially announce our courtship to the entire household."

"Why? What's tomorrow evening?" he asked.

"A party," she said. "Have you not heard?" He shook his head and she felt grateful to be able to steer the conversation away from such serious topics into telling him her reasons for wanting to use her own money to put on a big party for the household staff simply to express her appreciation for all they had done for her.

"What a marvelous idea," he said. "I only wish I'd thought of it myself."

They sat close together and held hands while she told him the plans being carried out for a fine meal in the main dining room, and some party games and dancing in the ballroom. Everyone had been given assignments to help with the preparations, so no one would have to put too much work into the occasion, and everyone could enjoy themselves.

"I was hoping," she said, "that you would come out of hiding and be able to join us. I'm glad that you did."

"So am I," he said and kissed her.

"And I think the children should join us, as well—not only so that some-one won't have to miss the party to watch over them, but so they can enjoy such an event with the people who do so much for *them*."

Sebastian smiled and said, "I agree, and I think you're a genius, my darling." He kissed her again and then gazed into her eyes while his smile broadened.

"What are you thinking?" she asked.

"I was thinking how very blessed my sons are to be able to grow up with you as their mother, and how everyone who works with us is also blessed to have a woman such as yourself in charge. But it is I who am mostly blessed."

Enid returned his smile and said, "I think it is the other way around." She only hoped that when some time had passed, and he had learned the entire truth about her, he would still feel the same way.

* * * * *

Enid felt as if her entire life had flipped over and she'd ended up on top of all that had so recently been weighing her down. Just being able to spend time with Sebastian and feel completely comfortable with him was not only miraculous, it soothed her soul and warmed her heart. The boys were thrilled to have both her and their father come visit them together, and Enid loved watching the comfortable way that Sebastian held Sarah, talking to her in a silly voice that made the baby smile and sometimes even let out one of her newly found laughing noises.

The party that Enid had been planning for weeks—with the generous help of others in the household—ended up being a huge success. Every person there had a wonderful time, but the highlight for Enid was when Sebastian quieted everyone down so that he could make a little speech. First, he thanked everyone for their loyalty and service, and he humbly expressed appreciation for their patience while he'd been going through an especially difficult time. He then motioned for Enid to come stand at his side before he announced that they would be officially courting, which brought on a hearty round of applause and even some whistling and joyful comments. When the small crowd quieted down, Sebastian said, "This amazing lady has brought me back to life, and with any luck after we've had some time to get past the difficulties we've both endured, she will agree to be my wife. In the meantime, I'll be glad to live in a house full of chaperones—since I think courting someone who lives under the same roof isn't very common." This was met with laughter, and Enid knew he was mostly teasing; she had no concerns about him being appropriate about such things, but she *did* appreciate his acknowledgment to all with whom they shared their home. Her relief at no longer having to try and hide their feelings for each other was deep, but even more so she was relieved over no longer having to avoid Sebastian. Instead she could spend as much time with him as their schedules would allow. Being courted by Sebastian Hawthorne—even if they already lived under the same roof—seemed as perfect as life could be.

Alone in her bed that night, Enid considered all that had changed and the probable future that lay ahead. She felt thoroughly thrilled and elated—until she recalled the aspects of her life that she'd not yet shared with Sebastian. A part of her truly believed he would be compassionate, and his feelings for her wouldn't change, but she couldn't be certain. Another part of her feared that he would be disgusted, or he'd twist her secrecy into some kind of intentional deception on her part. Enid forced thoughts of that inevitable conversation away, grateful that he'd promised her some time. Until spring began to appear, she simply had to enjoy his company and continue to assess by his daily behavior whether he had truly changed as much as she wanted to believe.

When Sunday came, Enid completely loved the way she and Sebastian rode together in a carriage with the children, and he held her hand as they went into the church—which brought on some not-so-discreet whispers from those around them. After the service was over, Enid noted how Sebastian seemed deliberately slow to leave the chapel, and he welcomed every opportunity to converse with other people—something he generally avoided. He was purposely taking the time to declare to members of the congregation that he and Enid were courting and he had high hopes of convincing her to be his wife. Enid knew that those he told would be quick to tell others the news, and word would spread through the area in no time. She hoped and prayed that when the time came to make the decision regarding whether they should be married—when everything was completely disclosed between them—that neither she nor Sebastian would have the embarrassment of causing the community to wonder what might have come between them and halted the expected nuptials. But she didn't think about that now; she just enjoyed the way he looked at her and the kind things he said about her as he spoke to those with whom they attended church.

During the following weeks, they settled into a comfortable routine, with their schedule centering around the children—except that now both she and Sebastian were spending time with the boys together when they were not having their lessons, and they also shared time with Sarah when she wasn't napping. Enid and Sebastian shared every meal, whether it was with the boys or in the kitchen with the servants. Neither of them had any desire to eat in the huge dining room where it was far too quiet, although occasionally the two of them shared a meal in a quaint breakfast nook on the east side of the house. It was a cozy room with large windows where the morning sun was abundant on cloudless days, and Enid couldn't deny that it was nice to eat alone with Sebastian occasionally, just so they could talk privately, or simply enjoy each other's company in companionable silence. She wanted her whole life to be this way, and prayed that time would prove such a prospect was possible.

Christmas came and went with much joy and celebrating in the house, then the new year began with a series of storms where the wind and snow made it difficult to leave the house at all. Thankfully they were well stocked with supplies, and everyone remained inside, doing their tasks as usual and keeping the fires well stoked in the rooms that were being used.

February was cold but less stormy, and Enid felt the evidence of time passing. Sebastian had kept his promise to remain patient, and he'd not said a word about the fact that she still hadn't told him the mysteries of her past. He also proved more every day just how sincere his declarations of love for her had been, and how deeply he'd changed. Her confidence in their relationship grew week by week as time proved his complete lack of anger toward her—or anyone else. His commitment to her was readily evident, as was his trustworthiness and the kindness and respect he always showed to her and those with whom they worked. She could feel herself healing from the wounds of the past, just as she could feel the evidence of Sebastian's healing as well. They talked occasionally about their deceased spouses, the struggles they'd had in their marriages, the love they'd felt in those relationships, and the grieving they'd experienced over such enormous losses. Sometimes they even cried together over the fact that Marie and Alistair were gone—and they were both keenly aware of the irony that the love they'd come to share would never have been possible if they'd not both tragically lost their spouses. It was a situation that created a deep bond between them as long as they were willing to be completely open with each other over the bouts of grief that occasionally popped up out of nowhere, and their need to address such feelings and help each other come to terms with them—rather than believing they could just move forward into sharing their lives completely, ignoring the fact that the past had left deep wounds that were still healing.

Sebastian told Enid more than once how grateful he was for her wisdom in giving their relationship some time to flourish, rather than rushing headlong into marriage. Given the changes he'd felt within himself, and the conversations they'd shared concerning their deepest heartaches and regrets, he'd come to see that he had not been nearly as whole inside as he'd wanted to believe, and before he became her husband he wanted to be his best self. Enid let him know that she very much agreed and felt the same; she wanted to be a good wife to Sebastian, but first she had to completely make peace with how her efforts to be a good wife to Alistair had only broken her heart. She felt herself healing more and more as weeks passed into months, and she was able to speak honestly with Sebastian about her feelings, without fear of any judgment or criticism from him.

March started out very windy and with another series of storms that were more rainy than snowy; then suddenly near the middle of the month the weather became especially warm, and hints of color were beginning to show in nature. Enid looked out her bedroom window to the lovely view below and all the evidence that spring had arrived. Sarah had grown and changed so much; she was now crawling and loved to explore anything that was in her path. The boys were each showing more of their individual personalities as they progressed in the things they were learning from their lessons, as well as the time they spent with Enid and their father. Enid couldn't comprehend the depth and breadth of the love she felt for these children, any more than she could the love she felt for Sebastian. Once again taking in the view, Enid clearly recalled her agreement with Sebastian that when spring came, she wanted him to ask her again to be his wife. He'd proven himself worthy of being a good husband even far beyond her hopes and expectations. The advantage of living under the same roof was that she knew he couldn't simply pretend and be on his best behavior all the time, any more than she could. They'd both seen each other at their worst in the past and they'd survived. There was only one thing that stood in the way of her feeling comfortable with becoming his wife, and she knew that telling him the truth about her past couldn't be put off any longer. For her to avoid it further would only make her look foolish. He'd given her no reason to believe that she couldn't trust him, and that he wouldn't hear what she had to say with an open heart—even though she felt certain he couldn't begin to imagine what it was she needed to tell him. But tell him she must. She just needed to gather her courage and do it. If Sebastian knew everything about her and decided he couldn't marry her, she needed to know; they both needed to know so they could get on with their lives. Right now, she couldn't think about what she might do if that happened. Perhaps she *would* have to move away and find a life elsewhere. But until Sebastian actually told her that marriage was not a possibility, she had to believe that it was. And she would never know until she told him the truth—no matter how terrified she felt.

Just after supper, Enid told Sebastian she needed to talk to him as soon as the children were down for the night.

"That would be fine," he said, looking concerned. He clearly sensed her trepidation. "In the library?"

"Yes," she said and walked away before he could sense the full depth of her dread regarding this conversation.

Once Sarah was sleeping soundly, Enid went to the library, taking a lamp with her. The fire there was dying down and she added some wood and stoked it up, but not too much. The weather outside was mild, and she didn't want the room to become overly warm. She lit two other lamps to illuminate the room more clearly, and she'd barely done so before Sebastian entered the room, smiled to see her there, and closed the door behind him. He leaned against it, taking in her countenance, and his smile faded. "You're very somber," he observed quietly. "Should I be nervous about this conversation?"

"I hope not," she said.

"What does that mean exactly?"

"It means that we need to talk, but I really have no idea how you will feel about what I have to tell you."

"If you're going to tell me you don't want to marry me," he said, "I will be utterly devastated. Anything else I think I can handle."

"I *do* want to marry you," she hurried to clarify. "My fear is that once I tell you the whole truth about myself, you might not want to marry *me*."

"You've said as much before, but I think you should just tell me and get it over with."

"Which is exactly what I intend to do," she said and motioned for him to sit down. She sat beside him on the sofa but didn't look at him as she began. "I know very well that you didn't like me when I came here as a bride; you didn't approve of Alistair's choice in a wife. Obviously, we need to clear the air over this. You cannot in good conscience ask me to be *your* wife without acknowledging your previous disapproval. Would that not be somewhat hypocritical?"

"I didn't know you then," Sebastian said, not sounding at all defensive. "I never allowed myself to get to know you. I don't know why I felt the way I did. I was clearly being prejudiced and judgmental. I'm not the same man now that I was then."

"Most of that is true," Enid countered. "There was one obvious reason you considered the match unsuitable. Alistair told me what you'd said to him; and I believe you said it many times. According to what he told me, you could overlook the fact that I was not from the same social class, given that I had sufficient ladylike qualities to fit in with the polite society of the community. But you could not understand why my family would have disowned me when I was so obviously improving my status through this marriage. My interpretation of that, Sebastian, is that the matter bothered you so deeply that it overshadowed everything else you knew about me, and no amount of my good qualities could dispel your uneasiness. Therefore, you simply assumed a stance of disapproval; I most often felt that you barely tolerated me."

"You make me sound like some kind of fiend," he said in a tone that sounded more confused than annoyed.

"I never thought of you in any such way," Enid declared firmly. "I only felt frustrated that you would not overlook what you simply could never understand and just accept me as I was. Marie did; but you never could. And now that we've ended up where neither of us ever imagined we could be, I'm absolutely certain that brushing those feelings under the rug will never serve our relationship well."

"I agree with that," he said. "You're absolutely right. Knowing nothing of your past *did* bother me, and I'm certain I let it bother me far too much. Or perhaps what really bothered me was the fact that neither you nor Alistair would offer any kind of explanation for the situation. A wedding with the complete absence of any of your family members, even though I'd been assured they were all alive and well in London, certainly came across as suspicious. Surely you can see that."

"I *can* see that," she said. "Whether or not either of us handled the situation correctly is in the past. The only thing that matters now is . . . well . . . you need to know the truth before you make a decision as to whether you're willing to commit your life to me."

Enid hesitated as she gathered her words and the courage to let them pass through her lips. She looked at Sebastian somberly and stated a sincere truth that he needed to know, "We were trying to protect you."

"*Protect* me?" he echoed, his brow furrowed with confusion.

"You, Marie; everyone here."

"I cannot even begin to think what you might be talking about."

Enid just said it, wondering how many years it had been since she'd even spoken the words. "I'm Jewish."

Following a stunned silence, Sebastian blurted, "What?"

Enid couldn't help but notice a sharp rise of agitation in Sebastian while he looked at her as if he'd never seen her before. Her heart pounded painfully hard and it took great willpower to keep her voice steady as she pressed forward. "Did you not hear me? Do you not understand what it means to be—?

"I heard you perfectly, Enid," he said, and she hated the astonishment in his voice. "And of course I understand what it means. What I do *not* understand is that I've observed much evidence of you living—and worship-ing—as a Christian; you went to Africa as a Christian missionary. Are you telling me that you've been living some kind of lie? That your behaviors are not consistent with your beliefs?"

"It would be more accurate to say that I'm a Jewish Christian."

Sebastian let out a one-syllable laugh that held no humor whatsoever. "Is that not a contradiction of terms?"

Enid was feeling hard-pressed not to cry while she searched for the words to answer his question. She stood abruptly and moved to a comfortable spot where she could look out the window into the darkness. Moments of silence passed while her mind remained blank and her heart continued to pound. If only to break the tortured silence she finally stated a fact that had always given her an inexplicably comforting perspective. "Jesus was a Jew," Enid stated, turning to look at Sebastian. He repeated the same humorless laugh and pushed his hands through his hair as if that might help him more clearly understand what she was telling him.

Sebastian looked away and said, "Yes, I'm well aware of that, Enid. But surely you can understand why all of this is very confusing for me."

"Yes," she said, looking down, "I can understand that." Impulsively she hurried back to the sofa, feeling a little weak, and knowing this conversation would not be brief now that she'd finally opened the door.

Before she could think of what to say next, Sebastian turned to look at her directly, and when he took her hand, saying gently, "Just talk to me, Enid. Help me understand," she felt hopeful that this might not be as bad as she'd believed.

Enid sighed and was grateful for all the times she'd silently rehearsed how she might tell him. The memory of those rehearsals came back to her now. "There are a great many details about my upbringing . . . my family . . . the situation . . . that we can talk about in the future; there is far too much for one conversation; it's my hope that we can have many more conversations, and this won't be the last—even though I have greatly feared that it would be."

"Why would you think that?" he asked, genuinely baffled.

"Why?" she echoed, unable to hold back the tinge of anger triggered by such a question. "I meant it when I said that I've forgiven you for anything hurtful that's happened between us in the past, but that doesn't necessarily mean we don't have to still sort it out and come to terms with it. Does that make sense?"

He thought about it for a long moment, "Yes," he said.

"The fact is that from the day I came here as Alistair's bride, I knew you didn't like me and didn't approve of my being a part of the family. And you wonder why I would be afraid to tell you that I come from a race—and grew up in a religion—that is greatly looked down upon and even shunned for the most part here in England. Given our complicated history, can you understand why I have feared the possibility that you could very well find the truth repulsive and use it as a reason to never speak to me again?"

Enid allowed a minute of silence for that to sink in, wondering if she'd been too harsh. Another minute passed, and she began to feel terrified that he would get up and leave the room, and all the progress they'd made would be completely shattered. If that were to happen, she doubted that after all they'd been through, it could ever be possible to repair their broken hearts.

Sebastian finally lifted his head to look at her, saying simply, "Talk to me, Enid. Just . . . tell me how you came to be a Jewish Christian. I want to know."

"Very well," she said with a sigh of relief.

"And, yes . . . I would be grateful if you'd share more details with me in future conversations."

Enid was surprised—though perhaps she shouldn't have been—by the tears that overtook her. She'd feared this moment since the first time she had acknowledged that she'd fallen in love with Sebastian Hawthorne. The evidence of his acceptance and his willingness to talk about the most difficult aspect of her life meant more to her than she could say.

"Hey, what is this?" he asked, noting her tears.

Enid couldn't speak. Instead she impulsively threw her arms around his neck, silently hoping to express her gratitude and hope. Her relief deepened from the way he wrapped her in his arms and held her tightly, guiding her head to his shoulder while he whispered, "It's all right, Enid. Everything is going to be all right."

"I do hope so," she said with a sniffle, lifting her head to look at him. "Forgive me," she added. "I've just . . . been afraid of how you would respond, and . . ." He handed her his handkerchief and she gratefully accepted it to dry her tears before she attempted to finish this conversation. "We had to hide the fact that we were Jewish. I've been told there are places in England where Jewish synagogues exist, and people can worship publicly, but I honestly don't know whether that's true or just a rumor, because I've never actually seen such a thing. What I know of the history of *my* family is that for generations back—in the families of both my mother and father—there are terrible stories of persecution and suffering. As I understand it, the laws of England have mostly leaned toward a preference of Jews living elsewhere in order to preserve the purity of the Church of England. But I'm not an historian, and certainly not a politician. I only know the stories as my parents told them. And I know that they were intensely afraid to be known in our community as Jewish. Because my parents wanted to be accepted in the community, and perceived as respectable, we attended church along with all our neighbors. Going to a Christian church meeting every Sunday was all part of a grand ruse my family was forced to play out in order to feel safe. We carried out our Jewish traditions privately and secretly within the walls of our own home."

"Were there no other Jewish people among your acquaintances?" Sebastian asked in a way that helped Enid feel more comfortable with this conversation, and she began to relax as her dread melted into relief.

"There were a few families. We gathered together often and we all knew each other well, but it always felt like we were continually hiding who we really were and what we believed." Enid sighed and forced herself to get to the important points. "As I grew from childhood into my youth, I told no one that my years of attending Christian meetings every Sunday had changed the way I felt about religion. I have a deep and abiding respect for my Jewish heritage; I know in my heart that all they teach and believe in concerning the Old Testament is true. But I have come to know with equal conviction that the New Testament is also true. My family believes that Jesus is a great rabbi; a wise teacher. I know in my heart that He is the Son of God." She sighed again. "But I never told them how I felt. I knew how deeply it would hurt them . . . even offend them."

When she didn't go on, Sebastian guessed, "And then you met Alistair?"

"Yes, actually. Ironically, I met him at church; he was staying in London so he could spend most of his time trying to assist people in need. I believe he wrote about that in his journals."

"Yes, he did," Sebastian said with some self-recrimination. "And I'd believed he simply enjoyed the London social life and he was there just to be among friends and have a good time. I should have allowed myself to know him better than that."

"It's in the past," Enid said, taking his hand.

"Perhaps once I more fully understand everything that happened, I will be able to put it in the past," he said, silently asking her to go on.

"I began helping Alistair with his project of purchasing food and passing it out to the hungry on the streets. I enjoyed it despite how difficult it was to see the way people were suffering. When he talked of going to some faraway place to do the same, I suggested many times that there was plenty of need right here in England." She took a deep breath and got back to the point. "Anyway . . . when he asked me to marry him and I believed it was the right course for my life, I had to tell my parents that I was going to marry a Christian man, which meant I also needed to tell them I had converted to Christianity. And that also meant telling them I was not going to marry the

Jewish man I barely knew—a marriage that had been arranged many years previously." She looked more firmly at Sebastian and declared, "And that is when my father told me I was dead to them." She felt tears trickle down her cheeks. "My mother wanted to know where I would be living in case she ever needed to contact me. My father made it clear they would never have cause to contact me, and I was not to share any information about my life from that time forward with any member of my family." Enid shrugged and passed the handkerchief over her cheeks to dry the tears. "Now you know."

"Yes, now I know," he said, looking at her as if he needed to assess her in a whole new light. She began to feel nervous until he said, "And you are even more remarkable than I ever imagined. I'm ashamed to think of how I assumed the worst—even though I couldn't imagine what the "worst" might be. Your courage to follow your convictions is . . . incomprehensible to me, including the sacrifices you've made." He pressed a hand to the side of her face and Enid leaned against the strength of his touch. "I love you, Enid; now more than ever. I only wish I had known the truth a long time ago—even though I understand why you didn't want to tell me."

He leaned forward to kiss her, and Enid wrapped her arms around him, marveling at how the absence of any secrets between them had lightened her spirit so immensely. Sebastian's relief and acceptance were demonstrated in his affection, and Enid felt more hope and more peace than she'd ever imagined possible during the tumultuous journey they'd taken to arrive at this point.

Sebastian kissed her once more, then relaxed with his arm around her. She leaned her head against his shoulder while a contemplative silence settled over them. Enid focused on the crackling of the fire while she absorbed the relief of having said what she'd needed to say, and knowing that Sebastian had received the information with love and humility. Now that they'd come this far, she truly believed that everything would be all right.

Enid closed her eyes and relaxed, knowing Sebastian needed time to take in all the information she'd laid out for him. She felt certain he had many questions, and it could take time to fill in all the details of her past, but she was completely surprised to hear him say, "It was a Jewish word. That's why I didn't know what it meant."

"What?" Enid asked, lifting her head to look at him.

"The day you put me in my place . . . not long after you'd returned; I remember it so clearly. You said, 'It's not like this situation is some kind of yibbum or something.' I asked you about it later, and you wouldn't tell me what it meant." Enid felt her face turn warm—which meant she was probably blushing—as she tried to look away, wondering again why she had ever let that word come out of her mouth. Sebastian took hold of her chin and turned her face toward him, giving her no choice but to meet his gaze. "What does it mean?" When she hesitated, he added, "I want to know why you said it, and why you have become so embarrassed both times I've asked you about it."

"I don't know why I said it," she admitted. "I suppose it was just . . . that Jewish part of me that slipped into my anger, and . . . it doesn't matter; it's nothing."

"It's not *nothing*," he said. "If you could see yourself right now, you would know why I can't accept that answer. Please . . . just tell me what it means."

Enid closed her eyes, not certain she could say it while looking at him. "It's a Jewish practice that has ancient roots; it's referred to in the book of Deuteronomy, and was once mandated by Torah law. Yibbum is also sometimes referred to as a Levirate marriage. It's not strictly practiced by all Jewish sects, but it's something I know my family believes in." Enid sighed loudly but kept her eyes closed.

"Marriage?" Sebastian repeated what she guessed was the one word that had really caught his attention, and perhaps had clued him into why she felt so embarrassed to be explaining this to him.

Enid took a deep breath and looked down; she could open her eyes as long as she was looking at the floor. *Just say it*, she ordered herself; *just say it and get it over with.* "According to the law, the brother of a man who died without children has an obligation to marry the widow." She actually heard him gasp, however softly, and she hurried to say, "Of course my bringing it up was completely ridiculous. The idea behind it is that when a man dies, it's important that his posterity will somehow be carried on; even though I had not yet given birth, Alistair did not die without posterity. But even if he had, you're not Jewish—and neither am I anymore. And . . . it's just ridiculous. I wish I'd never said it; I don't know what I was thinking. I was angry and I—"

Enid stopped abruptly when he touched her chin and tilted her face toward his. She was surprised to see a sparkle in his eyes and a seeming glow in his countenance. Trying to read his emotions she saw perhaps a hint of amusement, a mite of surprise, and a touch of relief. Most of all she saw evidence of his love for her. Her embarrassment fled along with every other doubt when he smiled and said, "I'm all right with that."

"With what?" she asked.

"Not because of any laws or expectations, but simply because I love you and I know in my heart that we should be together. Taking care of my brother's wife and daughter feels like the only possible choice before me, Enid." He let out a long, slow breath and smiled. "You told me that when spring came I could ask you again. Please tell me that you'll marry me—soon. I'm tired of being alone."

"As am I," she said, thinking of how she'd felt so alone throughout most of her marriage to Alistair. "Yes, Sebastian. My answer is yes . . . from the heart, with all my heart."

He laughed softly; a laugh that expressed perfect delight and relief. Then he kissed her, and kissed her again. And Enid felt more happiness than she had ever believed possible.

✳ ✳ ✳ ✳ ✳

Everyone in the household was thrilled with Sebastian's announcement that he and Enid would be married in less than a month. But no one was happier about it than Enid—except perhaps Sebastian. She loved the almost constant smile on his face as they spent nearly every waking minute together. For months now, the children had already been interacting as if they were all part of the same family; it seemed that making their family official was the most natural thing in the world.

When Enid and Sebastian were not spending time with the children, they never ran out of things to talk about. And now that Enid had told him a truth she should have told him a long time ago, it was easy to feel completely relaxed without having to worry about avoiding what she'd feared talking about. Now Enid told him all about her family, realizing how good it felt to talk about them, even if it did bring up some sorrow over the fact that she could never see them again. He was intrigued to learn that she was the eldest of five siblings, and she had been given a great deal of responsibility in helping care for them while their parents worked together to run the family dairy. He found it amusing to learn that Enid was very good at milking cows and caring properly for the animals. The house where she'd grown up was some distance from the property where the cows were kept and cared for, since Enid's mother had very much preferred living in the city, but their livelihood depended upon animals that needed to be kept on farmland. But Enid told Sebastian that there was great demand for fresh milk in London, and her father owned the property just outside of London that was ten minutes' ride from where they lived—therefore both of her parents were happy with the arrangement.

Sebastian loved hearing everything about Enid's former life; he was fascinated with Jewish beliefs and traditions, and he wanted to know everything. Enid loved being able to tell him such things as much as she loved hearing about his own upbringing, surprised at how much she *didn't* know about his family when she had been married to his brother. But she'd long ago accepted that Sebastian's brother had kept far too much to himself, even his love for her. She could only feel grateful to put that season of her life behind her and look forward to a new and better life.

Chapter Fifteen

ACCEPTANCE

LESS THAN TWO WEEKS BEFORE the wedding, Sebastian told Enid they would be having a special meal that evening with the entire household gathered together. All the servants and the children would be sitting down to eat in the enormous dining room of the house that had never been used at any time when Enid had been living in the house except for that one party, which had included the entire household. Enid was curious over the purpose of this gathering, but Sebastian told her it was a surprise and she just needed to show up and enjoy herself. When Enid *did* show up, with Sarah in her arms, she took a long look at the dining table, already set with a place for each person. But something was strikingly unusual—at least for *this* household. She knew very well what day this was according to the Jewish traditions in which she'd been raised, but just as with all things Jewish, she kept them to herself and honored them in her heart. However, in that moment, her old life merged into the new one as she observed the presence of a Seder plate at each place setting. Every Seder plate contained five items, each of which were a fundamental part of the Passover ceremony, symbolic of different elements of the great Exodus of the Jewish people from Egypt, as it was recorded in the Old Testament.

Enid stood frozen as she took in more fully what she was looking at, then she realized that Sebastian was standing in front of her. She met his eyes but couldn't find the words to ask any one of the many questions swirling in her mind. He smiled as he took her hand, saying quietly, "After doing some research, I spoke with Mrs. Thorpe about the possibility of beginning a new tradition in our home. She's been very enthusiastic about putting it all together, as has Mrs. Miller. I hope we got everything right; if not, we'll do better next year." Enid smiled at him but still couldn't speak. He motioned toward the table and said, "The sun has gone down. Shall we be seated and begin?"

Enid blinked back tears and allowed Sebastian to help her with her chair before he took Sarah from her arms and stood nearby. He spoke loudly enough to get everyone's attention, and every person sat down and quietly waited for the earl to speak.

"Many of you might be wondering about this new tradition I have decided to make a part of our household. As Christians, we celebrate Easter quite religiously, but it's occurred to me that we often forget the tradition of the Passover, which began when Moses led the children of Israel out of bondage, following a series of great miracles. Jesus Himself celebrated the Passover, which is recorded in the New Testament, and in fact it seems to be an important element of the final days of His life."

Sebastian put a hand on Enid's shoulder as he continued to speak, and she wondered if he might actually be so bold as to expose her heritage to those with whom they lived and worked. She felt decidedly nervous about such a prospect, not certain that some kind of persecution or difficulty might not arise from having other people know. She told herself that Sebastian surely knew as much, and she needed to trust him. She took a deep breath and waited for him to finish his explanation.

"My lovely fiancée has shared with me that there is some Jewish heritage in her ancestry," he said, winking at her as she looked up at him. She felt certain he had carefully considered how to word that sentence to explain why they were going to celebrate a Jewish tradition when it would otherwise make no sense to anyone else in the household, and he obviously knew as she did that it was best if no one knew she was Jewish by birth, and had been raised with Jewish traditions. Given that the servants had helped prepare this festivity, he had likely said the same thing to them prior to this moment. She just smiled at him and waited for him to go on.

"I've been doing some studying in the Bible and have come upon things that I've not given nearly enough attention to in the past. Most of you attend church every Sunday, and those of you who don't have always been respectful of the Christian beliefs that are paramount in this household. So, I would like to draw your attention to some details of the history of the Passover, which we are celebrating tonight."

Sebastian went on to explain that the tradition began after sundown on the night before the first official day of Passover. Enid could tell that he really *had* been doing some research when he described the Seder ceremony accurately. He finally took his seat, and everyone present became engaged in hearing Sebastian talk about the five symbolic items on the Seder plate; even the boys were being quiet and listening to their father. They were clearly relieved when Sebastian stated that it wasn't required for anyone to eat what was on the Seder plate, but rather the items were placed before them as a sacred reminder, prior to enjoying a fine meal. Tasting the items was optional for those who wished to participate more fully in the ceremony.

A certain reverence prevailed over the room as Sebastian explained that the small sprig of parsley dipped in salt water was eaten as a reminder of the sweat and tears of the people of Israel who had suffered in slavery for so many years. Enid noted that all the adults took a little taste of the salted parsley with expressions of reverence. Sebastian handed Sarah over to Tilly when she became wiggly. Tilly let Sarah crawl around while the nanny watched over her and remained attentive to what Sebastian was saying. The next thing on the plate that everyone except the children reluctantly but willingly tasted was a tiny bit of horseradish, which eaten by itself tasted very bitter—which was meant as a reminder of the bitter oppression of slavery and the heinous decree of Pharaoh to kill all the male infants of the Israelite people. Next was a mixture of chopped apples, nuts, wine, and honey, which symbolized the mortar the Israelite slaves had been required to make to build cities for Pharaoh. After that was a roasted shank bone, representing the sacrificial offering of the Passover, and then a roasted egg, which symbolized renewal and rebirth. Wine was served to the adults to symbolize the redemption of the Israelites, with an empty glass on the table for Elijah the prophet, which was meant to represent the hope of future redemption.

Enid found it difficult to keep her emotions in check as she listened to this man she loved so dearly telling the story she'd grown up hearing in her own home. She missed her family, as celebrating Passover in this way brought back many memories. But at the same time, she perhaps missed her family less, given the fact that Sebastian had just made it possible for her to be able to celebrate traditions she had very much missed. While she shared a lovely meal with these people who were all a part of her life—some more than others—she felt an inner warmth over the prospect of a future wherein she could honor her Jewish heritage and still live her convictions as a Christian. She exchanged more than one warm smile with Sebastian across the table, but they weren't seated close enough to be able to speak. It wasn't until she'd gone upstairs to feed Sarah and get her ready for bed that she looked up from changing the baby's nappy to see Sebastian leaning in the doorway.

"How did I do?" he asked. "If I didn't do it right, you can teach me before next year's celebration."

Enid picked up Sarah and smiled at her fiancé. "You did beautifully," she said and meant it. "I don't know if I could ever tell you what this means to me." The tears she'd been trying to hold back all evening tumbled out with her words.

Sebastian crossed the room and wrapped her in his arms while Sarah seemed content to be briefly sandwiched between them. "What's wrong?" he asked.

"Nothing," she declared firmly and looked up at him. "Everything is so right. Beyond missing my family, everything is perfect, Sebastian. To know that you went to so much trouble to honor something so important to me is just . . . well, I love you more every day." She kissed him quickly. "Thank you . . . for making it so clear that you can embrace this part of me, rather than just pretending it doesn't exist."

"Is that what Alistair did?" he asked.

"Yes," she answered, grateful that she could be completely honest. "He told me that he respected my heritage, but it was best if we just forgot about all of that and moved forward. Not once did we talk about it after that. When we'd agreed that we should keep it a secret from everyone, I hadn't expected that it would become completely ignored even between us. I realize now that I'd lost a part of myself, and tonight you gave it back to me. So . . . thank you . . . for everything."

Sebastian looked mildly embarrassed, as if he didn't want too much attention drawn to his deeds. But he smiled and said, "I'm just glad that my efforts produced the effect I'd hoped for."

She returned his smile before he kissed her, but their kiss was interrupted by Sarah suddenly declaring that she'd lost her patience with this situation. Both Enid and Sebastian chuckled before Enid sat down to feed the baby her bottle. Sebastian kissed the top of Enid's head, saying, "I think I'd better go drag our sons away from the party. They're getting so much attention, I think they'd stay up until midnight if I let them."

As he headed toward the door Enid said, "I love you, Sebastian."

He turned back and smiled. "And I love you."

"Yes," she said, "I know."

He left the room and Enid relaxed more deeply into the soft chair, holding Sarah close. That was the biggest difference between Sebastian and his brother, she concluded; Enid *knew* that Sebastian loved her because he demonstrated his love with his actions and behavior toward her. He really heard her when she spoke, and he was keenly aware of her whenever they were together. With Alistair she had felt invisible and perhaps subsequently insignificant; with Sebastian it was exactly the opposite. Feeling completely loved and thoroughly happy, Enid closed her eyes and mentally tallied the days left before she would become his wife. The prospect only deepened her happiness, leaving her undeniably content.

* * * * *

Easter Sunday came with a bright blue sky and the warmth of spring in the air. After attending a special church service, the entire household gathered together again, all seated around the table as equals to share a fine meal. Enid enjoyed the food and the company, but she felt preoccupied with a warm feeling surrounding her as she considered the beautiful balance and symmetry of life that she'd found here in this home with these people, and the traditions that would be honored throughout the remainder of her life.

Only a few days later, Enid felt as if she were living some kind of dream from which she never wanted to awake. Standing in the chapel, looking into Sebastian's eyes while they exchanged sacred vows, she marveled at how happy he'd made her, and at his goodness. The journey they'd taken to arrive at this moment flashed quickly through her mind, making it impossible to deny the miracles they'd been blessed with, and the healing that had taken place in their lives. The difficulties they'd endured—and even the terrible anger they'd felt toward each other at times along the way—somehow sweetened the prospect of sharing the rest of her life with this man. She'd witnessed the changes in him—and in herself—and she knew they were real. What could be better than that?

As Sebastian kissed her to seal their marriage, she couldn't keep from laughing, simply because she was so happy. He laughed as well and kissed her again before they returned home to enjoy a fine celebration with the people who mattered most to them. However, not long after they'd finished sharing an extravagant meal with their guests—some of whom had helped prepare and serve the meal—Sebastian stood and announced, "Thank you all for being a part of this day with us, and for everything else that you do.

You are all welcome to celebrate and enjoy yourselves for the rest of the day and into the night for all I care, because my bride and I will be leaving within the hour."

"We will?" Enid asked, looking up at him from where she sat.

Everyone chuckled at her ignorance of what they had all apparently known about. Sebastian looked at her and said, "Your bags are packed, Mrs. Hawthorne, and everything is in order. So, I suggest you go change out of your wedding gown into something more practical and we'll be off."

"Where are we going?" she asked as she stood, wondering why she'd never bothered to even ask him if they might be going somewhere for a honeymoon.

"That's a surprise," Sebastian said and kissed her before he shooed her out of the room. She went upstairs to find Tilly and Gert there to help her get out of the elaborate wedding gown, since they'd also helped her order the dress, and she never would have gotten *into* it earlier today without their assistance.

Sure enough, Enid found that the maids had packed her bags; since they knew her habits so well they had taken care of everything and she was ready to go in a very short time. It was difficult to say good-bye to the boys, and to think of not seeing them or her dear little Sarah for an unknown number of days. But she knew that all the children were in the best of care, and she also knew that having some time with her new husband away from home and their usual routine was important to creating a good marriage relationship.

Once all the farewells had taken place, Sebastian helped Enid step into the waiting carriage and they were quickly on their way. Enid was caught off guard by a fluttering in her stomach, which caused a little laugh to escape from her mouth.

"Is something funny?" Sebastian asked.

"No," she said and laughed again, "just happy."

"Amen to that," he said and wrapped his arms around her.

"Now that we're off, will you tell me where we're going?" she asked.

"Tonight we're staying at an inn that's less than two hours away, and tomorrow we will go on to London."

"London?" she echoed, her heart quickening just to hear the name of the city spoken—the city where she had lived her entire life prior to marrying Alistair.

Enid wondered whether Sebastian might have some ulterior motive for taking her to London, but he dispelled her suspicions when he smiled and said, "There are so many wonderful things to see and do in London, and I've not been there for many years. Although," he smirked slightly and kissed her, "I dare say we might be content not to go out at all."

"I dare say that's highly possible," she replied and urged him to kiss her again.

* * * * *

Enid came slowly awake, feeling more rested and relaxed than she had since Sarah's birth, or perhaps it had been since Alistair's death. Then again, it could be since she and Alistair had set out for Africa. Or maybe she just couldn't remember when she'd felt so perfectly safe and content; perhaps she never had.

Once she could hold her eyes open, Enid turned to look at Sebastian sleeping beside her. She'd never imagined being able to feel so much love— or to feel so thoroughly loved. Today would be their third day in London, yet she could hardly remember how it had felt to not be married to this remarkable man. Thinking of all they had shared as husband and wife made her smile as a tangible warmth settled over her. Already this marriage had very little in common with her first one. She'd simply never imagined being so happy.

Enid closed her eyes and thought about the children. She wondered what they were doing, and *how* they were doing. She missed them, but not enough to wish she was at home. Perhaps more days away would bring her to a desire to go back. For now, she just wanted to enjoy this time with her husband, and the opportunity to continue experiencing all the wonderful facets of London she'd never experienced during her growing-up years here, in a family where such luxuries had never been an option.

Enid thought of her family and wondered what *they* were doing; *how* they were doing. Being in London had kept them closer in her mind, simply because she knew they were so near, but the reality hadn't changed; they might as well have been halfway around the world. So she pushed thoughts of them away and stood up to pull back the curtains and look down to the street below, but in fact she couldn't see it. The fog was heavy and that was *all* she could see. But nestled in a beautiful room in a fine hotel with her husband, she really didn't care. She imagined a day of having meals brought to their room and having no need to go out at all.

"What are you doing all the way over there?" she heard Sebastian ask, and turned to see him watching her.

"I'm concluding that it's terribly foggy out there, and staying in would be preferable."

"I won't argue with that," he said, reaching a hand toward her.

Enid moved back to the bed and sat beside him, taking his hand as she bent over to kiss him. "Good morning," she said.

"Good morning," he replied, smiling with the same kind of contentment that she felt. His expression then sobered, and she knew his thoughts had shifted. Before she could ask, he said, "There's something I want to talk to you about, but I don't want to dampen the mood."

"It's possible you already have," she concluded from the intensity of his tone. "Go on."

"I think we should go and visit your family," he said. Before she could even think of responding, he quickly added, "I know it's difficult for you, and I know there's the risk that they will turn us away and it could be very upsetting. But I can't stop thinking about it, and I just have to say that . . . there's also the possibility they'll be happy to see you. Either way, I think we should try, and . . . if nothing has changed and they turn us away, I will spend the remainder of the week taking you to operas and ballets, and I will buy you a great many gifts, and—"

"Is that not what you already have planned?" she interrupted.

"I cannot deny it," he said.

Enid tried not to feel upset by his suggestion, or perhaps more accurately she tried not to let him see how upset she felt. She had to ask, "Is that why you chose London for our honeymoon? To try and talk me into seeing my family?"

"No," he said, adding somewhat sheepishly, "well . . . partly. We're enjoying the honeymoon I've imagined for months, and we will continue to do so until we return home. But, Enid . . . how can I not think of the fact that you grew up in this city? That your family is here? I know that *you're* thinking about it. How could you not?"

Enid looked down but kept his hand in hers. "I confess that being here has made me think about them a great deal, and I can't deny wishing I could go and see them, but . . . when I remember how my father turned me out . . . the things he said . . . I just don't know if I have the courage to stir up that kind of drama all over again—for myself as well as for my mother, my siblings."

"Well," Sebastian drawled, "why don't you think about it for a day, and tomorrow morning we'll decide. I'll honor your wishes, darling, but I cannot deny that I want very much to see where you grew up, and to meet your family—even if it's only for a moment while I'm being thrown out and disavowed." He chuckled wryly. "Look at it this way, at least you won't be disavowed alone. I'll be there beside you—no matter what happens."

Enid pondered the sincerity she saw in his eyes and simply said, "I'll think about it. Right now, I'm starving."

After sharing a lovely breakfast that had been brought to their hotel room, Enid and Sebastian both agreed that they would rather stay inside and relax and just be together rather than braving the fog and the chill in the air. Enid thoroughly enjoyed the day, even though Sebastian's idea about attempting to visit her family hovered in her mind. That night Sebastian lay sleeping close beside her, his head on the same pillow, his arm wrapped around her in a way that implied he would always keep her safe, even while they slept. She gently toyed with his hair and occasionally pressed a kiss to his brow even though he was oblivious, sleeping deeply.

Enid stared at the ceiling and toward the window, praying silently in her mind and trying very hard to examine the feelings in her heart so that she could make a viable decision as to whether Sebastian's idea was something she should take advantage of—or ignore. She fell asleep at last and dreamt of her family—most specifically her mother sobbing as her father had shouted at Enid, making no effort to mince his words over what a great disappointment she was to him, and how he could never abide laying claim to a daughter who would betray her family and her beliefs so boldly. In her dream, Enid was also aware of her siblings all witnessing the ugly scene, some of them looking stone-faced and perhaps in shock, others crying almost as much as their mother. Enid had walked away with what she could carry in two bags. In her dream she walked into a heavy fog and disappeared, finding herself lost, alone, and afraid.

Enid awoke to daylight, recalling vividly the images from her dream that were mostly the repetition of memories that had haunted her. She recalled how she'd left the house while her father had still been shouting and her mother crying. Alistair had met her a short way down the street with a carriage waiting to take them to Thornewell Hall, and Enid hadn't lived a day since when she hadn't wondered if they were all well, if any of them felt regret over her being banished from the family, or even if she'd been missed or thought about.

"Are you all right?" she heard Sebastian ask and turned to see him leaning his head on his hand, watching her.

"I just barely woke up," she said. "Why wouldn't I be?"

"You look . . . troubled," he stated. "Bad dreams?"

Enid sighed and admitted, "Bad memories in my dreams."

"Anything you want to talk about?" he asked, and while Enid was considering whether she *did* want to talk about it, the idea came suddenly to her mind that if she did not at least try to see her family while they were here in London, she would surely regret it. If they turned her out just as they had done before, she would certainly be disappointed, and undoubtedly in need of a good cry. But she would have Sebastian at her side no matter what happened. Even if it turned out to be a completely negative experience, she could at least know whether everyone was all right. Since much of her anxiety throughout the years had been her concern over simply not being able to know whether any of her family members were facing difficult challenges, she decided the risk was worth it, and taking on Sebastian's challenge suddenly felt not only right, but necessary.

Enid turned to look at her husband and asked, "Will you take me to see my family today? And will you hold my hand no matter what happens?"

He smiled slightly. "Yes, and yes."

Enid went on to tell him all her thoughts and feelings on the matter, finishing their conversation over breakfast. Once they'd eaten and were dressed for the day, Sebastian hired a carriage and Enid told the driver where to find the home where she'd grown up. At least the fog had cleared, and the day was sunny, which made their trek feel a little less ominous. Enid held Sebastian's hand tightly and tried not to betray just how deeply nervous she felt. She wanted more than anything to have both her mother and father feel glad to see her, to embrace her, to tell her they'd missed her. But in her heart, she knew that her father's principles and convictions ran far too deep for any such thing to happen. And even though her mother put a higher priority on the love and connection of family than she did on any disagreement over lifestyle or beliefs, she would never go against her husband's wishes; just as Enid knew her siblings—even though most were now adults—would not contradict their father's edicts.

"You're trembling," Sebastian noted, looking at her hand in his.

"Would you expect anything less?" she asked. "I'm utterly terrified." She blinked back the threat of tears as she realized how hard she had worked through these years of separation to push away thoughts of her family, and the grief and sorrow related to having lost them. She likely needed to give herself permission to grieve over such an enormous loss, rather than trying to ignore it, but now was certainly not the time. Still, perhaps it was time she fully came to accept and make peace with the fact that her family would never be a part of her life. She knew from other experiences that acceptance brought healing, and maybe that was the greatest purpose of this venture.

"I suspect it won't take long to know whether or not anything has changed," her husband said. "If they don't want to see you . . . or won't talk to you . . . then we will leave quickly, and it will all be over in a matter of minutes, and then we'll both cry over it before we find a lovely restaurant and share an extravagant lunch. And then we'll go and buy more gifts for the children—just because we can."

"That sounds like an excellent plan," Enid said, leaning her head on his shoulder, so grateful for his support in every respect. He would be with her while she faced this, and whether he literally cried with her, he would be completely understanding of her own need to do so, and he would do everything he could to distract her from a painful experience—which it was mostly likely to be.

The carriage halted sooner than Enid had expected, and her heart pounded as she looked out the window at the modest house where she'd been born and had lived until Alistair had taken her away. It was three stories high but narrow, sandwiched between two other homes that were all part of a long row of houses, all the same except for slight variations in the color of brick. Sebastian stepped out and helped Enid do the same. Her heart pounded as it took very few steps to get to the front door, since the row houses were very close to the street.

"Here goes," Sebastian said and knocked loudly at the door, not giving Enid a chance to hesitate even a moment. She attempted to take a deep breath but had trouble filling her lungs. With one hand, she tightened her hold on Sebastian's hand and took hold of his arm with the other.

The door flew open as if the family had been expecting someone, and Enid faced her sister Lucy for long moments of silence. She noticed Lucy holding tightly to the door, as if she feared losing her balance otherwise. Enid leaned more fully against Sebastian for the same reason.

While Enid sensed that Lucy was trying to think of what to say, Enid hurried to break the strained silence, "If you can't let me in . . . or even speak to me . . . I understand, but . . . we were in London, and . . . I had to at least try, and . . ." Enid lost her breath as Lucy stepped forward and engulfed her in a tight embrace that pulled her away from Sebastian as she wrapped both arms tightly around her sister, and she couldn't keep from weeping—especially when she could hear Lucy weeping as well.

Enid had four younger brothers, but Lucy was her only sister, and less than two years separated them in age. They'd always been close, and Enid had always known in her heart that the decision she'd made to marry a Christian man had likely been at least as hard on Lucy as it had been on her parents. She suspected her brothers would have been upset, but not as emotionally impacted. Now, Lucy was holding her tightly, seeming hesitant to let go, and Enid felt the years melting away with the evidence that her sister had not lost any of the affection they'd once shared.

"Oh, my goodness!" Lucy finally said, stepping back only to put both her hands to Enid's face. "How I have prayed you would come back!"

"You have?" Enid countered, genuinely surprised, knowing that her return was likely to cause problems of one kind or another.

"My dear sister, we have so much to talk about! Come in. Come in. And I'll find Mama and . . ." Lucy looked up at Sebastian, assessed him for a few seconds, then said to Enid, "This is not the man you left with, the man you were going to marry."

"No," Enid said and offered the briefest of explanations. "Alistair died." Lucy gasped but Enid hurried to add, "This is his brother Sebastian; we are married now."

Lucy looked overcome with such news and said, "It would seem you have as much to tell us as we have to tell you. Come in," she repeated and motioned them into the tiny entry hall, closing the door as Sebastian said, "Thank you."

"It's a pleasure to meet you, Sebastian," Lucy said.

"And you," Sebastian replied, nodding politely toward her.

"Please . . . sit down," Lucy insisted, motioning to the parlor, "and I'll find Mama."

"Will Papa not—" Enid began to ask, genuinely terrified of facing her father's wrath once again.

"It is only me and Mama here," Lucy said. "It's all right," she added, her voice filled with relief, which contradicted a sadness in her eyes.

Lucy hurried away down the hall, and Enid took Sebastian's hand to lead him into the parlor that looked almost exactly as it had when Enid had left here years ago, believing she would never return.

"Are you all right?" Sebastian asked, squeezing her hand.

"So far," she admitted but felt a quivering in her chest, as if her heart itself was overloaded with fear and hope and sorrow. She'd already been received more graciously than she'd expected, and she was grateful, but she had no idea what to expect now. She'd barely allowed the thought to settle into her mind before she heard hurried footsteps in the hall, and she turned to see both her mother and Lucy enter the room.

"God of heaven be praised!" Enid's mother exclaimed, putting her hands to the sides of her face while tears flowed in a steady stream down her cheeks. "Lucy said it was you; I could hardly believe it! I've prayed and prayed for you to come back!" She opened her arms, and Enid flew into her mother's embrace, now openly weeping as well. Her mother had been praying for Enid to come back! After the way she'd been turned out—with no uncertain terms—Enid never could have imagined such a reception.

After Enid and her mother had shared a good cry, holding tightly to each other, Enid eased back and wiped her hand over her face, laughing softly to see her mother do the same—and Lucy who stood nearby was also wiping at her tears. A quick glance told Enid that Sebastian was standing across the room, observing the reunion, looking entirely pleased with the situation, perhaps even mildly smug over having been right about needing to come here. But Enid just smiled at him; perhaps he had the right to be smug. She was certainly grateful for his nudging. But her greatest fear leapt into her mind, shattering the peacefulness of the moment. "Will Papa not be angry when he comes home to find me here and—"

"Sit down," her mother said, and Enid sat on the sofa between her mother and sister. Sebastian and Enid's mother exchanged a slight nod of acknowledgment, but it seemed that something important needed to be said before introductions were made. "Your papa died," Enid's mother said, and it took seemingly endless seconds for the words to penetrate her mind. Before she could ask the obvious questions, Lucy and her mother took turns explaining that he'd been having chest pains occasionally for quite some time, but had been stubborn about seeing a doctor, until one day he had collapsed after getting up from the breakfast table, and it seemed he had died immediately. The funeral had been a couple of months ago, and the family had all agreed that they'd never been comfortable with the harshness of how Enid's father had disowned her, and they'd all wished they had known where to find her. Enid couldn't believe it! Despite her father's very strict and sometimes heavy-handed ways, she had loved him dearly, and to learn of his death was a shock; something that would surely take time for her to come to terms with. In a strange juxtaposition of feelings, Enid was assaulted with grief and bathed with deep relief just to be back home, receiving such love and acceptance from her mother and sister.

Enid asked where her brothers were. She learned that they too had missed her and had grieved over the harsh separation. She learned that the eldest of the four had recently married, and had moved to Liverpool where he had a good job on the shipping docks; a job which he'd been able to get through a friend he'd made while working at the docks on the Thames. His current employment was a better situation with better pay, making it possible for him to provide a more comfortable living for his new bride and their expected baby. Ironically, in fact, this employment opportunity had been available for *all* of Enid's brothers, and they were all living together in the same home in Liverpool, having moved there the week after the funeral. Enid's mother and sister had received many letters from them and had been assured that they were all doing well, which gave them a great deal of peace, even though the house felt very quiet and lonely.

"And what of the dairy?" Enid asked, knowing that her brothers had been working with their father to keep it running.

Lucy answered. "There were some debts, and as soon as Papa died it became evident that we would be better off selling the dairy, and it was at almost the same time that this opportunity for the boys to get work elsewhere came up."

"It was surely the hand of Providence in our lives," Enid's mother said with obvious humility.

"Surely it was," Lucy said.

Once all the most important news had been shared and the shock had subsided slightly, Enid introduced Sebastian and quickly explained the situation of their recent marriage—which meant giving them a brief explanation of Alistair's death, as well as Marie's. Lucy and her mother expressed condolences over the losses that both Enid and Sebastian had endured, but they were thrilled to hear that Enid had a daughter, and that Enid had also become an official mother to Sebastian's two sons.

"Oh, I would so love to see them!" Enid's mother said, again becoming tearful. "To spend some time with them!" She turned to Lucy and declared, "I'm a grandmother!"

"You are indeed," Lucy said, beaming. "And I'm an aunt."

"We can certainly arrange to have you come and visit," Sebastian said. "I would be honored to cover all of your traveling expenses, and you'd be welcome to stay as long as you like."

Enid saw her mother and sister exchange an astonished glance before they both began to cry again. "What is it?" Enid asked, taking hold of their hands, looking back and forth at them sitting on either side of her.

"God surely is merciful!" Enid's mother declared.

"There are too many miracles to count," Lucy added.

Enid exchanged a confused glance with Sebastian while the other women were preoccupied with their tears. He shrugged, indicating he was equally ignorant as to why his suggestion for them to visit had brought on a new bout of emotion.

Lucy finally managed to explain. "It's just that . . . with so many changes, Mother and I have been feeling . . . perhaps lonely; the house is so quiet, even though we have each other. And we've just been talking about how we're somewhat bored; there's nothing of purpose with which to occupy ourselves, and . . . it's almost as if this place doesn't feel like home anymore, even with as many years as we've lived here."

"If your offer is sincere," Enid's mother said, looking directly at Sebastian, "it would surely be a blessing to come and spend some time with my grandchildren."

"I would *not* have offered if it were not sincere," Sebastian said firmly, and Enid loved him even more for his kindness toward her mother and sister. "And if you like it there and decide to stay indefinitely, that would be all the better in my opinion. Enid would surely be happier to have you there, and the house is ridiculously large. Putting empty rooms to good use is a blessing, in my opinion."

"Oh, you are incredibly kind!" Lucy declared. Enid's mother was too overcome with tears to speak.

"Mother?" Enid said, turning more toward her. "Are you all right?" She wondered if the ongoing intensity of her emotion was due to still grieving over the loss of her husband, the moving away of her sons, the return of her daughter—or perhaps all of it combined. But she sensed there was something more.

Enid turned to quietly repeat the question to Lucy, when all their mother could do was cry into her handkerchief. Lucy dabbed at her eyes and sniffled before she said, "We've sold the house, Enid. It's just too big for the two of us, so we decided it would be better to sell it and find a smaller flat that would be sufficient, and doing so would help conserve our resources. But," Lucy's voice quivered and she squeezed Enid's hand, "another week and you wouldn't have found us here; we might never have seen each other again."

"Good heavens!" Enid said, horrified at the thought—especially now that they'd all shared such a sweet reunion. "We have all indeed been blessed with many miracles!"

"Amen," the other women murmured.

They all talked a while longer before going to the kitchen to share a simple meal and more conversation. Enid was so glad and deeply grateful to be able to tell her mother and sister about all that was good in her life, and she thoroughly enjoyed sharing with them how Sebastian had surprised her with a Passover dinner to honor her heritage. This too brought up tears in the women, but it also prompted some direct questions about Enid's beliefs and how she truly felt about the religion she was raised with *and* the religion to which she had converted. Enid had never been given an opportunity to share such feelings before, and she was deeply grateful to be able to do so now, and to feel respect from her mother and sister, even while it was evident their beliefs differed greatly. But they all agreed that they didn't have to share the same beliefs to be able to love and respect each other, and it was time to make a fresh start.

That night as Enid stared at the ceiling of their hotel room, holding Sebastian's hand in hers, she couldn't even count how many miracles had happened that day. She resisted the urge to thank Sebastian once again for pushing her to go and visit her family. She'd already thanked him so many times that it had become redundant. She'd also thanked him over and over for his sincere offer to have her mother and sister come to their home and stay—and his completely genuine hope that they would decide to live there indefinitely. In all of Enid's wildest dreams she never could have imagined the wonderful life she'd come to share with Sebastian—but to also have her mother and sister become a part of that life was just too wonderful to comprehend.

"You'll get used to it," Sebastian had said more than once with a smile that made her believe opening his home to Enid's family had filled him with genuine happiness.

Knowing that he was still awake as well, Enid leaned up on her elbow, resisting the urge to once again gush with gratitude while recounting the miracles of the day. Through the darkness she saw him turn his head toward her. "I love you, Sebastian Hawthorne," she said in lieu of everything else; surely that was the most important thing for him to know.

"And I love you," he said, pressing his hand to the side of her face, "Enid Hawthorne."

Enid bent down to kiss him, savoring the experience as one of so many things she loved about being his wife. It was ironic that she hadn't needed to change her name upon marrying her deceased husband's brother, but being Mrs. Hawthorne *felt* different to her now. When she considered how her life had been after taking Alistair's name, she found little resemblance to how it felt to be married to Sebastian. Being Enid Hawthorne had never felt better or more right.

"You know," he said, pushing his hand to the back of her head to urge her to kiss him again, "I think this is what storytellers might mean by happily ever after."

Enid laughed softly. "I don't believe either of us are naive enough to think that life will necessarily be easy; the very nature of life has challenges."

"No, neither of us are that naive," he said and kissed her again. "Still, whatever we face in the future, we will face it together. And we are so very, very blessed."

"Yes, we certainly are," she agreed and decided to stop talking so that she could thoroughly enjoy the moment while he kissed her yet again.

About the Author

ANITA STANSFIELD HAS MORE THAN fifty published books and is the recipient of many awards, including two Lifetime Achievement Awards. Her books go far beyond being enjoyable, memorable stories. Anita resonates particularly well with a broad range of devoted readers because of her sensitive and insightful examination of contemporary issues that are faced by many of those readers, even when her venue is a historical romance. Readers come away from her compelling stories equipped with new ideas about how to enrich their own lives, regardless of their circumstances.

Anita was born and raised in Provo, Utah. She is the mother of five and has a growing number of grandchildren. She also writes for the general trade market under the name Elizabeth D. Michaels.

For more information and a complete list of her publications, go to anitastansfield.blogspot.com or anitastansfield.com, where you can sign up to receive email updates. You can also follow her on Facebook and Twitter.